I0614355

By SUSAN LAINE

NOVELS
Falling for Rain

SENSES AND SENSATIONS
A Luminous Touch
Love in Plain Sight
Sounds of Love
The Sweetest Scent

LIFTING THE VEIL
Book One: The Wolfing Way
Book Two: Genie's Wish
Book Three: Hunter's Moon

SECOND CHANCES
Accidental Chemistry
Twice by Chance

Published by DREAMSPINNER PRESS
http://www.dreamspinnerpress.com

The Sweetest Scent

Susan Laine

Dreamspinner Press

Published by
Dreamspinner Press
5032 Capital Circle SW
Suite 2, PMB# 279
Tallahassee, FL 32305-7886
USA
http://www.dreamspinnerpress.com/

This is a work of fiction. Names, characters, places, and incidents either are the product of author imagination or are used fictitiously, and any resemblance to actual persons, living or dead, business establishments, events, or locales is entirely coincidental.

The Sweetest Scent
© 2013 Susan Laine.

Cover Art
© 2013 Catt Ford.
Cover content is for illustrative purposes only and any person depicted on the cover is a model.

All rights reserved. This book is licensed to the original purchaser only. Duplication or distribution via any means is illegal and a violation of international copyright law, subject to criminal prosecution and upon conviction, fines, and/or imprisonment. Any eBook format cannot be legally loaned or given to others. No part of this book may be reproduced or transmitted in any form or by any means, electronic or mechanical, including photocopying, recording, or by any information storage and retrieval system, without the written permission of the Publisher, except where permitted by law. To request permission and all other inquiries, contact Dreamspinner Press, 5032 Capital Circle SW, Suite 2, PMB# 279, Tallahassee, FL 32305-7886, USA, or http://www.dreamspinnerpress.com/.

ISBN: 978-1-62798-012-8
Digital ISBN: 978-1-62798-013-5

Printed in the United States of America
First Edition
September 2013

I dedicate this to all the fans of the series and especially to one cocky brat who never shuts up.

Part One

Chapter 1

"WHAT the—"

Bro Sumner started at the noise coming from down the hall and pulled away from the most delectable kiss he had ever had the pleasure of partaking in. His cheeks flaming with embarrassment, he turned his head to find his older brother Sebastian standing there with his fiancé, Jordan Waters.

"I can explain...," he began, even while knowing he was mumbling too fast for his deaf brother to understand him. Still, getting caught almost literally with his pants down while making out with his girlfriend on the couch did not exactly incline Bro to enunciate clearly.

But he was proven wrong about his assumption when Sebastian said angrily, "What have I told you about leaving your stuff on the coffee table overnight? I don't want a rodent infestation here. Bro, take your dirty dishes to the kitchen this instant." Then peering over Bro's shoulder, Sebastian added with a smile and a wave, "Hi, Lacey." There was no malice in his words, and Bro sighed in relief.

From the couch, Lacey called out enthusiastically, "Hi, Sebastian," and added a girlish wave to the words. She was scrambling to an upright position, adjusting the hem of her dress to cover her exposed thighs.

Grumbling under his breath, momentarily thankful his brother could not hear him, Bro grabbed the dirty plates and glasses off the living room coffee table and headed for the kitchen, stomping around like an angry bull to make his point. He was seventeen, but that did not make him a domestic slave for the grown-ups of the household.

As he passed his brother and his fiancé, though, Jordan cuffed him on the head, mostly just tousling his black hair. "Sebastian may be deaf, but I'm not, so mind your tone, Bro, and watch the swearing. If you can't be bothered to keep the place tidy 'cause you're too busy making out—"

Bro snapped his head back and glared at Jordan, who smiled back congenially. "Okay, okay. Jesus fucking Christ. You're such a bully."

"Language," Sebastian immediately cut in, his hollow voice so familiar to Bro.

"Oh, please," Bro huffed indignantly. "Like you and Jordan never suck face—"

"Hard to smooch while cursing." Jordan laughed and moved off toward the loft kitchen, where he unceremoniously planted the food bags he had been carrying.

"Fuck you" was Bro's response as he flipped Jordan off.

"Bro!" Sebastian did not approve of his baby brother using foul language, especially in a situation that was utterly Bro's own fault. He had known his family was coming home, but he had been too caught up kissing his girlfriend to remember to clean off the coffee table.

Lacey.

At that moment, Bro realized that amid his fury he had totally spaced out on Lacey, and shame heated his cheeks. Turning on his heels in a flash, he glanced at Lacey, who was sitting demurely on the couch, her legs folded under her, as she observed the whole interaction with some amusement; that is, if the sparkle in her light-brown eyes was any indication.

God, he's so freaking beautiful. Yeah, she sure is.

Lacey Adair was Bro's girlfriend—only underneath the feminine clothes, he was a boy, or she was a boy, however you preferred to put it. She was beautiful, more so than anyone Bro had ever known. Her blond hair was cut very short, but it was still soft and wavy, sort of a cross between a boy's and a girl's hairdo. Her pink lip gloss made her full, pouting lips look wet and delicious—although most of it was smeared off now—and she also wore dark-brown eye shadow and eyeliner around her elegantly made-up hazel eyes. In sunlight Lacey's eyes glimmered almost golden sometimes, in Bro's infatuated mind at least.

Like one of those old-fashioned pinup girls, Lacey looked cute posed on the couch, her yellow chiffon summer dress flowing around her petite, delicate frame, giving her a casual yet stylish look. Bro loved that Lacey was slim but still had meat on her bones. They had done enough lovers' wrestling for Bro to know Lacey was no one's breakable little flower. Her feet were bare, as she had been sitting in Bro's lap before they had been so rudely interrupted.

As usual, simply seeing Lacey made Bro sigh contentedly, dishes forgotten.

"Here, I'll take those." Jordan wasn't bothering to conceal his mirth as he snatched the dirty dishes from Bro's hands and headed back to the kitchen, whispering loudly on his way, "I think something other than dishes needs your undivided attention."

Bro blushed at Jordan's insinuations, but it wasn't like the guy was wrong. With a small, grateful nod, he returned to the couch and sat next to Lacey, whose smile was as bright as the sun.

"Sorry about that," Bro muttered apologetically. He found a few strands of hair gone astray around Lacey's temple, so he brushed them behind her ear, caressing the soft shell of her earlobe along the way. She shivered.

This close to Lacey, Bro always noted her intoxicating scent. Lacey only ever wore women's perfumes, preferring the slightly more floral women's fragrances than those of men's colognes. What at first hinted of lavender and something citrusy, soon morphed into orchid, and finally lingered at a musky undertone that could be both male and female. The duality of Lacey came through clearly in her choice of ambiguous perfumes. In any case, the sweet scent suited her to a tee.

When they had first met and started dating, Bro hadn't been sure whether to call Lacey him or her. Lacey was, after all, a gay boy who, as far as Bro knew, did not want to physically become a woman. Yet with her friends, she identified more as female, and the same was true with Bro, so he went along with whatever she wanted. In bed, however, she took on a male persona with ease, matching with her, um, boy bits.

Lacey chuckled lightly, covering her mouth with her hand. "It's all right. We knew they'd be coming home soon. Jack and Kevin probably won't be far behind."

This was true, Bro thought, sighing longingly. He lived with an extended family of sorts in a huge loft apartment that took up two floors. What had started out as the household of the two Sumner brothers had grown to include the Waters brothers, and also one Thompson thrown into the mix. EMT Jack Waters was Jordan's younger brother, and Kevin Thompson was Jordan's partner at work—in the Financial Crimes and Fraud Unit of the MPDC—and Jack's partner in the relationship department. At times it felt like living in an episode of *The Secret Life of the American Teenager* or *Gossip Girl* or *90210.*

Bro sometimes believed their family would continue to grow into infinity if he so much as blinked.

At the moment, though, he had a lovely young thing in front of him.

"I have to get home anyway," Lacey said, her voice carrying a hint of sadness.

"What? Already?" Bro knew he sounded whiny, but he wasn't willing to let Lacey go yet. He longed to wrap his arms around her waist and pull her near enough to feel her heartbeat, to sniff her strawberry shampoo, to taste her neck….

Lacey chuckled, her full lips curved into a smile. "Come on, Bro. You know how my dad gets if I'm too late." Bro could only grunt in acknowledgment of Lacey's father, who was, for all intents and purposes, a drunken, belligerent asshole with no idea who his son was. "And if he tells me I can't see you…."

As Lacey's slender shoulders shivered, Bro wrapped his arms around her, comforting her, running his palms up and down her back. "Yeah, I get it. It's fine. Well, not fine, but I get it, 'cause he's a bit of a prick and—"

His voice was muffled by the brush of Lacey's lips against his own, then silenced entirely when Lacey's tongue slipped into his mouth, curling around his. As Bro tilted his head a bit more, the kiss deepened, and Bro could not have cared less if his whole high school sat as audience to their shared intimacy.

She tasted like cherries, and Bro loved cherries—with whipped cream. Her body, like her spirit, was at once frail and vigorous, yielding and defiant. These contradictions were, to Bro, more fascinating than anything he had ever come across, so when he had the opportunity, he took advantage, tightening his hold on her, tasting her, touching, caressing, kneading. Bro could feel her bones and muscles underneath her skin, knowing full well it was the guy he adored, not the girl. Well, mostly. Lacey was sort of both.

Lacey's lips were perfect for Bro. Her upper lip had a delicious curve, a feminine Cupid's bow he liked to trace with the tip of his tongue, as he did this time. Then there was the fuller lower lip, with its natural pout, created to be licked lightly and suckled softly, and once again, Bro indulged himself with Lacey's delights. He felt himself hardening in his jeans, and denim was not the most giving material, which made him groan into the kiss.

Lacey pulled back, her eyes hooded with lust and her lips red, glistening, and swollen from their intense kiss. "Bro, honey, I gotta go. As much as I'd love to stay and keep kissing you...."

Reluctantly, Bro loosened his hard hold, fully aware of the disapproving growl emerging from his throat. "Yeah, I understand. Sorry. I got carried away."

Lacey giggled and mock glared at him. "You're sorry for kissing me? Really? Should I be offended or—"

"I'm not sorry for kissing you," Bro cut in angrily. "I'm sorry 'cause I'm making you late."

Lacey's fingertips traced Bro's jawline tenderly. "I know, silly. You're just so easy to tease."

That comment made Bro snarl louder, and Lacey snickered, hiding her mouth behind her hand again. Bro did not particularly like that gesture because she was so beautiful when she smiled, but old habits.... "Call me when you get home, yeah? Just wanna make sure you—"

"I love it when you worry about me." Lacey's tone had dipped, becoming almost husky, and in those times, the adolescent guy she was came through. Her gaze was directed at Bro's mouth, and she bit her lower lip, as if trying to maintain control. That made Bro practically bounce with glee.

"Hey, Lace, you wanna stay for dinner?" Jordan called, popping into view from the open kitchen.

Shaking her head, Lacey replied, "Sorry, Jordan, I can't. I have to get home. If I haven't done my homework by the time Dad gets home…. I don't wanna get grounded."

Jordan nodded, grinning. "No prob. Next time."

Bro and Lacey rose from the couch simultaneously, and grumbling under his breath, Bro escorted Lacey to the foyer.

"You wanna come over tomorrow?" Bro asked, not bothering to disguise the hopeful tone.

Lacey snickered. "Of course. But later, yeah? You have football practice—"

"Shit, I forgot all about that."

"—and I have violin lessons with Mr. Teasdale after school. But after that, maybe?"

Nodding, Bro stared at Lacey, dazed, wanting the speeding moment to slow down and last a little longer. Then he accepted the facts and snapped back to reality.

After helping her into her cream-colored denim coat, Bro opened the bright-red metal door to the loft so Lacey could exit. The stairwell had huge industrial-sized windows on the highest floor, so it was easy to see the dark clouds as well as the striations the raindrops were creating on the glass.

"Oh no, it's raining," Lacey moaned despairingly, as though she were made of sugar and was likely to melt, which made Bro grin.

"It's okay, babe. I can drive you," Bro said proudly, as he did have a learner's permit. In Washington D.C., where they lived, he had gotten the permit when he'd turned sixteen, with his guardian's—Sebastian's—approval.

"Oh no, you won't," Jordan's voice interjected from behind him, and Bro growled in frustration. The man was so annoyingly sneaky, being a cop and all. "You know as well as I that, without adult supervision, you're restricted to driving to school and back."

"But—"

"No buts." Jordan remained adamant, and Bro knew he could not win this fight. Not that it was going to stop him from trying. But Jordan beat him to the punch. "I can drive you, Lacey. It's no imposition, I assure you."

"But—" Bro tried once more.

"Unless Bro here thinks I'm trying to get you alone, Lace, so I can ravish you in the car." Jordan may have been joking, but the mere thought of another man kissing Lacey made Bro's blood boil as jealous fury coiled inside of him. His hands fisted at his sides as he gave Jordan a murderous glare.

"*I'*m driving her," Bro said with as much conviction as an angry seventeen-year-old could.

"Bro…." Jordan sighed patiently, giving Bro a rather parental look, which had Bro teeming with fury. "Do I have to use the A-word?"

At that threat, Bro paled. "You wouldn't…," he muttered, glancing at Lacey from under his brow, a silent warning to Jordan not to cross any lines drawn in the sand.

Lacey's expression was both sympathetic and amused. It wasn't that she didn't know Bro's A-word, but like everyone else—except for a few misguided teachers who soon learned the error of their ways— she never used it. His parents had been cruel to name him… Ambrosius. Even if it was a family name.

Jordan nodded in satisfaction. "Come on, Lace. Let's get you home. At least with me, we won't be stopping at every light or intersection to make out."

"You'd better not, or I'll—" Bro started, but Lacey's body pressing tight against him stopped the flow of words and thoughts as she kissed him goodnight. Her velvety smooth cheeks were cool, but her lips were warm and soft, and Bro's knees nearly buckled with desire. He had been ever so patient up till now, not once acting too hastily and wantonly to avoid making her feel like he was pushing her too far too soon. But the underlying need for Lacey, for her scent, her taste, her everything, was always there.

It was Jordan's light chuckle that saved Bro from making an embarrassing scene, wanting Lacey so much it hurt. Offering a wordless thank-you to his brother's fiancé, Bro let go of his girlfriend with the utmost reluctance.

"Lacey, I…." The words of affection were there, hanging on the tip of his tongue, so close to bursting through his safeguards. Bro felt his mouth twitch open and closed as he almost said the words.

As Lacey blinked, her long golden lashes fluttered like veils in the wind, and Bro had a feeling they were both standing at the edge of the same precipice. Confessions of love, so close. Without speaking, though, and with a quick buss on his cheek, Lacey was out the door and down the stairs, a grinning and winking Jordan following close behind.

Bro flipped him off just before he disappeared around the stairwell corner.

Sighing sadly, Bro hurried to the other window, where he could see the front of the building. He watched longingly as Jordan held the passenger's side door of his monstrous SUV open for Lacey, like a gentleman, and then rounded the car in a rush as the rain started to pour. Biting his lower lip hard, Bro told himself he would not go all girly and start blubbering. Still, his gaze did not veer away until he could no longer see the car's taillights.

A gentle hand landed on his shoulder, and Bro knew without looking that Sebastian stood next to him, staring into the dark of the night where his man had also gone.

"You'll see Lacey tomorrow," Sebastian said encouragingly, his unusual hollow voice reaching Bro effortlessly. Although it was not like him to feel so emotional, Bro leaned back against his brother briefly for comfort, and that was enough to ground him and settle his anxieties. Yeah, he'd see his girlfriend the next day and the day after that and so on, hopefully so far into the future Bro never had to think about the alternative.

WHEN the heater began to warm up the car properly, Lacey settled more comfortably into the cushioned seat, sighing. The tactile memory of kissing Bro still lingered on her lips, making them tingle, and as usual, a goofy smile rose on her lips.

"Thinking of Bro?" Jordan's teasing voice was kind, and Lacey knew him well enough by now to realize he was supportive of their relationship.

"Don't I always?" she countered amusedly, glancing at her driver. Jordan was a very good-looking man with his muscular build, platinum-blond hair with lavender-colored streaks, green eyes like gems, and tattoos and piercings all around. Lacey had never kissed a guy with a tongue piercing. Then again, she didn't know if Jordan actually had one. Lacey had not taken that close a look, and she blushed at the thought.

"Listen, Lace...." Jordan sounded more serious now, so she gave him her rapt attention. "Does he...? No, never mind." He shook his head as if to clear confusing thoughts.

"What?" Lacey asked, curious now.

Jordan harrumphed, but the sound seemed directed at himself. "Bro's young. You're both young. So if he.... I mean, there shouldn't be any, you know, um, pressure... to hurry into...." His tanned face rarely showed his blush, but this time the reddening was definitely visible.

Suppressing a laugh as best she could, Lacey did grin at that. "Don't worry, Jordan. Bro would never force me into anything I didn't want, no matter how horny he got. He treats me like a lady. He's the perfect gentleman."

Jordan gave her an incredulous look, quirking an eyebrow. "This is Bro we're talking about, right? Boy, seventeen, black hair, blue eyes, athlete?"

Lacey giggled. "Yes. He's sweet. He'd never hurt me." Looking away, but feeling quite mischievous, she added, "And it's not like we haven't done stuff already." Now Lacey was totally messing with Jordan, since she and Bro had not yet done the big... *it*. Anal intercourse. That was a bridge they had yet to cross.

The car suddenly swerved sharply as Jordan's shock caused him to overreact. "Come again?"

Lacey laughed out loud, bouncing on her seat in full-on goading mode. "Oh, come on, Jordan. We're seventeen, not seven. And we use protection each and every—"

"Aw, I think I'm gonna be sick," Jordan groaned with a pained expression, though Lacey was certain at least half of that was exaggeration.

"Oh, come *on*, Jordan," Lacey reproached. "You're seriously going to sit there and tell me you never did anything before you were eighteen or, goodness, twenty-one? 'Cause that would definitely be a load of—"

"All right, all right," Jordan practically shouted, waving an impatient hand around to stop her from talking. "Fine. I'll take your word for it." Readjusting his position on the seat, he added, "For now."

Snickering, Lacey let it drop, because Jordan did have a point. Bro was like most of his friends, young and eager. But Lacey also knew Bro felt something deeper for her than if she were just a casual high school hookup. The two of them were in the final stretch of their senior year, having successfully navigated the major pitfalls of the high school house of horrors—so far.

And the possible threats in school were just the tip of the iceberg.

After a second's hesitation, Lacey asked, "Jordan?"

"Yeah?" His gaze remained fixed on the road ahead.

"Could you…? Would you consider…?" It was her turn to shake her head. "Bro has told me you're a martial arts expert."

Jordan grinned. "I know a few tricks."

"Would you teach me?"

Jordan's suspicious cop glare hit her dead on, and Lacey fought the instinct to squirm under his relentless scrutiny. "Teach you what, Lace?"

Licking her lips nervously, Lacey tried to add levity to the situation, so she giggled a little. "I mean, I'm…. Well, just look at me. A boy dressed like a girl—"

"Lace, is someone harassing or bullying you?" Jordan's serious tone had taken on a sharp, cold edge, and she shivered as a result. She was thankful she never had to be on the other end of this cop's interrogation tactics. Although at the moment, that was what this felt like.

Sighing as if feeling way more relaxed than she was, Lacey answered, "I would just like to learn how to defend myself *if* something were to happen. That's all." Though concerned Jordan might be able to read her face better than she would have liked, Lacey confronted Jordan's stare with her own pleading gaze. She did have a secret, but if she got Jordan's help, then she would not have to tell anyone. The problem would sort itself out.

It was obvious Jordan's suspicions had not been fully alleviated, but finally he gave a curt nod. "Sure. I'll show you some basic moves. In this day and age, everyone should know them. Just let me know when it's convenient for you, and I'll check my own schedule."

Lacey sighed in relief and smiled. "Thanks, Jordan." But before she allowed herself to completely let down her guard, she quickly added, "Jordan? Please don't tell Bro. He's got enough on his plate, and I don't want him worrying about me, not any more than he already does. And believe me, he worries plenty."

As he shifted awkwardly, Jordan's lips pursed in disapproval. "I don't like keeping secrets, Lace. You need to tell him at some point 'cause—"

"I will, I promise," Lacey hastened to say. "Just… not yet, okay? I need to prep him—and myself."

Jordan seemed to pause to think about it, and Lacey could relate. Having been brought up by emotionally distant parents, Bro had an unusually warm and close relationship with his deaf brother. He had a tendency to wear his heart on his sleeve, sometimes, and he could be very touchy-feely. Those endearing qualities made Lacey lov—um, like him more.

Her heart leaped at the sudden swell of emotions within her, and her breath caught in her throat.

Could I really be… in love… with Bro? Lacey had no answer to that. Yet.

Chapter 2

"WHAT the fuck?" Bro groaned as he fell to the ground with a heavy thud. Pain spread through him from his arm, and he cursed out loud. Though the grass lessened the impact, the springtime ground was cold and hard.

A low, intimidating sneer came from above him. "I thought you pansies were sturdier flowers than this. Can't take even one good tackle."

Peering through the flashing sparks of pain up at Deacon, the new guy in school and on the team, Bro shot him a furious glare. "What the fuck is your problem?" He didn't even have to touch his arm to know his shoulder was dislocated. It had happened twice before, both times during sports, but never from such vicious intent to harm.

Deacon chuckled. "Hey, if you can't handle a few bruises, maybe you should sit this one out. Or better yet, don't play at all. Find yourself a little flower patch to grow out of, yeah?"

Bro did not have an opportunity for a smart retort before the thundering sound of a dozen feet approaching nearly deafened him as the rest of the team gathered around.

"What the hell happened?" The deep, serene voice belonged to Bradley Carlisle, the captain of the team as well as the quarterback—and Bro's best friend.

Before Bro had a chance to make even a peep, Deacon laughed coldly. "The lily here couldn't take a little tumble."

With an awful lot of huffing and some serious physical effort—aided by Bradley's hand on his waist—Bro managed to climb to his feet, his face red with anger. "There's tackling, and then there's what you did. You attacked me. My fucking shoulder's dislocated."

"What?" Bradley's deep voice boomed with a mixture of concern and fury. Quickly, he studied the state of Bro's injuries with expert hands, and though it was painful, Bro didn't let out a sound. "Yeah, it is dislocated. The coach can set it, or the nurse—"

"So can you, B," Bro interjected, starting to feel queasy with the pain. "You've done reductions before. I trust you. Just do it."

Though Bradley was frowning, there was determination in his brown eyes, and with a tiny nod he began, letting his experienced fingertips carefully roam the bones, muscles, and joints of Bro's unmoving, straightened arm, searching for the one right place to effect a fix. When he found it, he moved the arm bone in tiny increments, and then he popped the joint in place—hard. Well, the maneuver itself was soft, but it felt... utterly excruciating.

Unable to squelch the grunt arising from the stabbing pain, Bro breathed through the ordeal. As soon as it was done, the sharp edge of the pain dulled into a constant but manageable ache that was beginning to die down. This kind of physical torment he was familiar with. Still, it was clear he would not be able to practice for a few weeks.

"Rake, what the hell did you do?" Bradley's tone was a warning. Not many knew how dangerous he could be, and apparently Deacon Rake was not among those privileged few.

Deacon shrugged, indifferent, as though he had done nothing wrong. "I was supposed to take the squirt down, and I did. It's not my fault if he's as fragile as a daisy."

The rest of the team shook with pent-up rage, but then they took one look at Bradley and swiftly stepped back, widening the circle around their captain, Bro, and Deacon. Bro noticed the subtle change in the atmosphere, while Deacon remained casually oblivious.

Bradley was the ideal jock, tall and broad as a barn, with bulging muscles of steel and the attitude of a consummate professional. He was going places, Bro had a feeling. But he was also a man who took shit from no one.

His dark-haired head tilted to the side and his eyes narrowed. "My twin brother Ricky is gay. Would you like to call him a fag? And me a queer by association?" Bradley closed the gap between him and Deacon so fast it was like he'd transported in front of him. Deacon swallowed, no longer looking so sure of himself. "This school *and* my team are 100 percent hate-free. If you have a problem with that, Rake, take a fucking hike."

It was curious how much the attitude of social leaders—the popular kids—affected the general atmosphere of a high school's environment. When someone like Bradley took a stand on a crucial social issue—like being progay and speaking out against bullies—everyone took notice, and like ripples in a pond, the student populace followed his lead. Bro watched silently as Bradley's words sank in for Deacon. The team around them nodded along with grim expressions, all aimed at Deacon, who tried his best to backpedal.

"Hey, man, I was just…. It was just a joke. I didn't mean to—"

"Fuck that," Bradley said, his tone even lower than before, and the fire in his eyes could have made even the strongest man burn to cinders. "We have a scrimmage against Lincoln High on Saturday. If we lose because Bro's not able to play, then that's on you, shitface—and you'll be off the team so fast *you* won't know what hit you." Pointing a finger at Deacon, who was two inches shorter than him, Bradley growled, "And don't even think about whining to the coach about this. You wanted to play in the big leagues. This is how real men behave, not bigoted assholes. So you decide if you wanna play ball, or get thrown out for being a dick."

Though it wasn't like Bro to let someone else fight his battles for him, Bradley was his closest friend. They'd have each other's backs any day of the week, and not only because Bro was gay like Bradley's brother. For that reason alone, Bro made an exception and ignored Bradley's intervention instead of verbally striking Deacon down himself to make sure the moron didn't bother him again.

Deacon gulped, his handsome face pale and coated with a light sheen of sweat. "Sorry, man."

"I'm not the one you need to apologize to, dumbass," Bradley said, stepping aside so he could see Bro and do the right thing.

It was clear Deacon was doing it reluctantly, but looking half-angry, half-embarrassed and shifting his weight around, he looked down at the ground and muttered, "Sorry."

Though Bro would have liked to torment the guy into a more profound apology and maybe some quality groveling, his arm was part throbbing, part numb, and he wanted to lie down. And he was a better man than that anyway. "Whatever, dude. Next time I'll kick your ass."

Bradley rested his big palm on Bro's healthy shoulder, locking gazes with him. "You gonna be okay? You need to get that shoulder X-rayed ASAP. The team needs you back on your feet, you know. You're our fastest runner, and you never miss catching the ball. The field can't hold you down." Suddenly, he grinned wickedly. "And I'm in no mood to hear you bitch and moan about your sore little hand—"

"Fuck you." Bro shoved the guy back with his right hand, glad his dominant hand, at least, was fine. "You're the bitch, you fucking turd." But he said it without vehemence and with humor.

Bradley chuckled, as did the other guys, and the situation was defused.

Accompanied by good-natured bickering, they returned from the football field to the locker room, where Bro spoke to their coach, Mr. Young, and got a pass to see a doctor. Deacon, however, got an earful. Thankfully, Bro only heard the first bars of the deafening shouting match, because he changed as best he could and walked out, dialing Jordan's cell to beg for a lift.

"YOU'RE feeling better today, I see," Mr. Teasdale said admiringly, and Lacey beamed while finishing her set. The last notes of Bach's sonata for solo violin in G minor flowed through the air, seemingly light and effortless, but actually requiring skill and precision it had taken Lacey years to master.

Lacey grinned as she lowered the violin from beneath her jaw, where the slightly rougher patch of skin was, and waved her bow hand to relax the tightened muscles there. "Maybe I should move on to the Irish fiddle next. All those jigs and reels would certainly give my fingers a challenge."

Teasdale, her violin teacher, laughed. "As a mistress of the vibrato, you could handle all those rolls and slurs, my dear, I have no doubt," he said in his posh English accent Lacey liked and yet found quaintly amusing. She wasn't all that sure it was genuine, either. Not that it mattered, because he was a good man and a great teacher.

"Gosh, Mr. Teasdale," Lacey teased. "You sure know how to make everything sound positively naughty."

Mr. Teasdale's cheeks reddened below his round spectacles, and he mumbled something incoherent as he rubbed the back of his neck. "Lacey," he scolded almost tenderly. "Did you try that *Romanza* by Martino yet?"

Lacey shook her head. "No. I've been working on the Liszt Piano Sonata in B Minor for Solo Violin. That's what you told me last week."

Mr. Teasdale frowned, recalling, and then his brow cleared. "Ah, yes. I'd forgotten that one. Good, good. And how's it coming along?"

Shrugging, Lacey said vaguely, "All right, I guess."

Mr. Teasdale smiled knowingly. "Not really setting your heart on fire, that music, is it? We'll have to find you something more inspirational, then."

"Maybe."

"At least we've managed to steer you away from Takemitsu's saddest tones."

Lacey bristled. "I'll have you know Takemitsu's 'Requiem' is just fabulous. On par with Mozart's." Under her breath she added, "Besides, without it I wouldn't have met Bro."

"Your boyfriend?" Mr. Teasdale asked politely with a hint of a smile. Though not by any means certain, Lacey suspected her violin teacher was, if not fully gay, then leaning heavily in that direction. Not that his potential sexual orientation made a bit of difference to Lacey. No one understood better than she that who a person slept with had no bearing on his talents and abilities.

"Yes." Lacey blushed, looking sheepish, as she had not intended to bring him up at all. "I was playing 'Requiem' in the music room on my first day at the new school. After my mom…." Her voice trailed off as the hollow space in her chest vibrated briefly with the sorrow of her loss.

"Forgive me, Lacey," Mr. Teasdale said empathetically, resting his hand on her slender shoulder. "I did not mean to force you to reminisce—"

"You didn't, Mr. Teasdale, I assure you. It's fine." Lacey gave him an encouraging smile, hoping to alleviate his anxieties about causing her distress.

Then she noticed his hand was still on her shoulder.

So did he, and he yanked his hand back as if it were on fire. "Oh, goodness," he sputtered, clearly distraught and embarrassed. "I, oh, I forgot. All these rules about, um, touching and.... I did not mean anything by it, of course, Lacey. Surely you don't believe—"

"It's all right, Mr. Teasdale," Lacey cut in kindly, determined to show nothing but self-confidence and maturity in an awkward situation. "I know you didn't. And I appreciate your sympathy. I think I'm old enough to be able to tell a comforting touch from inappropriate groping."

Mr. Teasdale fidgeted awkwardly. "My God, I would never...." Clearing his throat, and his thoughts, too, apparently, he added, "You are a very wise young woman, Lacey." Suddenly, he became aware of his second faux pas, and he was struck silent, opening and closing his mouth like a fish on dry land.

Lacey took pity on him because he was a nice man and a consummate professional in his field. "Mr. Teasdale, please, stop. I'm not offended, really. I don't mind being called a man or a woman. It's fine." To derail any further unpleasantries and awkward silences—and because she was curious—she changed the subject. "You played for the London Philharmonic, why did you leave them?"

Having expected sadness or longing, Lacey was surprised to see relief and humor in Mr. Teasdale's brown eyes. "In a word, stress." He sighed but not longingly at all. "The pressure to perform outstandingly was constant, and I learned quickly it was not a good atmosphere to cultivate strong mental health. I felt like I was headed for a burnout or a breakdown, so I quit. I became a teacher, and I have not regretted my decision to this day."

"That's good."

"Though it meant a demotion in career terms, it was the right decision for me." While Mr. Teasdale's eyes had glazed over a bit in self-reflection, now they brightened again as his gaze landed on Lacey in serious inspection. "Do you want to become a professional musician, Lacey? You show great promise, my dear. With your talent, it's absolutely something you should consider. Especially if you could get a music scholarship to a noteworthy college as we discussed."

That was a thought that had given Lacey many sleepless nights already, and she wasn't ready to talk about it, not even with her music mentor, not yet. "I'll sleep on it."

Cocking his head, Mr. Teasdale paused, and his scrutiny was evident, though nothing like the burning intensity of Jordan's cop gaze. "Of course, sweetheart. This is not the time for that choice, and I'm sure there are other people you might want to talk to about it first and foremost. Just so you know, Lacey, I only meant my words as encouragement. I was honored to write you a letter of recommendation and aid you with the video auditions. You have true skill, and I do hate seeing the most gifted squander their—" Suddenly, he paled and bit his lip nervously. "Oh my. I'm doing it again, aren't I?" He shook his head angrily. "Ignore me, my dear."

Lacey laughed companionably. "As if that were ever possible, Mr. Teasdale."

Chapter 3

"I'M GOING. And unless you're gonna tie me up and throw me in the basement, you can't stop me." Bro felt like growling, and he probably was too.

Jordan chuckled. "We live in a loft. There is no basement."

"But, Bro, you're still not well enough—" Sebastian said worriedly, his expressive face scrunched in concern.

"Bas, I'm fine," Bro snapped back, waving his hands about, half speaking, half signing his words. "And if you want to worry about something, worry about my mental health. I *will* go bananas if I can't see Lacey!"

At that comment, Jordan chortled so badly he actually doubled over and excused himself from the room. Blushing, Bro realized he could have chosen different words, but he was too pissed to care. He had already missed out on one week with his girl, and he wasn't about to lose a single day more.

A week and a half after Deacon had bruised him into an unplayable condition, Bro's shoulder had finally healed. A doctor had examined and X-rayed the shoulder, and there were no bone fragments or torn ligaments to suggest a permanent injury. Bro had been as happy as a clam, even though he had missed the scrimmage on Saturday. After his fiasco from before, Deacon had put in an effort at the game, and they had indeed won. Lucky for him, Bro had thought at the time, surly and resentful. He did not appreciate having to sit in the stands with his hand in a sling to watch a game he should have been a part of. Nonetheless, at least the injury had been temporary.

And tonight was date night.

His date with Lacey.

Bro had missed his girlfriend the whole time. Sebastian had allowed them to meet at the loft, but he had made sure with constant interruptions that Bro could not and would not exert himself in any sense of the word. Bro had been so mad. He could not tolerate his big brother serving in the role of chaperone.

And he wasn't having any more delays or diversions. Bro *would* go out with Lacey, dammit. "I'm going, and that's final!"

Sebastian's brow was furrowed, but Bro knew he wasn't angry so much as he was afraid. They meant the world to each other, and neither of them could honestly handle the idea of losing any more loved ones, not with their family history *and* their extended family all having hazardous professions. Understanding all that from Sebastian's expression alone, Bro's irritation went away.

"Bas, I know you can be a real mother hen sometimes, but I'm okay. The doctor said so. And... I miss her." He didn't bother to conceal the pleading in his voice or expression, because Sebastian was a reasonable brother and guardian. And Lacey was a good girl.

Sebastian's soft smile confirmed as much, and Bro relaxed. "All right. Go see your girl. But, Bro, curfew's at ten—"

Bro sputtered. "What? Hell to the no! Midnight!"

Sebastian's blue eyes narrowed as his lips pursed with disapproval. It was funny how he could always tell when Bro raised his voice even though he couldn't hear a thing. Finally, after what felt like the silence of the Inquisition before sentencing, Sebastian said serenely, "Eleven. And not one minute more. If you're late by ten seconds, I am sending a black-and-white out to find you and bring you home in the most humiliating way possible."

"Got that, squirt?" Jordan said from behind Bro, chuckling and tousling his hair as he walked by to crash down on the couch.

"Don't call me that, *Jordy*." They both hated being called by derogatory nicknames, which was why they called each other those things all the time. Bro threw a glare in Jordan's direction, but the guy was just sitting there, not looking at him, grinning. Well, at least he hadn't used the A-word. Something to be thankful for. "If I have to get back by eleven, I need the car." He was so blackmailing Jordan, but he was a good driver. In two years he hadn't hit a thing—except that one trash can, but honestly there had been previous dents in both the can *and* the car, so technically it wasn't his fault. The trash can had moved on its own!

Quirking an eyebrow in a way that suggested he wasn't buying it, Jordan looked up at Bro from the newspaper he was reading. The probing gaze made Bro uneasy, as always, but he was used to Jordan by now and knew all his games. This tactic of intimidation wasn't going to work, nuh-uh, no way.

"If you get pulled over—"

"I won't! I'm a good driver!"

"If you do, you're on your own. I may be a cop, but neither I nor Sebastian will make any charges disappear. We will bail you out of lockup, but that's it. Your mess, you clean it up."

Though the calm words sent a frisson of fear running up and down Bro's spine, he was secretly pleased to hear it. Jordan was going to trust him with his car *and* his integrity. Jordan was treating Bro like a man, telling him that actions had consequences, and though Bro would always have his family, he would have to take care of his own shit from now on. He was seventeen, after all, and not a kid.

"I'll just drive me and Lacey to the restaurant. Then I'll drive her home. No joyriding, I promise." Lifting his chin defiantly, he half expected Jordan to change his mind. But Jordan kept eye contact for a few seconds more before shrugging, nodding, and returning his attention to the paper.

Bro had won. And he felt ten feet tall, his chest puffing up with a surge of pride. His widening grin threatened to split his face in half.

"YOU look beautiful, baby," Bro said admiringly, and it wasn't an exaggeration.

Lacey had never looked more lovely, graceful, and sensual. She wore a light-gold, body-hugging knee-high dress with long sleeves and a turtleneck. A dark-brown ornament made of lace circled around the dress, snakelike, from bodice to hem. The tones of the dress accentuated her hazel eyes and blond hair. And it did not escape Bro's notice that she also had on golden silk stockings and black high heels.

The black velvet band around her neck gave her an almost collared look, like a love slave, and Bro felt his heart start thudding in his chest, his throat drying, and his cock beginning to swell in his jeans—the cleanest pair he had. His imagination provided a whole host of flashes of what she might have underneath her elegant dress. He had seen her naked before, and that sight never failed to get him so hot he thought he might explode. Lacey's nimble, slender limbs, thin waist, prominent hip bones, and silken skin were all apparently designed to drive Bro mad with want.

Lacey snickered, covering her mouth with her hand again. "You look great too."

Baffled, Bro stared down at himself with a frown. He had on his usual light-blue jeans, white sneakers, and a white T-shirt with the text "Jocks love balls" emblazoned on it in gray letters, a heart symbol in place of the word "love." Over it he had his sports jacket. This kind of outfit was nothing new to him, but he felt comfortable in it. Yeah, he was aware maybe he should have worn something more refined and stylish for a date, but he had tried that once—slacks and a button-down—and Lacey's lips had pursed in a disapproving way that conveyed her irritation without words. She was not a fan of Bro being someone he wasn't or behaving differently from his normal style.

The things he did have going for him, however, were his height— he was taller than his big brother Sebastian by two inches and hoping to add a bit more to the five-eleven he was now sporting—and his musculature. The variety of sports he engaged in, especially football, had given him hard, firm, bulging muscles. As a result, his clothes fit him to a tee, showcasing his arms, pecs, thighs, and ass to perfection.

The appreciative gleam in Lacey's eyes confirmed as much, and Bro beamed.

"So, shall we?" he asked, gesturing to the door.

Lacey nodded. "Where are we going?"

"Downtown, to Fiola. Is that okay?"

Lacey smiled, her eyes lighting up, and nodded. "Absolutely. Love the food there."

Just when Bro thought he could not have been more pleased, he was proven wrong.

THERE were definite advantages to having the corner table at Fiola, Lacey remarked to herself. The tiny rectangular rosewood tables, clean and polished, were situated almost indecently close to one another, barely leaving room to maneuver. Here in the corner, though, Bro and Lacey had some much-needed privacy, even though the general chatter in the place reminded her of lively cocktail parties—not very intimate for a date. But the lights were dimmed, and there was a soft golden glow all around, giving the place a luster somewhere between classy and cozy, enhancing the mood.

Not that the place itself mattered to Lacey, who couldn't keep her eyes off Bro sitting opposite her, smiling in that smitten, lopsided way she adored. "How's the football practice gone lately?" Lacey knew there had been trouble with some new guy, but nothing since then.

Bro shrugged. "Okay. Kinda boring. Brad still won't let me do everything I want to, and that dickhead—um, Deacon's been an asshole ever since he busted my shoulder. No rough stuff, or Brad would kick him off the team, but off the field…. He's just being Deac the Dick."

Hearing frustration color Bro's words—and seeing embarrassment over cursing coloring his cheeks—Lacey decided to cheer him up. "Maybe he's jealous of your mad skills, or for having the cutest girlfriend in town." She batted her eyelashes at him and winked.

Bro relaxed and grinned. "Could be." He placed his palm over Lacey's hand on the table, caressing the skin with his thumb. "But in case you're thinking of moving on from me to him, just know I will fight for you."

It was Lacey's turn to blush. Bro could be such a typical boy with his caveman routine sometimes, and clueless at other times—yet he had a big heart and was capable of such tenderness and warmth Lacey could not help but be impressed.

"From what I hear of Rake, you're definitely going to have to suffer my company a bit longer."

"No pain in that, only pleasure." Bro's voice had dropped an octave or so, and Lacey felt heat flash inside her belly. The sensation only increased when Bro's gaze raked all over her with single-minded intent. "You wanna maybe—"

They were interrupted by a waiter, who asked what they wanted to drink and if they had decided on what to eat. Lacey and Bro both jumped at the young man's eagerness, letting go of each other's hand. But the waiter only took a curious gander at both of them and then grinned, winking like a conspirator. Lacey ordered a water, while Bro went for a beer. When that didn't fly with the waiter, he settled for a nonalcoholic apple cider. The guy departed to fill their drink orders.

Once he was gone, Bro recaptured Lacey's hand tenderly, squeezing a little. "Those guys should wear bells around their necks."

Lacey giggled. "In here, in this noise, who'd notice?"

"What you gonna order?"

Lacey scanned over the possibilities. She did this even though she knew very well what Bro wanted, and she happened to like the same thing. Normally, she would have gone for a lighter meal, perhaps only a salad, but with Bro she not only wanted but needed the energy provided by a full stomach just to keep up with him.

"You know what?" She peered up at him through her lashes, smiling. "I'm famished. I'm gonna go for the grand platter of Tuscan-style grilled meats. Is that all right with you?"

The relief on Bro's face was quickly replaced with hunger—of both sorts. Her cheeks heating, Lacey bit her lower lip, and Bro's gaze dropped to her mouth, his eyes darkening.

"Cool."

When the waiter returned with their drinks, they ordered the grilled meats. Before the guy left, however, Bro called him back, got a chocolate mousse for himself, and then surprised Lacey by asking for coconut custard with Limoncello Granita—Italian ice cream—and yuzu, a Japanese citrus, as a dessert for Lacey. With a wink, the waiter departed, and Lacey had to shift on her seat to adjust her erection. She was wearing her silkiest, softest, loveliest underwear, and she knew her arousal would soon show if she didn't get herself under control.

Glaring at her boyfriend, she said, "What if I had wanted something else?" Bro blinked at the snarky comment and heat suffused his cheeks. Lacey cursed herself. "I'm sorry, Bro, I… I'm sorry. It's perfect." When Bro's frown wouldn't dissipate, she decided honesty was the best policy, so she leaned over the table to whisper, "It's just… I'm getting… a hard-on, you know, so… if you could please not do anything sweet?"

The mood lightened in an instant. Bro's furrowed brow smoothed and a wicked grin replaced the sad pout.

His tone was positively mischievous as he whispered back, "Does that mean no sweet-talking, sweet-kissing, or sweet-thinking? 'Cause I can't do all three. You're just too damn… sweet. All over."

Lacey couldn't take it anymore, not when she knew what she wanted. Closing the gap between them, she kissed Bro tentatively. And then Bro inched forward enough to deepen the kiss into something more sensual than a mere brush of skin. The slightly tangy taste of the apple cider on Bro's lips was sugary, and Lacey wanted more, swiping the tip of her tongue over Bro's full lower lip, savoring the taste.

By the time they parted, they were both breathless and flushed. Lacey's heart thundered as she felt a longing for closeness she knew could not take place at the moment, not here. She desperately wanted to be somewhere else, anywhere they could be alone, to hold each other to their hearts' content and sink into one another, into each other's bodies, to let go and experience what the physical side of love was like.

Once again, Lacey felt shaken inside that the word—and associated feeling—"love" kept popping up: in her head, in her body, *and* in her heart.

Bro was grinning like the proverbial cat that ate the cream, licking his glistening lips. "Just like I said. Sweet all over."

Covering her mouth, Lacey smiled and snickered. "So are you, honey."

A sharp clink of glass stole her attention, and she suddenly remembered they were in public. Nervously, she took a quick look around to see if anyone was watching, and right away felt silly having done so. What did it matter if someone ogled at them?

Bro had apparently come to the same conclusion. "It's just us, babe. No one else. Just you and me." His hold on her hand was smooth and reassuring, and Lacey forgot why she had been so jittery. With Bro, she always felt safe. Even when his smoldering gaze undressed her slowly, one piece of clothing at a time.

The same feeling of security had been present since the beginning. "You remember when we met?"

Bro chuckled, looking smug, grinning. "How could I forget? Best day of my life."

That Lacey agreed with wholeheartedly.

ON HER first day in a new high school, in the middle of the school year, near Christmas, Lacey had felt out of place and lonely, and she sought the safe familiarity of the school's music room. Without a word, she took her violin from the case, lifted it beneath her chin, and allowed the sad tones of Takemitsu's "Requiem" to carry her away to another place in time.

After the death of her mother in a car accident, Lacey had withdrawn into herself. And her dad didn't know how to handle her being gay and feminine, let alone her grief-stricken state and search for solitude. His solution was to move to another town, as if that could erase everything that had happened and wash her emotional slate clean. And then he had begun to drown himself in drink in seedy bars into the wee hours of the morning.

On that day Lacey had been crying silently, and not even music could distract her from her melancholy and sorrow.

"That's beautiful."

Startled, Lacey jumped at the sound of a boy's voice. She turned around to find a cute guy leaning against the doorframe of the music room, looking relaxed and comfortable, with a lopsided smile dangling on his lips. Wearing blue jeans, a gray T-shirt, and a school football jacket, he had a casual charm Lacey found more than a little attractive.

The shiny black hair—almost emo in style—and the bright-blue eyes only added to the effect.

"Um, thanks," she muttered, feeling emotionally exposed.

The boy's head cocked to the side as he inspected Lacey, who was getting more than a bit uncomfortable with every passing second. Suddenly, he looked bashful, even blushed a little.

"Hey, I'm sorry. I didn't mean to interrupt you, or anything. I just thought... you play beautifully." Standing up from his slouching position, he squared his shoulders—and for the first time Lacey saw how big the guy actually was. Not beefy, but tall and very fit. He gave a small, shy smile, lifting his chin in a quick good-bye gesture. "I guess I'll see you around."

As he started to turn, Lacey called out, "Yes, see you... around...." She had tried to sound confident and at ease, but it came out an undignified squeak. She knew he wouldn't stay now.

But the guy glanced over his shoulder, curious, and then he sauntered closer to Lacey, who suddenly found it hard to breathe—or look anywhere else but at the young man with eyes the color of forget-me-nots and a flirtatious grin tugging the left corner of his mouth.

He stopped in front of her, sort of swinging on his heels. "Hi, I'm Bro."

Lacey looked down, shy, and smiled a little. "I'm... Lacey." She wondered what it was he saw. Did he see a pretty girl in a lavender-colored dress, or a boy trying to be something he wasn't?

Bro's thumbs were hooked in front pockets of his jeans, and as such his hands framed his bulging crotch deliciously. All of a sudden, Lacey realized she was staring.

While she was busy blushing, he chuckled softly. "You're new?"

Lacey dared a quick glance up and saw only fascination in the boy's face. "Yes. We moved here two weeks ago. Me and my dad."

The boy nodded. "Welcome to DC."

"Thanks." Lacey became aware she was still holding her violin in one hand and the bow in the other, undecided as to what to do with them. Fidgeting, her hands seemed to move on their own, searching for the red fiberglass violin case, and she feared she might have given the impression of a broken robot, twitching away.

But then Bro was there, handing her the case from the chair nearby. "This what you wanted?"

"Yes, thanks." As she grasped the case and started putting her instrument away, not forgetting to wipe the excess rosin from the strings, Lacey noted she had probably thanked the boy half a dozen times by now. *God, what is wrong with me?* She was usually more articulate than this.

Lacey didn't have a boyfriend. Yet she wanted to get to know a boy. And this Bro was surprisingly kind and courteous. He must have had a great, supportive family.

That thought brought into the foreground her own recent loss, and she found herself shaking with sorrow, her eyes watering.

"Hey, hey," the boy said, his voice filled with concern as he placed his hand on her shoulder comfortingly. "I'm sorry if I—"

"It's not you, I swear," Lacey denied quickly, in between sobs, blinking furiously to dispel the moisture in her eyes. "You're nice."

His hand left her shoulder in a hurry, and when he spoke, his tone was darker, lower, more dangerous. "Has someone been... not nice to you?"

The boy's protectiveness surprised Lacey, who looked up in amazement. No one had cared about her well-being like that before, unless they were family. Bro's expression was akin to a storm cloud, and Lacey felt a sudden, strange feeling of safety flowing over her.

Smiling uncertainly, she said, "No, I haven't been here long enough. It's...." She bit her lower lip. "I lost my mom."

Bro's face overflowed with sympathy, and he took her hand very carefully, as if it were a fine piece of porcelain. "I'm so sorry. I've lost my mom too."

Lacey's eyes widened in shock. "Your mom's dead too?"

Looking sad and dejected, Bro shook his head a bit. "No. She just didn't want me, or my brother." Then he frowned, looking ashamed. "I suppose it's not the same."

"No." Lacey shook her head. "It's worse. Being alive and abandoning your children? Yes, it's definitely worse. At least my mom loved me." She gasped when she realized what she had said, how insensitive it must have sounded. "Wait, I didn't mean it like that—"

"It's okay." Bro smiled encouragingly, his eyes filled with levity again. "I know what you meant." Sighing in relief, Lacey squeezed his hand empathetically, and his hold of her nimble fingers tightened a bit. "I didn't intend to sound, you know, aggressive and shit—um, I mean all… caveman. It's just I thought you might have been… bullied, or something."

"Thankfully, no." Lacey offered her brightest smile, showing her white teeth, and the effect was instantaneous. Bro's eyes seemed to glaze over and a goofy, lopsided grin rose to his lips. Had this cute guy been into boys, Lacey would have hugged him. But someone that sweet probably already had a girlfriend anyway, so she quelled the instinct.

Then she was proven wrong.

Puffing his chest a bit, Bro nodded and said, "If you ever are, you know, bullied, you just come to me, okay? I'll straighten everything out." Lacey was about to interject that she did not need a knight in shining armor, especially one who thought he was protecting a girl, but Bro spoke first. "I mean… you look real pretty in that dress. Even if you are… you know… a guy."

Bro's cheeks reddened as he spoke, but to Lacey he looked chivalrous to the point of glowing. "Y-you don't mind?"

Then the self-assured, cocky grin was back in place as he winked. "Nah. I definitely don't mind. And I'd mind even less if you were my girl. Even if you are a boy. Fortunately for us, I'm a boy who likes boys."

He shrugged nonchalantly, and his laid-back attitude worked wonders with Lacey. At that promising comment, Lacey had to laugh out loud, the emotion and the following physical response bubbling inside her like champagne. It had been so long since she had felt true, unabashed merriment she almost went down on her knees to thank God—or Bro, whichever came first. The pain of losing a mother and the sadness at having a father who didn't understand or approve of her all seemed to melt away as she let herself go, emotionally and physically.

BRO had equaled comfort and safety that day, not to mention humor and vitality, and to this day Lacey had never forgotten the gift of laughter he had given her then.

"How did you know back then that I was a boy? I mean I was dressed like a girl, and I had makeup on." Lacey had always wondered about that, marveling at Bro's accurate perception. She leaned closer above the table, wanting the intimacy of truth to envelop her.

Bro grinned wickedly. "You really want to know?"

Lacey frowned, irked at her boyfriend's baiting. "Of course I do. I asked, didn't I?"

Appearing almost disinterested, Bro said, "I was watching you. As pretty as you were, beautiful as an angel, even, I was *really* looking. Your hips, your waist, your chest, your stance, even your cute face—"

"Cute?" Lacey narrowed her eyes, though she did not mind the words even half as much as she indicated. She was totally needling him back.

"Yeah." Bro smirked and winked. "So freaking cute and cuddly and adorable—"

"Oh, so there was a puppy in the music room with me?"

Bro laughed out loud, causing a few people at nearby tables to stare at them, frowning, but he didn't seem to care. "Like I said, sweet and adorable. That's you. That was you then, too, both girl *and* boy. Just perfect. Made for me."

Lacey blushed so fast and hard at those words, she worried her cheeks might go up in flames. And that warmth was nothing compared to the heat pooling in the pit of her stomach, giving her an erection. Squirming on her seat, she tried to talk her dick down, but the effort proved unsuccessful with Bro sitting opposite her, flashing that irreverent, toothy grin and winking with those blue eyes.

But Bro wasn't finished, and he whispered softly, "Perfect."

Lacey covered her mouth as she smiled at the lovely compliment, and then she sighed longingly, her gaze locked with Bro's. "I wish we could leave, just go home and make love."

Swallowing hard, Bro looked ready to jump up and drag Lacey off with him. But the arrival of the waiter stopped him, and Lacey had to grin at the utterly displeased expression Bro was sporting. He even growled a bit. The waiter placed two huge platters of grilled meats before them, and Bro wasn't the only one drooling. They might have been hungry for each other, but they were practically starving too, so once the waiter had moved off, they dug into their delicious, savory meals as the scents of well-done meat, salsa, and lemon enraptured them.

They did not speak during their meal. Lacey knew all boys were like this, unable to converse properly while eating, and she was no different. The smells, the tastes, all the wonderful sensations made it impossible to focus on anything else.

Even if Bro did play footsie with Lacey under the table the whole time.

When their immediate hunger was satisfied, they pushed their empty plates away. A virtually simultaneous sigh of contentment escaped from both of them, and with one look at each other, they began to chuckle in unison. For a while they simply interlaced their fingers, holding onto the connection between them, unmoving. Unaware of the passage of time, they both started when the waiter returned, took the empty dishes, and left.

"I'm beginning to see your point about them wearing bells around their necks," Lacey heard herself saying, dismayed, and Bro chuckled, nodding. "What do you want to do later?"

Bro wasn't one for planning their dates in detail, even though this night—a fine dinner in a fancy restaurant—proved to Lacey her boyfriend was capable of surprises.

Bro shrugged, but his look was pensive. "We could go see a movie."

Lacey crinkled her nose. "Not in the mood."

"Or we could go to the park for a walk."

"You mean camp out on the grass and make out while freezing our nuts off? No."

"We could go to a dance club and—"

"And not be able to hear a peep out of each other for the rest of the night? Pass."

"Okay, how about a coffee house? There we could talk and—"

"Coffee would keep me up all night."

Suddenly Bro grinned. "I don't see a problem with that." When Lacey gave him a reproachful yet playful glare, he asked, well on his way to being miffed, "Okay, so what do *you* suggest? 'Cause after all these refusals, you'd better have a stellar idea."

Now it was Lacey's turn to be mischievous, and she smiled wickedly. "How about we go back to my place, make out on the couch like a couple of horny bunnies, and then go up to my room for an exclusive slumber party—just big enough for two?"

Upon hearing that, Bro was practically out the door—without his dessert.

Chapter 4

IN THE end, they did remain long enough at the restaurant to have their desserts.

As they drove away from the restaurant at long last, Bro was licking his lips. The taste of his dessert—chocolate mousse made with Italian chocolate, accompanied by hazelnut ice cream—mixed with Lacey's unique, delectable flavor. Sexual hunger rampaged through his self-control like a beast in heat, and he could vividly picture his dick snarling inside the constrictions of his jeans.

Squirming on his seat, he asked quietly, "Will your dad be home?"

Lacey's face darkened, but not with anger or frustration so much as sadness. "Yes, probably. But he won't interrupt us. He's too worried he might see something... unseemly."

Bro's hold of the steering wheel tightened. "He's such a fucking—"

"Bro, don't." Lacey sounded miserable, and her eyes brimmed with tears.

"Oh, baby, I'm sorry," Bro rushed to say, touching Lacey's hand on her thigh, offering solace. "You know me, always a stinker of a foot in my rabid mouth. I'm so sorry."

"I know." Lacey smiled, and the impending rainstorm in her gaze receded. "I don't want him to ruin tonight. Let's just be together. Let's not think about anything else, okay?"

Bro grinned. "Sounds good to me."

For the rest of the drive, they held hands, fingers interlaced.

LACEY lived in the suburbs, though it was becoming clear her father could not maintain the house by himself. Soon they would have to move into an apartment building in town or away to another town. Bro swallowed hard at the mere thought, dread gripping his belly with ice-cold fingernails. He shrugged the notion off, determined to believe it would not happen, no matter how lost Lacey's father was when it came to Lacey and his whole life.

After all, perhaps he was coping the best way he knew how, the angel on Bro's shoulder reminded him.

But being a drunk, belligerent homophobe and a general mess around a teenage child was wrong of any adult, the devil on his other shoulder said, growling.

And Bro had to agree with the imp on this one. Roger Purcell wasn't much of a father. He even had a different surname. Still, he hadn't chosen that out of hate, but out of respect for Lacey's mother, Lexie. She had asked for Lacey to be an Adair because it was Lexie's family name. Roger had acquiesced because he loved her so much.

All Bro could hope for was that the man would soon rediscover his humanity and take his parental role seriously, not with hate and prejudice, but with love and understanding. Lacey was more than worth it in Bro's opinion.

After parking at the curb, Bro turned off the ignition and studied the house warily. All the lights were off, and not a peep came from the inside as they approached hand in hand. Right now Bro wished they had gone back to the loft instead. At least there, they would have a semblance of privacy, but more importantly, they'd have a loving family around them, a safe cocoon from the harsh realities of the outside world.

Lacey squeezed his hand and smiled encouragingly. "It'll be all right, Bro."

Not sure whether he liked being consoled by the person he was supposed to be giving reassurances to, Bro still nodded and returned the smile.

Lacey unlocked the door, and they went in. The house was as silent as a tomb, and no lights illuminated the darkness. Roger Purcell wasn't home, and Bro needed only to glance at Lacey to feel her sadness and disappointment and to realize if the man wasn't home, he was most likely in a bar, given his track record.

Bro pushed aside the depressing thoughts. He pulled Lacey into his arms. "Hey. Don't be sad, babe. We've still got each other. And besides—" He tried for levity by grinning and winking suggestively. "—it's not like we'd welcome his company anyway, not for what we're gonna be doing. Right?"

"Yes." Lacey sighed with visible relief, her whole body relaxing as she melted into the embrace.

Holding her close by her waist, Bro managed to steer them toward Lacey's room on the second floor at the back of the house, even though Lacey kept wiggling and giggling the whole way there. She was so cute Bro wasn't willing to let go even for an instant.

When they got to her room, Lacey pushed Bro off and let him close the door. He had always liked the look and feel of her boudoir, as she called it. The two pieces that made up the furnishings were a dressed-up vanity at one end of the room and a queen-size four-poster bed on the other. Lacey had told Bro that of all the pieces of furniture she had once had, these were the only two she had brought with her from Seattle, and only because she had picked them out with her mother. The bond she had with them was special, and she adored them.

Unlike a typical teenage girl's room, however, the colors were deep and rich, with dark gold, wood tones, and shades of gray. The underlying main theme was brown, various shades of it, from almost white to almost black. But all around the room there were little details and flashes of bright color, like the picture of a laughing girl in a bright-red dress next to the vanity, or the sunshine-yellow bookcase, or the olive-green pillows. Nothing was dirty or messy or out of place, and the scent of her perfumes wafted through the air from the vanity.

Lacey plopped down on the bed, bouncing a little and watching Bro. She bit her lower lip. "So…."

Exhaling and willing himself to relax, Bro leaned against the closed door, keeping his gaze locked with Lacey's. He wanted her so bad.

Only… it was the boy Bro wanted. The young male beneath the lovely outfit.

"So…" he murmured, waiting to see what she had planned. Technically, it was his date with her, but Bro wasn't against the idea of letting her call the shots. Yeah, there were plenty of things he wanted to do with Lacey, but he remained patient. In fact, he had been patient for nearly a year and a half, keeping the roaring beast at bay, for she was as fragile as a butterfly sometimes, and he didn't want to damage her.

But… he did want her. Bro wondered if Lacey wanted him back with equal fervor.

Lacey licked her lips sensuously, and all the blood in Bro's body seemed to rush down to his swelling cock until he felt light-headed. "Well? Take them off." She nodded at his clothing, and the teasing challenge in her eyes was evident.

Though they had been naked together plenty of times and done quite a few things, the idea of undressing in front of Lacey—while she remained fully clothed, enjoying the show—still unnerved him. His cheeks turned feverish as he blushed.

But there was no chance in hell he was ever going to refuse her anything.

So, almost violently, he grabbed the hem of his shirt and began to yank it off.

"No." Lacey pouted, frowning. "Slowly."

"I'm not a stripper," Bro growled back, eyes narrowing. Lacey's expression showed her disappointment, so he cleared his throat and said, "I'll do it, I never said I wouldn't. But why am I the only one undressing?"

In a flash her smile returned and she wrinkled her nose. "So I can watch you take your clothes off, and afterward you can undress me. Silly." She shook her head, playfully mocking him, and he glared at her, though not with serious intent.

In truth, Bro wasn't nervous about nudity. After all, he and Lacey shared the same equipment. Whatever Bro would reveal while undressing, Lacey had the same man parts, and he would thoroughly enjoy removing all her clothing in turn. Slowly, just like now.

And it wasn't like Bro had anything to be ashamed of in the cock department. Flaccid, his cock was almost five inches, and erect he sported a very healthy seven and a half inches. Well, eight if he was bragging. And Lacey... she had nothing to be embarrassed about either. Oh, just thinking about Lacey's cock made Bro squirm as blood pooled at the tip of his penis, making him feel like his dick weighed a ton. He needed her now.

Yet he forced his motions to remain enticingly slow.

He received an immediate reward for this sensual play when Lacey bit her lower lip anxiously and shifted on the bed, her cheeks turning pink and her eyes darkening to chocolate brown. Yes, Bro might have been the one getting nude, but there was no mistaking the naked hunger in Lacey's eyes and demeanor.

Lifting the hem of his T-shirt, he exposed his tight, flat stomach, his firm, muscular abs, and his sculpted chest with pronounced pecs. Lacey shifted again, tucking her legs beneath her and worrying her lower lip until it was all red and swollen. Bro wanted that effect to come from his kisses.

Shucking off his shirt, he lowered his hands to the top button of his jeans. Lacey's gaze was riveted, and it looked like she was holding her breath. Bro grinned at the sight as he popped the top button.

Lacey made a soft, strangled sound in the back of her throat, pushed off the bed, rushed to him, and dropped on her knees before him. Her meaning was clear, and Bro practically came in his pants, his cock pushing painfully against the cold zipper.

Even though her gestures seemed timid as her fingers fumbled with the zipper, Lacey had a curious sexual certainty about her, as though she had always known who and what she was. Bro had not been that lucky. Though his big brother Sebastian was gay, Bro had assumed this wasn't the case with him, and he had not really looked. That is to say, because he was horny 99.9 percent of the time, he had noticed both girls *and* boys, but discerned no preference.

Not until he had laid his eyes on the most beautiful girl he had ever seen.

Only… he had known from the start she was a he.

And now this elusive, magical creature knelt in front of him, quiet and demure, peering up at him, eyes wide with a question. "Do you want me to…?"

Bro frowned, hesitating. "Do *you* want to?"

Lacey nodded, relief painted on her face. "I do."

She pulled the zipper down, and the thin barrier of the cotton briefs between Bro's skin and Lacey's touch was no match for his dick, which tried to push through the fabric, the red glistening tip peeking over the waistband. With an excited sigh, Lacey pushed her fingers beneath the fabric and gently pulled them down to midthigh, exposing Bro's cut cock, now proudly jutting upward in a full erection.

Rapt, he watched as Lacey smiled happily, closed her eyes, and inhaled, pressing her lips against his warm, soft, almost hairless sac. Bro gulped, and his knees trembled. His hand sought her curls, raking through them until he got a tight hold. She did nothing more than slide her lips over the sensitive skin, back and forth, and he wondered if her lips tingled at the feel of it.

Pulling back, she palmed the sac with her right hand, jiggling it about, caressing and tugging. "You smell so good here. Strong. Love it."

Bro's mouth was dry, but his hands were sweating, and his cock twitched, wanting and needing something, anything, from Lacey. "Come on, Lace. You gonna…?" He left the question hanging in the air between them, crackling like electricity before a storm, and the hairs on the back of his neck stood up.

Lacey snickered, glancing up at him with a wicked grin gracing her full lips. "Boys…. You need to learn patience."

Bro grinned. "Just you remember, babe. Payback's a bitch."

"I can't wait." And she licked her lips hungrily, her gaze locked with his the whole time. Bro heard himself growl, the sound primitive and instinctive, beyond his rational control.

Lacey wrapped her left palm around the base of Bro's cock, pressing hard on his groin before inching up the cut shaft excruciatingly slowly, and then back down. With her eyes back on his face, she held Bro's cock firmly in place, pointing upward.

Tentatively, she licked the flat of her tongue across his crown, over his slit. Bro's hips bucked, and he groaned.

Looking down, eyes undoubtedly hooded with lust, he murmured, "You're a tease."

Giggling, she shook her head. "Untrue. I will give you what you want."

Another long, languid lick over his glans had him moaning. "Give it to me, then."

"Don't I always?" Lacey licked around the ridge before Bro had a smart retort ready, and then his brain fried, and he had nothing more intelligent, or even intelligible, to offer. She wrapped her lips around the mushroom-shaped head and sucked. Bro's whole body flushed with heat, and he almost doubled over. He wished they had been in bed, so he wouldn't tumble over her when she did that *thing* with her tongue and....

With precision and purpose, Lacey darted out her tongue and pushed the tip into his slit.

"God, oh sweet fucking God," Bro cried out, reaching out to one of the posters of her bed to keep himself standing. "Lacey...." He knew he was going to topple over, but he could barely get his voice to work.

She backed away, and she was a little breathless, not from exertion but from arousal. Her head tilted slightly, Lacey watched as a translucent bead of precome collected on the slit, growing in size. Before the pearl could slide off, however, she gathered it on her right index finger, staring at it mesmerized—and then she put her wet finger in her mouth.

That sight really was too much for Bro, who staggered to the bed awkwardly with his jeans and briefs around his knees. He practically fell on the bed, his knees jelly and his brain mush. "Jesus fucking Christ, Lace...," he panted, dropping down on his back, feeling too many things inside his head and in his body. This wasn't their first time, not by a long shot, but the way Lacey always made everything feel brand new, like the first time, made Bro nearly jump out of his skin.

Suppressing most of her lascivious giggle, Lacey came to lie on the bed next to him, watching him intently. "You okay?"

Dazed, Bro saw Lacey cover her mouth again as she smiled, the gesture shy but her eyes promising… not shy things. "What you do to me…." He ended the statement with a deep exhale.

Lacey's eyes darkened, and her lips trembled as she kissed him. A sugary taste with a hint of salty bitterness awakened Bro's taste buds, and he knew it was his own flavor. Still, her dessert zest of coconut, citrus, and ice cream mixed with it and with her own taste, too, until he parted his lips more to let her in. Since the beginning, Bro had loved the fact that Lacey was an eager kisser. She could spend hours making out, and her kisses started out lingering, but grew ferocious over time.

She tried to climb on top of him, but then seemed to change her mind, and she moved off, breaking the kiss. Bro made a loud disapproving noise, and Lacey snickered. "Patience."

With a quick pivot of her hips, she landed on her ass next to him and extended her left leg above his chest and face. "Your turn."

Shaking his head, amused, Bro got up to a sitting position, struggled out of his jeans and briefs until he was naked, and then proceeded to hold Lacey's silk-stocking-clad leg in his arms.

"I love that you wore these for me."

Lacey looked mischievous. "What if I wore them for *me*?"

Bro didn't look at her, but he did grin. "Then you wouldn't be making such a big deal of me taking them off." From the corner of his eye, Bro saw her purse her lips in a pout, but he knew she was pleased he had noticed.

While Lacey leaned back onto her elbows, Bro simply held her leg, one hand on her calf, the other on her ankle. She had such a slender figure. Had she really been a girl, Bro would have called her petite. But one didn't go around calling a boy petite, no matter what the circumstances. The silk of the stocking was smooth and soft, cooler than his feverish skin, and the golden hue of the fabric twinkled in the low light of the room. She had a dimmer, which he sort of envied.

Usually when they kissed, Bro felt the need, the overwhelming compulsion, to have her, to throw her down on the bed and take her, using his rough passions to force the issue. But every time he actually held her in his arms, he could not just ravish her. He longed to draw out the sequence of events, to take his time and claim her slowly, entice and seduce her until she'd be writhing in agonizing pleasure and pleading to come.

Bro kissed the sole of her foot. "What if I told you I was gonna suck your toes?"

Lacey tittered. "Do what you want."

That made him look up at her, surprised. A carte blanche to act as he willed? "Like... what do you mean?"

Blinking and frowning, not reining in either gesture, she dithered, but finally said in a low, hushed tone, "I mean... we can... go all the way... if you want."

Instant visions rolled across his mind's eye: images of flipping Lacey over, licking his way down her spine to the curve at the small of her back, dipping lower into her private place, opening her up with his tongue, fingers, and then his cock, inching inside that velvety heat, deep, to the hilt. Bro could not deny the thought turned him on to no end, and he felt too hot for his own skin. God, how he wanted to do that, to have her in every conceivable way, with a few innovations he had in store just for her.

But Bro hadn't missed the wavering of her voice, either. She wasn't sure, maybe she was even scared, and that clinched the deal for him. He raised her foot and caressed it with his cheek, and then he shook his head. "Nah. Not tonight."

Though there was frustration and doubt on her face, her expression confirmed her relief, too. "Why not?" She looked down, veiling her eyes with her lashes. "Don't you want me?"

With deliberate intent, Bro grabbed her other leg and yanked her forward into his arms, straight onto his lap. Bracing himself above her, he stared her down as firmly and gently as he could.

"Lace, I want you so bad I could come just from looking at you, or seeing you smile, or hearing your voice. But I don't want to rush it. And besides... we don't know if your dad's gonna come home tonight or not, and in what condition." She worried her lower lip, her brow furrowed, as she mulled over the idea of her father interrupting them *in flagrante*, which clearly hadn't occurred to her. "You are the best thing that's ever happened to me, Lace. I don't want you to... regret it, if and when we do... it."

For a moment Bro felt like the sensual moment between them had passed, that it had gotten too weird, but then a smile broke out across her full lips. And it was as bright as the sun.

"Thank you, Bro. You're… the sweetest. The best, the cutest—"

"Add adorable to that, and I'm calling the night off," Bro growled in a warning.

Lacey threw her head back and laughed, and Bro couldn't help but look at her throat, her neck, her exposed skin. The black velvet band didn't cover it all. Swooping down fast, he latched his lips over her pulse point, softly sucking and licking, and her laugh morphed into a moan. She draped her hands around his neck, pulling him closer, and then they were pressed together tightly, from lips to toes, moving in frantic unison.

Suddenly, her hands snaked down past his hips and grabbed his butt cheeks so firmly he felt her fingernails digging in. Grunting, Bro broke the kiss, startled by her actions.

She snickered a bit. "Just FYI, there is no *if* about, you know, *it*; only when."

It was Bro's turn to laugh. "Okay. When we do it." He grew serious and searched her eyes for a sign. "It'll happen, Lace. At the right time, in the right place, for the right reasons."

Lacey smiled in relief and contentment. "Yes. Just us. Just you and me."

Though Bro did look at other girls and other guys—and Lacey probably did too—he felt no real burning need for others. Lacey had him by the balls. "Yeah, just you and me."

Flicking her tongue over his lower lip, she teased. "So, you gonna undress me, or are you gonna take me fully clothed? 'Cause this is one of my favorite dresses, and I don't want come all over—"

Putting a stop to her flow of words, he kissed her silent first, and then he deepened the kiss and made her breathless. "Gotcha," he said with a grin as he pulled back to sit on his haunches and take her right foot in his hands again.

She chuckled. "You know, I'm not a ball in one of your games."

Bro quirked an eyebrow. "No. You've got two."

Insinuating his fingers upward from her foot to her knee and thigh, Bro eventually reached the clasp holding the stocking up and popped it open with a tiny click. The stocking was tight enough not to droop, but the silk did become a bit looser, and he used both hands to slide it off her right leg. Lacey shaved her body hair, so nothing but smooth skin greeted Bro as he finally held a bare foot in his hands.

Then he did what he had promised and sucked on her toes. Lacey was ticklish, and chortling, she began to squirm, trying to break loose. But Bro held fast, licking lazy circles around each and every delicious toe, every gold-painted nail. If he knew her well enough—and he did— the nail polish was likely the glow-in-the-dark variety.

"Bro, stop! It tickles!" She was almost screaming, her voice shrill. Lucky for them, her next-door neighbor was a little old lady with three cats and a poorly functioning hearing aid. "Mercy, please." Between giggling fits and cries, she was pleading, and Bro relented.

When he let her foot land on the bed, she was out of breath, her cheeks as pink as her ears and neck. This tint of arousal turned Bro on even more, his cock tightening and growing bigger and hotter with every heartbeat. Without another word, he made quick work of her other stocking as well.

Then there was only her dress left.

With happily dazed, slitted eyes, she watched his every move.

Winking, Bro hovered over her, and while kissing her soft, moist lips, he loosened the velvet band around her neck and took it off.

As he pulled back, her taste on his lips, Bro searched the dress with his eyes. "How does it come off?"

Smothering a snicker, she whispered seductively, "Buttons on the back."

"How the heck did you get it on?" Bro huffed.

"With the help of a friend."

"What friend?" Bro was immediately overtaken with the fires of jealousy.

"Audrey, you silly boy."

"Oh." Bro had the good sense to feel slightly embarrassed. Audrey was Lacey's best friend, after all. Then he refocused on his girl.

Before he could tell her, or do it himself, Lacey had rolled over onto her stomach, almost kneeing Bro in the groin. The golden fabric was sparkly enough to hide the buttons running from the turtleneck down to the small of her back. Swallowing and licking his dry lips, he fumbled with the buttons, which were tighter and harder to open than he had surmised.

"Dammit...," he muttered in frustration when his hands kept shaking, and he couldn't get a proper hold, let alone get at the fiendish buttons quickly or skillfully enough.

She turned her blond head toward him and winked. "No rush, Bro. I'm nothing if not patient. As much as I want you, you can take your time." A corner of her mouth rose as she smiled, closing her eyes with a sigh. "You're the best thing that's ever happened to me."

Bro's hands stilled. He could not fathom how he could be so lucky as to have her heart, for she was the sweetest, kindest, loveliest person he had ever known. He tried to voice his thoughts but nothing came out, no sound moved past the lump in his throat.

He wished kissing her now-exposed nape would get the message across. Judging from her soft chuckle, morphing into a low moan, Lacey definitely understood.

Sighing in relief and relaxing, Bro popped open the remaining buttons. He parted the sleek fabric and revealed her back, smooth creamy skin, sinewy muscles, and the delectable, inviting dip at the bottom of her spine, with the cutest dimples on either side. Though Lacey was not nude yet, there was no denying the bare facts of her unspoken promises, nor her masculinity. Her narrow waist, lean hips, and strong back were all male.

Inhaling fast, Bro was no longer seeing her.

Finally, there was only *him*.

Chapter 5

RELAXED and half-careless, half-reckless, Lacey let her eyes close as her heated cheek lay on the cool sheets. Bro was moving behind her, his big, strong hands gliding over her bare back. Then he was pulling the dress down her shoulders, past her arms, down to her waist and hips, trying to get it off entirely. She wiggled and lifted to accommodate him. He made quick work with her tight underwear as well, the unyielding fabric keeping her cock and balls in check, until finally she lay nude on her stomach, her privates snuggled comfortably on the cool sheets.

Lacey heard Bro gasp and then groan. His palms were feverish now as he kneaded her back, inching lower until he cupped her buttocks and pinched. She protested with a sharp mewling sound, and he chuckled, repeating the act.

"Meanie," she taunted, wanting him to remain exactly where he was, but not wanting him to think she was *that* easy.

But she should have known Bro would be on to her wiles. He leaned down and whispered in her ear, "Oh, you want me to stop, then?" His erection poked at her cleft, and heat radiated from his taut member, causing eruptions in the boiling pool of lust within her groin.

"You really are a meanie," she murmured, half grumbling. Then Bro licked at the soft shell of her ear and her exposed nape, making her shiver.

His whole body landed on top of her, his chest against her back, and his cock nestled between her ass cheeks, sliding easily with the slight rocking motion of his hips. Blood-hot precome dripped on her most sensitive stretch of skin, and her hole fluttered in anticipation.

More, her body screamed. *More*, her senses demanded. *More, more, more*, her heart and soul chanted in unison.

Closing her eyes and letting the sensations wash over her, Lacey knew at that moment, here in her bed with Bro, she was not a she, but a *he*. Lacey was a boy, with another boy on top of *him*, one about to make love to him. Here, right now, in his boyfriend's arms, Lacey felt like a boy—and it was okay. No, it was better than okay. It was fine, it was good, it was perfect. It took nothing away from the girl he was too.

"You're so hot, baby," Bro whispered, his voice hoarse. His body kept quaking above Lacey's, and his hands roamed everywhere, searching out every patch of skin he could reach. He even wormed his hands beneath Lacey to touch his chest. Bro tweaked Lacey's nipples into taut, fiery peaks; he petted the groove of his groin and thigh; he groped his buttocks; he smoothed and caressed his flanks, then ran his hands up and down his sides, feeling and tickling every rib and muscle; he stroked and pressed on his belly, just above the hipbone.

"Let me turn," Lacey begged breathlessly, needing the connection.

Almost instantly, he was taken a hold of and swiftly rolled over onto his back. With a grin, Bro welcomed him. And then Bro's gaze moved away from Lacey's eyes, and he ate up the sight of Lacey beneath him appreciatively as he held himself up with his straightened arms. Fiery hunger burned in his eyes like blue flames. "At last…. At long last you're mine…. My guy." He spoke as though he had never been with his boyfriend before, and it was utterly arousing.

Lacey shuddered. The deep, possessive tone was his undoing. When Lacey was with Bro like this, intimately, he didn't care about being a girl or a boy. All he cared about was that he was Bro's, that his heart and body belonged to his boyfriend. Though physically they were two young males, those small-minded, restrictive gender classifications meant nothing to Lacey. He suspected Bro felt much the same. Who Lacey was wasn't about labels, or categories, or verbal phrasings. It was about feelings. And Bro wanted Lacey as a boy *and* a girl.

So Lacey let him, and then he let himself go, to fly beyond boundaries, safe and loved in Bro's arms. "Bro, do it. Do *me* now. Kiss me."

Bro did not need to be asked twice. He plunged his tongue into Lacey's mouth, all but devouring him, staking a claim, apparently unwilling to stop for any reason. It was slick and wet and warm, and Lacey loved it. Bro's arms wrapped around Lacey, taking a fierce, unyielding grip of him, and he ground against him so hard Lacey was certain the friction would cause sparks to fly and set the bedroom ablaze. Bro was hot, hard, and heavy against Lacey, whose own cock throbbed painfully, needing release. Their erections bumped against each other, rubbing just the right way, the familiar feeling of closeness with its partner melding with the newness of the experience, the same but different every time.

Then mere frottage wasn't enough anymore, and Bro slithered his hand between their writhing bodies before fisting and mashing their cocks together. He massaged the lengths of their shafts as one within his steadfast grip. Hot precome dripped from both their slits, easing the way when Bro began to pump up and down in a firm rhythm. Lacey moaned as Bro's hand worked his cock like a pro, with enthusiasm and lust. And it was perfect.

His arms draped around Bro's neck and shoulders, Lacey held on as best he could, not sure if he could hold on much longer. His cock burned, too hot and big in the taut skin stretched to its limits.

"Please, Bro, *please*."

Lacey's words were muffled as he breathed them into Bro's mouth, the kiss breaking as they became too breathless to do anything other than pant into each other's mouths.

But Bro still managed to nod his understanding. "You close?"

"Yeah." Lacey wound his legs around Bro's waist, then locked his ankles around the small of Bro's back, anchoring himself against the onslaught of Bro's gyrating hips. His own body bucked up, demanding more pressure, more contact, just more of everything.

Bro rained kisses over Lacey's cheek and down to his neck, sliding his tongue over his ear and beneath it, sucking softly, then biting on the juncture of his neck and shoulder, undoubtedly leaving a noticeable hickey. Lacey didn't mind Bro's primal urge to mark him, so long as he could hide it if necessary. And seeing the red marks later in the mirror usually made him horny as hell as he relived their lovemaking.

"God, I love your taste, your scent, everything about you." Bro's voice had gone husky, barely discernible as anything but moaning and breathing.

All Lacey heard was *that* word, and it was so close, hovering between them once more, fluttering like a hummingbird, too quick to catch, light as a feather. Happiness bubbled inside his heart—and his cup overflowed as he started to come. A splash of heat accompanied the feeling of bursting apart at the seams as the spasms racked his body, pushing him over the edge again and again, until his balls emptied through the slit of his cock onto his belly and he had nothing more to give.

On top of him, Bro was still moving frantically, and his groans had reached a higher pitch. "Yeah, yeah, baby. Just like that. God, you're so fucking beautiful. Wanna make you come a second time, more than a dozen, a hundred fucking times."

Lacey pressed closer to him, burying his face in Bro's sweaty black hair, and whispered into his ear, almost goading, "Come, my boo, and then we can go again."

That was all Bro needed to reach climax. His whole body shook, his hips stuttered, and his cock spilled hot spunk between them, on Lacey's stomach and chest, thick creamy ropes of come that made Lacey's mouth water. Bro kept heaving and grunting, his eyes pressed firmly closed as he rode through the waves of his orgasm until the crest broke and he collapsed on top of Lacey in a limp heap of limbs and torso.

With a satisfied sigh, Lacey gathered Bro close and held him. Though he was practically out of it, Bro did the same, enveloping Lacey in his arms and then tightening his hold possessively.

In a way, the shared afterglow and the cuddling were more intimate than anything they ever did sexually. The fact that the post-sex nodding off into a haze of bliss resembled dreaming added the final touch.

A LOUD noise awakened them. Lacey recognized it as the front door slamming. She had no idea how much time had passed. Bro blinked at her groggily for a moment, then hastily they both scrambled from the bed, seeking out clothes to wear in the low light of the bedroom. The clink of bottles sounded from the kitchen, then the fridge being opened and closed, then something falling on the floor with a bang, and finally muttered curses echoed around the house.

Lacey stopped in the middle of pulling on her dressing gown, knowing from the noise alone that her father was drunk and in a foul mood. A jumble of emotions from anger and fear to sorrow and despair filled her, and she felt tears brimming in her eyes. The scene turned watery, and she couldn't see clearly. Her jaw and hands trembled as she fought to hold back the emotional break.

Instantly Bro was there, holding on to her shoulders in a gentle manner. "He doesn't matter, Lace. He can't take this away from us. What we feel. He can't ever diminish it. Unless you let him. Don't let him, Lace. I lo—I need you."

That made her stop fretting, and a mellow warmth spread through her from her heart, reaching her from head to toes. She couldn't help but smile at him affectionately and gratefully.

"Thanks, Bro. I really needed that. Need *you*."

Bro pulled her into his arms, her hands around his still-naked torso. "I'm here for you. I always will be. Don't you worry. I won't let him take you away from me."

Snuggling in close, almost wishing she could burrow within his tender heart and sweet body, Lacey sighed happily. Nothing could ruin this mood, this cocoon of, *yes*, love and safety Bro created around her, around them both, with just the circumference of his arms.

"You're the best thing in my life, Bro. Never, ever doubt that, okay?"

He kissed her forehead. "I promise."

Ringing in her ears were the words Bro had almost said, and that made Lacey happy for it meant what she felt, he shared. She held on to her boyfriend tighter, resting her forehead on the hollow of Bro's throat, relishing his warmth and solidity.

She was so wrapped up in Bro's embrace, she didn't hear the approaching footsteps until they were at her door, and then the door was pushed open so hard, it banged against the wall.

Guiltily and fearfully, Lacey jumped apart from Bro, who quickly yanked on his T-shirt, even though his chest was spattered with dried come.

Cautiously, she looked up at her father, trying to gauge his mood. His swaying back and forth in the doorway gave away how drunk he was, if the sloshing beer bottle in his hand or the watery eyes weren't enough of a clue. He squinted to see better, and then his eyes grew wide with fury.

Pointing a finger at Bro, he yelled, "What the fuck is that fag doing here, Lance?"

Bro's face darkened until his lips were a thin white line. "Her name is Lacey."

Lacey winced as her father took a step closer, his face red with wrath. "*His* name is Lance, not some stupid girly name. And he ain't a fucking faggot. Now get the hell out of here, or I swear I will—"

"You'll what?" Bro cut in, unafraid, standing his ground. Lacey knew her father could not take on Bro, who had youth, speed, agility, and strength working for him. And her dad was drunk as a skunk.

Still, Lacey placed a hand on her boyfriend's arm. "It's okay, Bro. You had better go." She pleaded with her eyes, and Bro stopped, listened, and obeyed. Quietly, with disapproval and worry written all over his face, he nodded, sidestepped Roger, and headed downstairs. A minute or so later, Lacey heard the front door close. She knew Bro hated abandoning her there, with Roger, but the man was Lacey's father. Unfortunately.

Roger took a step closer, pointing a shaky finger at her. "He's not allowed in this house ever again, you hear, Lance?"

"But I lo—" she started to say.

The slap came too fast for her to duck.

Across her left cheekbone a stinging, burning pain flashed, and it spread to her whole face, fiery tendrils with sharp claws. Hot tears made her sight cloud, but Lacey fought the flood because it was all she could fight against. Roger was her father, and she could not raise a hand against him. He was drunk, so he didn't know what he was doing, right?

As she stifled a sob, Lacey's legs turned to jelly and gave out from under her, and she fell on her butt on the floor while he glowered above her, hands fisting at his side.

"You will never see that boy again, do you hear me, you stupid boy? If you do, I swear I will teach you how to obey like a son should. And no more fucking dresses! You're a man, and you're gonna wear men's clothes!"

While Lacey was mildly surprised her father could still formulate coherent sentences, the cold shivers that ran down her spine at the sound of his threatening voice made her unable to confront his gaze, or anything else for that matter. She nodded—even though in her heart she knew she would disobey. She barely had any men's clothes aside from jeans. And... Lacey couldn't *not* see Bro. He was all that stood between her and despair, her and rock bottom, her and insanity.

Why does my own father hate me so? I cannot change who I am. I was born this way.

Muttering something vile under his foul breath, Roger turned around on his heel and stomped off down the stairs. Lacey let out the tiniest of sobs, feeling hollowed out inside, only to have that emptiness fill with a weight as heavy as a mountain and as deep as an ocean of sorrow. She felt so alone, so totally empty, she almost had no name for it. A family should have been a pillar to steady her, a foundation to build on. But for Lacey, the only thing family meant was the absence of one parent and the hatred of another.

The urge to call Bro and have him comfort her was foremost on her mind, but she knew she couldn't. Bro would get so mad he'd come right back and beat Roger to a pulp, which would solve nothing. If anything, it would only ensure Lacey could never see Bro again.

So with deep wet breaths, Lacey composed herself, still sitting trembling on the floor by the bed, vowing to herself to sort this out on her own. And that was when she remembered who could help her. A wave of relief washed over her as she contemplated her limited options.

But… at least there was a glimmer of hope.

Chapter 6

"HEY, those are my onion sticks! Get your own!"

Bradley just chuckled infuriatingly while Bro tried to snag back his small portion of garlic bread and onion sticks. Bradley's fingers were surprisingly nimble, him being such a big guy and all, so Bro grumbled low, frowning as he finally managed to snatch the basket in front of him, surrounding it possessively with his arms.

"Where's your girl tonight?" Bradley asked companionably. His eyes wavered toward the checkout of the café, where his girlfriend, Audrey, was busy getting a mocha latte. "Doesn't she mind all that stench soon to be coming out of your mouth? Do you kiss her with that mouth?"

Bro growled, but it was all in jest. "What does it matter? You ain't never gonna find out what kind of a mouth Lacey likes kissing."

Laughing, Bradley shook his head. "Guess not. Besides, Audrey would kill me."

"And why am I killing you this time?"

Though she was not his type, even Bro had to admit Audrey was a knockout. A babe. A hottie. She habitually wore the skimpiest of skirts and the tiniest of T-shirts. Today the checkered kilt-like dress almost exposed her rear end, and had her breasts been one size bigger, that tight white shirt would have been absolutely obscene. She had on long socks coupled with high heels and wore thin suspenders over her shirt, but somehow she made the combo work. It could have been the perky bosom, the narrow waist, or the long legs that did it. In any case, every man in the café was fixated on the pinup of a Catholic schoolgirl, undressing her with their eyes and minds. Her long black hair was held together in two extended braids, giving her a girlish look, but the artful sooty makeup around her eyes and bright-red lipstick on her full lips gave her a sultry, seductive appearance.

"Your boy's asking about the whereabouts of *my* girlfriend." Bro stuck out his tongue at Bradley, who grinned at that.

Sitting down next to Bradley and crossing her legs, Audrey quirked a thin eyebrow. "Is that so?"

Bradley leaned closer, kissing her temple. "Come on, baby. You know you're the only one for me. Who else would know how to...." His voice trailed off from Bro's hearing threshold as he whispered something in his girlfriend's ear—from the looks of it something dirty because Audrey giggled and blushed a little, squirming on her seat. Had she been a puppy, she would have wagged her tail.

Bro rolled his eyes. "Jeez. Get a room."

"Keep your heretical jersey on," Bradley chuckled, giving Bro a pointed look.

Bro pursed his lips, torn between flipping the guy off and tossing something edible and sticky at him. He went with profanities. "Fuck off." Bro was wearing his Denver Broncos football jersey, while Bradley had his Washington Redskins jacket, and the two of them always fought amicably over this—even though Bro secretly cheered for the Redskins too, and Bradley wasn't a die-hard fan. "Like your stupid jacket is any kind of fashion statement, dude."

"My allegiances aren't in question in this town, but yours are, pal." Bradley nudged his girlfriend closer to nuzzle her neck.

"At least I ain't a fucking turncoat," Bro replied, grumbling. He loved the Broncos, and just because he lived in a different town now, he hadn't abandoned his loyalty for the team.

"Never said you were, brother." Bradley's voice was muffled, but Bro could tell he was needling him to get Bro all miffed and huffy, which Bradley would find quaint and amusing.

Bro didn't dignify the comment with a response, just made a dismissive wave of his hand.

Audrey pulled away from Bradley but gave her boyfriend a totally smoldering look that might have left any man a pool of lust on the floor. "Where is Lacey? I thought she was supposed to join us. Is she rehearsing her violin today?"

Shrugging, Bro had to admit he didn't know. "She just said she had an errand to run." His face darkened as he remembered the previous night and Roger's menacing bigotry. "Her dad was a fucking asshole last night. Kept calling her... not by her name, and a... a fag. For a second I thought he was really gonna hit her."

"But he didn't, right?" Bradley had straightened in his seat. His handsome face was grave, his brow furrowed. He was ready to fight for Lacey, and for Bro, which made Bro feel better about it. Lacey wasn't alone; she had friends who would stand with her and would have her back if push came to shove.

Audrey's lips pursed with disapproval and anger too. "Was he drunk again?"

Bro nodded reluctantly. "Yeah."

"That son of a bitch." Audrey's fingers toyed with her napkin until it was in shreds. "I don't like Lacey being alone with that hatemonger. I'm afraid one day he's going to—" She stopped abruptly, blinking and realizing she may have said too much. Bro knew exactly how she felt. Lacey and Audrey were best friends, like Bro and Bradley were best buddies. The four of them hung out together a lot, and by virtue of four months seniority, Audrey felt very protective of Lacey, as though Lacey were her little sister. For Audrey, Lacey's physical gender didn't enter into it at all. "Aren't there any other relatives she could stay with?"

Bro shook his head, saddened. "No, not that I know of. It's just her and her dad."

Whatever else he might have said got lost when an annoying voice filtered through his consciousness. "Well, if it isn't our high school's own fairy patrol and his fag hags."

Bro's head jerked toward the owner of the voice, Deacon, who sauntered into the café like he owned the place, grinning maliciously. He was still on the school's football team, but he continued his shitty behavior and harassment of Bro every chance he got. Bradley, too, was getting sick of him, and Bro worried what their captain was going to do about the situation one of these days.

Yet of the three of them, it was Audrey who spoke. "Well, well, if it isn't this town's biggest asshole and bigot with his entourage—oh, wait, you don't have any 'cause your sorry ass doesn't have any friends. Get lost, creep." She tossed one of her braids around and stretched herself, like a lovely feline, making sure every eye in the joint was on her. "We should all go see a movie on Friday, yeah? I think Lacey would like that, and we can do girl talk while you boys shower us with hearts and flowers, not to mention condoms and candy."

The tension left Bro's body as he allowed himself to relax and focus solely on Audrey. Out of the corner of his eye, he could see Deacon's cheeks redden as he stared at Audrey like he wanted to strangle her or fuck her, but couldn't decide which. Finally, he stomped off.

Bradley shook his head, sighing. "You sure do know how to defuse situations, baby." There was a soft scolding in his voice, presumably because, like Bro, he could foresee trouble ahead, but Bro had never seen Bradley mad at his girlfriend about anything. He probably wasn't angry now, either, for they were a solid couple. Bro had a feeling they would last longer than the length of high school and college too. And he wished the same for himself and Lacey.

Audrey's green eyes flashed, indignant and furious. "Deacon's a fucking dickhead. If he insults my friends, you can be damn sure I'll respond in kind. If you want a pretty, quiet, demure doll of a girlfriend, I suggest you look elsewhere, because I will not—"

Bradley kissed her silent, and surprisingly, she let him.

Watching them kiss made Bro want Lacey there right the fuck now so he could kiss her like that, and then slowly pull her to sit on his lap, caress her hair and slender arms, kiss her lips and neck, and have her skin filling his mouth, her dress shifting upward with his hand as he explored her body intimately, lovingly....

"Hey, Bro, you with us?" Audrey was waving her hand in front of Bro's face, amused at his spaced-out condition. "Friday? Movie? Something action-y, so we can cuddle our boys. And then we can get a bite to eat."

Bro tried to swat her hand away in irritation, not because he disliked Audrey in the slightest, but because he missed Lacey. "Yeah, yeah. Now get the fuck away from me."

Audrey snickered. "Love it that there's a guy out there who doesn't want me."

"I'll want you doubly, honey, to make up for the loss," Bradley teased, his hand brushing against her knee and beginning to slide upward while she wriggled and giggled, barely trying to escape the attempt.

Bro rolled his eyes and harrumphed loudly in reproach. "Okay, I'm getting diabetes with this sugar overload. I'll see ya guys later. I'm off."

As he got out of the booth, all he could think about was how much he missed Lacey.

"KEEP your arms up. Come on, Lacey. Stop slacking off."

After a grueling hour of practicing self-defense moves with Jordan, Lacey was ready to fall down on the ground and cry in exhaustion, or alternatively, punch the guy's lights out. Well, bitch slap really, as she didn't have any strength left. Jordan was merciless, not giving Lacey any room to falter or stumble. He was a great instructor, but he was borderline cruel. Still, she knew he meant well.

Quickly, she brought up her arms to block his attack. Each hit hurt, even though she anticipated them, and she'd have bruises later. "I'm trying, dammit."

"Curse all you want," Jordan remarked, unrelenting in his assault. Though they were for practice and not for real—much—the impacts still made Lacey ache all over. "You're giving me poor performance. Now buck up!"

She was growling now in frustration, but she refused to give in or give up. Jordan avoided her face and focused on her body, trying to attack her torso or force her off balance by kicking her feet from under her. The moves themselves weren't difficult, as they were just a simple series of continuous motions that could be used to daze, incapacitate, or even seriously injure an opponent. It was sort of like dancing, only the other guy didn't want to dip her but throw her down.

Lacey gave the practice her all, even though her body cried out for a break. She was a violinist, after all, not a martial arts expert. She didn't go to the gym or do the kind of rigorous training Jordan and Bro did, although for different reasons. Yet she wanted to excel in this. Not to find something to brag about, but to hold her own against any foe.

Even if the foe was her father.

Lacey's damaged cheek hurt as blood thundered through her system with the exertion. Though the throbbing was damn near blinding in its intensity, there was a cleansing effect within as she relaxed and fell into the flow of the string of movements. Though Jordan was way better, she felt in control of her body, her choices, her life. She felt strong and capable.

"Your left hand is dragging, Lace. Pick it up!"

And then Jordan's words reminded her she still had a ways to go. She redoubled her efforts, keeping her feet moving, never sticking too long in one place. She kept her arms up but close to protect her upper body and her face. Whenever there was an opening, she took advantage. She doubted Jordan was really that vulnerable or exposed, but these moments gave her confidence.

She had fighting gloves on, not the heavy boxing kind. Her hands felt fragile, as though the small bones there might break or shatter at any second, when in truth the fighting gloves were designed to prevent any such injuries. Her tennis shoes were well used, so they didn't chafe, but she had been bouncing around on her feet for nearly two hours.

"Jordan, I'm tired."

"Not yet. Fifteen minutes more, Lace. Come on, honey, you can do it."

It was such simple encouragement, but it renewed her strength. Well, her strength of will anyway.

The gym Jordan had built in one of the larger rooms in the loft was spacious and airy, and Lacey felt comfortable there, free of pressure and tension, free from the feeling of the walls closing in on her. For the first hour, Jordan had shown her how to take a swing at or how to kick a punching bag, and that had relieved her stress and anxiety quite a bit.

With a live opponent, it was another matter. Jordan wasn't squeamish about any of his actions, even if it meant she learned something through trial and error, and with a swarm of bruises to boot. Lacey knew, however, that had Jordan been able to see the bruise on her cheek underneath the concealer, it would have been a whole other ballgame. Thankfully, the makeup had lasted even through the two hours of exercise.

"Come on, Lace. Front kick."

Growling, Lacey aimed a hard kick at Jordan's groin but missed. She did hit him just above the knee, and he grunted, backing off. "Ha!" she gloated, lifting her hands in triumph.

"You got lucky." Jordan's movements didn't slow or waver despite the impact. Lacey was certain a real attacker wouldn't either, so she carried on.

"Remember what I told you?" Jordan asked imperiously while circling her. "Disorient, incapacitate, flee."

Lacey nodded. Jordan had shown her, among others, some basic Krav Maga moves. Disorienting an opponent was a simple matter of attacking the senses, like blinding with a finger in the eye socket or deafening with a harsh slap against the ear or temple. Incapacitating meant using the extremities to hit vulnerable spots, like groin, knee, or abdomen, and as the attacker doubled over in pain, then making sure they went down permanently, for example with a punch on the back of the neck. Once the enemy was down or distracted by pain, the only thing left to do was run out of range to a safe harbor.

While she went over the instructions in her head, Jordan had managed to sneak attack her rear, giving her ass cheek a pinch. Crying out with indignation, Lacey gave his shin a rear kick and then finished with a hard elbow strike back, straight in the gut. Grunting, Jordan doubled over, holding his belly.

"Good one, Lace." The compliment stroked her ego like no other comment before.

"I think you've done enough for the day." Jordan straightened slowly, rubbing his belly, which must have hurt at least a bit, but he was grinning. Lacey was certain this was because Jordan took pride in his achievements, especially if they were designed to help someone he valued or cared for.

"So do I."

Startled, both Lacey and Jordan turned to the new voice.

Bro was standing in the open doorway, his eyes narrow with irritation, his lips a thin line, his feet apart, and his arms crossed over his chest.

Lacey winced, then bit her lower lip. This was not how she had planned this encounter to go down. "Bro, I...." Then she ran out of words, knowing an explanation of her reason for training with Jordan was only going to make matters worse. The alternative would have been to lie to her lov—boyfriend. And she couldn't do that either. So Lacey ended up standing in place, fidgeting, and opening and closing her mouth like a goldfish.

Bro wasn't stupid, and he caught on pretty quick. His narrowed gaze hit Jordan square in the eye, asking a silent question. Jordan exchanged a glance with Lacey, who was well aware she was pleading with her expression, and then he sighed.

"This was my idea, Bro. Lace dresses up like a girl. I thought it would be a good idea if she learned a few basic self-defense moves."

And that was the extent of his explanation. Take it or leave it, and Lacey swallowed hard, praying Bro wouldn't question it. For she had no other answers to give him right now, certainly none that would defuse the level of tension in the room, let alone the tension in the set of Bro's broad shoulders.

But then there was none. Bro's rigid stance eased, and he let out a breath, giving Lacey a concerned look with a hint of sadness and pity. "Why the fuck didn't you tell me?" There was no vehemence behind the words as Bro closed the gap between them and laid his hands on Lacey's hips, gently pulling her closer.

Emotions constricted Lacey's throat. "I... I didn't want to worry you. You already think I'm in danger from every shadow in the streets." She shrugged, reluctant to continue.

"Babe...." Bro let out an exasperated huff but said nothing more, only hugged Lacey to his chest.

Lacey protested weakly. "I'm all gross and sweaty."

Bro chuckled then, and the knot twisting Lacey's gut unwound. "I've seen you sweaty before, babe. Lots of times." And his arms grew tighter around her. Taking a deep breath of spicy cologne and male musk, Lacey circled Bro's waist and buried her head in his neck, feeling safe and happy again. Bro seemed to have that effect on her every time.

"Lace?" Jordan spoke from behind them, his tone neutral, not giving anything away. "It is late. Wash up, change, and I'll drive you home." Bro must have been about to argue, because Jordan cut all protests short. "The only place you're going, little boy, is to bed—by yourself. Now hop to it."

"Sir, yes, sir," Bro grumbled, and Lacey giggled against his chest. Bro peered down at her, smiling. "Why wouldn't I obey? The sooner I get to bed, the sooner I can dream about you. Lewd, dirty things." He waggled his eyebrows, and Lacey burst into laughter.

"Sounds like a plan," she said at last, winking. Bro's eyes darkened.

"Now, please," Jordan cut in, impatient yet clearly amused.

"Bully...," Bro mumbled and then cussed a blue streak under his breath. Lacey was the only one who heard the long line of obscenities, and she snickered behind her hand, blushing. Her guy sure had a potty mouth.

With a much too quick kiss, Bro let Lacey go. "I'll see you tomorrow, yeah?"

"Duh." Lacey gave him a lengthy good-night kiss of her own before dashing into the changing room. It wouldn't do for her father to find out what she had been doing. If she smelled too sweaty, he would suspect the worst. If she smelled of soap and water, he would really go berserk. It was a fine line. She used a warm, wet washcloth to clean up most of the sweat and then added some deodorant, hoping that would be enough to mask any bodily odors. Besides, if he was drunk, maybe all he sniffed would be alcohol anyway.

At least Bro had retreated to his room when she came out. One less distraction.

Five minutes later, Lacey sat in Jordan's monstrous, pimped-out SUV once more as he drove her home. Only… it wasn't home. It was just a house she lived in right now. It had never felt less like a home, no matter what she did to spruce up her room to make it cozy. A home was a place that housed the people one loved. Lacey loved her dad, but a little less every day, and that saddened her. She felt alone, exposed, and vulnerable, naked and visible to the whole world, a wreck without a safety net. She felt more at home with people not her kin, like Bro, Jordan, and Sebastian, Audrey and Bradley. Her friends were her new family more than her one surviving parent, and her house was not a home.

"You okay?" Jordan's soft voice cut through the interference.

Shaken, Lacey nodded. "Yes. Jordan, I…." She took a deep breath to calm her nerves. "I'm sorry I wasn't frank with Bro. I just—"

"I understand. Next time." Jordan's cool was an armor that almost never cracked. He meant it too, Lacey could tell, and she was grateful.

The rest of the trip passed in companionable silence. When they parked on the curb, Lacey peered toward the house and saw the lights were on, and a shadow moved across the drapes. Her father was home. Shrinking against the seat physically and into her own head emotionally, she had never felt less inclined to enter the house she was supposed to call home.

"Lace?" Jordan asked in a concerned voice.

Taking a quick breath, Lacey plastered her most endearing smile on her lips. "I'm off. Thanks for the ride, Jordan. Good night."

"Wait." Jordan grabbed her arm, but it wasn't hostile or harsh. Instead, he eased his hold to plant a business card in her hand, closing her fingers around it. "My number's on here. And so is my private cell. I can tell there's something going on, Lace, something major you don't want to talk about. Just know that if you ever need me, I'm one phone call away, okay?" With a quick, reassuring squeeze, he let go of her.

Feeling slightly bereft and ashamed of keeping her loved ones in the dark, Lacey nodded, tucking the card into her jacket pocket. "Okay."

She left the car, releasing the breath she had been holding only after Jordan had given a quick chin lift and eased the car into the street, disappearing into the dimness of the early evening. She covered her trembling lips with her hand, hoping no one saw her shaken state, and quelled the sobs threatening to burst out. The people around her offered their help again and again, and every time Lacey was certain it would never get so bad she would have to leave her birth family behind.

Even though a part of Lacey wanted that. Her dad broke a little bit of her heart every day, never giving her the love of a parent. The trouble was that she could remember the man he had been before the tragedy that had robbed them of her mother and his wife. Back then, Roger Purcell had loved Lacey unconditionally, like a true father, supported and cared for her, listened to her woes, and given her his precious time. At the time Lacey's girlish ways hadn't seemed to bother him that much. When they lost the third vital member of their family, Roger had lost himself and built up walls so high no one could climb over them. Hidden inside his fortress of loss, he grew to hate the world—and his gay son. Sometimes it felt as though Lacey had come to embody everything that was wrong with his life, and Roger poured all his pain, anger, and blame on her.

As she reluctantly strode over to the door, Lacey thought about how tired of it she was. She was only seventeen. She should have felt full of life, bursting with youth and love for her special guy and giddy about the promise of a better future. Yet when she felt those joyous feelings stir inside her, a shadow fell over them. Knowing it was because of her father just amplified her sadness.

Lacey hadn't lost one parent; she had lost two.

Suddenly, the door was practically ripped open, and the huge, swaying silhouette of Roger Purcell stood framed by the hallway lights.

Lacey started, taking a step back. "Oh, Dad, I didn't see—"

"Where the hell have you been, Lance?" her father demanded, the smell of beer wafting over her. "You've been with that little faggot again." A sound halfway between a burp and a hiccup interrupted his rant for a few seconds, and he teetered over the threshold, his watery eyes unfocused and blinking. "I told you you're never to see him again. You won't turn into a little pansy-ass fairy like him."

Lacey felt conflicted, wanting to cower before her father's hatred and to stand up for her boyfriend. The last instinct won. "Bro's a jock, the most manly—"

Roger growled, advancing on Lacey, and then the back of his hand made contact with her face. Pain shot through her, a jolt so hard it forced her to step back. Her neck hurt, as did everything else. His knuckles had landed solidly, and his wedding ring had scraped her cheek. She smelled and tasted blood, and her teeth clattered. Her jaw felt looser than before. Her legs wobbled, nausea set in, swirling in her belly, and bile rose up in her throat.

Roger was shouting now. "You little shit! I told you not to—"

Lacey responded with the new skills she had spent the past hours practicing. She brought her foot up fast and hard and kicked Roger in the thigh. Groaning, Roger fell to his knees.

Without trying to do more, Lacey spun and started running. Tears were flowing down her cheeks, and the pain made her stumble every other step, but she couldn't stop. It was as if she became the essence of escape, sprinting forward at such high speed her soles barely grazed the ground. Lacey had only one destination in mind, and she prayed they would welcome her in her greatest hour of need.

Chapter 7

"WHAT the heck is all that ruckus?" Bro rubbed his bleary eyes as he sauntered into the living room, having been stirred from his half-asleep state by the sharp noises from the door.

He stopped dead in his tracks when he saw Jordan and Sebastian standing in the foyer, both of them furious, with a shaky, sobbing Lacey before them. Bro's heart froze in fear, and he had to fight to breathe. Then his feet were moving on their own, finding their way to the sad girl he loved more than anything.

Without speaking, Bro pulled Lacey into his arms, holding her fiercely, wanting nothing more than to protect her forever. When she wrapped her arms around his waist and sniffled into his chest, he spoke softly.

"What's happened, honey?" He rubbed her back soothingly, up and down, unceasingly. He was so worried he wondered if his soul could take it.

Lacey's hot tears wetted Bro's T-shirt, the fabric soaking them all up, and he wished he could do the same thing with her pain, absorb it like a sponge and store it inside of him. Then she would never have to feel sorrow again.

"Dad."

The one word was enough; wrath boiled inside him. "What did he do?"

Lacey shivered hard in his arms and burrowed her way deeper into his embrace. Her muffled voice cracked with the swell of emotions. "Called you names. When I tried to defend you, he... he hit me." Bro's heart did stop beating then. "I kicked him, and then I ran." Her sobs became louder, more distinct. "Why does he hate me so? I never did anything to deserve it. Deep down, he's a good man, I know—"

"No, baby. No more," Bro cut in, adamant, trying to rein in his own temper. "No more excuses. He's had plenty of chances to change. A year's worth of opportunities. Now he's crossed the line. You know that. You gotta stop defending him."

"But... but he's my dad...." The utter loss and misery in her small voice made Bro grimace and then tighten his hold, cradling her and rocking in place gently. She felt so tiny in his arms tonight, so frail and alone. If Bro had his way, Lacey was never going to be lonely for the rest of her life.

"Being a dad is a privilege, not a right. And as far as I'm concerned, the dickhead has lost that right," Bro growled out through gritted teeth. He knew he might be making the situation worse, but he had to speak his mind—and voice what was in his heart.

"Lacey, my brother is right," Sebastian said in his hollow voice, his hand coming to rest on her slender shoulder. "He and I both know biology alone does not make a good parent. The minute your father chose violence as his recourse, his parental rights ceased to exist. Nothing excuses his actions. Not even his own sorrow or pain, let alone who he used to be."

With teary eyes Lacey looked up at Sebastian, but Bro could tell she was reluctant to agree with their position. It was a huge deal to admit to others, as well to oneself, that a parent had only hate in his heart. Bro didn't envy Lacey's position, having to decide for or against her father.

Yet it wasn't her decision alone anymore. Cops and officials had to get involved now.

Finally, Lacey nodded feebly, looking devastated. "Now what?"

Bro was on top of things, taking charge. "Now, baby, you're gonna stay with me here and be safe and happy. Your daddy's gonna pay for what he's done to you. I'll be your family."

Her eyes widened as she stared at Bro, not surprised exactly but definitely shocked a little. It was then Bro realized how determined and uncompromising he had sounded. Though he felt he might need to take things down a notch, he couldn't bring himself to retract any of what he had said.

Lacey seemed to understand as a small, fragile smile lifted her trembling lips a bit. "I'm glad you're with me, Bro."

He cupped her delicate face, locking their gazes. "I'll always be with you." To keep the moment just between them, Bro hugged Lacey again, feeling her body turn pliant and relaxed. He felt his chest puff up with pride. He had successfully alleviated her anxieties, even after what had happened to her. She was still capable of trusting people, and that was a good sign.

"I'm gonna call Kev, and we're gonna get an arrest warrant for Roger." Jordan's level, low voice drifted into Bro's calming cocoon, reminding him why Lacey was in his arms in the first place. He stiffened as a result and not in a good way.

"I'm coming with you," Bro said harshly. He had a feeling he was going to rip Roger a new one the moment they shared the same space for longer than two seconds, and he sure didn't regret that impulse.

Lacey pulled back to look at him pleadingly. "Please, Bro. Don't. I need you here."

With that shattered tone and those appealing words, Lacey owned Bro, and the urge to attack left him. "Shh. You're right, Lace, as usual. Everything's okay. I'm not going anywhere, I promise. Jordan can kick his ass way better than me anyway." He added a little grin at the end to show he was joking, and Lacey's relieved expression told its own story.

"In the meantime," Jordan interjected, all business now, "you need to document her injuries. Sebastian, you've got one of those digital cameras, don't you?" Nodding, Sebastian touched Lacey's healthy cheek gently, then was off to fetch the camera. Looking at Bro and Lacey sternly, Jordan continued, "Bro, I expect you to be an adult here. When we're gone, lock the door, and let no one in—"

Bro stopped him. "I was gonna call Bradley and Audrey over. I think it would help Lacey to be among friends right now." He looked at his girlfriend shyly, suddenly afraid she might want to hide away in shame from those who cared about her. He was sure that would be detrimental to her mental health and well-being. Her father might be an asshole, but if she turned into an emotional recluse, he would have won. "I mean, if that's okay with you."

"Yes." Lacey sighed and returned to hugging Bro.

Bro glanced at Jordan. "I'll make sure no one else comes here. I don't think Roger even knows where I live. He's never shown any interest in tracking me down."

"Good. Let's keep it that way." Jordan's intense gaze followed Sebastian's progress down the spiral staircase. Sebastian smiled and waved a black digital camera in his hand as he approached. "Take pictures of Lacey's injuries, both close-up and farther away," Jordan instructed, and Bro nodded his understanding and compliance. "Sebastian, you're coming with me and Kev. If Roger really is as drunk and violent as Lacey says—"

"You think she's lying, you shithead?" Bro all but shouted, his ravaged emotions causing him to react without thinking. Immediately, he felt Lacey cringe in his arms, and he regretted his tone, his accusation, everything. "Babe, I'm sorry. It's okay. I'm sorry I yelled. I won't do it again."

Jordan's voice was neutral but with a hint of iciness. "I meant he might be passed out by now." Bro swallowed down his embarrassment and nodded, hoping Jordan would understand and forgive him his outburst.

"Lace?" Jordan went on, "Did he hit you anywhere else?"

"No."

Jordan paused. "Has he hit you before?"

For a moment there was silence. Then Lacey started crying against Bro's chest again, shivers wracking her frame. Bro felt tears burn in his eyes as he realized the truth. Now he was shaking too, wanting to hunt the man down and tear him limb from limb.

"Once before," Lacey confessed, her face still hidden.

Distressed, Bro had to ask, "Because of me…?"

Lacey shook her head hard, and waves of anger emanated from her. "No. You're just an excuse to him. It's me he hates. My name, my clothes, me being gay, my girliness, my violin. I'm not enough of a man for him. I will never be." She looked up at Bro, tears falling down her cheeks. "It's not your fault. Never was, never will be. It's all him."

Though it was painful to capitulate to that fact, Bro knew she was right. Some people needed no reasons beyond the first excuse that popped up on their radar.

Quickly, he cupped her face once more. "I will never let him touch you again. I promise."

Lacey's eyes were grateful yet sad. "Don't make promises you can't keep, Bro. I have no other family, so he could keep custody—"

"*We're* your family—" Bro started, his tone rising.

Jordan cut through, like an icy knife. "Bro, cool it. Lacey, there are options for custody. We're going to explore them all. We'll all do whatever it takes, okay? You're not alone."

Lacey slumped. It looked like a visible weight had dropped from her shoulders. "Thank you, all." She tried to say more, but her jaw quivered, and she couldn't seem to manage another word.

Bro held her tight to his chest. "You're welcome. Come on, babe. Let's get that face on film. Then the courts will let you stay with me— um, us."

Jordan gave a chin-lift good-bye before heading out, yanking his leather jacket on and holding a cell against his ear as he went. "Kev? Yeah, sorry to bother you this late, but we've got a situation. Lacey's dad's...." His voice trailed off as he disappeared into the stairwell. Sebastian gave Bro the camera, hugged them both, and ran out to follow his fiancé. The red metal door shut with a heavy bang.

Without another word, Bro steered Lacey toward the downstairs bathroom. She followed meekly, still holding on to his waist, her steps slow but steady. The cool bathroom light greeted them, showering them under a soothing glow. The scent of air freshener floated about with the air conditioning.

Bro lifted Lacey up on the counter, between the two sinks. "Show me. Please."

That "please" was clearly welcomed. Lacey sighed, relaxed, and tilted her head to show him her cheek. The bruise had not yet fully formed, but the swelling was obvious. Bro bit his lip hard to prevent another rage-filled explosion. She would not have understood that his anger wasn't directed at her right now.

Bro's hands felt heavy, sweaty, and shaky as he lifted the camera, pressed the on button, and snapped several shots, a few up close and a few from farther away. The visible, recorded evidence of Lacey's suffering made Bro's stomach clench. It took serious effort for him not to act like a total dickhead, scream and shout and break things and fight for the girl he adored.

"We should wash your face first, before I put anything cool on it, okay?"

Lacey furrowed her brow as she contemplated this. Then she blushed, looking small again, and Bro really hated seeing her so timid.

"Can I take a shower? I feel… filthy."

Bro tried to capture her lovely face, but she squirmed away. Bro felt like gnawing a bone for some reason, this weird primitive urge probably stemming from his frustration. "Baby—"

"I just want to be alone," Lacey whispered, hanging her head as if ashamed.

Feeling a little faint, Bro realized he had started breathing really, really fast. "Baby, please, listen to me." He finally caught her deer-in-the-headlights gaze, holding onto the tenuous connection between them. "Lace, you're the sweetest, best person I know—"

She sniffled, wiping her nose with the back of her hand. "No. I'm ugly. Inside. I must be 'cause he hates me so."

The fresh burst of anger at Roger within Bro made him grunt and blink tears from his eyes as he hastened to say, "You're beautiful, honey. Inside and out. You always will be. He's the one who is all festering hate and pain and sorrow. Not you." With aching tenderness, he kissed her soft, trembling lips. "I know. Because I lo—because you're mine. And I know you, heart and soul. I've never known anyone as full of light as you. You shine, baby. You blind me."

Now Lacey's face crumpled, and she started to cry.

"Baby, please don't...." Bro wanted to hold her, but his hands stuttered in front of him, hesitant. "I'll never let him hurt you again."

Lacey shook her head, drowning in her emotions, and Bro felt so helpless he wanted to scream. "It's not that. Jordan showed me how to defend myself." She wept in between harsh gasps, in the heart of the tempest, only there was no calm center there. "My mom.... Now my dad.... I don't have anyone." Bro started to speak, but Lacey's feverish, clammy hand pressed against his mouth, preventing him. "You're so important to me, Bro. You have no idea. Brad and Audrey too, and even Jordan and Sebastian. But... you're not the family I was born to. Yes, I can rebuild a family from all of you, and I don't even think any of you would mind. But...." She rasped the words out, like sickening lumps. "To know my dad hates me like that, that he doesn't want me as his child, that he'd rather hit me than hug me.... It hurts, Bro. It hurts so fucking much. I don't know if I can bear it."

She cursed so rarely, it shocked Bro to silence. But when Lacey draped herself over him, clinging to him like a lifeline, he wound his arms around her again, squeezing her as close as humanly possible without their becoming one person. How trite it would sound to say everything was going to be all right, so Bro held back those words.

Instead he mumbled the second thing to come to his mind. "You know, love is kind of like tears, isn't it? I mean, it's in your eyes first, as you look at the one you love. Eye of the beholder and all that jazz. But then love, like tears, falls down to your chest, sort of like... like soaking into your heart, filling it. Only... it's not sorrow, but love, all warm and soft and scary and exhilarating and perfect." Bro nodded, wanting so badly to believe the words he was uttering. "You know how I know? It's because when you cry, your tears are my tears. 'Cause I love you, Lace. So very much. More than anything, more than anyone. I love you."

Lacey pulled back fast, her eyes wide like saucers as she stared, flabbergasted. For a long while she said nothing, just ogled him without comprehension, her lips an impeccable O. Then she made a strange, strangled sound in her throat, and deflated, looking overjoyed and miserable at the same time.

"I love you too, Bro. A *lot* a lot."

The relief that swamped Bro at that moment was almost as powerful as the burst of joy in his heart. A smile rose to his lips, and he doubted if he'd ever be able to stop. Lacey's beautiful lips joined him with a similar gesture. For a moment, the horrible recent experiences receded, and there were only happy heights of the heart.

Nodding over and over again, Bro leaned forward, pressing their foreheads together, and their gazes remained locked. "You're perfect. My sweet love. My lovely baby." The nonsensical endearments kept rolling out of his mouth, and when the tension left Lacey's body, he knew he had done well keeping the confession to himself until this moment. She was shattered, but Bro hoped his love for her would repair at least some of the damage.

In fact, he prayed so hard his soul ached for the wish to be fulfilled.

But then Lacey's warm body pressed against his as her arms wound around his neck, and he knew everything really was going to be all right.

"My strong guy," she murmured in his ear, her hot breath brushing over his skin and hair. "I'm never lost with you. You always find me. When he slapped me, I fell, Bro. I fell into this deep, dark hole, and I couldn't get out. I ran, but...."

"I've got you, love," Bro soothed her, rubbing her back gently. "You don't have to run anymore."

"I know." Lacey sighed, and the contentment in her voice was all he needed to hear. Suddenly she giggled a bit, though the sound was watery and choked. "But I also know I want to take a shower. I want his touch gone from my skin." She parted from Bro, who felt an acute fear gripping him. Lacey must have interpreted his terrified look right, because she softly admonished, "I'm not going to cut my wrists in the shower, Bro. I won't let him have that. I have a life and a future, and it's with you. Whether he likes it or not."

Relieved, Bro kissed Lacey. Her lips, though soft, were dry and salty from crying. He didn't want that taste to cling to her lips ever again. Only sweet and happy things would grace her lips from now on.

"Okay. I'll be right outside. I'm gonna call Audrey, okay?"

With a brave smile, she nodded and straightened up. Lacey seemed like herself again. Bro knew it was too soon to expect it to be truly so, but he had hope. Jordan and Kevin would take care of Roger. They would make sure he never got the chance to lay one finger on Lacey again. In the meantime, she could stay with them at the loft. God knew it was big enough to accommodate new arrivals, of which there seemed to be more every year.

"I'll ask her to come soon, okay?"

Lacey smiled. "Yes. I… I'd like her here." Her face darkened a bit, doubtful. "You think she's gonna be mad at me? You know, for not telling her sooner?"

"Audrey loves you like a little sister," Bro said emphatically, denying the mere notion. "Will you be fine in here all by yourself?"

"Yes. So stop fretting." She hopped down from the counter, then winced but smiled to take the edge off.

"Never." Bro gave her one more quick kiss and then left the room. Before closing the door, he said, "Towels are in the cupboard. Washing stuff's in the stall—"

"I know where everything is, silly goose." Lacey gave a light laugh that didn't last very long, but Bro accepted it nonetheless as a sign of better times ahead.

So he closed the door and let her have her privacy. More picture taking lay ahead once she was clean. He moved away from the door, then slumped down on his bed, burying his face in his hands, feeling the tremors of absolute horror wracking his mind, body, and soul. *God, I nearly lost her today.* Tears stung in his eyes, and he had to blink hard to be rid of them. With trembling hands and a chill racing down his spine, he pulled his cell phone from his jeans pocket and sent a simple text—*L's dad. Bad sitch. Loft. ASAP*—to both Audrey and Bradley at the same time.

Then he set out to await their arrival. And to keep breathing until then. No conscious thoughts ran through his mind. Only emotions swelled inside him, and he let them take over as he sat still in place, unable to move an inch, wanting so desperately for things to be all right once more. He was held together by a thread, a tenuous tether to ground him to reality. In his fantasies, Bro hurt Roger back, many times, until there was no man left to speak of. He saw it with crystal clarity in his mind's eye. He didn't want to be this person, the kind of man who solved his problems with his fists. Especially now, when Lacey had known enough violence from someone who was supposed to love her. Bro shook his head vehemently. *I'm not like Roger. I'm not like that violent fucker. I will never be.*

So with deep breaths, he fought to clear his head from all the noise and settled into a patient holding pattern yet again. He closed his eyes, hurting all over, on his skin and deep inside his soul. *I love you, Lacey. Always will.*

His cell beeped to indicate a text. He read Bradley's text from the screen: *ETA 5 min.* It had to be enough, Bro thought. Then he could crumble too.

"HOW are you, honey?"

Audrey hugged Lacey, showing just how much strength lay in that tiny body. Though she felt like she was being crushed, the close contact of her best friend nonetheless felt like a protective circle around her, and Lacey embraced her back.

"I'll be okay." She glanced at Bro, who sat at the end of the bed with Bradley, their heads down as they spoke in hushed tones, and immediately she felt her knees turn to jelly. Bro's love confession had made mush of her brain and pushed out all the sadness within her heart, replacing the empty space with a warm, cuddly feeling that made her toes curl and her face break into a smile.

For that Lacey was grateful. It wasn't like she had planned on spilling blood under the shower spray. Yet, she had hit rock bottom within her heart, having lost touch with the last human part of her father, feeling disconnected and inhuman, like a piece of trash, not worthy of being loved and living her life in peace. Was there anything Roger liked about his child? Being feminine and gay were definitely out. What about her music? Each time Lacey lifted the bow and drew out the first soft chords from her violin, the world made sense, and she remembered her mother's smile and all the happy times they had shared.

No. She shook herself inwardly. Lacey would not allow her father to steal these things from her. They gave her life meaning and purpose. As she played, the sad notes of the violin ripped through her soul and yet soothed a healing balm over the many gashes there. Sometimes Lacey felt like she was bleeding a drop every day, wondering if one day she would run out of life essence.

But then Bro always made his presence known, and Lacey couldn't help but feel happy and normal again. He really was her rock to stand on, to rebuild on. Without Bro, Lacey would not have known what to do.

As though he knew Lacey was thinking about him, Bro peered up at her, smiling reassuringly. "You okay there, Lace?"

"Better now." Though Lacey was first and foremost talking about the cooling gel Bro had applied over her forming bruise, she also hinted at his declaration of love. That made her face flame up, and in a perfect accompaniment, Bro's cheeks reddened as well. His smile turned into a salacious grin, and Lacey's body responded to the suggestive gesture as if to a real touch.

"What's going on here?" Audrey asked, pursing her lips knowingly with her hands on her hips, mock glaring at both Lacey and Bro.

"Mind your own business, your nosiness," Bro growled back, never taking his eyes off Lacey.

Suddenly Audrey's face cleared and she got a smitten look on her face. "Aww...."

"What?" Bradley frowned, his expression confused.

"Nothing," Bro ground out, his lips thinning, and his chin lifted in that defiant look Lacey knew so well. So he wanted to keep it private between the two of them for now. She was fine with that. The outside world had intruded upon their relationship enough for one day.

Bradley snorted, waving a hand about. "Okay, whatever. Excuse my intrusive girl over there." He pointed his finger at Audrey, who huffed, indignant, and shot him a scary glare. Bradley just grinned and made a lewd kissy face. Audrey rolled her eyes. "Anyway," Bradley went on, serious again. "Lace, whatever you need, we're there for you, okay?"

To think that a little over a year ago, Lacey had barely known these people who now called themselves her friends and made her all gooey inside. So her father was a drunken bigot. At least she had her friends to stick with her and by her.

"Thank you, Brad. That means a lot to me."

Audrey hugged her again and then rested her arm around her shoulders, giving her comfort. "You mean a lot to us too, Lace. Why didn't you tell us? I'm not trying to make you feel bad; you have to know we're not here to judge you. We only want to help and stand with you."

"I know." Lacey bit her lower lip, hanging her head. "I was… ashamed."

"What happened was not your fault, and you didn't do anything to deserve it," Audrey countered, her green eyes flashing intently. "Your daddy's a dick. And that has nothing to do with you. If it wasn't you he hated, it would be something else. Anything to avoid having to look inside, let alone deal with his own loss of…" Audrey stumbled, swallowing hard and looking bashful. "Oh, sweetie, I'm sorry. I didn't mean to remind you of—"

"Don't apologize." Lacey gave her a quick peck on the cheek in a sisterly manner, and Audrey blushed sweetly. "I don't ever want to forget Mom. And I don't mind talking about her. Dad never talks about her anymore. Not that he talks about anything with me anymore."

"Okay then." Audrey straightened up and glanced at the guys. "Time for you boys to skedaddle so we can have our girl talk. Scram." She thumbed behind her shoulder to point at the door, and grudging Bro and grinning Bradley got up and left the room. Bro kissed Lacey on the lips before he left, however.

Once the door closed, Audrey smiled at Lacey. "Let's talk."

Lacey lay down on her side on Bro's bed, smelling his young male scent in the sheets. Audrey lay next to her, propped up on an elbow, looking at her expectantly.

"Lexie was a great mom," Lacey said quietly, staring at the ceiling. "Alexandra Adair. I chose my new name to resemble hers." Audrey smiled, as she already knew that, but she let Lacey direct the conversation. "When she was around, Dad was different. He never said anything about me being... well, not like the other boys."

"Your mom's influence was pretty strong," Audrey agreed slowly, cautiously. Lacey had a feeling she wanted to say more but held back. Lacey knew her best friend would die rather than hurt her in any way.

"I guess Dad thought it was okay for me to emulate her then, like an idol, as kids do with their parents sometimes." Lacey shrugged but felt anything but indifferent. "But when she... died—" Lacey swallowed hard, the pain in her heart fresh and slicing. "—she took away the reason for me to be this way. At least in Dad's eyes. When Mom was alive, my dresses and makeup faded into the background. When Mom died, who I am jumped into the foreground. Dad couldn't handle it, I guess."

"Oh, Lacey." Audrey's sigh was both empathetic and irritated, and Lacey heard them both, frowning a question. "You always make excuses for him. As if his pain is somehow more important than yours. As if it explains and justifies everything."

"I never said that," Lacey defended herself. Still, she knew Audrey had a point. But Roger was her father. *His* father. Whatever. Lacey was Roger's child, and he was the only parent she had anymore. She wanted to believe Roger would pull out of his grief-stricken, drunken haze and once again become the father she needed him to be.

Deep down in her soul, in a dark and unhappy place, Lacey was beginning to see that maybe that transformation was beyond Roger's capabilities.

"He's the only dad I have."

"You're not alone, Lace. You gotta know that." Audrey's hand rested on hers, and the warmth of the touch held nothing back.

"You're my friends. But you're not my parents. You never could be." Lacey wished she didn't sound so miserable. It was strange to *know* she had friends who could become her new family, and yet *feel* like she had no one. She wished her head could rule just this once.

"No, we can't be your parents. But we can be your family." Audrey's wise, tender gaze left nothing uncertain. She meant what she said, and Lacey's dark world got a little lighter.

Then Audrey's sharp, narrow gaze landed on Lacey's cheekbone, where the bruise was slowly forming. It was already swollen but glistened wet now. "Does it hurt, sweetie?"

Lacey raised her hand and almost brushed the cool, slick skin. "Yes and no. It's sort of throbbing, but it's not a sharp pain, you know. Bro applied some ice gel to it."

Suddenly Audrey smirked. "Yeah, I bet he did!"

Laughing, Lacey rolled her eyes. "God, you have such a one-track mind!"

"Yeah, yeah, I'm a total slut." Audrey snickered. Lacey pursed her lips, disapproving of her self-characterization, as it was untrue. Whatever conflicting messages Audrey sent with her appearance, she loved and was faithful to Bradley. Lacey was pretty sure Audrey chose to look and act the way she did because she was rebelling against other people's expectations of her. Looking flirtatious and alluring was her facade and shield. Few knew who she really was. Lacey was proud to be among those chosen.

"You know I hate it when you call yourself that," she scolded her best friend.

Audrey winked. "Yup. But this way you can stand next to me and appear so innocent the angels themselves will weep to love you."

Now Lacey really rolled her eyes, making a loud *tsk-tsk* sound. "Oh my God. I'm just going to pretend you're not even here." She lay down on her back, staring at the ceiling defiantly.

Then she felt Audrey's thick hair and warm arm near her as she rested next to Lacey. Her flowery scent assailed Lacey's nose. "You can't pretend 'cause you're so sweet. And I can get really loud. And teary-eyed. If you make me cry, then what will all those angels think of you?" It was her turn to make disapproving clucking sounds.

Lacey burst into laughter and felt better. Maybe things would work out after all.

"ROGER'S hit Lacey before," Bro admitted reluctantly, miserable down to his soul as he sat on the living room couch. Bradley sat opposite him, on the coffee table of all places. "She didn't tell me. She just hid it from me and the world with concealer and lies."

"Oh, come on, Bro." Bradley sounded annoyed and reproachful. "Give her a break. You know it's not easy to talk about stuff like that. To say out loud how you've been victimized by someone you've trusted. It's hard to shake off that sense of shame. Especially if one's a guy, and the one doing the hurting is a parent."

"Yeah, I know that. Jesus fucking Christ." Bro cursed a blue streak, ran a hand through his hair harshly, and muttered, "It's just that.... Well, me and Lacey. We're the same, you know. We both have lost a parent—her mom and my dad—and the surviving parental unit hates our guts with a vengeance. Sure, my mom's a cold-hearted bitch with ice water running through her veins, while Lacey's dad is a raving lunatic all fired up by booze and bigotry. I mean, Lacey and me, we come from a similar situation. Did she think I couldn't understand, or sympathize, or accept that bad shit happens. Why couldn't she trust me?"

"Fuck, Bro." Bradley's typically level tone dropped to a dangerous low, and his eyes blazed with irritation as he shook his head. "What the fuck does it take to get through to you, pal? This has nothing to do with trust, let alone you. You know Lacey adores your sorry ass. But these things are so damn hard to address, to talk about, to confront. Despite what the shrinks say. Who knows? Maybe she thought it was an isolated incident—"

Bro snorted loudly. "Yeah, right!" Bradley's patience rarely waned, but Bro had a feeling he was testing his best friend's limits.

"Look," Bradley argued. "A child instinctively trusts his or her parents, wants to believe in them, trusts them even after some seriously fucked-up shit. Or maybe Lacey just needed a breather, some time to decompress, to try and figure it out, to process by herself. And you sure as hell can't blame her for that, dipshit."

Never one to back down from a fight but not one to hide from the truth either, Bro nodded slowly. He felt too weary to think clearly but knew his best friend had a point. No, more than a point. Bradley was more insightful and wise about this than Bro, who couldn't separate his raging emotions from his failing logic. "I guess...."

Bradley sighed, clasping his hands together between his splayed knees as if praying for patience. "Geez, Bro. You gotta cut her some slack, man. Ease up. She doesn't need the added stress of you wigging out on her right now."

It wasn't like Bro didn't know his best friend had him dead to rights. He wanted so badly to be there for Lacey, but he also felt like nothing he did was going to be enough. "I know that, man. I swear I do. It's just... I feel so fucking helpless, you know? So useless—"

"That's bullshit," Bradley countered, all but growling. "Grow a set, why don't you?"

If only it had been that simple, Bro thought. To just man up, give Lacey his support and time and strength. But there were all these other feelings inside him, raw and primal, urging him to fix this problem for good.

"I... I want to kill him." His confession tore through his conscience, eating him alive, cutting a sliver of his innate goodness from him.

Bradley reared back, stunned, his eyes wide, blinking. "Jesus, Bro.... No."

Laughing bitterly, Bro felt these compulsions festering inside him. "I see it in my head, you know. I see myself doing it, hurting him good, making him pay—"

Bradley grabbed Bro's trembling hand, then squeezed it hard. "You absolutely cannot go down that road, brother. You do that, and you lose everything. I mean all of it. Your family, friends, your future, freedom—and Lacey."

"I know." Bro closed his eyes, trying to swallow past the lump in his throat, his chest constricted with the weight of utter desperation within. "I can't do it. I know I can't, and I shouldn't. And I'm not even saying I'm gonna.... But it's there, you know, inside. Like a fucking cancer, eating at me." Bro wanted to cry, to scream, to hit, to tear apart, to run, to fight. Yet he simply sat there on the couch, feeling lost and exposed, like a raw nerve, unable to shield himself from the attacks from the outside world, from adults who knew nothing but their own cruelty. "I hate that I have all this rage inside me—"

"We're her friends too, Bro," Bradley reminded him, steering his storming emotions toward a place of calm. "Me and Audrey, we feel the same way. We want to stop that asshole too. We want to see him go down, unable to ever get up from the mud. We want him to end up behind bars, never to emerge back into the light of day. But... Lacey doesn't need stupid heroics right now. She needs stability and serenity."

"Yeah, I fucking know that, all right?" Bro all but yelled. Glancing over his shoulder into the hallway where the door to his room remained closed, he took a steadying breath. "I'm trying to bury these thoughts and feelings as deep down as I can, but it's so fucking hard. Especially when I see how sad and broken and lonely she is. I don't want her to suffer anymore."

"Neither do we, brother." Bradley was once again in charge, his cool demeanor a pool of tranquility for Bro. "We'll stick together, yeah? Return to normalcy. Reassure both her and you this whole sordid business is not the end. Can you do that, man? You gotta step up to the plate on this one."

Bro had no doubt in his mind his best friend was absolutely correct. If he had any hope of getting Lacey out of the emotional and physical swamp she was mired in, he had to keep a cool head.

"Fuck, man. I gotta get this under control. I gotta rise up above it." He nodded to himself, and Bradley's touch helped ground him to reality. "I gotta be there for Lacey. So, yeah. I will try to let this rage go and just... just be normal and soothing for her. Yeah." Then his gaze found Bradley's. His best friend smiled encouragingly and nodded as well, agreeing and offering support. "I'll best these instincts before they ruin my relationship with Lacey, or my sanity, whichever comes first. I promise."

Bradley smiled, relieved. "I know you will, brother."

Just as he let go of Bro's arm, the front door opened and brought Jordan, Kevin, and Sebastian into the loft. As Bro got up, he saw their grim faces and knew they were the bearers of bad news.

"Fuck!" he cursed, and for once Sebastian didn't reproach him for his outburst.

Right then the bedroom door opened, and side by side, Lacey and Audrey came out, apparently having heard people arriving. While Audrey looked confident in her expectations, Lacey appeared more hesitant, nervous. Yet Lacey didn't seek out anyone but Bro, who unfortunately couldn't keep the frustrated disappointment from his expression.

Her hand flew up to her mouth, but this time not to cover up a smile. "Oh no...."

Before the gasp left her lips, Bro was at her side, embracing her steadfastly. "He's not gonna get away, babe. I promise you."

Jordan stepped forward, his face schooled to neutrality. But from the corner of his eye, Bro could see he was less calm than he appeared. He said only one thing, and Bro felt his stomach plummet so far down it might as well be buried underground.

"Roger's done a runner."

Chapter 8

"YOU okay there, Lace?"

Audrey's concerned voice reached Lacey in the depths of her depressing thoughts, and she jerked back to full awareness. "I'm fine… ish."

She sighed, staring out across the high school football field as they sat side by side in the bleachers, spring whipping cool air their way and rustling the trees around the field. Football practice hadn't started yet, so they were waiting for the team to arrive from the locker room. They would cheer the boys on. Lacey was eager to see Bro back in the game, even if this wasn't a real competition like the games in the fall.

Audrey took her hand, interlacing their fingers. "I'm here for you, Lace. Whenever you need."

Smiling, Lacey bumped her best friend with her shoulder. "Thanks."

"You're not going to end up in the system, are you?" Audrey's voice had dipped low in the register, concerned.

Lacey shrugged, uncertain. "Jordan, Kevin, and Sebastian talked about a lot of things with me yesterday. Jordan got a temporary order of protection for me from a judge who is sympathetic to victims of domestic abuse." She shuddered, realizing from now on she too would be another number on a case file, a statistic, one in a million, a drop in the ocean, a new gear in the relentless, merciless machine.

"That's good, at least." Audrey's hand never left hers.

"The temporary protection order is only valid for two weeks, but considering how my dad is, another one will probably need to be filed sooner rather than later." Lacey repeated Jordan's words, having heard them many times last night, feeling both safe and vulnerable at the same time. Could she trust the system to help her?

"What happens then?"

"My situation is reviewed by family court. If they decide Dad's done nothing wrong, I could end up back with him."

Audrey shook her head, her lips a thin, angry line. "No fucking way, Lace. We'll put a stop to him. He's never gonna hit you again. What else did they say?"

Lacey sighed wearily. "I don't know. A lot. Too much really. They spoke about the age of majority in Washington DC, and emancipation of a minor, and domestic violence support groups, and.... Well, I guess they wanted me to know there are options for me. That regardless of what my dad does, or if the civil protection order is continued or not, I won't be discarded or dismissed. That I will have other opportunities to fight my dad's custody of me, especially if he continues to... to hurt me again."

"It's good to have options," Audrey agreed with an encouraging smile.

"Yeah. Legal protection and... and all of you by my side." Lacey glanced bashfully at Audrey, who nodded and chuckled, bumping her arm against Lacey's shoulder.

"You know...," Audrey started, dragging out the words. Lacey looked at her funny, and Audrey smirked, apparently in an effort to lighten up the mood, which was a welcome gesture in Lacey's mind. "What happened between you and Bro before me and Bradley got there? 'Cause I can tell something did." She leaned closer, whispering, "You know I won't tell anyone."

That was true. Lacey had told Audrey a lot of private stuff about her past, her dreams, and her relationship with Bro. Not once had Audrey broken a confidence.

"Yes, I know." And a part of her wanted to speak about what had transpired with someone so it would be... more real. Lacey snorted at her ridiculous notions. "He loves me."

Audrey's eyes sparkled with glee, and her grin widened. "Wow. He said that?" Unable to say it with her quivering voice, Lacey merely nodded. "Oh. My. Fucking. God." For a second Audrey just breathed really, really fast, and Lacey was getting concerned. Then Audrey let out a loud whoop of girlish glee. "Oh, Lacey. I'm so freaking happy for you." She hugged Lacey so hard her bones crackled under the loving onslaught. Lacey laughed with her best friend, embracing her just as heartily. Suddenly, Audrey pulled back a bit. "So, where *did* you sleep last night?"

Lacey scoffed, playfully outraged. "Not in Bro's bed!"

"Oh." Audrey managed to sound somewhat disappointed, but then she grinned. "Well, plenty of time for hanky-panky later. He loves you, and we all love you, too, honey."

"Me too. Love you all, I mean," she said. She hoped her confession of Bro's love for her was one she could share with others in the future, and no one would bat an eye at her homosexuality. Unfortunately, that line of thinking brought her back to the only family member she had left, who couldn't stand the sight of her. Despondency reared its ugly head again.

As if sensing the shift in the mood, Audrey said softly, "You're not alone, honey. I'm here for you, and so are a bunch of others. Families are forged through fire, and we're all definitely battle-hardened bitches."

Lacey had to chuckle upon hearing that. "God, Audrey. You're so bad."

Audrey's arms tightened around her as she sighed smugly. "Perfectly bad."

"Now you're fucking girls too? Finally you're acting like a man, but you've still got a damn dress on? Get up, Lance. I'm taking you home."

Both girls jumped at the sound of the man's harsh voice. Lacey started at the sight of her haggard-looking father, who hurried toward the bleachers, his clothes rumpled and reeking of booze. His eyes were bloodshot, and he snarled at Audrey.

"Dad...." Lacey stood up, shocked and afraid.

Audrey got up too, her worry palpable. "Want me to call for help, Lace?"

"*His*. Name. Is. Lance." Roger shook his fist in front of Audrey. Having successfully climbed the two rows of seats, he was now right on their level.

"No, it's not." Audrey's body had gone rigid, yet Lacey could tell she was primed for a fight.

"Stupid whore," Roger swore under his breath and closed the gap between him and Lacey. "You're coming home, boy, where you belong. And I'll whip this nonsense from your mind if it's the last thing I do."

Even as the words came out of his mouth, Roger grabbed Lacey's hair and yanked her with him. Lacey fell on her knees, feeling a sharp pain and her clothing rip as she cried out. As she struggled to break free, her nails dug into the skin of his hand, but he slapped her across the head and made everything spin and wave and sparkle. Nausea roiled in her stomach, and bile rose in her throat. Pain rattled inside her brain like seeds in a calabash.

Suddenly, Roger grunted, and his grip on her hair loosened.

Lacey heard a shrill shriek. "Let go of her, motherfucker!" And as her vision cleared, she saw Audrey draped over Roger's back, her arms around his throat.

By then Roger was cursing loudly, using words Lacey had never heard and hoped to never hear again. He tried to shake Audrey loose. Finally, he got a fierce grip on her arm and tossed her over his shoulder. Audrey landed on the wooden bleacher bench with a thud, all the air whooshing out of her lungs as she gasped in agony.

In horror, Lacey saw Roger wrap his hands around Audrey's throat and squeeze.

It was all too much. Lacey knew the man she had called father was gone for good.

"Let go of her," she screamed, throwing herself on him.

In a heap of flailing limbs, they fell down on the bench below with Roger on his back and Lacey on top of him, slapping and punching and scratching and kicking. Deafened by the roar of blood in her ears, she was faintly aware of an animalistic squeal that seemed to be emanating from within her. But then everything faded to the black of instinct, shot through with red and white flashes of anger and pain.

"WOULD you hurry up already, you slouch?" Bradley's taunting voice ribbed at Bro's expense, and he flipped his friend off, causing nothing more than a chuckle in response.

On their way out to the field, Bro slowed his step. As much as he wanted to see his girl in the bleachers, he worried about her state of mind. He wondered if maybe this attempt at normalcy was premature. Perhaps she wasn't ready to watch him play ball all afternoon, sitting there with nothing to do but twiddle her thumbs and think about all the crap that had been flying at her lately. Bro didn't want her thinking too much, because he knew where that would lead her. His shoulders slumped in defeat.

"Geez, Bro. You look like you've already lost the game." Bradley punched him lightly on the arm.

"Pansies get stepped on." Deacon brushed past them, hitting his shoulder on Bro's arm hard on purpose.

The rough bullying act had the opposite effect on Bro of what was intended. Deacon may have wanted to crush Bro's spirit. Instead, he got a fighter on his hands. "Enjoy your winning days, *dick*. Once you're out of high school, all you'll be doing is asking "You want fries with that?" and I'll be there with a video camera in hand to record it for all time."

Bradley wasn't the only one who laughed. Deacon's expression darkened.

Then one of his teammates, Spencer, called out, confused, "What the hell is all that ruckus?"

Everyone stopped in midstep to listen.

Bro's heart froze in an instant when he recognized the desperate cries of the girl he loved.

His feet were moving before his brain caught on. He felt as if he were on fire, as if his feet had wings, never touching the ground. Behind him he heard more feet running, the thumping loud in the open space between the school buildings and the field.

As he rounded the corner of the bleachers, he came to a halt, sensing Bradley right next to him.

What he saw chilled him to the bone.

Roger Purcell was fighting on the lawn with Lacey and Audrey, all of them tumbling and shouting and ripping into each other on the ground.

"Oh my God…," Bro managed to gasp.

And then he was running again, his feet finding their way to the girl he adored.

"Stop!" he yelled, grabbing onto the first limb he could reach amid the tussle.

The arm belonged to Audrey, who growled and fought back, probably indifferent to whoever was holding her. "Fucking let me go! He's hurting her!"

Bro all but tossed her aside, knowing Bradley would catch her. *"Lace!"* he shouted, so desperate to get her to safety his vision blurred. An elbow landed on his chest, and from the size and strength, he surmised it belonged to Roger, though he doubted the man realized who he had hit.

Other people joined in, trying to pull the two fighters apart as best they could.

Finally a slender arm came into reach, and Bro yanked Lacey up. "Stop!"

Lacey's eyes were glazed over and disoriented as she stared at Bro, clearly not recognizing him. Her nose had bloody blotches, as did her busted lower lip. She had scratches all over, and her dress and stockings were torn.

At long last, she blinked hard, frowning. "Bro…?"

"Yeah, babe. It's me. Snap out of it." Bro barely heard his own voice but was aware of the high-pitched quality.

The light of comprehension lit up Lacey's eyes, and she straightened up, looking over her shoulder at Roger, who was restrained by Bro's teammates, about to get up on his feet.

"He... he attacked Audrey...."

"*What?!*" Bradley's booming voice made everyone still, worried.

"She was trying to protect me," Lacey explained. She sniffled, but her eyes remained dry. "He was going to drag me back home and give me a lashing."

Bro pulled her into his arms. Lacey shivered; not the way she did when she was crying but in a strange stilted manner, so Bro assumed she was in shock or something. "He's not going to get the chance. Ricky, call Jordan and tell him to get his ass over here, pronto." Bro tossed his cell phone to one of the guys surrounding them. He almost never left it in his locker, not even during practice. One never knew when it might be needed in an emergency.

Like now when his girlfriend had been attacked by her drunk father.

Though not one of the team, Ricky Carlisle, Bradley's twin, often came by to watch his brother play. Today was no exception. He looked a lot like Bradley with his broad shoulders, ripped physique, and narrow hips, not to mention his brown eyes and dark-brown hair. In fact, he had an almost Latino appearance with his tanned skin. Bro wasn't as close to him as he was to Bradley, nor had Bro ever been attracted to him. Ricky wasn't Bro's type.

"Got it." Ricky flipped the cell lid open, found Jordan's contact info, and dialed. He made swift progress in explaining to Jordan on the other end what was happening. From the sound of it, Jordan had hung up almost immediately, which told Bro he was on his way here.

"He'll be here in five. He was close by," Ricky told Bro, handing him his cell phone back.

Bro tucked it in his jeans pocket. "Thanks."

"You had better calm down, Mr. Purcell. You don't want to get into any more trouble." Mr. Young, their sports teacher and football coach, was trying to pacify Roger. Even with his low, soothing voice, the middle-aged African-American man was having a hard time reaching his target, as Roger continued to spew curses.

"He's my son, you son of a bitch," Roger growled. "Get the fuck away from him. He's coming home with me, where he belongs."

"*She* isn't going anywhere with you," Bro spat out, barely holding on to his rage. He tried to rein his emotions back in control, but it was difficult. "Mr. Young, there's a temporary order of protection on Purcell. Jordan will explain everything."

Ennis Young took one look at Lacey's battered face, and his own expression hardened as he nodded. "Understood." Turning back to Roger, he said slowly, "You need to calm down, Mr. Purcell. You're only making this worse for yourself. The police are on their way—"

"Good!" Roger shouted, his cheeks red, his eyes wild and wide. "They'll give me my son back. These faggots are keeping him from me."

Lacey broke out of Bro's hold, though he attempted to keep her close. "Dad, stop. I'm not going anywhere with you. These are good people. They are my friends."

"No! They turned my boy into a pansy-ass little girl!"

Lacey was shaking now, but Bro saw it was anger. "I was like this long before I came here. Mom knew and understood—and she accepted me for who I am."

By then Roger was almost bellowing. The guys had a hard time holding him in place. "It's not enough you got her killed. You had to go and make yourself look like her and sound like her, even taking her name. You robbed me of my wife. You're no son of mine." At that, Lacey was by no means the only one staring in utter disbelief. Then Roger crumpled, started crying, and fell down on his knees, his whole body shaking. "If Lexie hadn't left the house to fetch you from your stupid violin lesson, she wouldn't have crashed and died. It's all your fault. You killed her." Then he was sobbing and babbling incoherently.

Bro couldn't believe any father would say that about his child. To blame his only child for something so heinous when it was only a tragic accident. It was too horrible to think about. Especially since Bro knew better. Lacey had told him this story a long time ago.

Glancing at Lacey, Bro saw her look at Roger with such sadness and despair it took his breath away. Yet, Lacey apparently wasn't going to say anything.

So Bro would. "That's not true. That's not how she—"

Lacey's hand clamped over his mouth so fast and rough Bro's lips tingled. "No."

But without relenting, Bro yanked her hand away from his mouth. "Tell him the truth, for fuck's sake."

"Does it look like he could listen, let alone understand, right now?" Lacey pointed at the man who had slumped on the ground, half-crying, half-muttering, completely out of it. "Now is not the time." Lacey's chin jutted out defiantly, daring a comeback.

Bro frowned, wondering what made her suddenly behave this way. He had expected her to fall to pieces, but she had no moisture in her eyes, and her stance was that of a warrior, not a victim. This was the strongest he had ever seen her, and he didn't know what to do. So he said nothing.

"Bro." Jordan's level voice cut through all the other interference within his head. Jordan came to stand at his side, his gaze sweeping over Roger coldly, then turning to Lacey with concern, and at long last landing on Bro with a question.

"We're okay. Lace might need to go to the emergency room—"

"I'm fine. A few scrapes. Nothing I can't handle. I want to go home."

Anxious and baffled, Bro wanted to grab her and shake her until she explained why she was acting like this, so cool, distant, and indifferent. But Jordan beat him to it.

"Kevin will take your father to the station and formally charge him with assault, Lace. I'll take you and Bro home in Bro's car." He turned to Bro. "Got the keys?"

"They're in my locker," Bro said shortly, adding, "I need to change."

Jordan nodded, his expression serious. "Okay. Make it quick."

The thought to do otherwise hadn't even crossed Bro's mind. It was all Bro could do to leave Lacey's side even for a minute but he managed to put one foot in front of the other. He still lingered though and watched silently as Jordan's partner, Kevin Thompson, attached handcuffs to Roger's wrists, brought him up on his feet with his considerable strength, and escorted him off the field toward the SUV by the curb. Blue lights flashed across the front grill, turning the private vehicle into a uniformed one.

Then Bro rushed to the locker room, changed back into his T-shirt and jeans, grabbed his backpack, and charged back to the field. It had seemed to take forever, when all he wanted was to be with his girl, but the tableau had hardly changed when he returned, as if in his absence time had frozen in place, just waiting for his reappearance.

He handed the keys to Jordan wordlessly, and then watched as Jordan guided Lacey toward the school parking lot where Bro's weathered, maroon-colored Dodge Durango—he had gotten it used for three grand a year ago—waited for them. Jordan kept a constant hand on Lacey's shoulder, but she remained stiff and silent as they walked; not once did either of them look back at Bro.

Audrey caught up with them, hugged Lacey wholeheartedly, and exchanged a few words Bro couldn't hear before they parted ways. After that, Audrey returned to Bradley's side, letting her boyfriend hold her. Her beautiful face wasn't mangled either, save for a few scrapes, so it looked like both girls had been incredibly lucky today.

Bewildered, Bro stared at Lacey's retreating back, not having a clue what was happening with the girl he loved. With the boy he loved. With Lacey.

"You'd better go after them." Bradley's deep tone brought him out of his glum reverie, and the nudge on his arm helped out too.

"Yeah." He had more to say but couldn't find the words, so he moved off, following Jordan and Lacey, very confused.

As he passed Deacon, who stood close by staring in the direction where Kevin had taken Roger, Bro couldn't help himself. "Take a long, hard look at that asshole, Rake. An adult bully. Must be an idol for you. That's your future right there."

If Deacon replied, Bro didn't wait to hear it. Slouching, he felt worn to the bone, and the stress in his stomach tightened his intestines into knots, one after another. He should have been happy to witness Roger's outburst. The order of protection would definitely be continued after this incident. He could even end up doing hard time. Bro should have been elated.

But he felt nothing but a hollow of perplexity. Lacey had seemed so rigid, so detached somehow, almost alien. No tears, no visible reactions. Maybe it was shock, he concluded. After all Lacey had been through recently and before, surely she was allowed to feel and behave any way she wanted. Bradley had been right all along. Bro needed to give her time and space to work through her issues.

Swallowing hard, he realized he had no idea how to do that. Not when her ache was his ache too.

LACEY'S smell had changed.

It was the first thing Bro noticed once they got to the loft. Jordan took her statement, and Sebastian made them all a late lunch, or early dinner. Bro honestly didn't care.

Her typical half-feminine, half-masculine perfume, *oh so sweet*, now held the bitter, coppery tang of blood. It clung to her skin ever after she had cleaned up in the bathroom—alone. She hadn't allowed Bro, or anyone, entry.

Deciding to give her privacy, Bro retreated into his bedroom, closed the door, and let Jordan interview Lacey one-on-one. Lying on his back on the bed, his hands behind his head, Bro stared at the ceiling, unmoving. His head was empty apart from the flickers of emotions, like candles in a dark room, igniting and flaming out. But they flew by like fireflies, and he had no will to catch even one of them for closer inspection.

Only Lacey could answer these questions inside his head and heart.

He closed his eyes and only then realized how hurt he felt all over. Physically weary, bruised and battered. His eyelids were heavy like concrete, and his eyes itched, like they were dirty or burning with unshed tears. Yet, he didn't feel like crying, or screaming, or punching a bag, or anything. He simply lay there, waiting in silence.

Unaware of the passage of time, Bro startled a bit when he heard the door creak open and then close. Shuffling of feet, rustling of clothes, and the dipping of the mattress signaled the arrival of another person. Then the sweetest perfume assailed his nostrils: Lacey's natural scent. Not even a hint of blood anymore. Fragrances of bergamot-scented soap and strawberry shampoo hung thickly in the air, indicating she had indeed showered and changed before coming to him.

A warm arm wrapped around his waist, and a head rested on his pectoral muscle. His own arms came around the other body instinctively.

For a while it was quiet.

Then Bro had to say something out loud. "Did Jordan and Bas go back to the station?" Lacey replied with only a nod he felt through his T-shirt. "Are you okay?"

She was still and silent for a long time, and Bro thought she might have fallen asleep as her breathing was even and slow. But then she whispered, "I guess." Wanting to say something encouraging and yet soothing remained a mere intention for Bro before Lacey continued. "I can't cry anymore. I don't have any more tears left. I'm tired of blubbering my eyes red or pouring my heart out. I don't want to do it any longer. Dad…. He's not going to get one more drop from me."

Bro stroked her hair, still damp and slick from the shower. "Okay."

"Does that make me a bad person…?"

She sounded so small saying that, it made Bro shiver. "No. Of course not. People can push you too far sometimes. And then your emotions just sort of… dull, you know. Lose their edge. And it doesn't feel the same anymore; it doesn't make you react the same. It's okay. It's just human." He fell silent, wanting Lacey to take the lead and guide him wherever she needed to go.

She sighed, and her hold of him tightened for a moment. "I know you're mad at me—"

"No, I'm not."

"You wanted my dad to know his accusations weren't true."

"Yeah, but I'm not angry with—"

"He wasn't in a state of mind where he could process anything. Certainly nothing as important as the fact that Mom had gone to the mall to buy a present for Dad for their upcoming anniversary, not to come pick me up from my violin lessons."

"He's gotta find out at some point, Lace. Or he's gonna go to his grave believing it was your fault when it wasn't. But... I am *not* angry with you. Not now, not ever." Licking his dry lips, he prayed for guidance and patience, and a bunch of other things just for the hell of it. "What I am is confused. Or I was. I get it. Why you didn't tell him. Why you didn't cry. Why you feel so...."

He let his words trail off, not wanting to finish that statement of how alien she had felt then. Maybe Bro had gotten too used to Lacey's girlish side and expected her to always need his masculine protection and strength. Now he was lost when she didn't appear to need him for those things anymore.

Lacey shifted upward until she was able to nuzzle Bro's neck. The physical response was immediate as Bro's cock stiffened in his jeans and heat rose all over his skin, prickling.

Against his skin, she whispered, "I feel like I grew up today, Bro. Like I have been a child all this time without realizing it, and today I came face-to-face with the real world. The adult world. It hurt, all that stuff he said, what he accused me of." Suddenly she snorted, the hot puff of breath tickling Bro's skin and giving him goose bumps. "Mom would've kicked his ass for saying that."

Bro smiled a bit. "I wish I had met your mom."

"She would've loved you." Lacey kissed his pulse point. "Not like I love you, but still. My mom's death broke my dad, and he just can't get over it. I miss her too, every day. But I can't live in the past, not like he's trying to." Then she shuddered violently. "But I didn't realize my appearance reminded him of her all the time."

Bro felt a chill in his spine. "So, what? Now you're gonna change to appease him?" He tried so hard to keep the venom from his voice but knew he had been unsuccessful when Lacey let out a long-suffering breath. "I'm sorry, Lace. I'm so fucking sorry."

"I know, honey. I know." Lacey kissed his neck again, and Bro felt the hot moisture of her lips like a sweet benediction, granting him deliverance. "Before this whole mess, I was thinking about transitioning." Bro's heart nearly stopped then as he envisioned the boy he knew becoming physically a girl. The process was supposed to be about the goal of matching an inner sense of gender with an outer one.

That was all well and good—but where did that leave those who were in a relationship with a transitioned person? Lost? Confused? Angry? Afraid? Happy? Still in love…?

Bro got up so fast Lacey dropped down on the mattress. God, he'd really hoped he could have displayed better self-control than this, but he failed. His head was spinning, and his vision grew hazy. He felt like he was having a panic attack. Pressing his tight chest, he aimed to regain his composure. But he failed at that too.

"Lace…," he mumbled, his knees so rubbery he fell down on his butt on the floor.

Right away Lacey was there, angling her way onto his lap, cupping his face until they were looking into each other's eyes. "I said I was thinking about the process *and*… I like my dresses and stockings and bra and makeup. *But*… I like being a boy. You know, just for you. Like I'm… candy wrapped in shiny paper. Colorful and sweet, to be unwrapped by you for the delicious treat inside."

Bro stared, his jaw hanging open. "Candy…?"

At that, Lacey actually giggled, covering her mouth with her hand in such a familiar gesture Bro felt most of the tension leave his body. "Yes. For you. *And* for me too, really. I don't want actual breasts, or a… a pussy. I like my boy bits. I like that *you* like my boy bits."

"Yeah, I love your boy bits." Bro grinned but quickly sobered up. "I'm sorry I freaked out. I just…. Everything's moving so fast, you know?"

"And we're just trying to hang on that bucking bull for our dear lives? Yes, I know exactly what you mean." Lacey pressed her forehead against his, and Bro surrounded her with his arms, embracing her close. "I guess I was thinking about transitioning into a woman because I miss Mom. As much as I like my girly things, a part of me maybe chose them because of her. I always idolized her. I wanted to be pretty like her."

"You *are* beautiful," Bro said determinedly, but feeling anything but confident. "You want to stop being a girl?"

Lacey gave him a long look he couldn't decipher. "I'm not a girl."

Bro gave an exasperated sigh. "Yeah, I know that. But… you know what I mean."

Shrugging, Lacey looked sad. "I like being a girl, or looking like one, anyway. It stopped being about Mom a long time ago, even if the inspiration did come from her. I like the way I am now. I didn't understand Dad saw her in me every time. I'm sorry he feels that way, but... but I can't ever be what he wants me to be. Nothing but a boy."

"You're more than that. And that's fine. It's perfectly fine."

Lacey smiled, and Bro felt warm, as if the sun shone on his face. "Thanks, honey."

"You're my girl," Bro said, this time with absolute faith. "*And you're my boy.*"

Lacey snickered, brushing her lips gently over his. "I sure am."

The kiss was soft and tentative at first, mere flicks of tongue and nipping of lips, but soon it grew hotter, wetter, needier, and more open. Lacey delved inside Bro's mouth, and he groaned, seeking more by sucking on her tongue and lips almost desperately. Craving her was like requiring the heart to beat; living was impossible without it.

Lacey's hands dipped low and slipped beneath Bro's T-shirt in search of skin. Bro was happy to oblige.

"Make love to me, Bro."

Lacey's whisper caused all the blood in Bro's body to rush south of his belt. "Yeah."

Then she spoke so low Bro almost missed it—and a part of him wished he had indeed missed it. "Tonight, I want you inside me."

Chapter 9

"ARE you... all right...?" Lacey searched Bro's shocked face for clues that he didn't want to have anal sex with her right then, or perhaps ever. After all, it wasn't like they had never spoken of it. It had been understood for a long time they were going to do the big *it* at some point.

Then she learned that instead of doubts about the act itself, he questioned her motives. "Why? Why now?" Bro's voice was low, strained, nearly rough. Lacey knew instantly the reasons behind the query and the tone.

"It wouldn't be like a Band-Aid, I swear. It's just...." She swallowed hard, clasping the front of his shirt in her hands. "He said such horrible things. I want to erase this feeling like... dirt, you know. In his mind this is wrong. He thinks that two guys shouldn't love each other, that it couldn't be beautiful and loving. I don't believe that."

Bro sighed, dropping his gaze to her hands, and covered them with his own. "Making love because of your dad? Not exactly how I pictured it." The bitterness came through in waves.

"No, not because of him." She shook her head furiously, and Bro looked up at her, frowning. "You and me?" Lacey cupped his face, smoothing out the wrinkles on his forehead with her thumbs. "We're A-okay. He's not getting between us. In fact, he's gone. I'm not thinking about him."

"But you just said—"

"You didn't let me finish. Since we met in the music room, being with you has been all I think about. Well... a lot of what I think about." Lacey let out a breathless snicker, and a ghost of a smile flickered across Bro's lips too. "Since Mom died, it's like I'm stuck in a storm, and it never ends. The only thing that ever made everything calm and not spin was my music. And then later... you."

Bro nodded, clearly shaken. "You too. I mean...." Seeking the right words turned into a silence, and Lacey could relate.

"I know, honey. Yes, I'm feeling lonely. Yes, I'm sort of alone now. Yes, Dad's still in my head, in some distant, dark places. But no, he's not why I want you to make love to me."

Bro swallowed visibly, his Adam's apple bobbing frantically. "No...?"

"I've been inside the storm for so long I almost can't imagine my life without it. With you, it doesn't feel so bad, or so daunting and depressing. With you, the storm's kind of... hot."

Lacey was running out of words, and she needed her guy to understand. She watched Bro frown again and bite his lip, but she interpreted the look as puzzlement instead of as a rejection.

"Hot?" he repeated.

Lacey struggled to find words to the meaning within her heart. "Like... like fire... and water. Your hot love and passion for me. And your cooling presence. Two in one."

Bro's head cocked to the side, and Lacey could practically see the gears turning in his head. "So...." He spoke slowly, as if figuring it out as he went along. "Your life's in turmoil, and I make things calm for you?" Lacey nodded, letting out a breath as he was starting to get it. "But at the same time, I also keep things a bit wild, kind of like a storm, and you're used to it, and it's hot because it's me?" Bro sounded less certain now, but Lacey felt only relief as she nodded again, at last able to smile as tension left her. "Lace... that's a bit...." Suddenly he seemed to change his mind; he shook his head as if to dislodge unwanted thoughts and exhaled. "Okay."

"Okay?" Lacey hoped he meant what she wished he was saying.

Bro smiled. "Yeah. Okay. I get it. There's been crazy shit going down lately. You want a break. But you also want to... to just get fucked." The wildfire-like blush that spread across his cheeks in a heartbeat made Lacey want to kiss him so badly she trembled at the impulse.

"Yes." She smiled back, reassured. "Only gently. At first, anyway. Then we can go, you know, hard and fast."

Bro brushed his fingers across her cheek and jawline. "No. No hard and fast tonight. *I* want to go slow. I want the pleasure to build, and build, and build until you beg me to come." His eyes narrowed. "I'm not gonna back down on this. It's my way or no way."

Lacey didn't know if she was pleased at the way Bro wanted to handle things or upset he was calling all the shots. But deep down, she knew his motives were pure and selfless as he didn't want to hurt her, so she let go of her indignation. And the thought of him manhandling her into rapture was a definite bonus.

She smirked. "Okay."

Bro studied her face the same way he had a while back, searching for signs of doubt, fear, and other obstacles to overcome. Apparently he didn't find any. "Okay then. Up on the bed."

Lacey giggled. "You're such a romantic."

Nonetheless, she wiggled herself out of his lap and dropped down on the bed. Bro stood up—and froze, staring at her, lost and confused. But Lacey understood. Her attire from before had been torn, so she had to borrow clothes after her shower. Now she had on a simple T-shirt and sweats, both baggy and gray, totally unlike her.

"My dress got ripped, and it's filthy. You didn't have anything of mine here. Unless you're hiding a skirt of your own in the back of the closet. Are you?" Lacey quirked an eyebrow in jest and as a dare.

"What if I told you I am?"

Lacey's eyes grew wide in shock until Bro's smirk told her all she needed to know. "If you did, I'd tell you to put up or shut up." She waggled her eyebrows, daring him.

Kneeling on the bed between her spread legs, he grinned wickedly. "I don't have any dresses here, it's true, but I may have at least one pair of your stockings buried in the back of the closet. I might put them on for you—for a price."

A thrill shot through Lacey at the image of Bro in stockings and garters just for her, the silk glowing in the dim light of a bedroom, in expectation of a sensuous rendezvous for two.

"Oh, God," she gasped at the visual fantasy.

Bro laughed low, seductively. "If I put out for you, I'm sure you'll put out for me."

"Oh, it's like that, is it?" Lacey teased.

Grinning, Bro nodded. "Yeah, it's just like that, baby. And you can't say no."

"No?" Lacey's eyebrows rose.

"Nope." Bro's gaze scoured Lacey's clad figure even though Lacey couldn't imagine him being able to see even an inch of exposed skin. Then she remembered he had seen her naked numerous times, and heat flashed through her body. The crotch of her sweats tented.

"Why are you the only one allowed to say... that word?" she insisted.

"'Cause very soon I'll be the master of yes."

As the echo of his words and meaning died down, Bro dipped his head to brush his lips over the peachy skin beneath Lacey's ear. He tugged the fabric of the shirt out of the way as he glided his mouth down the curve of her neck and finally sucked up a mark on her shoulder. His barely-there touch followed the elegant lines of her muscles and tendons and traced the edges of the delicate protruding bones.

Lacey sucked in a breath, desperate for anything to cool her flaming insides. "Yes, my master," she whispered, only partially joking.

Licking his way to her mouth, Bro proceeded to kiss Lacey breathless.

Until she grimaced in pain and let out a cry.

Immediately Bro backed off, frightened. "What?"

Embarrassed, Lacey blushed. "It's my lip. It hurts." In the scuffle with her father and Audrey, her lower lip had taken the brunt of a blow, and blood had gushed into her mouth. At least she hadn't lost any teeth. Though the split had closed quickly, the coppery taste of blood hadn't disappeared for a long time. The side of her face throbbed unpleasantly every once in a while, and her ears had been ringing after it had happened too.

"Why the hell didn't you say anything?" Bro growled with displeasure and moved off her.

Clutching at her boyfriend's T-shirt, Lacey yanked him back, though not hard enough to keep him as close as he had been. "I didn't want to stop—"

"You must think me really callous if you believe I'd want to fuck you—and hurt you with every kiss." The anguish Lacey felt was mirrored on Bro's face, and she felt horrible for giving him cause to doubt her so.

"I'm sorry." She felt like shrinking but couldn't in reality fold herself into a neat knot no one could ever force open again.

She heard Bro sigh ruefully. "Don't apologize, Lace. Come on. Let me see those pretty peepers of yours." The silly lure worked, and Lacey looked up to see Bro's expression soften as he smiled. "There you are." He took a deep breath, as if to steady himself. "Lacey, I get why you want this. And God knows how much I'd love to just—" He shook his head, caught off guard with his wayward thoughts. "But one man has already hurt you today. I won't add to that."

"But—" Lacey stammered to speak.

"No buts." Bro was adamant, his chin lifting decisively. "Honey, you're hurt. It's okay to admit you're not a hundred percent right now."

Lacey waited until Bro stopped talking. "Can I talk now?" Bro rolled his eyes, but for effect nodded his acquiescence. After everything she had been through today, she wanted warmth, physical closeness, the intimacy of love and all that came with it. But at what cost?

As she looked into Bro's hesitant gaze, Lacey had her answer. "I love you. Another day, then."

When Bro cocked his head to the side and looked at her amusedly, Lacey's stomach suddenly lurched. He was so up to something. "Just because there's stuff we can't do, doesn't mean there's nothing we can do, right?" He waggled his eyebrows, and stuck his tongue out between his teeth.

Lacey burst out laughing, but stopped when her sore muscles and ribs ached. "Ouch." Bro was about to leap to her aid, but she held out a hand. "I'm fine. Just don't make me laugh so much, you fiend." He managed to look sheepish, which prompted another giggling spell from her. "So, what do you want to do?"

"No." Bro shook his head, still kneeling between her splayed legs.

"No?" Lacey frowned, wondering what the problem was now.

"No. This time it's all about you, babe. I want to give you pleasure. Wanna make you come like a rocket or a shooting star."

Lacey swallowed. Such a sweet promise and loving endeavor. "Why does it have to be one-sided?"

Bro winked. "I was hoping you'd say that, baby. We could do sixty-nine." At the porn-quality images flashing across her mind's eyes, Lacey blushed deeply, her skin too hot for clothes. "Of course, we'd need to be naked for that."

With a hard shove, Lacey pushed the chuckling Bro out of bed so she could shed her loose-fitting outfit in a flurry of movement until she was a *he* again, a naked, young, aroused male about to have sex with his boyfriend. Bro on the other hand took his time, smirking and giving Lacey a show by peeling off every garment with deliberate slowness. Lacey was ready to slug Bro by then.

"Impatient much?" Bro needled as he observed his frustration.

"Cruel much?" Lacey goaded right back, and Bro chuckled.

"I'd never hurt you, love." At that remark, Lacey felt like crying. "You okay?"

"I'm fine," Lacey snapped back, blinking to be rid of the moisture gathering in his eyes, and annoyed at letting himself get so riled up. Maybe it was the inevitable consequence of an emotionally stressful day. "So what *are* we going to do?"

"Seeing as how you can't really do anything with your mouth, I'll be in charge of the blowjob tonight." Bro used an irritatingly posh accent as he said that, and Lacey heard himself purr when he had intended to growl. Sometimes having a voice more high-pitched than most men was agony.

"Well?" Lacey flirted, shimmying his bare hips on the bed enticingly. "You gonna put your mouth where your money is, or—"

Bro swallowed Lacey's cock to the hilt before any more words came out, and then all Lacey could do was moan at the blinding pleasure engulfing him. The wet, hot suction made his toes curl and his hands fist the sheets as his back arched off the bed and his hips bucked helplessly.

Damn, his guy had gotten so good at sucking cock that Lacey wanted to drag Bro off to be able to draw breath, and simultaneously push him down farther until all of Lacey's shaft was embedded in that glorious mouth. Bro's lips fastened tight around Lacey's leaking dick, squeezing every drop of precome out of him, and Lacey never wanted the moment to end.

"Oh, yes," he sighed, spreading his legs more and planting his soles against the bed to give Bro the opportunity to wrap his arms around Lacey's thighs and keep him unmoving and close.

Bro cradled Lacey's balls in his hands, fondling and tugging them softly. Lacey felt every yank all the way down to his toes, and his groin was boiling over. Then Bro's mouth moved from Lacey's cock to his balls and sucked them in, first one by one, and then both at once.

"God, Bro…," Lacey moaned, thrashing about on the bed.

After letting Lacey's sac fall out of his mouth, Bro grinned. "Want more?"

"No. Yes. No. I wanna come." Lacey knew he was babbling, but he couldn't stop. He needed to come right now. "Please, Bro. I need—"

"Gotcha." Bro dipped his head and took Lacey's cock deep in his mouth again. He sucked and licked relentlessly. No one in the world could possibly have resisted such sweet delight. Lacey's brain felt like it was turning inside and out, and his body was hovering above an abyss of pleasure.

Then Bro's tongue danced and swirled around the head of Lacey's penis, following the ridge. He licked all over, like Lacey's dick was a popsicle, and then applied pressure on the nerves below the mushroom head, on the frenulum. He flicked the tip of his tongue over the spot, and then laved across the slit.

By then Lacey was frantic to reach release. His whole body overflowed with heat, like a pressure cooker. "Bro, *please*."

As an answer to Lacey's prayers, Bro wrapped his other hand around Lacey's aching cock and pumped fast and hard, in unison with the fierce suction of his mouth. That combination of mouth and hand was all it took.

In a heartbeat, Lacey tipped over the edge headlong into bliss. His cock erupted and spilled loads of come into Bro's eager mouth, while his lover swallowed each and every drop.

Lacey fell back on the bed, limp and sated, not even aware how he'd gotten off the mattress. Breathless, he observed only physical responses, like his chest heaving, sweat covering his skin all over, the tremors within his muscles, the still devouring flames within his groin, the pulse of his heart in his drenched cock.

"Better?"

Lacey cracked open one eye to watch Bro above him, grinning, his palms resting over Lacey's thighs. "Uh-huh." That was really all he was capable of at the moment.

Bro kept looking at him and smiling happily, and Lacey fell more in love.

But without speaking, Bro lay down on the bed beside Lacey and spooned him from behind. His hard, hot cock was wedged between Lacey's butt cheeks. "I'll be gentle," Bro promised as his hips began to sway.

Slowly he rocked his dick against Lacey's most intimate spot, and Lacey felt his hole twitching at the nearness of Bro's sizable member. Then he felt the moisture there and realized either Bro had lubed up his dick for smooth mobility, or precome alone was giving them this. Lacey was still sure Bro wouldn't attempt anything more, not today.

Lacey placed his hand over Bro's thigh and the curve of his ass, encouraging his boyfriend to do more. "I love the feel of you *there*. I can't wait till you claim me as your own for real."

Lacey's soft whisper seemed to push all Bro's buttons, since he picked up his pace and slid up and down the hidden crevice, made warm with precome and slick with lube. "You feel so good," Bro muttered, his voice hoarse with desire. He clutched at Lacey's waist and chest, keeping them plastered together from head to toes. "Can never get enough."

Then Lacey turned his head, and Bro dipped down so they could kiss. Lacey tasted his own come on Bro's tongue, and traces of the sticky substance still lingered there too. They shared his essence together as their tongues danced lazily, entwining as one.

"Oh, fuck, I'm gonna come," Bro panted into the kiss.

A spurt of hot liquid splashed over the small of Lacey's back as Bro's hips rocked and shimmied convulsively. Bro was groaning, and his passion was undeniable. His arms tightened around Lacey's body, and then they cradled each other, their motions slowing when Bro stopped coming. His body lay languid in the pleasant buzz of afterglow. Lacey knew this because it was a state they shared right then.

"God, that was so fucking good," Bro murmured, his hot breath fanning over Lacey's sweaty neck, giving him gooseflesh.

"Yes," Lacey agreed, sighing with joy, and he let himself drift off to sleep in the wake of one of the best lovemaking sessions the two of them had ever had. Behind him, he felt Bro do the same, and it was the perfect end to a less-than-perfect day.

Chapter 10

ON FRIDAY, the four of them—Bro, Lacey, Bradley, and Audrey—went to the movies. They chose an action flick with romantic undertones to keep it light, funny, and sweet. Or that was at least how Bro had put it to himself when they had gone over their choices.

And it had been a good decision. Lacey was tucked under Bro's arm, feeling just right, as if she belonged there. The day after Roger had attacked Lacey and Audrey, they had gone with Jordan and Sebastian to pick up some of Lacey's belongings from her house. Thankfully, Roger had not been there. Jordan had told them Roger would spend most of the day in lockup, and then in court trying to get bail, which he might or might not get. He didn't have a criminal record, so the former was more likely.

But none of that mattered when Bro had his sweetheart pressed against his side, safe and sound, and from the looks of her, happy too. He kept stealing furtive glances at her, and when she noticed, she gave him a kiss. So naturally Bro made sure Lacey noticed him often.

"You like this movie?" Bro whispered in Lacey's ear, and made sure he flicked the soft shell of flesh with his tongue.

Lacey squirmed and giggled, ticklish as she was. "It's okay. Nothing to write home about."

Bro felt her tense up as she obviously hadn't meant to say that, but he held her more firmly, and she relaxed again. "No sad stuff tonight, okay, babe?"

Lacey all but burrowed into him as she snuggled closer. "Nope." She looked up at him. "Kiss me."

Happy to oblige, Bro kissed his girlfriend, softly at first, but then more thoroughly, probing deep. He cupped the back of her neck, keeping her close. He wanted nothing more than to make sure she would be all right, but he wasn't sure how to make that happen.

A wolf whistle put a stop to things escalating from there.

"Get a room, you two." It was Bradley's voice, sounding proud and amused at the same time, as if he saw Bro as something of another kid brother as much as a best friend. He was sitting three seats down from Bro, with the girls nestled in between them. He winked shamelessly and then glided his own hand under Audrey's dress.

Audrey, however, swatted the invading hand away hard. "Nuh-uh, mister. Watch those hands, or they might get bitten."

"Oh, honey, you know just how to turn me on," Bradley murmured seductively, with laughter in his voice.

"Jerk." But Audrey was smiling, and then she rewarded her boyfriend for nothing at all with a good, long kiss. At Audrey's side, Lacey snickered, and Bro chuckled too.

"What do you wanna do after this?" Lacey asked Audrey, who immediately stopped kissing, much to Bradley's obvious chagrin, and smiled happily. Audrey and Lacey were best friends, and though she would be hard-pressed to admit it, Audrey had been shaken by Roger's attack at the football field. Jordan had offered to take her to an emergency room for a checkup before he had driven Lacey home, but Audrey had refused. Both girls had minor scrapes, but after a week, most of them had healed.

Audrey paused for thought. "Wanna get something to eat? There's that new sushi place at the mall."

Bro and Bradley exchanged grimaces. "Raw fish? Why you gotta torture us?" It was Bradley who was whining about it. Sure, he could eat it, but it wasn't his favorite, and neither was it Bro's.

Lacey and Audrey shared whispered giggles. "Boys can be such pussies," Audrey said tauntingly.

Next thing they knew, Bradley had wrestled the squealing and cackling girl onto his lap and was mercilessly tickling her. They all laughed. Then the usher came by with his flashlight and told them to pipe down or get thrown out. Everything settled after that—although Audrey made sure to punch Bradley in the gut with her elbow, but not vehemently if both their grins were any kind of clue. And two seconds after, they were smooching intently, all tongues and groping hands.

Lacey was laughing, burying her head in Bro's neck. Bro kissed her temple, and she looked up, so bright and cheerful it took Bro's breath away. At that moment he knew without a shadow of a doubt he loved her more than anything. She leaned up and kissed him, and then they were subconsciously mirroring their friends' make out session.

After the end credits had rolled and lights turned on—none of the four of them much the wiser about the movie itself—they strolled out of the movie theater, arms around each other's waists, two pairs side by side.

They didn't get far, though.

"Hey."

All four of them stopped dead in their tracks when Deacon walked over. He stopped just shy of touching distance, and his gaze was directed squarely at Lacey, who inched away from him a bit. Bro tightened his protective hold on her.

"Um, hi." Deacon looked uncomfortable, shifting in place, his hands tucked deep into his pockets. "You, um, are you... okay?" He spoke to Lacey, and Bro could feel her surprise.

"Yes. Getting there. One day at a time." Lacey's tone was soft and vulnerable.

Deacon nodded in response, looking like a jack-in-the-box. "That's good. Getting better, I mean." He cleared his throat, and his head trembled a bit, as though his instincts told him to turn away, but his mind ordered him not to. "Your dad's, uh... an asshole." His cheeks pinked at the remark.

"Takes one to know—" Bro started, but fell silent when Lacey elbowed him in the gut.

"He's not really a bad man," Lacey said. She didn't sound defensive so much as sort of sad. "Losing someone's not an easy thing. Guess just because one's a grown-up doesn't mean—"

"Yeah, yeah, I guess that's true," Deacon said, nodding again. Then he closed his eyes briefly and looked really ill, as if he were five seconds from puking. "Listen, I, uh… I just wanted to say I'm, you know, sorry about the way I treated you and—"

"Are you fucking kidding—?" Again Bro tried to cut in, angry, but Lacey's elbow in his ribs prevented him from finishing the sentence once more.

"It's nice that you're sorry—if you mean it," Lacey said, her voice more confident now. "But it would be better if you didn't do those things. Bullying. Then you wouldn't have to go around apologizing later."

Deacon cringed, but stayed put. That was way more than Bro would have expected from him. "I, uh, I don't wanna be like your dad."

At that Bro didn't even try to interject. He honestly didn't know what to say. His first instinct told him the guy was lying. But why would he do it in public like this?

Lacey smiled a bit, encouragingly. "Making a decision is the first step. I'm glad to hear that. I'm sure we all are."

"Right. Right. Yeah." Deacon apparently noticed his bobbleheaded dog imitation because he suddenly stopped, swallowing visibly as his Adam's apple jumped nervously. "Well… I gotta get going." He took a step away but stopped abruptly. "You're a bit crazy, you know that? I mean, he's twice your size, and you just took him on." A ghost of a grin tugged at the corners of his lips. "Nice."

Then it seemed his embarrassment quota had exceeded itself because he hurried off, picking up the pace with every step, until he was nothing but a blur amid a sea of people.

"Well, that was, um…." Audrey started to say, looking flabbergasted.

"Nice of him," Lacey finished for her, smiling a little. She looked up at Bro, who was, as always, taken by her sweet outlook, trusting people even after being disappointed.

"I love you," he said.

Lacey's eyes widened at the public declaration of affection, and then an utterly pleased expression made her positively glow. "I love you too, honey." Then she kissed him, and Bro wanted for nothing more.

"Aww...." Audrey's enchanted voice reached them soon, though. "God, you two are so fucking adorable together."

"Dree," Lacey chided but grinned at the same time.

Audrey hugged her, practically shoving Bro out of the way.

"Hey!" Bro protested loudly, his arms wide.

"Oh, leave them be," Bradley said, chuckling. He wrapped a friendly arm around Bro's shoulders and leaned in close, as if taking his friend into his confidence, before whispering loudly, "I mean, two girlfriends can kiss, so let them."

Both Audrey and Lacey turned to face Bradley, their lips pursed with mock rebuke.

"Your boyfriend's a perv," Lacey said to Audrey.

Audrey shrugged. "So's yours."

Lacey smiled. "Guess we're both lucky, then."

"Ain't that the truth." Audrey laughed, Lacey chimed in, and hand in hand they walked off, leaving two dumbfounded, entranced boys in their wake.

"Wow." Bradley's deep rumbling voice was filled with pride and awe.

"Yeah." Bro felt the same way, plus some enchantment as well.

A slap on his shoulder had Bro stumbling over, almost falling on the floor. "Come on, buddy. Let's catch up to our sweet young things before we lose 'em."

"Asshole," Bro muttered, rubbing his shoulder. But he followed a laughing Bradley to find the girls.

Just when they caught sight of the girls window-shopping for dresses and chattering away, a new voice hollered at them. "Bro! Brad!"

Ricky Carlisle, Bradley's twin, ran toward them. It was amazing how much he resembled Bradley. Those wide shoulders, slim hips, strong arms, and long legs were sure to catch anyone's eyes. His dark-brown hair flopped over his eyes, his tanned skin giving him a glow of life Bro might have found attractive if his appetites didn't run in other directions.

"Hey guys," Ricky said once he had caught up with them. "Whatcha doin'?"

"Just hanging," Bro replied.

"What are you doing here?" Bradley demanded to know with the authority of his one hour and twelve minutes of seniority over his twin. "I thought you had practice tonight." Bro didn't know anything about Ricky's extracurricular activities, he realized. It couldn't have been football, or he would have been able to work out with the high school team, since his brother was the captain.

"Come on, Brad," Ricky said, pouting and whining. "It's Friday night!"

Bradley seemed ready to argue, but Bro put a quick stop to that. "Just what kind of practice do you have on a Friday night?"

Ricky blushed, managing to look all of five years old instead of seventeen. "I, um…." He glanced at Bradley, and Bro realized he was silently asking his twin's permission.

But the only emotion Bradley sported was pride. "Go ahead. You can tell him."

Ricky grinned, relieved. "Cooking class, twice a week. I usually have it on Tuesdays and Thursdays, but the teacher, Ms. Mills, couldn't make it yesterday."

Bro was surprised; Bradley couldn't cook for shit. "Wow. You can cook?"

Ricky laughed, his pitch a bit higher than his brother's. "Yeah. I'm way better than that lunkhead." He pointed at Bradley, who crossed his arms over his chest menacingly but rolled his eyes amusedly. "At least I'm better at something than his majesty, Bradley the Bold, the golden boy of—" Ricky ducked lightning fast when Bradley tried to swipe his head with the palm of his hand.

Bro laughed with the brothers. "So you're gonna play hooky tonight, is that it?" With a wink to Bradley, he said to Ricky, "That's gonna cost you."

Now Ricky appeared nervous, frowning. "What does that mean?"

Bro shrugged nonchalantly. "We could go back to my place—and you could cook for us. I'm tired of microwave dinners, candy, popcorn, and all that shit. What do you say, dude?"

All of a sudden Ricky chuckled. "Is that all? I love to cook. Sure, it's a deal."

Pumping fists with the guy, Bro was glad he had asked, even though it had been an unethical sort of extortion. But Ricky seemed fine with it. So the three of them headed to the girls, who were staring at new shoes on display at a store window, practically drooling over some velvety-looking high heels Bro would love to see Lacey wear—in and out of bed.

Five minutes later they were driving toward the Waters-Sumner-Thompson loft.

As they parked and got out, three men came tumbling out of the apartment building front door. One was a gorgeous, tall blond with a few faint facial scars from a fire, and another was a big, bulky bald man with several fire-themed tattoos. The third man, a grizzly-bear-like barrel of a man, watched the other two laughing away while he shook his head in mock reproach. Him they had seen at the football field earlier, taking Roger away.

"Oh, hey, Bro," the cute blond called out and waved to him. The other two men did only the chin-lift greeting, trying to steady Jack's step, though he wasn't drunk, only eager.

"Hey Jack, Kev, Luke," Bro replied. "Off somewhere?"

"A couple of drinks at the local dive, and then we're off to shake this old booty on the dance floor," Jack shouted back, shimmying his hips like a professional dancer—a go-go dancer.

"Have a good time."

"Oh, we will." Jack winked wickedly, leaving no room for misunderstandings, and the bald muscle-bound god next to him laughed out loud with a deep, guttural, rumbling noise.

The three men were busy climbing into a huge SUV when Bro heard Ricky ask in a quiet voice filled with awe, "Who is *that*?"

Bro followed Ricky's wide-eyed gaze to the bald, bulky man. "That's Luke Kennard, Jack's best friend. He's a fireman for FEMS." Jack Waters was Jordan's younger brother, a down-and-dirty party boy as well as an EMT. The quieter man with Jack and Luke was Kevin Thompson, Jack's boyfriend and Jordan's partner in the Force, a man they had seen before. Bro relayed this information to Ricky, too, but doubted he'd heard a word past "fireman."

"He's... amazing." Bro turned back to Ricky and saw his instantly smitten look, nothing short of rapture in his brown eyes, a fire Bro had seen reflected back in the mirror more than once when he thought about Lacey. Luke was definitely an eye-catcher, a brawny hunk with a bad-boy image, and his very essence exuded masculinity and raw sex appeal.

Wondering if Bradley was okay with his twin crushing on a guy publicly, Bro took a cautious peek at his best friend—only to witness Bradley's half-worried, half-understanding gaze settle on his brother.

"You okay?" Bro whispered to his best friend, leaning closer.

Startled out his thoughts, Bradley blinked and then nodded. "Yeah, fine. I've known about his orientation for a while. Ricky hasn't dated a guy yet, not to my knowledge anyway, but he can handle himself. And that fireman? Hot!" Shrugging, he added, "Let's go inside."

Bro touched Ricky's arm. He had been watching with rapt attention as the SUV drove off and jumped at the contact. Then he looked sheepish, glancing at his big brother warily. Bro guessed he wasn't sure of his brother's reaction either, which told Bro Ricky didn't habitually show such blatant interest in guys, especially not in front of his straight big brother.

Bradley chuckled and yanked Ricky into a playful chokehold, tousling his hair. Ricky laughed, and the tension was broken.

"You know, as long as you don't start fucking a guy in front of me or in public, you gotta know I'm cool with this, you being who you are, ogling hot guys," Bradley chided his brother softly as he let go.

"I was scared. I didn't want you to think less of me for... um, ogling that guy." Ricky sounded embarrassed.

"Like I ever could." Bradley winked, then grinned. "Now who's the lunkhead?"

"You are," Ricky shot back, twisted out of the hold, and ran for the front door of the building. Cussing, Bradley sprinted after him, spewing out loud threats of bodily harm if and when he caught the brat. More laughter followed. Audrey rolled her eyes and dashed after the twins.

Lacey giggled, slipping under Bro's arm, and they walked in too, though at a more leisurely pace.

Jordan and Sebastian greeted them inside the loft, but they soon went off toward their own bedroom, for which Bro was glad. He did love his big brother and his moody cop fiancé, but this was a night to hang out with friends.

It took Ricky thirty seconds to rummage the kitchen for supplies and appliances, and then he started on teriyaki beef and noodles plus stovetop lasagna with such swift efficiency Bro found himself staring spellbound. The kid had moves and skill in the kitchen, absolutely. Still, regardless of his enthusiasm and talent, he didn't mind the girls helping him out.

Bro and Bradley went to sit on the couch overlooking the open kitchen, feeling useless yet somehow glad they didn't have to slice or dice anything, especially their fingers. Whatever finesse they had on the football field, it didn't extend to food preparation.

"How long's Ricky been into this?" Bro asked, curious.

Bradley smiled, his fond gaze aimed at his laughing brother in the kitchen. "Forever. When we get to college, he's going to be a home economics major, or whatever it's called these days."

"Wow. He's gonna get a lot of flak for that." Bro regretted saying it the moment the words left his lips. "Hey, man, I didn't mean—"

"I know." Bradley sighed. "I worry about him too. He's not girly, not like Lacey, and he can hold his own in a fight—"

"So can Lace," Bro reminded, grinning.

"Yeah." Bradley chuckled. "That girl of yours. She's a spitfire."

"Ricky's gonna do fine, too. He's gonna become a world famous chef, and everyone who's ever given him grief is gonna suck up to him to get even a whiff of what he's cooking."

Bradley's warm eyes landed on Bro. "You're such a romantic."

Bro growled. "I prefer idealist. Lacey's taught me to try and see the positive." He took a quick gander at his girlfriend chopping up an onion, chuckling, teary-eyed. "After everything that's gone down lately, I can at least try to count our blessings. Things could have gone a hell of a lot worse."

Bradley watched him intently; Bro could sense the speculative gaze. "Have you and Lacey talked about colleges? You two don't exactly share the same interests...." It was a leading question, Bro thought, or was it even a question? No, it was more of a statement. Bro knew it was true: Bro was going to focus on football and whatever else came his way, but Lacey had her eye on music. And precious few colleges, if any, had programs for both. Especially since Lacey wasn't a beginner with the violin. She was on her way to the big leagues, to study under musical geniuses.

Where did that leave Bro and the two of them?

He shrugged, feigning casualness. "We'll see. There's still time."

"Uh-huh." Bradley's noncommittal noise reminded Bro they weren't that far from graduation day, less than two months. Most of the student body, those who wanted to advance scholastically anyway, had already been accepted to colleges based on their strengths and preferences. Bro had received scholarship offers from a few schools in the area, and he did not have much time left before he had to make a choice.

At that moment Bro had a horrible epiphany, a shocking realization that his path might diverge from Lacey's significantly. She might go to a college in another town, or another state, or halfway across the country, or even the world.

Suddenly, his breath caught in his throat, and fear kept it clogged up tight.

To divert away from those dreadful, painful images of a life without Lacey in it, Bro broached the subject from a different angle. "What about you, Brad? Or Audrey and Ricky?"

Bradley frowned, rubbing his cleft chin. "I knew before I got together with Audrey that, regardless of her choice, I'm going to the same college as Ricky. Gotta keep my eye on him. You and I have those football scholarship offers from some of the same schools, but there aren't many that focus on home ec as well."

"What'd you come up with?"

As he asked, Bro became aware that they had spoken about furthering their education only in broad terms, never this specifically. As their high school days drew to a close, he realized they were almost adults, with their own lives and goals, maybe far away from each other. His best friend, his girlfriend, his friends, his family.

Apprehension gave way to nearly full-blown panic. Not only about the loss of people he held dear, but stepping onto a path of responsible adulthood—when he still had no idea what he wanted to be when he grew up.

"Howard looks good," Bradley said, startling Bro back to reality. "It has a human ecology program that's close to home ec. Otherwise it would have to be out of state, maybe even somewhere I don't have a scholarship offer, which would make it tough on the folks with two of us in school at once. And for Ricky, this town is home, same as for me. I don't want him to have to choose between his family and his dreams just yet. He agreed to let me find out what place would fit."

Bro glanced over his shoulder at Ricky, Audrey, and Lacey preparing their meals in the kitchen, laughing and jesting, and was it just his imagination or was there a leek flying around the kitchen like a guided missile? "What about *your* girl?"

"Ah-hah." Bradley grinned. "That's where it gets interesting. Audrey wants to go to law school."

"Really?" Bro's eyes widened in surprise. Audrey had a mouth on her and opinions up the wazoo, so maybe it wasn't that much of a surprise, come to think of it. "Like, political law?"

Bradley chuckled, casting an affectionate glance at his punk of a girlfriend. "Maybe both. I don't know the specifics. At first I thought she might have been joking, but…." He shrugged.

"Joke or not, why is that so freaking interesting?" Bro asked, baffled.

"'Cause she's been accepted in the pre-law program at Howard."

Understanding dawned on Bro immediately. "Oh, right. Then all three of you could go to the same college." Bro was awash with emotions, at the top envy and jealousy, and he hated feeling those things because it was looking less and less likely that he could do the same with Lacey. "That's great, man. If it all works out—I mean *when*—it's all good."

"You've had an offer from Howard, too, right?" Bradley asked, and Bro saw the sympathy in his eyes. Damn him for knowing his best friend so well.

"Yeah. Among others." Bro looked down at his hands as he wrung them in his lap. God, why couldn't there be a college in the area with both a good football program and a highly rated music department? Why did all this grown-up bullshit have to be such a rending experience, ripping everything familiar from him? His father had been distant, first, and then ill, and his mother…. They could write psychological treatises on her dysfunctions as a mom to two gay sons, one of them deaf to boot.

"Wait a second." Bradley seemed lost in thought, his brow furrowed. "I seem to recall there's a music program at Howard, too."

Bro's head popped up so fast he worried he might have whiplash. Hope stirred in him. Maybe Lacey wasn't lost to him after all.

He didn't get the chance to comment, however, for Ricky announced dinner was served in his worst imitation of a British butler.

Hungry, both Bradley and Bro jumped up on their feet and rushed to the dinner table the girls had set and filled to the limit. The delicious smells of beef, noodles, garlic, onions, cheese, basil, and cilantro whiffed their way. Bro's stomach grumbled as he sat down next to Lacey, giving her a kiss on the cheek for a lot of reasons.

"Mmm, smells nice," Jordan said as he walked past the table with his cell phone in his ear. He looked wistful, damn near salivating, and Bro wasn't the only one chuckling. Muttering a few select curses about impudent kids, Jordan put on a jacket and left the loft. Must have been work related, or so Bro assumed.

For a while they ate, drank, and chatted idly, enjoying each other's company.

While Ricky, Bradley, and Audrey were busy arguing about the merits and problems of professional cooking shows and reality cook-offs, Bro leaned over Lacey and whispered in her ear, "Thanks for dinner, baby."

Lacey beamed. "I didn't really cook anything, just chopped up vegetables and boiled water. It's Ricky you should thank."

"I will," Bro promised, glancing at Ricky, who was obviously enjoying the debate with Audrey. Then he lowered his voice even more. "Listen, I've been thinking. I found out that there's a music program at Howard University. They've offered me a football scholarship too. Brad, Dree, and Ricky are all going, if Brad and Dree get accepted. We could all be together. What do you think?"

Was it Bro's imagination, or did Lacey look shocked, even sad? "Bro, I...," she started, but the sound of the front door sliding open fast and hard caught all their attention.

In the foyer, heading slowly toward the table, was a woman in her midforties. Her glossy black hair was mussed up from the night wind, and her brown overcoat made her look three sizes bigger than she actually was. Though he didn't know her, Bro thought there was something familiar about her features, bewildered by the instinctive notion.

Suddenly, Lacey's chair scraped the floor with a screech a she got up fast, shock evident in her eyes. "Aunt Valerie?"

The woman blinked, surprised. Her smile faded. Bro saw that she had been looking at Bradley somewhat hopefully. When she spoke, Bro knew why. "Lance...?"

Bro got up in hurry, his tone less than friendly. "*Her* name is Lacey."

The strange woman looked hopelessly lost, and she didn't seem to know what to say. Lacey rounded the table and stopped in front of her. "Um... Aunt Valerie, these are my friends and family. Everyone, this is Valerie Adair, my mother's sister."

"Wait, back up." Bro's head was spinning. "I thought you had no other relatives besides Roger."

Lacey's lovely face crumpled as she clearly fought off tears. "Dad said my mother's family wanted nothing to do with us, and that's why we moved from Seattle to—"

"Oh, Lance, nothing could be further from the truth." Valerie placed her hands gently over Lacey's arms, squeezing a bit. "Roger forbade us...." She paused in midsentence, as if trying to figure out how to say what she knew. "After Lexie died...." She sniffled, wiping tears from her eyes. "After that Roger just took you. At first we gave him time to sort things out, but then.... We've been looking for you ever since." She turned to Jordan, who stood behind her. "Detective Waters found me due to the missing person's I had filed on you, Lance—oh, sorry, Lacey, is it?"

Lacey nodded, worrying her lower lip. "Yes, Lacey." She sounded timid, and Bro had to fight the urge to growl and shout that she had every right to be a Lacey if she didn't want to be a Lance. "Jordan found you?"

"Yes," Jordan replied quickly. "Once Roger was in the system, we started getting info from Seattle as we looked into the possibility he might have a criminal record there. Once alerted, Valerie found her way to the station here. I was on my way to pick her up when you all started to eat your dinner."

"I'm so glad I found you," Valerie said, embracing Lacey wholeheartedly.

Lacey was sobbing softly and hugging back. "Me too." Soon, though, she parted from her aunt. "How long can you stay? Where are you going to stay? Are you still working at the IRS?" Lacey had turned into a fount of questions, and she blushed when she realized this.

Valerie frowned, confused. "I don't, um... I mean, you have only been here in DC for a year or so. Seattle is where you come from. I've come to take you back home."

Bro's world, the one he had painstakingly built around himself, one family member at a time, shattered.

Chapter 11

LACEY stood before the bathroom mirror, her eyes directed at the reflective surface but not seeing it. Mechanically, she washed her hands, but her thoughts were a million miles away. Well, roughly three thousand miles, anyway, across the whole continental US.

Seattle. Once she had called it home. But then she had lost her mother, and what had been safe and familiar had become excruciatingly painful and dangerous. When Roger had packed up for DC, she had resisted at first, but it had turned out for the best in the end. Well, kind of.

Here in DC she had a new family who had taken her in without asking for anything in return and given her a new lease on life. And she had someone here who accepted, understood, and loved her beyond all comprehension.

Tears slipped down her cheeks as she thought of Bro.

He had sat so still on the sofa while Lacey and Valerie had talked. He had listened, but his blue eyes had a glaze over them. His handsome face had been blank, and it hurt Lacey to know she had brought that on.

Because she hadn't said no to Valerie right then and there.

Instead, Lacey had sat with her aunt, chatting about Seattle, her maternal family, the court case against Roger, and Valerie petitioning for temporary custody of Lacey. At that moment she had been glad she wasn't going to end up in foster care. She would soon be eighteen, which was the age of majority in DC, but for a few more months now, she still needed a legal guardian. If Valerie got custody, Lacey would be leaving for Seattle right after graduation.

And she remembered Seattle had been her home, the city of her birth and childhood.

Lacey felt conflicted, so she hid in the bathroom, waiting for everyone to retire for the night before creeping out to her bed—which was in Bro's room. Would he be asleep by now? Lacey sighed, knowing he wouldn't be. And she was tired of talking about it all tonight. Yes, she did want to give Bro some reassurance their relationship would still be….

Only, it wouldn't be, would it?

She didn't know what to do, so she stayed in the bathroom, having already showered and gotten ready for bed. Every time she felt the flow of tears might have dried up, a new well of them began to fall. She was going home—yet she was already home.

God, what am I going to do?

Rationally, she was well aware she couldn't stay in this room forever.

After turning off the faucet and the lights, Lacey sneaked out of the bathroom and into the bedroom across the hall. The room was dim, the only illumination streaming in through the narrow slivers between the shutters. There was a shape in bed, motionless, and Lacey felt both relieved and disappointed.

In the dark, she found her way to the cot bed between the bigger bed and the closet, far away from the only window. Typically, the two of them would sleep side by side in Bro's bed, but tonight she felt as though there was an insurmountable chasm between the beds, when in reality it couldn't have been more than five inches. Tonight they had to sleep in separate beds because of the distance.

Lacey slipped under the covers, wearing nothing but her tight undies. Normally she had a warm, firm body next to her own, but not tonight. She pulled the covers over her and lay in silence, watching the gray ceiling, where shadows danced whenever a car's headlights brought the shutters alive. She clutched at the thick blanket, a chill expanding throughout her skin, but it had nothing to do with the room temperature. She was missing a piece of her life, but she didn't know how to get it back.

"Lace?"

Bro's voice was barely a whisper in the night, yet it echoed loudly from the walls.

Lacey was out of her bed in a jiffy, and she snuck under Bro's blankets.

This was familiar, she thought when their bodies melded, plastered together tight from head to toes. And then they were kissing. Their hands groped and fondled while their kiss turned downright feral, nibbling teeth, sucking lips, and dueling tongues. Lacey whimpered, her mind emptying and her body filling with heat, pressure, and need. The passion present in their grinding bodies was a whole new level of lust for Lacey, the want so strong it surpassed all reason. It was as if they both longed to give increasing amounts of pleasure to the other, like it was their last chance ever to show how much they loved each another.

In the pitch darkness, they had no sight. They had to rely on other senses and on memory to find each other and the places where a mere brush ignited a new flame of desire.

But it didn't matter because Lacey's body knew what it craved.

"Bro, please. I beg of you. Make love to me tonight. Take my virginity."

In mental preparation, she went over all she had learned about that kind of sex, focusing especially on what not to do. She knew now not to use soap as lube, not to scissor fingers inside the anus, and not to be shocked by involuntary bodily functions, like passing gas, after the deed was done. What she had seen in porn and read about in erotica was one thing; what she had learned with Bro was another; and talking to brazen but knowledgeable Audrey had provided the rest.

Busy sucking on Lacey's pulse point and then on her earlobe, Bro took a moment to grasp the demand and another to respond. His head came up, his eyes almost black now with arousal, the blue iris a mere thin ring around the pupil.

"Lace...." Though out of breath, Bro sounded concerned.

She didn't want any of his apprehension. "Please, Bro. I'll be gone soon, and I want it to be you. My first. I *need* it to be you." In the quiet of the night, her voice sounded strange even to her, pleading with a whiny quality she didn't recognize in herself. Was she doing this for him, or for her, or for all the wrong reasons? But then again, was it so damn wrong for her to wish for the guy she loved to be her first, to claim a piece of Lacey no one else could ever possess?

Bro stilled, shaking his head in confusion. Then he took a deep, shuddering breath, and Lacey could sense the mood was broken. "I love you, Lace. More than anything. But this is wrong. I don't want... *that*... to be our good-bye." He was talking about anal, not sex in general, Lacey knew, and she felt ashamed for pressing. "It should be our beginning, not the end."

Furiously, she tried to extricate herself from under his strong, lean body, but he held her down. Then Lacey was really crying, out-of-control profound shivers ran through her entire being, pushing a flood of tears. She was shaking, but Bro embraced her tightly, not once letting go. He petted her hair, her skin, her heart.

Right then she realized leaving *here* would destroy her.

"Oh, Bro, please. I don't want to go." Her misery came through in palpable waves.

Kissing the wetness of sorrow from her eyelids, cheeks, and lips, Bro nodded. "Then you won't. We'll talk to your aunt tomorrow, and to Jordan and Sebastian. You don't have to go, or do anything you don't want to do, Lace. I swear."

Lacey longed to believe Bro's comfort and reassurance, but she had learned long ago that adults pretended to know better about a lot of things, and they took away a young person's freedom to choose in all the wrong places. It was as if they forgot what it was like to be a teen and to discover things for the first time.

He kissed her lips and deepened it into a maelstrom of mad desire that knew no limits or doubts. She yearned for him with every fiber of her being, so she wrapped her limbs around him and ground against him.

All too soon Bro pulled away—but thankfully only to remove their underwear.

And then, when Lacey was a *he* once again, and Bro landed on top of him and pressed tight against him. Bro's hands sought out the curve of Lacey's ass, the firmness of his thighs, the expanse of his back and chest. Lacey did the same, seeking every point of contact available. Their cocks, muscles, limbs, and skin rubbed and glided in unison. The heat expanded within Lacey, and he needed to come more than breathe.

Bro was right there, anticipating Lacey as always. He mashed their erections in his hand, and the leaking precome eased the way, though at times their slick cocks slipped out of Bro's hold, no matter how firm and relentless the touch. Then he started a fast stroke, his grip so hard Lacey saw stars in his field of vision. His hips bucked of their own accord, needing this connection with his boyfriend, his lover.

And all that time Bro's mouth was fused with Lacey's. No words were needed, and none were offered. They panted, and thrust, and the sex was exhilarating and wild, intense and intimate, demanding total and utter submission from both of them to the desire they shared. Only, it was more love than anything else, a desperate cry not to lose the love they had found in each other.

Before he knew it, Lacey was coming, his balls drawing up so painfully he felt as if they would get sucked into his body, only to spill out through his slit. Hot liquid splashed on his chest, and then Bro's cock twitched and swelled against Lacey's softening dick, and a new wave of sticky come landed in thick ropes between them.

Bro fell on top of Lacey, but he didn't care about the extra weight that kept him from getting his bearings or breathing steadily. Lacey wound his arms around his guy's neck to keep him close, and Bro reciprocated immediately. Gradually, their heart rates slowed, and the world stopped spinning, the kaleidoscope muting back to the dull gray of the night.

Stiffly, Bro pulled back to land next to Lacey with a soft thump. "God almighty, what you do to me." The tone was filled with awe, happiness, and best of all, love.

Lacey smiled, snuggling at his boyfriend's side. "I know *exactly* what you mean."

Limply, Bro rummaged the nightstand in the dark, mumbling something inaudible that sounded an awful lot like cursing, and produced a fresh washcloth. He wiped them both clean of come and tossed the smeared cloth to the floor.

Then Bro surrounded Lacey with his arms once more, and Lacey was in heaven.

Which was good since tomorrow was going to be hell.

"GOOD to see you again, Lacey," Mr. Teasdale said with a big relieved smile. "I heard about what happened to you from Detective Waters here. I'm glad you don't mind practicing here today."

Lacey grasped quickly that Mr. Teasdale had been referring to the incident with her father, not the latest development with her aunt. She smiled, grateful she didn't have to hash out all her business with her violin teacher, too. "Thank you, Mr. Teasdale. I'll be all right. You're sure *you* don't mind rehearsing here?"

"Of course not." Mr. Teasdale waved a dismissive hand about. "The loft's acoustics are excellent."

Jordan laid his big, scarred hand over Lacey's shoulder. "I'll make sure we mongrels won't bother you playing too much." With mock irritation, he peered over his shoulder toward the open kitchen of the loft, where Jack, Luke, Kevin, Bro, Bradley, and Audrey were all making their presence known, loudly, as they tried to make breakfast without agreeing to anything, not even what they should be making, let alone by what method.

"It's fine." Lacey giggled. Her eyes veered to Bro, who wholeheartedly joined in the playful arguments with the others, but who had seemed subdued when they woke up this morning. That made her mirth recede. They needed to talk, but she had no idea where to start.

So instead of a bathroom, she found refuge in her music.

"Let's start with arpeggios, Lacey," Mr. Teasdale suggested, though she considered this nothing more than handling the bow to create sounds. Nonetheless, she enjoyed the relaxed familiarity. She smelled the rosin on the strings and the varnish on the wood and inhaled them deeply, letting them fill her lungs and suffuse her very being as a musician.

"Which one?" she asked, no longer focusing on anything but the instrument tucked under her jaw, where the slightly rougher patch of skin always lingered from long hours of contact with her violin.

Mr. Teasdale shrugged. "You decide."

She avoided touching, or even brushing against, the few strings she had recently replaced, noting casually that they were tighter than the others. She laid the bow down and began to play, starting with E major and moving down to E minor through the descending scales.

"Ah." Mr. Teasdale sounded pleased. "Paganini's Caprice No. 1. Good choice."

Lacey smiled, finding the rhythm of the composition. It wasn't an easy piece by any musician's standards, but for her it was like coming home. Her bow felt like it was flying over the four violin strings, creating sweet chords that warmed her heart and cooled her mind.

"Andante," Mr. Teasdale reminded her when she played the piece too slow, letting it linger. "Don't forget the rhythm. Walking pace." His hands motioned with the correct tempo, and though he wasn't a conductor, she followed his lead.

Vaguely, out of the corner of her eye, she observed how the rest of her family had stopped wrestling in the kitchen and steadied themselves, calming down and stopping to listen to her play. It was a heady feeling to be able to entice a bickering group to fall so very silent. The high-pitched voices of her audience turned to the occasional high-pitched notes of the complex composition as they ricocheted within the instrument and then gushed out in a feverish melody, devilishly hard to emulate.

The piece wasn't long, though, and she was soon finished.

The silence after her performance, however, didn't last long.

"Is it supposed to sound like that?" Jack asked from the kitchen, frowning. "So, um, discordant?"

Mr. Teasdale burst into hearty laughter. "It only sounds like that to the unobserving, to the unknowing ear. And... the majority of violinists cannot play this adequately, and even fewer can play it as masterfully as Paganini himself."

Lacey winked at the man. "That's because he sold his soul to the devil."

"Pft, vicious rumors. As a child Paganini played half the day, every day, that's why." Mr. Teasdale waved a dismissive hand but then studied Lacey with enormous pride. "But you, child? You are by far the best violinist I have ever heard."

Lacey blushed so hard she felt like her cheeks might burst into flames. "Mr. Teasdale...."

He silenced her with a raised hand. "Play Caprice No. 2 and show your family what you're made of."

In her opinion the next piece wasn't as technically difficult as the first, but she obeyed. Starting in B minor, she proceeded through the slower, more romantic beginning toward the harder, more strained use of the bow and fingers. Though only one note sounded per bow drawn across a string, the skill was in making it sound like all the notes joined as one continuous, or even overlapping, resonance.

As the pace quickened, Lacey lost herself in the music, in the sharp, aching melodies she brought out of the tiny instrument, rising toward the highest, fastest peak, the masterpiece part of the composition. Paganini must have been insane to write this, she often thought, totally batshit crazy. The piece may typically have been played moderately, but in her opinion, that was an oversimplification, because the required dexterity alone could drive a violinist mad.

And it didn't help matters that her emotions were all over the place, definitely too stormy for caprices.

In midmovement, she replaced Paganini's caprice with a new song, this time "Smooth Criminal." She heard laughter from the kitchen and saw Mr. Teasdale mock glaring at her, but she didn't care. Lacey had been struck down by her own crescendo, and the melody flowed out of her memory with ease. She preferred the 2Cellos version over the original anyway. It was a fun, though slightly challenging, piece to play. Still, it was nothing like Paganini.

When she ended, everyone applauded, with smiles on their faces.

Lacey beamed. "Thank you." She curtsied, lifting the hem of her dress an inch. It was such a feminine gesture, and she wondered where she had picked it up. Surely she hadn't done a lot of that as a boy.

"Not your usual playing, but fine indeed," Mr. Teasdale complimented.

"Well, in truth I was just trying to avoid doing all twenty-four caprices."

"Careful, or I will make you perform Ravel's *Tzigane* right on the spot," the teacher warned, but his smile belied his harsh words.

Lacey shuddered. That piece was one of the more difficult violin pieces in the world, and she sure as hell wasn't ready to tackle that one. She had practiced Paganini for a long time, wanting to learn the technically challenging pieces, but she knew there was so much else out there. "I'll consider myself forewarned," she retorted amusedly.

"Oh, speaking of which!"

Mr. Teasdale dashed to his valise and pulled out a thick pile of glossy pamphlets. "I got these brochures from the places we discussed last month. The music schools." He handed the first to Lacey, who froze in place but mechanically took the offered papers. "As we expected, the Curtis Institute of Music is the best, but there's something to be said about Juilliard and Carnegie Mellon, too, or the New England Conservatory." Mr. Teasdale kept absentmindedly shoving new brochures in Lacey's lap while she was trying to precariously balance the fiddle too. "The worthiest music schools close by would be Washington College or the Peabody Conservatory. That is at a manageable distance, if I do say so, but there just don't seem to be any notable options for a violinist of your caliber in the DC area or—"

He stopped abruptly when he noticed Lacey standing rigid in place. She could feel the blood draining from her face, so she must have looked pale, like a ghost. Her skin felt cold and clammy, and she wanted to hide her head in a hole in the ground.

Months ago, before the New Year, Lacey and Mr. Teasdale had spoken about the best music colleges on the eastern seaboard, and he had even helped her with the video auditions. She had focused on this part of the country because of Bro. But this was not how she had planned on discussing it with her boyfriend.

"Oh. Oh. Have I stepped in it again…?" Mr. Teasdale muttered, horrified. It wasn't his fault, really, that Lacey had kept these future career plans to herself. She wasn't ready. "I thought when you auditioned for them…. Oh, goodness, I'm only making it worse."

"It's all right," Lacey reassured him, though she knew it wasn't.

Mr. Teasdale kept mumbling and shifting the papers in his arms, clearly at a total loss as to what to do now. "I'm so very sorry, my dear," he whispered finally, unable to look at her, and he plopped down on the sofa, limp as a wet noodle.

"When did you audition for these schools?"

Bro's voice sounded distant and detached, and ice ran through Lacey's veins. This was all too much. She was at the end of her rope.

"I meant to tell you, but I just…." She couldn't finish, the lump in her throat blocking the words she needed to say, all of them refusing to come out.

Lacey's eyes misted with unshed tears, but she still found Bro standing in front of her, though not within touching reach. "When I mentioned Howard, that was the time to say something. Instead you made me think there was a chance you'd stay and we'd be—"

A hand on Bro's shoulder stopped him, and he glanced at Sebastian's delicate visage.

"Now is not the time," Sebastian said. His hollow voice had such a curious sound that the musician in Lacey had found it fascinating from the start.

"When, then?" Bro argued back, getting pissed now, if the reddening of his cheeks was any indication. And with him, it was alarm bells ringing. "She's gonna be gone next week anyway!" He turned back to her, and Lacey saw the hurt in his eyes. "Guess you made up your mind, then."

He stormed off. The sound of a door slamming echoed in the loft.

By then Lacey was crying. Couldn't he see she had been looking into these places so they could be in nearby cities, a few hours' drive away from one another? Baltimore was an hour away, Philadelphia two to three hours, New York four hours, and Boston seven to eight hours away. Not in another country. They could handle these distances if they tried.

But with everything that had happened lately, maybe cutting their losses was the only sensible thing to do.

Sebastian's arms wound around her, and he stroked her back gently. He whispered in her ear softly, soothing her. Sebastian felt like a big brother to her, and she relished the warmth of affection and sympathy he was offering.

Only... Lacey had blood relations in Seattle.

These people had taken her in, cared for her, and helped heal her. Bro most of all. But were they family?

Deep down in her heart she knew they were, and she would miss them like crazy. All this talk of music schools was moot anyway if the West Coast was going to be her future. She and Bro were supposed to talk today about her not leaving, but if he thought she wasn't going to be around anyway.... Maybe getting angry made it easier for Bro to deal with the impending and inevitable loss.

But Bro wasn't the only one losing here. Lacey wanted to stay. She had felt confident because she'd had Bro at her side. Together they could have convinced their parental—or guardian—units that Lacey's place was here, not in Seattle.

But without Bro, what did Lacey really have here?

She wanted to seek comfort, but she didn't know where to find it.

Then she recognized something else that was keeping her here. And at least this was a problem she could face dead-on, and maybe find some self-confidence and closure, too.

She pulled out of Sebastian's hug and looked at Jordan, whose face was an enigma.

"I want to see my father."

A KNOCK on the door, timid and almost inaudible, aroused Bro from his sullen mood.

"Go away!"

The door opened anyway, and Mr. Teasdale's embarrassed face peeked in. "May I come in?" he asked with a shaky voice.

"Whatever." Bro wanted to stay mad, and this music teacher would be the perfect target. All the recent changes in his life had come to a head, and he wanted to scream and shout, kick and break. He wanted everything to stop spinning out of control so damn fast and slipping through his fingers. And most of all, he wanted Lacey with him. Forever, if at all possible.

Mr. Teasdale came in, closed the door, and leaned against it. Then he broke the silence by suddenly asking, "Do you know where the music schools I mentioned are?"

Bro gritted his teeth and leaned against his bed's headboard, staring stubbornly out the window. "Seattle?"

"No." Mr. Teasdale shook his head. "They are all on the East Coast."

That got Bro's attention, and his gaze snapped toward the shy man floundering by the door, seemingly trying to decide whether to walk closer to the young man or stay put. "What?"

"The Curtis Institute of Music is in Philadelphia, Washington College in Chestertown, just across Chesapeake Bay, and the Peabody Conservatory in Baltimore. The last two are the closest to DC. And surely you know Juilliard is in New York, as is Carnegie Mellon. The New England Conservatory is in New England, of course. Boston, to be precise. Right from the start, when Lacey and I first spoke about her options before the turn of the year, it was obvious to her she would want to stay on the East Coast, to stay close to you."

Bro trembled. Had he mistaken the situation so goddamn badly? Had he let his teenage hormones get the better of him, addle his brain so badly he couldn't even remember where some of those world-famous schools were, control him with undeserved fury? *Fuck!* "I...."

Mr. Teasdale's expression changed to a more patient, serious one, and his tone reflected that. "You do understand Lacey is one of the finest young violinists out there, and not just any college will do for her? She has a gift, a true natural talent, and it needs to be cultivated, encouraged, and nurtured. She wants to make a career in music—" He paused, frowning. "—but she also wants to be with you. That is why she focused on conservatories and colleges relatively close to DC. Her home."

The shame Bro felt then knew no bounds. God, how could he have been so stupid? He had assumed most of those fancy places would be all over the country, maybe even in Seattle. Bro knew he couldn't go that far to live, not even for Lacey. He couldn't leave his family behind, not when he had lost so many family members already. His father was dead, while his still-living mother was a coldblooded, reticent woman who felt no love for her two imperfect sons. The mere thought of leaving Sebastian and the new family they had formed was too horrible to contemplate.

But to realize that Lacey had understood and was willing to sacrifice some of the best schools of music in the world to be with Bro…. God, he had fucked up so royally.

He bounced up on his feet, heading for the door. "I have to talk to Lacey before—"

"She's not here," Mr. Teasdale said, causing Bro to stop in midstride.

"Where is she?" He squelched the urge to grab the man's lapels and shake him until answers fell from him like ripe fruit from a tree. He wasn't a violent person, though, and besides, this had been his mess, so it was his responsibility to clean it up, without bitching.

Mr. Teasdale spoke matter-of-factly as he said, "She wanted to see her father. Jordan and Kevin agreed to take her."

At that Bro was stunned and terrified beyond belief. He ran out the door as if the devil were on his heels.

"ROGER'S been released on bail, so he should be home." Jordan's words were as cool and calm as ever, and they soothed Lacey's frayed nerves as she sat next to him in his SUV. They were driving to her home, or former home. Kevin sat in the back, silent.

"Thanks." She wondered if her voice sounded as foreign to him as it did her.

"You still wanna do this?" Jordan asked. His concerned, wary gaze landed on her with its usual intensity.

"Yes, I do." About that she was adamant. "For closure, you know."

"It's not necessary, certainly not right now."

"It is for me, and what better time than right now?"

Jordan sighed a little. "Look, Bro didn't mean—"

"I don't want to talk about that right now," Lacey cut him off sharply.

"Okay." Jordan shrugged, but Lacey had an inkling Jordan was far from done with this subject. She had been given a reprieve, but in true family fashion, it wasn't over, not by a long shot.

Jordan slowed down, steered to the curb, and parked the car close to the house. Lacey saw lights on inside, in the living room but nowhere else. She shuddered. Her father had not been a bad man for most of his life, so Lacey still stubbornly refused to believe Roger had gone off the deep end with finality. During the fight, she had felt that way, but the hope within wouldn't die.

With that thought in mind, she got out of the car and walked to the front door. She felt Jordan and Kevin flank her and was grateful for their support and protection. Yes, with her new martial arts skill Lacey would probably have been able to take her father down alone if he tried anything, but that was hardly the point of this meeting.

She hadn't realized she'd been standing there in front of the door for a minute or so until Jordan touched her shoulder, silently asking her what she wanted to do.

Nodding, Lacey used her keys to unlock the door.

The light in the hallway was off, but one was on in the living room. Roger sat on the couch, a beer bottle in hand, his unseeing gaze directed at a black TV screen. Lacey noticed how lifeless he seemed, how slumped his stance, how motionless his very being, gaze dull, face blank. And he looked older, too, at least twenty years older than he was in reality. Was it a consequence of all the drinking, or the sorrow of loss, or remorse for his misdeeds? Lacey swallowed, feeling small and fearful. She still loved this man—who apparently didn't love her.

Maybe blood isn't thicker than water.

When he heard the door close, Roger glanced up. At first there was no recognition, but then his eyes widened, and he struggled to get up. The beer bottled dropped from his hand onto the rug, spilling its foamy contents, but he picked it up and placed it on the table. Lacey observed he hadn't used a coaster, and Lexie would have given him hell for it.

"Hi, Dad," Lacey said quietly.

Roger's hair was a shaggy mop, his skin pale, and his clothes rumpled. Yet, as he came closer slowly—not staggering, exactly, but less than steady on his feet—Lacey smelled no alcohol on his breath. Was that a good sign? Wait, hadn't he had a beer bottle in hand a second ago?

"Lacey." Roger said only the name, then appeared stumped. She didn't think he even saw the two men standing at her sides. "I, uh… I didn't expect to see… I mean, um…." Then his jaw trembled, and he shook violently. There was wetness in his eyes and on his cheeks now. "Oh God, son. What have I done?"

He held out his arms, as if waiting for Lacey to run right to him. But she couldn't. She didn't have enough trust in the genuineness of the gesture. So Lacey pointed at the couch. "We should probably sit down."

Awkwardly, Roger nodded and then walked back to the sofa, slumping down like a weighty puppet. "Lance, I have behaved so—"

"My name is Lacey," she cut him off. She was surprised to hear how calm she sounded even to her own ears. Was she in denial, or in shock, or losing her mind? "I know I'm not the kind of son you wanted, but this is who I am. I could change for you, because you're my father and I love you. But I won't. I. Will. Not."

Roger's face twisted, but to Lacey it looked more like agony than wrath. "I know."

Though that surprised her, Lacey ventured onward. "All that's happened to you lately, Dad… it's not my fault. You always tell me to grow up and be a man. You should follow your own mantra. I did not put the bottle in your hands and force the alcohol down your throat. You did that all by yourself. I did not make you hit me, either. You did that, too, by your own choice." She paused to take a calming breath. "I miss Mom too. So much sometimes it kills me. But no matter how many drinks you consume or how many times you slap me around, she's not gonna come back."

Roger said nothing. His jaw kept twitching, though, and he was wringing his hands. Then, finally, he said quietly, "I wish I could say it was just the drink talking, Son. I really do." He brushed his forehead, sweaty and pale. "I wish it was just about your mother, but it's everything. Oh, God, I didn't want you to find out like this…."

"Find out what?" Lacey's heart damn near stopped.

Roger let out a guttural groan that turned into a sad sob. "A month ago I… I lost my job because of the drinking."

"Dad…." Lacey's head was spinning, and so was her life, and her father's life. Their life as a family.

"But for the better part of the past year, even before I lost my job, I took money out of your college fund to pay the bills and… everything else."

Booze, you mean, and maybe some gambling too, or whatever. Lacey felt her own hands shaking, though her mind felt blank and sort of numb. *Shock again, huh? Familiar territory for you, sister.* "Dad, how could you?"

"I was going to replace it all, but… but things just spiraled out of control." Roger was desperate, she could hear it. He was sorry, but it was too late now.

"How much is left?" Dread settled into the pit of her stomach as Lacey watched with her mind's eye as her future as a violinist, as a college graduate, slipped down the drain with her father's drinks.

Roger's miserable expression turned to one of defeat. "A few… hundred. A thousand. Maybe."

Lacey felt her heart break. Again. "But Mom had made sure I had a college trust fund from Granddad's will."

"As your legal guardian, I had access." Then Roger stopped talking and simply sat there, saying nothing, doing nothing.

Lacey wanted to scream, to cry, to fight, to curse the injustice of it all. Even if she had a full-time job while in music school, she wouldn't be able to make that kind of money, not for one of those places. The stress, lack of time and sleep, pressures from all sides—she might be able to handle it. But it would all show in her music, that much she knew. Music was the language of the soul, and hers was damaged beyond repair, cut off from all sides.

She longed to hurt this man, Roger, for how could she call him dad anymore? What kind of parent did this to their child?

But Lacey understood sorrow. No matter how despondent or mad she got, she couldn't hurt him. Not even with the truth of what had happened on the day of her mother's accident, and the true reason she had been behind the wheel. For the sake of them both, that would remain buried for all time.

Now Lacey also knew she had no choice but to go to Seattle with Aunt Valerie.

There was no other way. She could not and would not ask her new family—*not for much longer, sister*—to foot the bill for years in a high-priced conservatory. Her aunt was her only option now. That and getting a job that paid big bucks, hopefully at least somehow tied to music.

"You unbelievable bastard. You miserable piece of shit."

Bro's voice from the open doorway startled them all. He looked wild and frantic and desperate and furious—and so much like a knight in shining armor to Lacey. Her brave champion.

She got up and dashed over to him, and when he saw her coming, he opened his arms, and she went to him, melting into his embrace. "You came."

"Of course I came," he mumbled into her hair. Lacey felt his heartbeats, his warmth, his solidity. *My rock.* "I'm so fucking sorry, Lace. I shouldn't have gotten mad at you. Teasdale told me all those music places are on the East Coast. But you see, I thought…. Fuck, baby, I'm so sorry. Please, forgive me."

"Of course I forgive you, silly." Lacey was just glad he was there, holding her. She knew it was wrong to give in to this feeling, especially since she was going to have to leave, but she needed the contact right now.

"I feel like a… like a carved tree trunk, hollowed out and empty." Roger's voice from the couch was deep and resigned. "There's only sorrow there, and I can't make it go away. I drown it every once in a while, but—"

"Dad, you have got to stop this." Lacey moved away from Bro and sat on the coffee table in front of her father. "You have got to get help. I don't want read your obituary in the paper. I don't want to stand at your funeral, watching them lower your casket down to the ground. I don't want to say good-bye like this."

Suddenly Roger moved, grasping at Lacey's hands, squeezing them, his eyes pleading. "I've been so horrible to you. You look so much like your mother." One of his hands came up in an attempt to caress, but he pulled it back at the last minute. "I know it wasn't your fault. What's happened to me, who I've let myself become. And… what happened to your mother."

Lacey gasped in fear of what was to come. "Dad—"

"Children are capable of such forgiveness," Roger muttered, looking deflated. "Not all parents deserve that." He glanced up at Lacey. "I know Lexie wasn't on her way to pick you up, but to get me an anniversary present." He shook his head fiercely when Lacey tried to speak. "I know I accused you of her… death. It was wrong of me. I've been wrong for a long time. Without Lexie, I don't seem to know how to put myself back together again…." His eyes brimmed with tears. "And now I have lost you because of it. Just like I lost her."

"I'm not dead, Dad." Lacey wanted to hug him, but she couldn't move her muscles to do that. There was too much bad blood between them. Or so she thought. Just when she thought the bond between them severed for all time, her hands seemed to move on their own, and she hugged him. Cautiously, Roger hugged her back, patting a bit.

"I know, Son. But you aren't going to be with me anymore."

Lacey pulled back and saw Roger's eyes dart to Jordan, Kevin, and Bro. There was some resentment, but mostly acceptance, and a little bit of pride too. She had to set the record straight. "Valerie's here, Dad. She's petitioning for custody. Then I'll go to Seattle with her."

"What?" The question came from two mouths at once—Roger *and* Bro.

Lacey ignored Bro's outburst, unable to deal with it right then. "Dad, I have no other choice now. I have relied on the kindness of my friends for far—"

"We're your *family*," Bro cut in, and she heard the desperation in his tone.

"—too long, but now I have to make my own way, and not be a burden—"

"You're *not* a burden, dammit!" Bro was getting well and truly angry, Lacey noted.

She sighed. "I have to go to Seattle, Dad, now that you drank my college fund. I have to get a job to support myself, and get a place—"

"You have a place *here*, Lace." Bro sounded breathless now, as if trying to outrun the inevitable train wreck that lay ahead.

Roger was the one to speak next, before Lacey got the chance. "Your, um... boyfriend is right. What you have to do, it wouldn't change regardless of which coast you're on. And...." He hesitated, swallowing hard. "And I know I have no right to ask, or to expect, but... I would miss you if you left."

"Why did you tell me Lexie's family didn't want to have anything to do with us?" she asked.

Roger exhaled deeply. "Because I knew they would see right through me, to the drunk underneath, and take you away from me."

"But you haven't wanted *me* to begin with." Lacey was confused.

Roger fidgeted in discomfort. "It's hard to have a son like you—"

"What Lacey is or isn't, it has nothing to do with you, you self-righteous prick," Bro snarled. "You didn't fail as a parent by siring someone as wonderful as Lacey. You did fail when you turned away from her, and accused her of—" Jordan's touch on his arm was the only thing that stopped him from continuing, and he huffed with barely held back, justified fury.

"I know," Roger said quietly. "A father should never take out his frustration on his child. A father should never hit his child. I failed in both of those."

Lacey couldn't say out loud it was all right. "I know it feels bad, Dad, but you need to try harder. You must. For both our sakes."

Roger looked up from his hands to search Lacey's face for who knew what. "God, how much you remind me of her. So beautiful...." His hand lifted to brush her hair behind her ear. "I thought if you were more like a boy, I wouldn't be haunted by her image in you every time I saw you. It was stupid of me. You are who you are." He hid his face in his hands, shaking his head, and the sound of sobs emerged. "God, I can't believe I was so out of it that I attacked you and your friend—" His head whipped up in utter horror. "Oh my God, is she...?"

"Audrey's okay, Dad," Lacey reassured him softly.

Roger's shoulders slumped. "Thank God."

"Thank Bro instead. He and his friends stopped you, remember?"

"It's hazy," Roger admitted slowly, frowning, as if trying to recapture a fleeting dream.

"Not for any of us," Bro murmured in the background, still steaming.

"Bro, please, stop it." Lacey locked gazes with her boyfriend, but for the first time she saw no understanding there. She knew why, though. He was withdrawing, shutting down, moving away from that which caused him heartache.

"Whatever." Then Bro took off, walking out of the house and slamming the door shut behind him. Lacey couldn't reproach him, but it still hurt.

"I did this to you. To you both. All of you," Roger whispered.

Lacey was angry, too. "Dad, the time for self-pity is over. Either you get up from this mire right now, or you'll be here for the rest of your life." She stood up, intent on finding Bro. "But I will not be here to see it."

She stepped aside, but Roger's hold of her arm kept her where she was. Faintly in the background she heard a car start up and drive off, tires squealing. *Bro's gone.* The emptiness in her heart felt too big for the fragile shape to contain.

"I'm sorry, Lance—um, Lacey," Roger said. "I am so sorry. I will do whatever I must to make things right."

"That's nice, Dad." Lacey removed his hand from her arm. "But I fear it's already too late." She turned to Jordan and Kevin. "I'd like to go home now."

For as long as the place would still be her home.

"BRO, can I come in?"

Lacey's apprehensive voice reached Bro muffled through the door. "Whatever."

Bro lay in bed, hands behind his back, his eyes closed. He knew he was being utterly selfish, demanding all or nothing from Lacey, who was already between a rock and a hard place. Yet he couldn't stop himself. He could accuse his raging teenage hormones for that, but in the end he was well aware it was his breaking heart that was responsible for the furor. Perhaps the heart truly was the most selfish organ.

The door opened and closed. Silence lay thick and heavy in the bedroom. Which was ridiculous because normally there was nothing they couldn't talk about.

"I'm sorry, Bro," Lacey said timidly. "I can't stay, not now."

Bro couldn't keep his big mouth shut. "Would it be so bad to stay here with us—with me—and go to school here?"

"No." Her voice was barely a whisper, and Bro heard the sobs kept at bay.

"Then why—"

"I already owe so much to all of you—"

"Damn your pride!" Bro opened his eyes and jumped up to his feet. Lacey stood by the door, lovely as ever in her pretty white dress and stockings, frail like a fine piece of porcelain. And Bro felt like the proverbial bull in the china shop, stumbling around wrecking things. "You don't owe me anything! I'm the one who owes you everything I have, my whole life. For loving me, and for letting a silly oaf like me love you back...."

"I love you, Bro. I do love you. So much." She was looking at the ground, as if trying to fold in on herself and be as small and invisible as possible.

"Then don't leave!" He was yelling now, and he never did that with her, not given her background. Lacey winced and looked even more delicate and breakable. His rage forgotten, Bro begged, "Stay with me, Lace. I need you."

"I can't." She shook her head a bit, appearing shell-shocked and tired, too. "Valerie's here. We're gonna pack, and leave as soon as we—"

"What, now? Already? What about graduation?" Bro asked, petrified at the speed at which everything was moving, specifically rushing away from him.

"I'll have to miss it, or go to it in Seattle." Lacey was leaning against the door, as if she didn't have even enough strength to keep herself upright. "I don't mean to be cruel, Bro. But if our roles were reversed, would you be so casual about living on the pity and charity of others?"

He wanted to embrace her so bad, and force her to see it had nothing to do with pity. "It's not charity. It's love, and family, and us."

"It's money you and your family don't have, and a place in the household reserved for guests—"

"You're not a guest, Lace. You're my...." Only she wasn't his girl anymore, was she? Bro's words trailed off, and they didn't come back. He would have fought for her and for the two of them through thick and thin, all the way to the bitter end. Now the fight had been taken from him. He was too late, and in a few moments she would be gone forever. Maybe there was no reason to prolong this agony they both clearly felt.

Lacey made a move, as if to come to him, but then she didn't. Bro was partially glad. He couldn't have let her go if she ever came close enough again. They would need the Jaws of Life to detach him from her then.

Quietly she turned and left the room, unobstructed. He had wanted to commit Lacey's face, body, and personality to memory with a slow exploration, but now all he had was memories of times gone by and no more chances to add new ones to that pleasant cavalcade.

Bro stood in place, feeling like the world had caved in on him. Though he didn't want them, streams of tears flowed unbidden mere seconds later. From now on he would be alone, living with half a soul.

Chapter 12

IN LESS than two hours, Lacey was sitting on an uncomfortable green plastic monstrosity called an airport waiting area seat. She hadn't cried yet. Her eyes were devoid of moisture. She felt numb, as if all of this was happening to someone else, an alien entity within her body, taking over her life only to destroy it.

"You all right, sweetie?" Valerie asked next to her, touching her arm gently.

Lacey gave a weak smile. "Yes."

She held her fiberglass violin case in her lap but wondered if anything but blue notes would ever ring out of it again. She clutched it with both hands, like her last lifeline.

She had spoken with Audrey on the phone as they had driven to the airport, but she couldn't make herself see her one last time. A good-bye with her best friend would surely end her, and then she would be reduced to a mere puddle of tears. Audrey had been both sad and angry that Lacey would leave without saying good-bye, but in the end Lacey hoped she understood her position. They had ended the call with promises of frequent contact, and Lacey hoped she would be able to deliver on her word. Audrey was one of the best things that had ever happened to her.

"Would you like something to drink, Lacey?" Valerie asked, startling her. "I could get you some tea from the café. That always calms my nerves." Her warm voice was indicative of who she was as a person, kind and empathic.

"Sure, that'd be nice. Thanks." She prayed her poor attempt at a smile worked better on her aunt than on her own mood.

Valerie moved off with a smile, in search of tea. Lacey slumped deeper into the horrid chair.

Then she just couldn't take it anymore and leave things the way they were.

She dug out her cell phone and dialed Bro's number. *Please, pick up. Please.* The wait was excruciating and felt like forever as the ringtone sounded again and again.

Finally the line clicked open, but Lacey heard only heavy breathing.

"Bro…?" she asked tentatively.

"Lace?" He sounded hoarse and muffled, and rustling came from the background. He was in bed, and judging from his raspy voice he had been crying. Not that he would ever admit it to her.

"Yes, it's me." She was worried beyond belief. "Is everything okay?"

Complete silence fell in an instant. "You're fucking kidding, right?" came the snarky, incredulous reply.

Lacey didn't want to argue anymore. "If I were with you right now, lying next to you in bed, what would we do? What would you do to me?" He may not have been there beside her, but whenever she closed her eyes, even blinked, he was there, gorgeous and young and laughing and teasing, and everything was all right.

The awkward silence dragged on. "A-are you serious…? This is one of… *those* calls?"

Lacey gave a weird, hollow laugh. "Yes. Tell me, honey. Please. I want… I want to remember you like that, when you play with me, laugh with me… love me. Please…?"

Bro sneezed, and then his voice came through clearer. "If you were here, Lace, I'd give you the sun and the moon and the world and everything."

"That's a lot." Lacey blinked away hot, itching tears. Her feet came up from the floor, curling beneath her as she folded herself together, compressed tight.

"I'd kiss you, baby. First I'd kiss your cheeks where the tears are."

Was he psychic or what? She wiped a few big drops off before they slid down any farther, and she closed her eyes, sinking into the sea of sensations his voice created. "Then what?"

"Then I'd kiss your hands 'cause I can feel them shaking. I'd kiss each of your fingers, one by one, and I'd take my time."

"Sounds wonderful." Her own voice cracked, and those stubborn tears kept on coming. She inched to lie down on two seats, curled into a ball, and let the images draw her away from this place of disconnectedness.

"I'd move to kiss your cheeks, to swipe away the salty wetness, and then I'd slide down to nip at your shoulder, and under your ear, and lick there until you shivered."

The warmth of memory within her of Bro doing just that wasn't ample protection to ward off the chills of realizing she would never get that again in real life. "Then what?"

"Then I'd undress you, baby. Slowly, just the way you want it. I'd push up your hands and then your dress to reveal that lovely chest, those pink nubs, those delicate bones, that pale skin. And then I'd bite down hard, mark you as mine."

"Yes, please," Lacey urged him quietly, her lips trembling, her body wracked with sad vibrations. "Love it when you claim me as yours."

"I'd suck up a mark, and then a dozen more, all over. I'd yank the dress off, and then I'd go down on my knees, and take off your undies and your stockings."

He was sounding breathless in a different way now, and Lacey wished she were in a private room somewhere, able to let herself recall his arms around hers, his fingers digging into her backside and thighs, his body firm and lustful against her. But she was lying alone on a crappy seat at the airport, with no privacy to speak of, let alone intimacy.

"I love you, Bro. I love you so much. I need you here. Need you to hold me." Saying the heartfelt confession out loud wasn't even half as torturous as it had felt keeping it inside for fear of upsetting him more. "Wish I was there with you. Wish I could feel your arms around me. Wish your breath would tickle my neck. Wish you would...." She couldn't finish because by then she was sobbing fully in a public place. *Great, just how I want to go.*

"I'll come there if you want, Lace," Bro said in a ragged whisper. And in that one sound all that was between them could be heard.

It tore Lacey to shreds, and she was really crying then, uncontrollable bursts of grief and loss. Honestly, how could she stand to lose anyone else?

A touch on her shoulder brought her out of her sorrow, and through blurry eyes she saw Valerie's concerned face looming above. "Lacey?"

"Hang on," she said to her. Lacey wiped off most of her tears, cleared her throat, and sat up straight. "Bro, I... I gotta go." Any more good-byes and she would just die. "I love you. Never ever forget that, please." Then she pushed disconnect, and artificial silence took the place of Bro's puffs of air.

"Here's your tea, sweetie." Valerie offered Lacey a white plastic cup with chamomile tea, the scent wafting her way with the columns of steam.

"Thanks." Lacey blew gently on the surface and then took a sip, burning the tip of her tongue. "Ouch. Hot." She smiled sheepishly back to her aunt. "Thanks."

"You've said that, Lacey." Valerie's concerned look shifted to a more decisive one. "Listen, I'm gonna ask you something, and I want you to be completely honest." Lacey frowned but nodded, nervous about her plain tone. "Do you really want to come with me now, and live in Seattle with me and my family?"

"You are my family," she said unequivocally.

"Yes." She smiled and petted her hair tenderly. "But I'm not your *only* family, am I?" Lacey swallowed hard, not knowing how to answer that. "The reason why I came to find you is because I was certain your father had not been able to deal with his loss and therefore neglected or mistreated you. I also assumed you had never gotten used to DC, and still considered Seattle your home." She took a deep breath, but her gaze was level. "Only one of those is true, isn't that right? This is your home now, isn't it?"

Lacey looked at her lap, clung to her violin case like to a baby, and replied, "You are my family, my mother's sister."

"Yes, honey, and I always will be. That's not going to change even if we were to live on different continents." Valerie put her arm around Lacey's shoulders and carefully pulled her near. "But that's not what I'm asking, and I think you know it. Would you rather stay here?" Suddenly she looked stern, as if anticipating opposition. "And don't you dare ask me whether I want to have you around because I think you know the answer to that, too."

Lacey nodded pensively, at the same time elated and afraid. "I... I want to stay here. He needs me. And I need him, too. Maybe one day things will be different, but... but not now."

"What about the music schools?" That had Lacey in a bind. Money would always be an issue for her from now on. Valerie chuckled a bit mockingly. "Oh, honey. Didn't it occur to you that you can get the same scholarships on the East Coast as the west? After all, people from all over the country apply to the best colleges all over the US, and beyond. You could live in Seattle with us on paper but still go to an eastern school." Lacey opened her mouth to speak, but Valerie got there first. "But, as you said, you have built a life here and forged a new family. I think that is something I have to take into account."

The possibility of a full ride truthfully hadn't registered in Lacey's mind at all. She thought about all the conservatories and institutions of music she had applied to, and only now realized most all of them must offer stipends and other financial aid for promising students. *How could I have been so stupid as not to think of those options?* Probably because she had always believed there was plenty of money in her trust fund and had never had to think in those terms, of needing funds to finance a higher education. But all that was no excuse for such blatant thoughtlessness. She shook her head in disbelief and then harrumphed with guilt and remorse, and finally sighed with renewed hope.

But that wasn't the only concern or problem left to be solved.

"B-but what about custody?" Lacey stammered, hope kindling inside her so strongly it was burning away all doubts.

"The order was temporary to begin with," Valerie replied, full of resolve and practical drive. Lacey really liked her, and that made her smile. She didn't remember them, as a family, having much contact with Valerie when they had lived in Seattle. Roger must have been an influence there too. "I'm sure Detective Waters can arrange for a third temporary custody order for you. Let's all trust that will be the last one. Third time's the charm." Then she bussed Lacey's cheek and smiled wickedly. "And don't worry. My family and I will see you soon when we come over to celebrate your graduation *and* your birthday with you. After all, it's frequent-flyer miles." She winked conspiratorially.

Lacey didn't know whether to laugh or cry. So she did both. Then Valerie hugged her, and for a time all was right with the world. Or for Lacey, anyway, since the world stopped hurtling out of control and finally let her take in the scenery. Valerie soothed her with rubs to her back, crooning in her ear.

"Thank you, Aunt Valerie," Lacey whispered. "Thank you so much."

Valerie leaned back, wiped the tears from Lacey's cheeks, and smiled encouragingly. "So, you about ready to get out of here?"

"BRO? You coming to dinner?" Sebastian peeked past the doorframe.

"Not hungry." Bro lay on his bed, staring at the ceiling, not seeing it.

He held his cell phone in his hand, hoping and praying that whatever interruption Lacey had had—he checked the time on the cell—forty minutes ago, it wouldn't recur, and she would call again. Her sadness had been so palpable, and just when Bro had been sure his heart was broken into so many trillions of pieces already it couldn't possibly get any worse, it had broken a little more. Bradley had called him once, but Bro had ordered him off the phone just in case. So far, though, nothing.

Bro more sensed than saw his brother come in and sit on the bed, which dipped a little as a result. "Lacey wouldn't want you to stop eating, or living for that matter." Then he added with signs, "*Well, would she?*"

"No." Bro sighed, but his eyes were dry now. Fuck, for a change. But he wasn't having a lot of luck believing the flood had been permanently averted. Maybe in a decade or two he could function like a regular person again. "But I'm not hungry. Leave me alone." He turned to his side, away from his brother.

Sebastian's hand landed on his hip, resting at first, but then shaking.

"What?" Bro turned back, irked.

"Sorry. I couldn't see if you were saying something," Sebastian retorted innocently.

Bro shifted on the bed until his back leaned against the headboard and he had free rein over his hands. "*I'm on to you, brother. I know all your tactics and games. You're not fooling me,*" he signed.

Sebastian smiled sweetly and bowed his head in recognition. But then he signed, "*If you're not out and sitting at the dinner table in five minutes, Ambrosius, we're all coming in here to have dinner with you. And trust me, we don't want to. It smells funny in here.*"

Hating the use of his whole name, even signed, Bro rolled his eyes and made a big deal about sniffing the air. "I'm a teenager and a jock. What'd you expect? I'm nothing but odors, dude."

Sebastian scrunched his nose cutely. "*Don't call me that.*"

"*I'll call you worse if you don't get the fu—out.*" Bro pointed at the door. It was a silly, childish gesture, and as expected, Sebastian just chuckled.

"I'm here if you want to talk, Bro. I hope you know that." The fact that Sebastian said that out loud told Bro he was serious, and the understanding look in his eyes confirmed as much.

"*I know, Bas. I'm not ready.*" He ignored the pain inside, making his signs as casual as he could.

"*Are you hoping Lacey will choose not to go and come back to you?*"

God, his brother had a master's in mind reading for sure. "*Is that dumb?*"

"*Hope never is. But sometimes you have to let go of impossible dreams.*" Sebastian's hands were eloquent, and Bro blinked away tears, but then he was pulled into a profound hug. Sebastian whispered in Bro's ear, "But there's no harm in keeping hope alive for one more day. We'll talk more tomorrow."

Then, with a spring in his step, Sebastian was gone.

Bro was grateful for the reprieve to think things through. Lacey's good-bye had been cut short. Maybe she would still call before the flight to say a proper farewell. Perhaps she would make that kissy sound she did when she got off the phone with him, making his heart flutter every time.

With no conscious awareness of the passage of time, since the ceiling looked the same no matter what, Bro went back to lying on his back on his bed, which now felt too big and empty for him. It could have been a few minutes, or half an hour or more, but Sebastian returned. Despite his threat earlier, he came alone, and bearing gifts: A bowl of macaroni and cheese, and a glass of milk.

"For the sporting hero," Sebastian exclaimed, and placed the tray over Bro's lap after he had once again moved to lean against the headboard.

"Thanks, Bas." It wasn't until he smelled the fresh herbs, the melted cheese, and all the other ingredients, that he felt a bit like himself again. "Oh, *you* made this," he complimented in sincere adulation as he took in the added ground beef, breadcrumbs, three different kinds of cheese, and hot sauce to burn off your tongue and tonsils. "Wow, you didn't need to."

Sebastian chuckled, his head tilted to the side as if puzzling something out, but still looking absolutely pleased. "I didn't make it just for you. The others are eating it too." He lifted his chin toward the door. "Wanna join us?"

Bro looked down and shook his head. "I'd just be a mood killer. Not tonight, okay?"

"Okay. Anything you sign." Sebastian winked playfully as he said the last word, and Bro grinned. It was an old joke between them, but the familiarity of it lifted his spirits. "*Later.*" And then he was gone again.

Grateful for the privacy, Bro dug into his food heartily. His stomach grumbled. Then he flashed on a memory of him spoon-feeding a giggling Lacey with this carb bomb. They had both gotten hot, sticky cheese sauce all over their clean sheets. Sebastian oversaw their progress, like a prison warden, as he made them clean up every last drop and wash the sheets twice. With a snickering Lacey at his side, as she brushed a kiss over his face every few minutes, Bro hadn't minded the cleanup routine one bit.

Anticipating that the food would taste like ash in his mouth, he was surprised to find the flavor enhanced by the memories, as if the meal itself wanted to remind Bro of all the good times he'd had with the lovely Lacey. Savoring every bite, Bro ate slowly. He relished the sensation of images and tastes in equal measure.

He had no idea how long it had taken him to eat half his bowl.

But then he was interrupted by a knock on the door.

Sighing, resigned, he yelled, "Come in." He guessed there was no avoiding concerned family members visiting his fortress of solitude tonight.

Bro placed the tray aside, waiting for whoever it was to come in. When he glanced up from the nightstand, he found Lacey standing there. Her back was to the closed door, her hands were behind her back, her stocking-clad legs crossed a bit, and she was worrying her lower lip.

He didn't care why.

Bro jumped up from the bed, ran to her, cupped her face, and kissed her. It was soft at first, but when he realized she wasn't a mirage, he kissed her more passionately.

Then Lacey whimpered, her knees buckled a bit, and she melted against him. And Bro was definitely on top of the world. No, this was paradise. She parted her lips more, and he stole his way inside, craving her more than air itself. Bro felt Lacey's hands fist in the back of his shirt. As he wound his arms around her, he knew it was real.

She's here, and she's all mine.

When they finally parted enough to see each other, they were both breathless, and their bodies shimmied with desire in unison. Bro's cock swelled to full erection in his jeans, and he could feel her equal reaction. But it was his heart that filled the most, with hope, love, desire, and all those things he had feared might never be his again.

Suddenly, Lacey made a face. "Eww!" Then she giggled, undoubtedly at the sight of Bro's shock. "Mac and cheese, eh?"

Bro smirked. "Oh, come on, babe. You know you love it—and me."

She laughed, and all was definitely right with the world. He had to feel her again. He pulled her into his arms once more and inhaled the scent of her hair and skin. As always with her subtle perfume, lavender and orchids made their entrée before the more masculine musk took their place. There was not even a hint of blood, but the memory of that smell clinging to her after her confrontation with her father at the football field made him shiver every time.

Bro was brought out of his reminiscences when he distinctly heard loud whoops of joy and happiness coming from outside his bedroom door. Lacey covered her full lips with her hand in that familiar coy gesture, and Bro fell more in love with her.

Still, he didn't forget to call out, "Walk away, nosy busybodies, or face my wrath."

A few seconds later Sebastian replied amusedly, "Ah, youthful bravado. Lace, honey? You want to eat some dinner?"

"I'd love some, thanks." But despite her speaking to Sebastian, Lacey stared up at Bro, her golden lashes fluttering around her hazel eyes, her gaze dreamy and earnest. "And I love you, Bro."

At that Bro grew serious, and he asked in a low, worried voice, "Did you come back to stay? Or to say a proper good-bye?"

Lacey's smile faded, but her hands came to rest over Bro's chest. "To stay."

"Why?" He hadn't wanted her to go in the first place, but he needed answers.

She looked uncertain for an instant, but it dissipated quickly. Still, the weariness had not disappeared entirely. "When we spoke on the phone, I was crying. Valerie saw me. She asked me if I really wanted to go back to Seattle. I said I didn't, but I didn't feel like I had any choice." Bro started to speak, but Lacey shushed him with her fingertips on his lips. "Then Valerie told me I was being a fool."

"She called you a fool?" That angered Bro to no end.

Lacey saw the protective response and snickered. "My brave knight. The truth is I had been a fool, in a manner of speaking. I was so caught up on everything that's been going on I felt like the world was closing in on me, and I was backed into a corner, with only one way out. I didn't want to be indebted to you—" Bro started to hastily speak again, but again Lacey stopped him with her hand over his mouth. "Yes, I know that was silly. I may look like a girl, but I am a boy underneath, and I have that pesky male ego thing going on." Bro grinned at that, and Lacey smiled back. "I was thinking about money and family and independence and… a lot of things. In any case, Valerie reminded me that with my skills as a violinist, I might be eligible for a full scholarship. *And* that those schools where I got the full ride might be on either coast. And that really clinched it for me. That… and you. Well, mainly you."

"Me…?" Breath hitched in Bro's throat at the sound of those promising words.

Lacey wrapped her arms around his neck and brushed a kiss over his lips. "Yes, you." Then she grew serious, too, and a bit scared. "Bro, you do know I can't go to the same college as you? Not unless it has a strong music program as well as an athletics—"

"Yeah, I know." He nodded his acceptance of that fact, and the relief visible in her told him everything he needed. "Teasdale told me about the conservatories, but he also warned me you're not ordinary, and you need to nurture your musical talent."

Lacey snorted with amusement and disbelief. "He said nurture?"

Bro shrugged cavalierly. "Might have been me who said that. But… I didn't need him to tell me you're extraordinary, but I did need the reminder as I was wallowing in self-pity." Then he quickly added, "That's not gonna happen again, just so you know. I'm properly toilet trained now."

Lacey laughed, and Bro considered that success.

A knock came from the door, and Lacey started.

"Dinner's ready, sweetheart," Sebastian's hollow voice declared cheerfully.

Dutifully, Bro stepped back from his girlfriend—*mine*—and gave Lacey enough room to open the door, grab a bowl of steaming hot macaroni and cheese, thank Sebastian, and then close the door again. She turned to face him, but her gaze was lowered to the food.

Her pretty nose scrunched. "Oh, if I eat this, I won't be able to fit into my stockings for a week," she groused cutely.

"I don't mind. I usually take them off you pretty quick anyway." He winked at her.

Lacey blushed, partly in arousal and partly in indignation. "Oh? Is that how it is? So...." She lifted the hem of her thin, natural-white dress to reveal the tops of her long stockings as they attached to her round thighs, accentuating her slender form, her tight muscles, and her pale skin. "So... *these* do nothing for you, and you wouldn't mind seeing me completely without them all the time? Very well, I'll discard—"

"No!" Bro's alarmed voice rose to a panicked shrill. "I mean, uh... no. No, you don't have to do that. I *do* like them. A lot." To prove his point, Bro let his fingertips slip over her thighs to the point where fabric met skin. "Yeah. A *lot* a lot."

Lacey giggled, playfully wiggling under his touch. "Really?"

Bro's eyes narrowed, and Lacey's taunt vanished as apprehension took its place. With deliberate slowness, Bro took the food bowl from Lacey's hand, placed it on the dresser by the door, and then opened the door, took Lacey's hand, and tugged her with him as he headed across the hall to the bathroom. Once they were both safely inside, he closed and locked the door, and then he grabbed her hips and lifted her onto the clear space between the two sinks.

As Bro spread Lacey's legs while maneuvering his own hips between them, he grinned wickedly. "Still feel like teasing, baby? I can tease you right back." He yanked her forward so their groins pressed together, and she moaned low.

Slowly, as she stared at him with something like worshipful awe and absolute love and trust, she shook her head, while biting her full lower lip.

Seeing her submissiveness, Bro lost all self-control. He put his arms around her tight, plastering them against one another, and kissed her hungrily. Lacey wrapped herself around him, and then there was only slick heat as tongues entwined amid the growing need of their writhing bodies.

Pretty soon they were both too heated to continue. Bro felt his cock press painfully on his zipper and feared he would get the metallic imprint on his dick in a matter of seconds. Lacey pulled away first, out of breath, her cheeks and neck tinted rosy red, her lips glistening and puffy, and her eyes dark with lust. Bro had no doubt he mirrored that rapturous sight.

"I need, baby" was all he said as he dropped down on his knees before her.

As Bro wiggled his fingers under the hem of her dress and onto the waistband of her tight undies, Lacey obediently lifted her hips to let him remove them. Bro drew her forward so that her backside was half over the edge. He pushed her splayed thighs apart more with his shoulders, and he was rewarded with the vision he never grew tired of.

"God, you're so fucking beautiful," he murmured, breathless with want. "I thought I'd go mad without you."

"Me too," Lacey confessed, her voice soft and heady. "Please, honey…."

With a flicker of a grin, Bro mashed his face against Lacey's warm testicles, the sac soft and thin and wrinkly against his skin, elusive whenever he tried to capture it with his mouth.

Lacey squirmed and chortled. "Oh, that tickles."

After toying with Lacey's balls for a moment, licking and mouthing and sucking tenderly, Bro advanced onto the pretty prick before him. Pink turned to darker red as Lacey's cock filled with blood, the shaft rigid, pulsating, and the slit leaking copiously.

"My lovely boy," Bro said just before he sucked the tip into his mouth.

Lacey's hips rolled and bucked. She was a he again as far as Bro was concerned; he saw Lacey as a *he* the moment his privates were exposed, and this time was no different.

"Oh God, *yes*," Lacey babbled, his tone dropping to husky. That made him seem like a boy more than anything else, except perhaps for his cock and balls, Bro thought.

Bro proceeded to drown Lacey in pleasure as he gradually took the length of Lacey's penis into his mouth and down his throat. He used his hands to keep Lacey's trembling hips firmly in place as he sucked on the head, followed the ridge, and traced the slit with his tongue, flicked over the bundle of nerves under the glans, and kissed all over the shaft, wherever he could reach. Bro loved giving head, and he absolutely adored it when the cock in his mouth belonged to Lacey.

"Oh, Bro, yes," Lacey muttered in between whimpers and pants. The soles of his feet kept banging against the small of Bro's back the more aroused he got, and Bro loved it.

The need for Lacey had built steadily within Bro since he first laid eyes on her as she stood against the bedroom door, just back from the airport. Now Bro couldn't in good conscience, or for his own sanity, dawdle much longer. Not when Lacey was spread out before him like a sexual smorgasbord, ready and willing to be devoured.

So that was exactly what Bro did. He ate Lacey up. Speeding up his pace, he bobbed up and down on that lovely piece of meat in his mouth, going down in one fell swoop and coming up with agonizingly strong suction and his cheeks hollowed. Lacey was groaning wantonly now, and his hands threaded through Bro's hair to grip hard.

Even if Bro had wanted to tell Lacey to take it easy, he wasn't going to. Not when he knew how good it felt to be on the receiving end of such pleasure. And he had missed her—and him—so damn much.

Making quick work of it, one of his best performances to date, Bro sucked, licked, nibbled, nuzzled, and kissed Lacey to the edge of delight—and, by adding his hands to the mix with a few hard pumps from one hand and the cradling of his balls with the other, pushed him over the edge.

Lacey cried out, his fingers almost tearing Bro's scalp clean off, and his feet hit Bro's back repeatedly as he convulsed in the throes of passion. Bro's mouth filled with bitter-salty-sugary goodness, the proof of Lacey's climax, as he swirled it inside his oral cavity before he swallowed the offering.

What had started out as frissons of electric pleasure within Bro became an insistent, demanding pressure within to find release. He popped his jeans open, pulled out his cock through the slit of his boxers, and with a few painfully hard tugs and yanks he was coming too. His fingers were wet, hot, and sticky with spunk, but he didn't care as he hummed and groaned through his own release.

All that mattered was the blinding orgasm he had brought on in both of them with his mouth alone. It was a moment of clarity, and he knew everything was going to be all right.

They would graduate with their best friends in a month or so, and then they would go on to their respective institutions of higher learning, but nonetheless remain close to one another, and still be a loving, devoted couple. Yeah, it was all good.

Panting hard, Bro slowly released the softening dick, and it fell from between his lips. Above him a fully sated nymphet stared back at him from under heavy lids.

"Thank you, honey," Lacey rasped, sounding like she smoked a pack a day, and her hem dropped to cover her crown jewels. "That was the best ever." Then she frowned slightly, her eyes opening more as awareness crept back. "You want me to—?"

Bro grinned, shaking his head. "Nah. If you were to touch me now, you'd get a handful of come."

Surprise widening her eyes, Lacey readjusted her slumped stance to lean forward and peer over the edge toward the floor until she saw Bro's come-soaked cock. "Oh." She sounded disappointed.

Staggering back up to his feet, Bro chuckled and offered his sticky hand to her in jest. "Here, have this, so you don't feel left out."

But Lacey grabbed Bro's wrist so fast and hard he stumbled, and then he wobbled a bit more when Lacey sucked his fingers into her mouth, one by one, licking him clean. Though spent just a moment ago, his cock began to refill as, enthralled, he watched the vision before him.

"Oh God," he mumbled, hardly getting any sound past the lump in his throat.

Lacey didn't stop until Bro was pristine. All the while she hummed happily, a smile on her full lips, and her eyes closed as she ate her dessert. At some point the touch began to tickle, but Bro would sooner have cut off his arm than have told her to stop.

When she was finished with her ministrations, however, she resembled the proverbial cat that ate the cream, and Bro damn near creamed his pants again.

"T-thanks…," he managed to say, his voice cracking.

"No, thank *you*," Lacey replied smugly, her voice level once more.

Bro smiled and rested his forehead against hers. "So good to have you back, baby."

Lacey smiled too, her eyes watering a bit. "Yes. It's great to be home again."

Part Two

Chapter 13

About five months later

"GET off me, you big oaf," Lacey giggled breathlessly.

Bro's merciless tickling assault didn't stop for an instant. "Yup, I sure am big all right," he drawled in a horribly clichéd seductive accent.

"Stop it, or I'll use the A-word." It was the only weapon left in her arsenal, so she used it shamelessly.

Those nimble fingers halted, and the grin above him faltered. "Y-you wouldn't...."

It was the perfect opportunity to turn the tables, so Lacey used her own body strength and flipped them over on Bro's bed in their shared room at the loft. Then she was straddling her boyfriend's lean hips—and the noticeable bulge in his crotch.

"Got you now," she taunted, and he relaxed beneath her, smiling ardently.

"You sure do, and always will." Bro's earnestness was evident in the twinkling of his forget-me-not blue eyes beneath his dark, untamed, almost twink strands. Lacey loved his eyes, for the way they looked at her, the way they mirrored his soul, and the warmth and love in them.

And the rest of him wasn't bad either, his athletic figure sporting broad shoulders, narrow waist, washboard stomach, and delineated musculature in streamlined perfection. This was the body of a high school football player, and Lacey adored the visual every day and night.

She dipped down and kissed his inviting lips tenderly, cupping his face, feeling the start of stubble on his jaw and the soft skin of his temples. Bro's hands slid up her back, toying with the thin fabric of her dress. With the tip of his tongue, Bro coaxed Lacey's lips to part, and he stole his way inside, taking her breath away. For a while they kissed, touched, and held each other as the slow fire between them simmered.

A reverent knock came from the door.

Bro groaned, displeased, and Lacey snickered at her grumpy lover.

"Dinner's ready, you two," came Jordan's amused shout from outside the door. At least he didn't peek inside, Lacey mused gratefully.

Bro growled some more, his eyes closed tight. "Fuck. I was just getting into—"

"Me?" Lacey teased.

Bro's eyes shot open, and in one fell swoop he had her pinned down on the bed. "Be very careful, little rabbit, or this big bad wolf will eat you up." Lacey laughed, and Bro grinned. "In fact, I might just push up your pretty dress and gobble up your sweet cock right now." His hands brushed against the waistband of Lacey's tight undies, reaching for her swelling dick, and managing to successfully graze the hardening length trapped beneath the strict, unyielding fabric.

She swatted his hand away. "If you give me wood at the dinner table, I'll wring your neck—or some other body part."

Bro chuckled, not the least bit concerned about the threat aimed at his crown jewels. "Oh, baby, you can squeeze the life out of any part of me." He smacked a big, sloppy kiss on her lips, and she scrunched her nose playfully. "You already have my heart in a chokehold."

Lacey blinked away some unneeded moisture in her eyes. "You say the silliest things." But she didn't mean it. In all honesty, she loved him for saying them. And she just... loved him.

Winking at her, Bro obviously wasn't fooled by her reproach, and then he confirmed his magical mind-reading prowess. "And you love me for it."

What could she say to that? Lacey wrapped her hands around his neck and pulled him down for a deep, hungry kiss that seemed to halt time itself.

Five hot, sweaty minutes later they sat down at the dinner table. Their awfully amused family members sat around them, and most of them were grinning ear to ear at the sight of Lacey's flushed face, mussed up short blond hair, and feverish hazel eyes, and Bro's just-try-me glare aimed at each and every one of them.

"Sure hope you two worked up an appetite," Jordan commented placidly. Jack, his younger brother sitting across the table, burst into hopeless cackles.

"My brother's appetite is insatiable," Sebastian remarked next to Jordan with equal calm. At that point, Jack was chortling and banging on the table with tears streaming out of his eyes, and even his typically stoic boyfriend Kevin chuckled a bit under the concealment of his napkin.

"Fine!" Bro huffed, indignant, red-faced. "Everybody take a potshot at me!"

Jordan frowned in mock confusion. "I thought we already were."

Lacey giggled, covering her full lips behind her hand in a demure gesture. Bro let go of his temper in favor of worshiping his girlfriend, who was in actuality a boy in a girl's dress. This point of view Lacey knew well because Bro's eyes glazed over when he was lost in his feelings for her, and she loved him all the more for it. Not because of the adulation itself, but the way Bro saw her never failed to make her appreciate the bond between them. That tie had gone through its share of frays and tears within the last year, but solidified into a stronger connection.

The summer break was almost over, and their freshman year at college would start in less than a week. Worst of all, they would be going to different places: Bro would go to Howard University right here in DC on a football scholarship, with his best friend, Bradley, and Lacey's best friend, Audrey—Bradley to play football, too, and Audrey to study law—while Lacey would be headed for the Peabody Conservatory in Baltimore, over an hour away from DC by car. It was a manageable distance, though not one she expected to enjoy on a daily basis.

But for Bro, Lacey would do anything, make any sacrifice. Not that the Peabody was such a hardship. The school had an excellent reputation, and Lacey was looking forward to getting her bachelor's degree in music with the string department. And who knew? After that accomplishment, the next step along her career would be a master's, and then perhaps, if she studied really hard and dedicated herself to her trade, a doctorate in musical arts. Violin performance would be her tool in achieving these goals, and then… take the world by storm?

Sometimes she was so excited about it all she could barely contain her enthusiasm, let alone sit still. Yet, she didn't feel like rushing it. This past summer had been the best of her life, and she didn't want it to be over yet. In four days, on Thursday, Lacey had to go to Peabody for orientation. And then she had one last weekend of peace before her time would be dominated by studies, research, and practice, practice, practice.

"Mr. Teasdale's going to drive you to Baltimore?" Kevin asked Lacey between bites of the pepper steak Jack had made. It was pretty much all Jack could make, but the steaks were damn juicy. Even Lacey, who rarely ate meat, had to admit that. She wasn't a vegetarian, but she was beginning to lean in that direction, not just to satisfy her ecological convictions, but because of the fresh, light taste.

"Yes." Lacey nodded. "I think he's as eager as I am to see the conservatory. He studied in England and Italy, so this is a change for him."

"Aww, your first fan," Jack stated with childish glee, half of it fake.

Lacey snickered. "I'll have to start selling tickets to my performances next." Then she glanced at her boyfriend beneath her lashes. "You'll have a special boyfriends-only backstage pass."

Bro grinned and blushed endearingly. Lacey just had to kiss him, tasting pepper steak, mashed potatoes, gravy, and vegetables, all with one lick. Friendly chuckles and one wolf whistle accompanied her actions.

As he pulled back, Bro stared at her dazed, like he always did after they had been smooching. Lacey felt heat suffuse her own cheeks, and felt her cock jump in her tight underwear, pleading to be let out to play.

As if sensing her discomfort, Bro asked, "We've still got four days. What do you want to do?"

During the past month, the six of them—Bro, Lacey, Jordan, Sebastian, Jack, and Kevin—had traveled quite a lot of the Chesapeake and Ohio Canal National Historical Park, by car, on bikes, and on foot. It had been an awesome six days, though they had scarcely seen all there was to see. Lacey had loved the outdoors. "I was thinking we could go camping for a couple of nights in the Shenandoah National Park."

Bro was a sporty, outdoorsy person too. The twinkle in his eyes and the widening grin told her that her idea was grand. "Yeah, that sounds fucking great. I've never been there before."

"Bro," Sebastian admonished him for his cursing, pursing his lips in playful distaste.

Bro rolled his eyes, but for his deaf brother's benefit signed, "*Sorry.*" He turned to Lacey, buzzing with excitement. "Yeah, let's do it. We'll go tomorrow."

"Tomorrow's Sunday," Kevin noted. "I recommend waiting until Monday."

"Why?" Lacey asked, curious.

"I've stayed at Shenandoah before. During the weekends, the campsites are crowded with children, precious few of them on their best behavior. It'll be noisy. Weekdays are best. I recommend Loft Mountain Campground. It's not necessarily the most popular site for families with kids, with no tourist shops close by. Oh, and do try to get there early. The A lots are the best. They come with some semblance of privacy, not to mention some killer views. But they go out fast." As usual, Kevin delivered his information with a deliberate lack of sensationalism, in an impassive manner. He rarely showed his feelings to people, and his boyfriend, Jack, was one of the few who could coax a truly emotional response out of him.

"Thanks, man," Bro said, his expression grateful and happy. Lacey adored seeing him like this, so effervescent, bubbling with life.

"It's at least four hours to drive there, so you better leave early," Kevin advised. "You could call them to make a reservation for a specific lot, but it's really first come, first served out there. Eat or be eaten."

"God, I love it when you get down and dirty poetic," Jack murmured wickedly next to him and leaned closer to nuzzle the big bear of a man's stubbly cheek. It wasn't Lacey's imagination that Kevin's face reddened at the teasing of the gorgeous blond.

Kevin cleared his throat and dug into his steak, lowering his face practically to the plate before him. Jack chuckled. Then Kevin suddenly jumped in his chair, while Jack looked all innocent. Lacey had a distinct feeling there were naughty things happening beneath the table, but she wisely chose to look the other way and say nothing.

Jordan had no qualms about scolding his little brother, though. "Jack, shut up and eat."

"You mean let your partner eat without getting his junk manhandled under the table," Jack said back, his tone ready for an argument.

Jordan and Kevin were partners in the Financial Crimes and Fraud Unit of the Metropolitan Police Department, while Jack was an EMT for the District of Columbia Fire and EMS Department. Sebastian was a volunteer police officer on account of being deaf, but he worked for the same department as Jordan and Kevin these days, tending to the evidence locker and to the mountains of paperwork generated by the department, being so diligent and energetic.

While Jordan and Jack bickered good-naturedly, Sebastian watched the row with rapt amusement, and Kevin buried his face in his plate, Bro was free to fondle Lacey under the table too. She felt his fingers sliding beneath the hem of her dress, trailing their leisurely way up her thighs. Lacey swallowed hard, feeling hot and perspiring again. She took a gulp of water from her glass, but then Bro's fingers found their way to her hardening cock and rubbed along the length with precision and stealth.

His downright evil grin made Lacey's heart pound. "Stop it, you fiend," she whispered, all but hissing.

"Make me," Bro dared with a low, seductive chuckle.

The only way she could do that was by causing a scene.

Lacey lifted her water glass above his head, warning with her eyes she was about to pour. "You need to cool down, boy."

Bro's hand stilled, and his wary eyes glanced at the glass, then her, then back at the glass again. Lacey could tell he was wondering if she would really carry out her threat. Then, with a total shit-eating grin, he said smugly, "Nah, you wouldn't." And his palm rubbed over Lacey's cock once more, insistently this time.

Then he let out a shrill yelp when Lacey spilled a glassful of cold water on his head.

Giggling, Lacey jumped up from her seat and ran around the table with a growling, water-spewing Bro on her heels and a tableful of men guffawing after them.

ON MONDAY morning, Bro and Lacey sat in Jordan's SUV on their way to Shenandoah. They had left early, around 5:00 a.m., both of them too excited to sleep. They still had about twenty minutes to go as the car climbed up along Skyline Drive as it wound its way up to the rocky, woodsy ridge. There was so much green around Lacey felt like she was swimming in it.

"You okay to drive the rest of the way?" she asked. They had changed seats midway.

Bro nodded with a grin. "Well, I might get a boost if you—"

"Don't even think about it." Lacey knew exactly what dirty things her boyfriend had in mind, and no way were they going to do that in the car while driving on a steep mountain road.

"Spoilsport," Bro countered, huffing in mock anger and pouting. Lacey was sure he would have been more surprised had she said yes and actually blown him right there.

Lacey laughed, shrugged, and turned her attention to the wilderness spreading outside the vehicle. She wanted to roll down the windows for lungfuls of crisp mountain air, but since they would already be sleeping outside in a tent for a couple of nights, they would be getting enough fresh air soon enough. So she snuggled into the soft, cushioned seat and enjoyed the warmth inside the car.

The Blue Ridge Mountains surrounded them, a lush jungle of vegetation with emerald-green grass and deep-green pine trees, sloping valleys and rising hills, and clouds of mist rising from the few waterfalls in these woodlands. Lacey had grown accustomed to high mountains and gushes of rain when she had lived in Seattle, in the shadow of the Cascade Mountains, and though this range had gentler inclines, it felt homey.

Although, DC was her home these days. She felt little to no longing to return to her old stomping grounds in Seattle. Her aunt, Valerie, lived there with her family, and during the summer Lacey had gotten the chance to visit her. Bro had tagged along, unsurprisingly. It had been a great sojourn, but it had gone a long way to prove to Lacey it was no longer her home.

Bro was, and she hoped he would continue to be for eons to come.

They arrived at the Loft Mountain campsite, asked the ranger what the availability was, and learned the cold morning and misty moisture had kept people away. They had gotten there at 8:30 a.m. Lacey knew Sebastian would have had a fit had he known his little brother had driven there this fast, cutting their traveling time by half an hour. Jordan would call Bro the A-word and then strangle him for speeding.

On account of their early arrival, they did, however, get a great spot on the A line, a relatively secluded section with a few concealing shrubberies around. They were able to park the car close by, forty feet away from their campsite. The ground was flat, well trod, brown and green, but that was good because they were able to pitch the tent with ease and speed, and it didn't list to any side.

In fifteen minutes, they were done and got the chance to take a leisurely look around.

They sat on the blanket in front of their tent, Bro holding Lacey in his arms, and just stared at the view. Rugged woodsy hills spread all around, with several peaks showcasing their magnificence in the distance, and deep ravines fell down toward the river, which was too far down to see. The scenery featured specks of yellow and red amid the green, too, and a light fog veiled parts of it.

"According to the map, that's the Doyle's River Trail," Bro explained, pointing down to the gully. "We're gonna take that trip tomorrow, yeah?"

Lacey leaned her head against her boyfriend's shoulder and sighed happily. "Sounds wonderful." His strong, muscular arms tightened around her as he nuzzled her neck, and she giggled at the feel of him. Her back was against his chest, which was good since the wind up on top of the mountain was harsher and colder than she had expected. It was late August, so autumn was on its way. She wondered if there was going to be snow on the trail. "What are we going to do today?"

Bro kissed her temple gently. "Relax and enjoy ourselves. Nothing complicated."

"Can we snuggle in the tent?" she asked in a whisper, though no one was around.

Bro chuckled, hot puffs of breath wafting over her ear. "Abso-fucking-lutely."

Yet neither of them made a move toward the tent.

They watched in silence as the winds swept away the gossamer fog and revealed the beauty of the midmorning wilderness landscape. The sun came out, but it looked like the day was going to remain slightly chilly.

They both lost their sense of time. Once it got a bit cold, they went into the tent and took a nap after the long drive. Lacey laid her head on Bro's chest, hearing his heartbeats in her ear, and slept like a baby. When they woke up, rested but groggy, they ate lunch—turkey on rye and apple slices—and drank hot chocolate. Dressed in their best boots, they walked about, checking out their surroundings. The sun was up but partly covered by thin clouds, and the wind had picked up. Very few people were about, and most of the tent sites were empty. It was quiet and peaceful.

Lacey held Bro's hand as they walked around the campsite, keeping on the traveled paths and not venturing into the wilderness without proper gear. The high elevation afforded them some unforgettable vistas, but they knew they would descend into deeper forests tomorrow. Most flowers from spring and summer were gone now, but the oaks, hickory, and maples provided a lush, rich feel that wasn't hampered by the inevitability of winter. There was moisture in the air, though it wasn't quite raining.

They returned to their tent slowly, in no rush, after hours of aimless wandering. Bro went to pick up dead branches and twigs for their campfire while Lacey prepared a cast iron frying pan for their evening meal, which was macaroni and cheese, premade at home and easy to reheat, plus made tastier with a few dried herbs. Bro got the fire going quickly, beaming and blushing in the light of Lacey's admiring gaze, and in less than ten minutes they were able to sit down and dine.

"Mmm, this is delicious, babe," Bro complimented Lacey, and she felt the same warm tightening in her chest she always got with him.

"I wish I could take credit for it, but I'm pretty sure Sebastian made it," Lacey replied humbly.

Bro shrugged. "Maybe. But Bas doesn't do the seasoning as well as you. And Jordan would have burnt this whole thing into a crispy, black mess by now."

Lacey laughed. "You're cruel."

Bro grinned wickedly. "Nuh-uh. I've lived through Jordan's cooking, and I can proudly state I'm a survivor."

Giggling some more, Lacey nearly choked on her meal.

Chapter 14

ONCE they were finished, they cleaned up after themselves, locking the remains of the food into a plastic container and hauling it back to the car. It seemed easier than burying it or placing it far away from the tent, as advised. Whatever midnight snacks they felt they might need if peckish—candy bars, crackers, water bottles, marshmallows, peanut butter, and dried vegetables and fruits—Bro stored in a tight plastic box and buried it under his smelly, sweaty clothing while Lacey snickered at his inventive streak. No bear would think to try and find food under that pile of odors!

Afterward, they decided to take turns in the showers located at the entrance to the campgrounds, by the store. Bro was ever the gentleman, and offered to go second, so Lacey went off on her own, taking their trash with her to dispose of in the designated dumpsters. She took the car, because she didn't want to traipse back wet, as the place was a ways off from their tent.

It was barely six p.m. once she got to the group of buildings, and still no one was around. Because of the sense of privacy she got, she looked at the women's side of the showers.

Only when she took a step toward the door, she heard a man's whistle. He wasn't a park ranger, but looked like a regular camper, an average height middle-aged man with thick hair and a scruffy beard, with an equally scruffy dog at his side.

"That side's for women. Can't you read?" he commented, snorting.

Lacey's cheeks flamed, and she couldn't find her voice.

The man laughed fully now, checking her out head to toes. "Maybe you're one of them she-boys. What you got under that dress?"

She looked down at her clothes. Lacey wore simple, tight but comfortable dark-gray sweats, a long-sleeved shirt with a slightly longer than normal hemline, and a jacket over it. There was nothing that screamed girl about her. For the purposes of this trip, she had even dispensed with her typical eyeliner, mascara, and lip gloss.

She didn't dignify him with an answer, and headed for the men's showers. Just as she was about to enter, he called after her, "Need a real man to wash your back, pretty boy?"

While not above playful teasing, Lacey did not appreciate mean taunting, especially not in a situation where a guy like that could do anything to her. So she chose to remain silent as she ducked into the dressing rooms. Her heart beat frantically as she made her way to a tiny bench, sat down, and willed herself to calm down.

There was someone in the showers, as she could hear the water running. She decided to be quick about it. Choosing a locker, Lacey undressed in a hurry, grabbed her washing kit, and made a beeline to the closest shower.

On the way there, she saw her own reflection in a mirror. Lacey was indeed a boy, no matter how much she liked girl's dresses and makeup. Blond hair, cut short in a feminine style, was ruffled by the winds, and her sun-kissed caramel-hued skin prickled in the heat of the shower room, the steam giving her goose bumps. Her slim figure had barely an ounce of fat, giving her form a petite quality instead of whip-thin or bony. Her cock wasn't as thick as she might have liked, not like Bro's, but it was of decent size, straight, and pink, and aroused it sported a very enviable length indeed. Yet hazel eyes stared back at her, huge and fearful, like a deer caught in headlights. She hated that a stranger had the ability to rattle her so.

She entered the shower space, picked an empty one, and turned on the water, placing her washing supplies on the empty metal rack.

She wet herself down, washed up, and rinsed, all in haste and in fear of some violent bigot's or closet rapist's imminent arrival.

"Soap?" a man's low, husky voice asked, and Lacey's spine went ramrod straight and cold with chills. Images of prison movie shower scenes flashed before her mind's eye. Swallowing hard, she turned, practically hearing the creak of her joints. There was an older man in one of the showers across from her, and he was offering a bar of soap, an unassuming question in his eyes. "Need to borrow?" he asked, simple kindness in his voice.

Lacey tried for a polite smile but felt the gesture was halfhearted. "Thank you, but I have my own."

The man nodded in understanding and returned to his own showering.

As she went back to her washing up, she wondered if it was always going to be like this. Men seeing a pretty little boy, ready to be a punching bag or to be gang-raped. Would she ever be able to just be herself and not raise any eyebrows or animosities from people who knew nothing about her? Though it was many months past, she could still feel the sting on her cheek where her father had struck her, hatred in his eyes and soul for a son who was "wrong" and not manly.

Warm waters washed away her hot tears, and she smothered the sobs that threatened to spill out.

Picking herself up emotionally, she turned off the water, dried herself, grabbed her stuff, and walked back to her locker. The other man was sitting on the same long bench, toweling his hair. He offered a friendly smile but didn't linger with his gaze, as if not expecting anything.

The door to the locker rooms opened loudly. A young man with visible resemblance to the older man peeked his head past the lockers. "Dad, you about ready? We're gonna head out to the amphitheater."

"Two minutes, son," the man replied with a nod. The teenager flashed a flirty grin at Lacey, and he was gone. "He's cocky, but he means well. I'm sure he didn't mean to startle you."

Lacey watched the man aim his words at her, and she forced a smile on her lips. "Oh, I'm just a scaredy-cat today. I thought it was a bear." She thought a jest might lighten the mood.

The man chuckled. "Ah. Well, Edwin can sure eat like a bear at times. Sometimes I think he's packing away to hibernate in a cave somewhere."

Lacey laughed in spite of herself. "Bro, my boyfriend, is exactly the same way." Then she realized what she had said, and the laughter died on her lips.

But the man merely nodded. "Teenage boys... I thought college tuition was all I had to prepare for. But no. I feel like I'm feeding an army."

Relieved, Lacey dared a small titter. "Occupying forces."

"You staying at the campground?" the man asked, giving her an honestly curious look.

"Yes." That was all Lacey had the courage to say. Small-time vandalism was one thing; sneak attacks during the night with murder on the brain were something else.

"So are we. In the RV section. Brought the family with us. Last romp before college starts, and then it's work, work, work." He winked as he said it, and the gesture immediately put Lacey's mind at ease. He extended his hand. "I'm sorry. Where are my manners? Irwin Hudson."

Lacey smiled and shook the offered hand. "Lacey Adair."

"This your first time up here?"

"Yes."

Irwin nodded. "The Appalachian Trail is amazing. We do it every year. Well, perhaps not next year, if we can't convince the boy to come back from college to stay with us old farts."

Lacey giggled at that, covering her mouth and feeling mildly embarrassed. "Sorry."

Irwin grinned. "No need." He waved a dismissive hand about. "You have a wonderful, memorable, and fun trip, Ms. Adair." He rose to get dressed, and Lacey followed suit. Suddenly the man spoke again, his voice lower, just above a whisper. "Is the reason you're so skittish because someone's been harassing you?"

Lacey fell silent, but only for a moment. "Some jerk mouthed off when I came in. No biggie."

Harrumphing, Irwin asked, "An unkempt little prick with a dog?" Lacey nodded, not quite sure where this was going. Irwin sure didn't sound like he was friends with that moron. "That's Miles. And you're right. He *is* a jerk." He dug into the pocket of his slacks and produced a business card. "Here's my number. If you run into trouble with Miles, you call me. We'll be in the area for another week. If you need backup with the park rangers, you just let me know."

"You believe me?" Lacey was surprised a complete stranger would take her at face value.

"That idiot was making rude remarks to my wife and son too, so yeah, I believe you." Irwin's gaze was steady and encouraging. "Be sure to call me if something happens."

"I will." Lacey nodded gratefully, tucking the card into her pocket.

"We better walk out together," Irwin suggested, putting on his coat. "Not that I think you couldn't handle yourself, Ms. Adair. But strength in numbers, as they say. Just want to make sure he's not outside waiting for you."

Lacey finished getting dressed and thanked Irwin again. They left the dressing rooms side by side, and sure enough, Miles was outside, throwing a stick to his dog, who fetched time and again. His gaze swept over Lacey and Irwin, then turned away.

After saying farewell to Irwin, Lacey climbed into her car and drove back to her tent.

Bro was waiting for her, eating a licorice stick in front of the tent. He smiled when he spotted her approaching. "And here I thought the view couldn't possibly improve."

Lacey giggled, glad to be back with her special guy. "Play your cards right, mister, and you might see something private that no other man has ever beheld." She sat down between his legs and lay back against his chest, feeling safe again.

"That sounds like a promise," he teased, kissing her temple, and his breath smelled like licorice. Lacey sighed, the tension leaving her shoulders. "Shouldn't a shower have made you less tense, not more?"

The cold dread in the pit of her stomach had melted in Bro's embrace, so Lacey felt no apprehension about sharing her recent experiences in the campground showers. Once she was done talking about Miles and Irwin, Bro was serious and inching toward angry.

"That piece of shit motherfucker," he growled out.

"Irwin was ever the gentleman and knight in shining armor," Lacey cut in. "That other guy, he doesn't matter. There's always going to be some miserable, hate-filled meanie who has it in for us. Let's just forget about him and enjoy our vacation, all right?" She turned in his arms, facing him. "I love you, Bro. Now you go take a shower, and then we can cuddle late into the night." Then she grinned naughtily. "And by cuddle, I mean—"

"On my way, gorgeous." Bro was up on his feet before he even finished his sentence, and Lacey snickered. With his supplies tucked under his arm, Bro walked to the car and drove off.

Lacey settled in to wait. She saw another couple setting up camp farther away, within eyesight but not earshot. Nonetheless, it was good to know there were people around if something were to happen. The campfire was lively, and she watched the evening wane, darkness falling over the wilderness like a shroud. White dots colored the blackening sky as the stars came up, and Lacey felt at peace.

Nothing was going to ruin this time with her boyfriend.

Chapter 15

THE dickhead mouthing off at the showers wasn't there when Bro arrived, and though he remained vigilant, Miles didn't make a reappearance. That was a good thing, Bro decided, since if he had, Bro might have been tempted to put the guy in a hurt locker.

But he got to shower and clean up all by his lonesome.

He returned to the tent and found Lacey sitting by the open flaps, watching the stars. The air was getting colder but also drier. The wet weather from earlier had gone and left a cool, crisp night in its wake.

Lacey's light-brown eyes held concern and a silent question, and Bro shook his head. "No one. Guess he took off."

The relief in Lacey was visible, and Bro went to hold her after he put his clothes and towel close to the fire to dry. He embraced his girlfriend and then snuggled in close. As usual, her hair smelled like strawberries from the shampoo, and he inhaled it deep into his lungs. When she was going to be gone for most of the day, every day, in Baltimore, Bro was going to have to learn not to think about her obsessively. The prospect sucked big hairy donkey balls, he thought glumly, after two years of seeing each other every day and nearly every hour.

They waited for their towels and damp clothes to dry before putting the fire out and cleared the site to get ready for bed. It was only 9:00 p.m., but they'd had a long day, and Bro was sure Lacey felt as exhausted as he did.

They zipped their sleeping bags together, undressed down to their underwear, and slipped in under the covers. The chilly air gave them both gooseflesh, but soon they were pressed skintight against each other, and the cold didn't matter.

Then Lacey found Bro's lips, and nothing counted but their erotic, loving intimacy.

After removing both their undies, Bro flipped Lacey on top of him so he was able to leisurely run his hands down Lacey's silky chest, smooth flanks, and satiny back, to cup the round mounds of flesh and give them a light pinch that made *him* whimper and wiggle about. When naked, Lacey was all man, a him. *My guy*.

And Lacey did indeed moan low into the kiss, so Bro got the chance to delve deep into his mouth, claiming him for all time.

The heated urgency gave way to passionate exploration, as if they hadn't slept together just last night. Lacey straddled Bro's hips, settling their cocks side by side between them, and then he started to hump and grind. Their dicks, soon slicked by precome, slid together smoothly and hotly.

It was Bro's turn to groan with pleasure.

Whenever they were together, each time felt better than the last. Rationally, Bro knew this high couldn't keep on going forever, but when he looked into his future with his mind's eye, the only constant was Lacey. He couldn't and didn't want to imagine life without him.

Bro nibbled on Lacey's full lower lip before sliding his tongue between his lips. Their slick, hot tongues met, then they entangled, and it was glorious. Bro couldn't stop kissing him. His arms tightened around his body, and Lacey shivered.

"You want to… maybe?" Lacey asked breathlessly against his lips.

Lacey's meaning was clear to Bro. They had been together for a year and nine months. It was almost two years, and they'd not had anal sex. They had done a lot of other things just as hot and intimate, but though they had talked about it many times and even started a few times, it had never come to pass.

Bro felt Lacey wasn't ready. "In a tent? Outside in the cold? Where anyone can hear us?" Bro sighed but kissed him softly to show him he understood. "I know why you want to. God knows I want to! But... just because we're going to college, doesn't mean we should rush into this. Besides, I'd like a chance to seduce you and take our time, and preferably in a proper bed." He chuckled as he spoke, hoping the sound brought enough levity into the situation.

As usual with this topic, he saw relief and disappointment war on Lacey's face. He had no doubt they both wanted to do the big *it* at some point, but there was a time, place, and a good reason for having anal sex, and none of those criteria were met here, in the semiprivacy of a national park with bears, bigots, and chilly winds just outside the thin fabric of the tent.

Finally, Lacey kissed him back, cupped his face, and then threaded his fingers through Bro's thick black hair. "I know you get it, honey. It's just... I know this is gonna sound stupid, but I don't want to go to college a... you know, a virgin." The last word was nothing but a whisper.

Laughing gently, Bro flipped them over so Lacey was underneath him. His legs wrapped around Lacey's waist, and the soles of Bro's feet bumped Lacey's round butt. "Baby, I assure you, you are *no* virgin." He thrust his hips and ground against his lover, eliciting a moan. "After all we've done, there's no way in holy hell you could be classified as a virgin."

It was Lacey's turn to giggle and blush cutely. "I guess."

Bro kissed his lips, staking his claim. Lacey wound his arms around him, and then they were pressed tight together from lips to hips. "Besides, that would only matter if you plan on advertising your experience all around campus. And babe? You had better not even think about it!"

Lacey whined playfully. "No? Darn. I was going to have it tattooed on my left cheek."

Bro snickered. "Left cheek, huh?" He grabbed the body part in question, squeezing the delectable mound. "What about the right cheek?"

Lacey looked up at him solemnly even though he was still smiling. "I was thinking of *Property of Bro*."

That statement made Bro still his motions and stare, dumbfounded and way more than a little aroused. "Huh?" His lack of the finer points of speech he attributed to the fact there was barely any blood left in his brain. All of it seemed to have rushed south, below the belt.

Lacey laughed wholeheartedly, and Bro joined him. Then they were kissing, caressing, and making love, and the outside world faded away.

THE next day, they had a quiet, relaxing breakfast, feeding each other cereal with milk and banana bits and chuckling goofily for no reason. After that, they put on their hiking gear and started their sojourn.

They chose the Doyle's River—Jones Run Trail. It wasn't the easiest trail, with a lot of uphill and downhill traversing, but the scenery more than made up for it. During their over six-mile hike, they saw three wonderful waterfalls, pools, and cascades that gushed with autumn's rains. They walked by magnificent, giant deciduous trees with colorful foliage, and amid lush ferns, nettles, and mosses that formed the thick undergrowth present everywhere. Old pastures with rich beds of fall wildflowers, rugged ravines and steep gorges, and crystal clear waters running from springs and rocky, stepped waterfalls appeared around every bend. All of these were amazing sights as the morning sun shone coldly through the green, golden, and ruddy leaves of tulip poplars, chestnuts, and maples. A light fog covered most of the panoramic views over the mountainsides, and it even veiled some of the paths into the forests, giving the woods an eerie, ghostly feel. Cool moisture hung in the air, dampening their clothes and squishing their hair. The rich smells of an autumn forest were the best. The earthy, crisp scent of fallen, decomposing leaves and the musty whiffs of ancient trees covered in moss drifted around them. The brisk air carried the odors of the season, of plants and animals, as nature transitioned from full blossoming to harvest and chilly winter, the time to slumber.

The trip demanded quite a workout from both of them. By the time they got back to the tent, they were exhausted. Still, they were excited, since they had seen white-tailed deer, gray squirrels, cottontail rabbits, and lots and lots of birds, all chirping and chattering away. They had taken pictures with their digital camera. Lacey had leaned against a large sycamore tree, smiling and waving, while Bro had posed in a quirky mock-militant stance by the Doyle's River Cabin, his cocky grin firmly in place.

They had enjoyed a few grilled chicken sandwiches and chocolate-orange coffee on the trail, making sure they were close to Skyline Drive and a parking lot, so no bears felt tempted to check them—and their snacks—out. Nonetheless, as they plopped down on the blanket in front of their tent, they were both starving and weary. The day had gone by like a whirlwind, and without them realizing it, five hours had flown by.

Bro stared at the hills in the distance, the green of the woods blending into sea green and sea blue shades, but he didn't really see it. He was too focused on breathing. "So… shower?"

"God, yes!" Lacey exclaimed in between giggles.

His legs shook as he got up again, and Bro had to lean on Lacey for a moment, and she did the same. On unsteady feet, they grabbed their washing kits, towels, and a change of clothes, and headed for their car. They drove up to the shower building and made their way inside.

As they were undressing in the empty locker room, Bro whispered in Lacey's ear, "So, you wanna play in the shower?"

Between snickers, Lacey swatted off his hand, which was following the trail of her hipbone far too suggestively. "If we do that, you'd have to carry me back to the tent, I'm so tired."

"Mmm, love my pretty damsel in distress," Bro retorted, grinning salaciously.

"Oh, God," Lacey moaned, half joking, half genuinely frustrated. "Behave, will you?"

"Never!" Bro exclaimed and stood up, posing like a hearty hero and holding up an imaginary blade. "I shall never yield, never—"

Lacey slapped a hand fiercely over his mumbling mouth, rolled her eyes, and dragged him toward the showers. They washed up next to each other, giving each other furtive glances filled with heat and love. Yet they didn't touch, except for washing each other's backs.

The hot water cascading over Bro's shoulders smoothed the aches in muscles he had barely acknowledged before this trip. They hadn't carried much of anything in their backpacks, but the constant climbing up and down had been a test of their abilities and strength. Bro felt sleepiness wash over him, but he resisted the alluring siren's call. His rumbling stomach reminded him of more pressing needs.

He got out of the shower and returned to the lockers, drying himself off.

As he got there, a scruffy-looking man was checking out Lacey's closed locker door.

"Can I help you?" Bro asked, and the man whipped around, startled.

His gaze was definitely not amiable. "Who the fuck are you?"

The man was shorter and older than Bro, and not in good shape, not like Bro, whose life revolved around football and a variety of other sports. There was no way the guy could take him on, so Bro snorted, quirking an eyebrow. "I could ask you the same thing. But since I know that's not your locker, why don't you shove off?"

"What's going on here?"

A third voice joined in. A man dressed in a park ranger's green uniform came into view, his blond hair peeking out from under his green ball cap. He eyed the interaction between Bro and the man he now knew to be Miles, the jerk, warily.

Miles sneered loudly, looking at Bro. "That faggot came on to me."

At that Bro scoffed. "Yeah, right. In your dreams, asshole. I have someone special in my life, and she ain't you."

Exactly at that moment, Lacey rounded the corner, drying her hair, and then she stopped dead in her tracks, her eyes wide in surprise.

Miles laughed, but it wasn't a joyful sound. "That's your *girl*? Man, you've been duped big time!" He shook his head, his disgust evident. "Fucking faggots…. You've got no place here among us good folk—"

"You must be referring to someone else, *pal*, because *you*'re not good folk by anyone's standards," Bro growled out vehemently.

Miles stepped forward, his face twisted into a snarl.

The ranger stopped him with a hand over his chest. "Don't even think it, mister. Time for you to go. Now." He emphasized the last word with his tone, which had dropped so dangerously low it reverberated around the room.

"You're taking their side?" Miles shouted, incredulous and pissed off. "What the hell kind of man are you?"

The ranger's blue eyes narrowed, and Miles stopped. "I'm an officer of the law. And you? You're two seconds away from being hauled out of here in cuffs."

Blinking hard, as though he couldn't believe what was happening, Miles grumbled under his breath and then stormed out. The door slammed shut with a loud bang after him.

Bro let out a breath but then straightened his back, ready to face the consequences. "I'm sorry, sir. I shouldn't have taken that tone with him. I saw he was angling for a fight." He felt Lacey's warmth press at his back, and he leaned a bit into the touch.

The ranger shook his head. "No, it's all right. You had the right to defend yourself." He looked at Lacey behind Bro. "Dad told me Miles had been up to no good yesterday, so I made sure to keep an eye on him. Good thing he doesn't know rangers don't carry cuffs." He winked at them in a conspiratorial manner.

"Dad...?" Lacey asked, bewildered.

The ranger grinned. "Yes. Irwin Hudson. I'm TJ, his other son. I work here."

Lacey stepped forward, despite having only a loose towel around her hips, and shook the man's hand. "I'm Lacey. Your father was very kind to me."

TJ shook her hand with a smile. "Nice to meet you. Dad spoke about you a lot last night. You made quite an impression on him."

Lacey ducked her head and blushed like a forest fire.

Bro hastened to speak to spare her discomfort. "I'm Bro, Lacey's boyfriend. Thanks for all your help. It could've gotten ugly. We didn't come here to make a scene or cause trouble. This is our first visit here."

TJ nodded. "I've told the other rangers to keep an eye on Miles. He comes here every year, and he's being a prick more often than not." He looked at both of them, curious. "Listen, this may not be what you want to hear but, uh… Dad wondered if you would like to join us for lunch tomorrow."

Lacey exchanged glances with Bro, and he saw her bubbling excitement. "We'd love to. Thanks for the invite."

"Good." TJ gave them a comradely chin lift, as if they had known each other years instead of a few minutes, and headed for the door. "I'll see you two tomorrow, then. In the meantime I'll keep my eye on Miles." Then he was out the door.

Bro hugged Lacey, who shivered in his arms. "I'm sorry, baby. I shouldn't have egged that moron on."

"If he bothers us again—" Lacey started, worried.

"Then we'll get the rangers to intervene. It'll be all right." He petted her still-wet hair, and stroked down her long, slender back. "Come on. Get dressed. I won't have you getting sick this close to start of college, got that?" He let her go and slapped her butt through the terry cloth.

"Ow!" Lacey protested, rubbing her behind with exaggerated annoyance. Bro laughed, and she finished getting dressed.

Once dry and dressed, they returned to their car. TJ was in the parking lot, talking on the radio of a patrol vehicle, a white SUV with a green stripe and the words "U.S. Park Ranger" on the sides. He nodded kindly as Lacey and Bro got into their car and drove off. Apparently Miles had taken a hike, and that was good news as far as Bro was concerned.

They returned to their tent. Bro made them a quick meal of previously grilled chicken and mashed potatoes, reheated in the frying pan, while Lacey took out her violin and started to play a flickering piece of music that sounded like water dripping and then wind whistling, sorrowful and yet hopeful.

"What is that piece?" he asked, curious and enchanted by her talent, as usual.

Lacey smiled. "'Silk Road' by Kitaro. Typically played on a synthesizer, but I love the melody so. I know I can't do it justice with just one violin, though."

"I think it sounds wonderful."

"You would say that 'cause you're biased."

"Nope. Actually the opposite is true. I already know I can get into your pants so I can afford to tell you the truth."

Bro winked at his lover, who blushed deeply, obviously pleased with the compliments. They smiled at each other for a while, without a care in the world and caring about one another so much, and the soft sounds of Lacey's violin carried off with the winds.

The notes drifted off, and Lacey set her instrument aside, and they sat down by the fire to eat.

"Oh, this is quite good," Lacey commented, nudging her boyfriend with her shoulder.

"Thanks—I think," Bro grumbled, knowing full well his talents did not lie in cuisine.

"Don't be so grumpy. I meant it. This is more than edible."

"I didn't make it, just reheated it."

"If you were Jordan, we'd be eating something burnt to a crisp."

That did lift Bro's mood, and he perked up, smiling. "You're right. At least I'm better than one man on the planet when it comes to cooking."

Lacey laughed, and the sound made Bro ridiculously happy.

After dinner they spent the rest of the day with Lacey playing the violin softly, not to bother any nearby campers, and Bro listening, lying on his back on the quilt, staring at the sky and damn near bursting with love and joy.

As the evening waned, they retired to the safety of their tent and nestled side by side in their sleeping bag, making out leisurely. The lovemaking lasted for the better part of an hour until the tide swept them away, and the wave of pleasure crested, leaving them in a heap of tired limbs and heaving chests. With weary hands, Bro cleaned them up with a wet napkin, and then they promptly fell asleep.

Chapter 16

"MR. HUDSON? Good morning, sir," Lacey greeted the old man by a huge white RV.

Irwin's smile widened with recognition, and immediately he walked up to her and Bro, extending his hand. "Good to see you both. Glad you could make it. Please, come and sit with us."

There was a tarp attached to the roof of the RV, and the canopy spread out to cover the patio-style folding chairs and table by the side of the vehicle. An older woman with ash blonde hair with silver streaks was sitting on one of the chairs, knitting away.

Irwin gestured toward her with obvious pride and love. "This is Bethany, the old ball and chain." He winked as she glared at him and then smiled too.

"And that old coot you've already met," she said. Her voice was high-pitched, and Lacey found herself wondering what her singing voice sounded like. "Hello. I'm Bethany, but you can call me Beth." She put the knitting aside, rose up, and extended her hand. "You must be Lacey." Lacey shook her hand, nodding. "Irwin was quite taken with you yesterday. It's great to see young people unafraid to be who they are."

"Aww, Mom, you're sounding like a teachers' infomercial again."

The owner of the whine was the teenage boy Lacey had seen yesterday at the showers, Edwin. That meeting had been over before she knew it, but now she got the chance to study him more carefully. He had dark hair like Bro, but unlike Bro, Edwin's hair curled more and was a lighter shade. His eyes were a deep sea green, and his muscular body, encased in raggedy jeans and a worn gray hoodie, suggested he was into sports. He had a five o'clock shadow, which gave him a rugged look, older than his teenage years, adding to the natural, sexy look.

Beth pursed her lips as she shot a fierce glare at her son. "Ignore the lack of manners my son Edwin is sporting. He's the runt, you see, and thinks he can get away with anything."

"And that's usually right, too," Edwin laughed and nodded his greetings to both Bro and Lacey. "Oh, and it's Eddy, by the way. Not Edwin."

It wasn't Lacey's imagination that his gaze lingered on Bro a bit longer than normal and those appreciative eyes checked Bro's body out with a hint of a smile. It sparked Lacey's jealous streak, but she held her tongue. At least it seemed Bro was none the wiser.

Beth shook Bro's hand as well, and another round of introductions went by.

"Is that a violin?" Beth asked, all excited, pointing at the fiberglass violin case Lacey had felt reluctant to leave in the car.

"Yes. I play the violin. I'm starting my freshman year at the Peabody Conservatory."

"Oh, that's amazing," Beth declared, her eyes sparkling. "Will you play for us?"

Lacey hesitated, but after an encouraging smile from Bro, she nodded. "All right." She placed the case on the table, opened it, and pulled the violin out. "Any requests?"

"Something fast," Eddy opted, leaning back in his chair to listen.

Lacey acquiesced and started the tight-paced melody of "Shadows" by Lindsey Stirling, an original song by the talented young violinist. Lacey didn't have any electro house instruments to add to the score, but she managed well. It was one of her favorite modern violin pieces, and she let herself fly as the notes soared higher and faster with every nuance, until the music took flight along with the movements of her slender frame as she swayed in place, her hips in constant motion.

Closing her eyes, she lost herself in the rhythm, adding to the beat with her foot tapping against the ground. Her bow hand flew and her fingers danced on the strings, seducing her audience and enticing more and more out of her delicate instrument.

When she finished it was eerily quiet, and she opened her eyes, wary of her welcome.

Everyone had sat down around the table, and they were staring at Lacey, eyes wide with wonder and mouths gaping open. Even Bro looked dazzled, smiling.

"My God, that was beautiful," Beth said, sighing deep, and her eyes were moist.

Lacey blushed in the face of such a reaction and bowed slightly. "Thank you kindly."

Eddy was in pretty much the same condition as his mother. "Wow... I've never heard anything like that with a violin. Fucking amazing."

"Eddy," Beth reproached mildly, her eyes still on Lacey, who felt like squirming but resisted the urge.

"There's an electro beat to the actual song, but I left my drums in my other jacket."

Laughing, Eddy said, "Cool."

"You are a very talented young woman," Irwin said with admiration and respect, smiling. "Peabody's lucky to have you." His gaze focused on Bro. "Is that where you're going too, son?"

"No, sir." Bro shook his head, rueful. "Not a musical bone in my body, unfortunately. I'm going to Howard U in DC."

"Really? That's where *I'm* going." Eddy's enthusiasm increased the unease in Lacey. The guy was handsome, totally hot, and Bro had never been with a guy who wasn't Lacey, but maybe now.... She didn't even want to think about the many temptations college was going to offer a guy like Bro, who was everyone's best friend. "Wow, this is so cool. We can hang out."

"Sure." Bro grinned widely, genuinely, and Lacey felt her stomach plummet down to her feet. How could either of them resist all those enticements their new separate lives would throw their way?

Eddy might not have seemed like Bro's type, but Bro hadn't played the field—yet.

Suddenly Lacey wanted to leave, to crawl into her sleeping bag, draw the covers over her head, and bury herself into a dark, warm place where her boyfriend was still hers.

Irwin was a sharp man, though. "Well, I know we may be asking a lot of you, Lacey, but would you do an old man a favor, and play something else? I'm sure we would all love to hear more."

With a tiny nod, Lacey lifted her violin back under her chin, the resin warm and a little bit sticky on her skin, and started the song. A slower, haunting melody spread from her violin into the crisp mountain air, the nearly shrill notes rising higher, taking them all on a journey. Soon the intensity grew to a crescendo, and then the melody suddenly dropped back to slow, delicate, and small, with only a few faint sounds here and there.

When she ended, Irwin was exalted, his voice hoarse as he asked, "What was that piece?"

"Yeah, it sounded kind of familiar," Eddy remarked, frowning in contemplation.

Lacey smiled. "It was 'Misty Mountains' from the first Hobbit movie."

Eddy clapped his forehead. "That's right! Damn, I must've heard that song like a million times, since that's about how many times I've seen the movie, so… I'm so stupid for not realizing sooner! But hey, that was fucking brilliant."

"And appropriate too," Irwin cut in, grinning. They were in a national park, after all.

Lacey giggled. "Thank you."

"Come on, let's eat," Irwin said and returned to his grill, from which gray plumes of smoke and delicious aromas of beef rose and scattered into the winds. He picked up a big plate and gathered steaks, ribs, and sausages on it. Beth had gone into the RV, and brought out potato salad and green fruit salad.

Bro made room next to his chair for Lacey, who put her violin away and sat down, keeping the instrument in her lap, as close as always. His hand clutched hers under the table, and it no longer mattered what kind of googly eyes Eddy may have directed at Bro. Relieved and still very much in love, she squeezed back.

As she took a few bites of every dish, Lacey asked Irwin, "What do you do, sir?"

"For a living? Nothing, not anymore. I'm retired. I was a member of the National Park Service, in the mountain and wilderness search and rescue back in the day."

"Ah, I see. That's where your son TJ gets the drive."

"Yes, TJ's into the family legacy all the way." The pride in his voice and expression were evident. "And, please, call me Irwin."

"Irwin. Thank you for telling your son to look out for us."

Irwin's face grew serious. "TJ told me Miles harassed you two again in the showers. I swear that cocky bastard gets more aggressive with every year that passes."

"Irwin, language," Beth scolded, but gently patted his hand on the table.

"What are you going to study at Howard U?" Bro asked Eddy to change the subject. "You gonna be a ranger like your brother and father?"

"Nah. Computer sciences, and maybe communications too, plus I run track. You?"

"Football. And… other stuff, yet to be determined." Bro's cheeks turned ruddy with the admission, but Lacey held his hand tighter, silently conveying her feelings toward him. Bro had yet to determine what besides Lacey and football he wanted out of life, and figuring out a major to study was still in the wind.

Eddy nodded with complete understanding. "I hear ya. I'm taking computer classes 'cause I know the buggers, and it allows me to run track. Other than that, I've got no clue about what I want to do the rest of my life."

Bro grunted back in total agreement. "It'll come to me, right? I'll figure it out in time. Hopefully before they boot me off the team."

Eddy stared at him with amused disbelief. "You can't be on the team since you're not in school yet."

Bro shared a conspiratorial wink. "No, I'm not. But I will be."

"Oooh, self-confidence." Eddy's tone indicated he was much impressed with Bro.

"Balls of steel." Bro said it matter-of-factly, with a serious expression and grave tone. And then he and Eddy burst out laughing, virtually in unison, already buddies.

Lacey plastered a smile on her face, though she felt like an outsider all of a sudden.

There's no doubt about it. Eddy wants Bro for himself. And them being so far away at Howard, how could I stop either of them making a move on one another? Lacey swallowed hard but tried to keep up a brave face. Insecurities had never run amok in her head, not like this. She had never had cause to doubt Bro's fidelity.

But then again, all three of them were eighteen, on their way to college, and whatever came with that was bound to be exciting and enticing. Besides, Eddy surely was hot as hell and sexy as sin. And most importantly, he would be there while Lacey was in Baltimore, over an hour away. What kind of competition could she be for a determined, seductive pursuer, if that was the way Eddy wanted to go?

Irwin seemed to sense the change in the mood because he said, "Don't you boys make too-hasty plans. Eddy's there to study and get a profession, not to hang around parties and sleep the days away. If I hear otherwise...." His stern expression was half-serious, half-playful, but Eddy nodded.

"Yeah, yeah, Dad. I'll be hitting the books morning, noon, and night, nonstop until I get a heart attack or nervous breakdown from all the stress, and end up back home living with you guys as a no-good bum."

He and Bro chortled together, and Lacey realized then that apart from Bradley, Bro didn't have a lot of close friends. In fact, he knew a lot of guys, but they were teammates or chums, not bosom buddies, so to speak. Perhaps Bro was simply longing for male companionship, a bonding of like minds, and Eddy fit the bill.

God knew Lacey had entirely different dispositions and pursuits. She was far from the kind of masculine ideal a man was supposed to be, while Bro personified the all-American jock from head to toes.

Did Bro want a career in football? Lacey wondered. He'd said so a couple of times, but college could change a person's plans. So far, though, Bro seemed into the sport. But did he want to make it into a living? Because if he did, he would be in for a rough ride if he was openly gay. Especially if he was in a relationship with a feminine boy like Lacey. But if Bro were with someone like Eddy, a muscular sports god, they could snuff out a lot of misconceptions about homosexuality. Sure, some people would still ask who was the man and who the woman because they were ignorant idiots, but others would see it as more natural in the sporting world than a player with a girlish boyfriend.

And that was the first time since she and Bro had gotten back together that Lacey began to feel maybe the two of them would go on to lead completely different and separate lives. And maybe that was for the best for both of them.

Lacey's chest constricted in pain at the mere idea of a future without the man she loved with all her being. Unshed tears brimmed in her eyes, and she lowered her gaze, fighting back the waterworks. The ache inside was born of doubt and fear, and those things were difficult to quell once they got a hold of you.

"Are you okay, Lacey?" Irwin asked, concerned, his voice low enough to be muffled by the rapid-fire talk between Bro and Eddy.

"Yes, I'm fine." She dug into her meal, faking high spirits. "Mmm, this is good."

Irwin was unconvinced of her apparent cheerful mood, and his grim gaze took in Eddy, then Bro, and finally landed on Lacey. "Eddy's a flirt. He wouldn't try to steal your—"

"No, no, of course not. I'm not worried. I had, um, music stuff on my mind." Lacey hoped she had been reassuring enough. She was his guest and did not want to go about accusing his son of being too friendly with her boyfriend.

Irwin and Beth seemed to be communicating without words, with eyes only, and then Beth said, out of the blue, "Okay, who's ready for some apple pie? Eddy, would you be a dear and fetch it for us?"

Startled by the sudden address, Eddy blinked a few times and then seemed to get his head in gear. "Yeah, sure, Mom. Coming right up." He got up and disappeared into the shadows of the RV.

"I hope you've all saved room for pie," Beth said with levity, chuckling as she picked up the dirty plates and replaced them with new ones—all paper.

"Who wouldn't want pie?" Bro said with incredulity, a mock shocked expression on his face, and Lacey had to smile. "Honestly."

"How silly of me." Beth went along with the joke, adding a self-deprecating comment and shaking her head. Irwin laughed heartily.

Eddy returned with a dish of apple pie. There was no steam, so it must have been made earlier and simply reheated. Lacey wouldn't have minded eating it cold. "I brought vanilla sauce too, Mom," Eddy said with a grin as he set the tray down, took the transparent plastic top off, and put a slice of apple pie on everyone's plate. He placed a tiny carton of vanilla sauce in the middle of the table and then sat down with the others.

"Dig in, everybody," Beth said happily.

"Is there any left for me?" came a voice from down the path, and TJ came into view.

"Always, honey," Beth replied sweetly as TJ joined them at the table and greeted their guests with quick nods before devouring his piece of the pie and sipping a cup of coffee. "Easy there, or have you turned into a hungry, hungry hippo?"

"More like a bear," Eddy needled and growled loudly.

TJ ignored his mother and brother and turned to Bro and Lacey. "I got a report from another park ranger. Miles has gone into the woods. We have no idea where he's gone. If he tries to camp out, we'll find him."

Bro frowned. "You're doing a whole Dr. Kimble manhunt 'cause that dickhead—um, guy—couldn't keep his bigoted mouth shut?"

TJ shook his head and swallowed down his pie before speaking. "Nah. Since we've been keeping an eye on him, we saw him vandalize a vehicle at another car park nearby. He went off into the woods before he could be apprehended. That guy's bad news all right."

Lacey was worried, and she bit her lower lip, anxious. "Is he dangerous?"

With an increase of pressure, Bro kept a fierce hold of Lacey's hand. "I won't let him hurt you, babe. Not in a million years."

"Should we get a room at a motel, or something?" Lacey knew she sounded like a frightened child or, dare she say it, a girl. The trouble was she had history with physical abuse, and violence made her shudder deep down inside, even after all this time of being safe with Bro and his family. *Their* family. "Bro...." Her voice trailed off.

With that one word, Bro obviously knew how she felt, even though he usually wasn't the type to back down. "If it'll make you feel better, we can check into a lodge nearby."

Why was violence, from family or strangers, always going to ruin her life? No way, not this time, she decided. "No, it's all right. This is our vacation. No one's going to make me tuck in my tail and run. Not anymore."

Irwin frowned. "I take it there's a story behind there." When neither Lacey nor Bro had an explanation to offer, he simply nodded. "TJ will take care of you, no matter what you decide."

Lacey was grateful. There were still good and decent people around, though it was hard to remember sometimes. "Thank you kindly."

"No need to thank us," Beth said with a smile. "You've given us the gift of music, and I for one couldn't have imagined a better way to spend the day."

WHEN Lacey and Bro returned to their car and drove back to their tent, the evening was well under way. They had spent the whole afternoon with the Hudson family, sans TJ, who had to return to work, and it had been a great day making new friends.

The moment the tent flaps opened and Lacey was able to climb inside her sleeping bag, she fell into a stupor of exhaustion. Thankfully, Bro remained to guard her, or so she thought when she felt the covers being drawn up to cover her back as she lay on her stomach.

She dreamt of feverish images of romps through the woods with a naked Bro giving her chase, a maddeningly smug laughter echoing through the lush, tropical vegetation.

When she awoke an hour or so later, she was confused, and not in the least because she couldn't recall if the gigantic god of muscle-bound delight called Bro had caught her in the dream and rammed his gargantuan dick inside her.

In any case, she was a sweaty, trembling heap as she sat up and stared around with bleary eyes, searching for her guy—who was nowhere in sight.

"Bro...?" Lacey called out, but no one answered. Though slightly concerned, she was sure she was overreacting. He must have gone to take a shower or something. Lacey was certain he would be back soon.

Groggy and stiff all over, she groaned as she got out of the tent and straightened up, pressing her hands on her lower back to help with the task. The stars had risen, and she checked on her cell phone, tucked into her pocket, and saw the time was 8:33 p.m. There was a light mist hanging above the ground and woven into the foliage.

"Hey."

She turned around, expecting Bro, but came face to face with Miles, the bigoted jerk.

Stunned into silence, Lacey backed up a step instinctively. "W-what do you want?"

Miles grinned, and his gaze wandered over her body. "What's the matter, little girl? The company of a real man scares you?"

Lacey felt her belly tighten into a heavy knot, but her rage also stirred inside her, the spark kindling into a flame. "Funny. I don't see any real men when I look at you."

Miles's smile vanished, and a vicious snarl replaced it. "Watch that fucking mouth of yours, little she-boy."

"Make me." Lacey wasn't as tall or heavy as Miles, but she was fast and strong in a way that violent man could never understand. To get up, dress up like a girl, and leave the house every day to face ridicule, hate, and even the threat of violence was a feat few of these so-called real men could do. Oh yes, Lacey was as powerful within as they came.

Closing the gap between them in a flurry of movement, Miles made to grab at her arms. Lacey's foot came up swiftly and she kicked him in the knee. He fell down on the other knee, shouting vehemently.

"You fucking bitch!"

What Lacey kept to herself was the martial arts training she'd received from Jordan. With that in mind, she could hold her own for a time in order to facilitate running away.

And that was what she did, dashing around him toward the paved road—where their SUV was shining in its conspicuous absence. *Where's Bro? I need you.*

Then she remembered her violin was still in the tent. She couldn't afford to leave it to be destroyed. Her whole future depended on it.

Stilling, she turned around.

Her eyes widened in shock. Miles was stumbling toward her as fast as he could with a bum knee, cursing like a pirate of old, and he had some kind of blade in hand. And he was so damn close already.

Bro, where are you?

Chapter 17

"LACE, get down!"

Lacey recognized Bro's voice and hit the ground before the words had rang out. The hairs on her nape stood out when she heard an electric rattling sound, then a sharp grunt, and then a heavy thud when Miles's body landed not three feet away from her.

But then strong, familiar arms picked her up, came around her swiftly, and Lacey was safe again.

"Oh God, Lace. You okay, babe? Talk to me." Bro's alarmed litany came out in a tight string of fast-paced words.

Lacey hugged her boyfriend hard and buried her face in his neck. "If you'd let me get a word in edgewise, I'd tell you I'm fine. I'm all right now." Her body still tingled and hummed with the excitement and adrenaline of the moment, but her heartbeat began to calm the instant Bro was wrapped around her. His effect on her was instinctive and encompassing.

"Oh, Jesus fucking Christ, Lace," he whispered in her ear, a quiet desperation making his tone tremor. "I about died when I saw you kick him, and him coming after you like some kind of monster from those shitty horror movies."

"I wouldn't know. I don't watch those. Too scary. My life's plenty scary as it is." She managed a soft chuckle. "I'm in the mood for a romantic comedy this upcoming weekend."

"Sure, Lace. Anything you want. Anything." He held her tight, swaying them both in place. Time became irrelevant as he enveloped her with his muscular jock's frame.

Until a courteous cough caught their attention, and they reluctantly drew apart.

It was TJ, and his handsome face was grim. "Lacey, how are you?"

"Shaken and stirred. But no worse for wear." The appearance of nonchalance was more important to her now than ever, for she got enough crap about being too girly.

A ghost of a smile graced TJ's lips for a second. "Did he hurt you?"

"No. He didn't get that far."

"Why the hell did you stop running?" Bro asked, anger in his voice.

"In the rush I forgot the violin in the tent. If Miles had smashed it, I'd have to kiss my future good-bye. I can't afford a new violin."

Bro looked up into the sky, as if praying for patience or guidance. "Oh. My. God."

"That's enough about my reprehensible actions," Lacey commented, her own body flaming with anger. "Where were you all this time?"

Bro looked embarrassed then, and he sucked in his lips the way he only did when he was both ashamed and furious. "I went to get some stuff from the car after you'd fallen asleep, and I found…. Well, let's just say Jordan's car is gonna need work."

Lacey felt the blood draining from her face. "What?"

It was TJ's turn to speak. "Bro drove up to show me. Miles keyed your car. Now it says faggot, cocksucker, and queer on the sides and the hood of the car." He looked about as angry and embarrassed as Bro had a moment ago.

Lacey's shoulders slumped when she sighed. "Jordan's gonna kill me."

"No, I do think he's gonna kill *me*," Bro countered, thumbing at his own chest. "Fuck. I promised nothing would happen to his precious pimped-out ride."

"Jordan loves you like a brother. I'm the one who isn't part of the—"

"Don't you fucking dare finish that sentence!" Bro's eyes shot lightning at Lacey with a kind of righteous indignation that made Lacey feel loved, appreciated, and safe. And it wasn't like it was true, anyway. Bro's family was Lacey's family now. There was no refuting it. The words may have come from a place of shame, guilt, and fear, but with these good people around, she didn't need to be alone.

"Sorry, honey." She bowed her head but peered up at her boyfriend from under her long lashes. "Forgive me?"

"Of course." Bro hugged her again, and all was well.

Only, it wasn't. "Is Miles dead?" she asked, both concerned and... not concerned.

TJ shook his head, glancing over his shoulder, where two other rangers had picked up Miles's body and carried him toward a park ranger's truck, grunting with the man's weight. "Nah. We just tasered him. He'll be out for the count. We'll take him to an emergency room for a checkup—in handcuffs. He's got multiple charges on him now. Your car, unfortunately, wasn't the only he vandalized."

"Great. What a grade-A asshole," Bro muttered under his breath.

TJ dug in his pocket and extended Bro a card and an official form. "Fill this out and send it back to me. It's so you can get reimbursed by your insurance company for fixing the damage Miles did. And... so you know where to direct the call if this Jordan fellow wants to talk to someone about what happened to his car." TJ gave a weak smile to Lacey. "I'm just glad we got here before he did anything... worse." He tipped his imaginary hat to both of them. "It was nice meeting you both. Have a safe trip home."

Then TJ Hudson walked off with his comrades, and Bro and Lacey were left alone.

At the exact same moment they looked at each other.

"Motel?"

"God, yes!"

THE next day passed by without incident.

Bro and Lacey checked into the Big Meadows Lodge, and as compensation for their ordeal they got one of the separate rustic cabins on the grounds. The room, of light-toned wood, was warm and inviting—though it had two single beds instead of a queen or a king. But it didn't matter. They simply made their home on one of the singles for the night. It was a close squeeze, but it was by far the best thing as far as Lacey was concerned.

Sure, there was no air conditioning or TV in the cabin, but since they spent only one night in there it was inconsequential. They hiked along nearby trails, met a couple of TJ's ranger friends, and had a full meal in the fireplace-warmed dining room at the lodge. And having their own private bathroom was a definite plus, though they didn't fully get to enjoy it on such a short stay.

Their stay at the cabin for one night and two half days crowned their vacation, last one of the summer before college. Two half days filled with early autumn nature culminated in a single night filled with pleasurable, slow lovemaking. It was as if Bro was determined to relish and worship every inch of Lacey's body, from lips to toes, and he spent an almost indecent amount of time sucking and licking his nipples, neck, and even fingers.

"Love these tiny fingers," he said once, taking them into his mouth and licking around them in the same lazy circles he did Lacey's cock. "They're so unassuming, yet so powerful. They make such beautiful music."

"You play *me* like an instrument for sure," she teased him gently, and her reward was a thorough kiss on her lips. Then a series of devout smooches landed on her as he went down, and finally a delicious open-mouthed kiss enveloped her cock whole, and Lacey was a heap of jelly.

These precious shards of time crystallized within her memory, and she never wanted to forget.

But… all too soon their vacation time was at an end, and the long drive back home lay ahead. They checked out of the lodge just before three on Thursday afternoon and got home after eight, both tired from the journey—and two bouts of morning sex, once in bed and once in the shower. So if they were worn out, it was their own fault, mostly anyway.

Jordan and Sebastian came out to greet them. Then Jordan saw the car and flipped out. Well, Lacey saw it more as internal combustion, with only a tiny visible tick on his jaw.

"Jordan, I'm so sorry," Bro whispered, his face ashen and all but crumbling.

Lacey stepped forward to try and explain. "There was a man at the park. He called me names and kept following us. Then he did this and attacked me—"

"What?" From Jordan's expression, a stormy one of an angel of retribution, it was clear he didn't give a rat's ass about his car anymore.

"Bro, tell us everything," Sebastian asked, his face as grave as his fiancé's.

And so Bro did, with Lacey providing additional information about Miles, the bigoted jerk. They both ended their story with swift assurances that the man was injured and behind bars. Bro gave Jordan the official form. "TJ gave us this. It'll clear things with the insurance company, he said."

Jordan took the papers without so much as a glance at them. There was that tick again, and then he grabbed Bro into a fierce embrace, as if wanting to reassure himself Bro was safe and unharmed. Then he gestured for Lacey to approach, and once Lacey came closer, she too was yanked into a familial group hug, with Sebastian throwing his arms around all of them as well.

"Oh, is it group hug time already?" came a mock cooing baby voice from the doorway into the apartment building. Jack stared at them, amused, like they were all crazy, but when the huggers drew apart, the view to the car was unblocked. Jack inhaled sharply. "What the fuck?"

Bro repeated the story, and Jack's expressive face showed every nuance of the narrative in his emotional reactions, from curiosity and anger to frustration and fear, all the way to relief that the tale had a happy ending.

"Jesus fucking Christ, you people can't be left alone for two fucking seconds—"

"Shut up, brother, or I'll make you swallow those words," Jordan growled. Lacey was well versed enough in this blended family dynamic to know how protective they were of each other. They had all lost people from their so-called real families, for a variety of reasons, so they clung tight to the ones they had gathered around each other.

Jack apparently got the message loud and clear too, and he hung his head. "Sorry."

Lacey smiled to alleviate the tension and said, "If you think you just got a scolding, you should've been there when Bro chided me for not running away from Miles." She shuddered in an exaggerated manner and gave Bro a mock bashful look with a theatrical trembling of her lower lip, most repentant.

Bro burst into laughter. "That's true. You should see her red backside too."

Reddening up to her scalp, Lacey gulped hard. No spanking had occurred, but Bro was trying, like her, to bring levity to the grim expressions around them, so she understood. She winked salaciously and sent her guy an air kiss.

Bro snickered, and then his eyes darkened.

"Okay, let's take this show inside," Sebastian suggested, chuckling at the shift in the mood toward the erotic.

But Bro stopped in front of Jordan. "I'll pay you back for—"

"No, you won't. I'm gonna make that dickhead pay for this, mark my words." Jordan's green eyes glinted like emeralds, and even from the sidelines it was clear to Lacey the detective wasn't going to back down. If Bro had wanted to butt heads, the two of them could easily have been at it all day, but thankfully Bro relented and nodded his quiet consent.

Hand in hand, their fingers interlaced, Lacey and Bro walked into their home.

NEXT day, Lacey drove up to Baltimore for orientation at the Peabody Conservatory.

It was pointless to argue with Bro, who had decided to donate his personal college fun-and-emergency fund so Lacey could get a car.

That boy could be so stubborn! Uselessly, Lacey had declared she could get a used car, but that was when the whole gang (read: blended family) joined forces against her and vetoed her suggestion. Instead, everyone added to the slush fund Bro had started accumulating since he hit thirteen, and lo and behold, Lacey had a new ride, a Toyota Land Cruiser Prado. And this midsize compact SUV was painted golden yellow because Bro knew it was her favorite color.

Though overwhelmed by the generosity of her new family, she accepted the offering and vowed to come up with a suitable return gift for all of them. She'd have to put her thinking cap on for this one. At least Bro didn't need a car since he already owned a used maroon Dodge Durango he had gotten a year ago for a couple of grand.

Though orientation didn't start until 10:00 a.m., Lacey started the trip at eight, just to be on the safe side. She hated being late for anything, least of all for something important. Though it was a busy working Friday, traffic was leisurely and steady on the Baltimore-Washington Parkway, with no sudden jerks from other vehicles to impede her or force her off the road.

And the company was delightful too.

Mr. Teasdale was Lacey's violin teacher and friend. Well, maybe not a close friend, but a friend nonetheless. After all, he was an adult, and Lacey wasn't always sure how to bridge the age gap. "Are you excited?" he asked. He was already bouncing on his seat, more than eager to see the famed conservatory.

"I'm trying not to throw up." Lacey felt nauseated, and all her anxieties were revving up her internal worry engine. "I know I got in, but I'm sick to my stomach. What if I'm not good enough? What if they kick me out? What if—?"

"Lacey, I assure you from the bottom of my heart you have nothing to worry about."

She wished she had her teacher's confidence. "Really?"

"Absolutely. Now stop fretting, and drive." Mr. Teasdale wiggled on his seat. "Gosh, I need to—" He stopped abruptly and reddened up to his eyeballs. It wasn't difficult to tell what was wrong.

Lacey suppressed a snicker and felt at ease again. The simplest things calmed her. "It'll be a half an hour still. Can you hold it, or should I get off at the nearest exit and find a gas station, or something?"

"I'll be fine, thank you very much," Mr. Teasdale replied, straightening up on his high horse and lifting his chin defiantly. With his glasses and mussed-up hair, he epitomized a scholastic nerd, and Lacey burst into laughter.

After that, the half-hour ride was a piece of cake.

They had an unobstructed view of the traffic circle around the Washington monument and museum as they parked in front of the tall, white building with big windows and an impressive facade. A promenade with tall trees added some greenery to two sides of the building. There was a two-hour parking limit, but Mr. Teasdale vowed to take care of any problems that might arise.

For a moment Lacey felt conflicted about all these people who weren't her flesh and blood, doing her favors and asking for nothing in return. It was a tad unsettling. But one stern look from her teacher, as if he were a mind reader, changed her mind about discussing it now.

Instead, they walked into the grandiose building in search of the admissions office.

Nervous once again, Lacey allowed Mr. Teasdale to lead and briefly considered the wisdom of having her high school violin teacher accompanying her. She doubted anyone else had a babysitter/chaperone with them. Yet as she walked down the halls, no one seemed to notice or take an extra gander at them. Perhaps they thought he was her father, if they thought about it at all.

There was a small line inside the admissions office, but after waiting ten minutes she got to speak to a nice, welcoming woman at the desk. Her nametag said Nancy Willows. Her hair was dyed far too bright red, while her lipstick was a bit too dark for her complexion, but Lacey took an instant liking to her.

Since most of the admissions process was taken care of online beforehand, right down to the first year's tuition—she'd gotten a full ride—there were only a few personal information checks and a couple of signatures. Nancy gave Lacey her student ID, and she was set to go.

Outside in the hallway, Lacey beamed. Now only orientation was ahead, and that she was to handle alone.

Mr. Teasdale studied her expectantly. "Everything all right? That wasn't so bad, now was it?"

"No. I guess I overreacted." Lacey blushed but smiled through the embarrassment.

"All right, then." Mr. Teasdale nodded firmly and looked around. "I assume you're going to get the full tour of the place at orientation. The parking is only for two hours, and it's been half an hour already. Tell you what. You go to orientation, while I take the car for a spin. I'll be back early to take you to lunch afterward. That sound good to you? Unless you want to have a bite to eat with any new friends you make."

"No." Lacey was determined not to get sidetracked. She'd come here for orientation, and nothing else. All that stuff could wait until Monday next. It would be rude to ditch her traveling companion for people she just met, and she wasn't that kind of person. "You scour the place good, so we can go straight to lunch once I'm done. Making friends here, if I do, will keep until Monday."

"That's nice of you," Mr. Teasdale said. From his inconspicuous attire and appearance it was hard to see the master of music he was, having performed on the grand stages in Europe and the U.S. "Now, if you don't mind, I'll have to, um…." He flushed red and glanced toward the restroom sign.

Lacey chuckled and nodded. It was curious how even men who knew her regarded her differently when she was wearing a dress. It was as if they forgot she was actually a *he*, and treated her as such. Talking about peeing and toilets in front of a girl was a no-no, and Mr. Teasdale was no exception.

When Mr. Teasdale ducked into the lavatory, Lacey meandered around the hallway, checking out the bulletin board. There were notes of all sorts: advertisements for roommates, couches, used cars, keggers and frat/sorority parties, lost kittens, music and vocal lessons, etc. Lacey smiled at the diversity of it all, and yet a sense of predictability came over her. Bulletin boards like these were commonplace. Still, she'd never seen it *here*, which gave it some luster.

Suddenly someone bumped into her from behind.

"Oh dear, a thousand pardons, my lady," a posh voice said, apologetically.

Lacey swerved around, not seriously injured, though with a bruise or two forming on her shoulder. "I beg your pardon?"

"No, no. It is *I* who must beg *your* pardon, dear lady."

Lacey stared. From the antiquated speech and the British accent, she had expected an adult, perhaps a teacher or a professor.

What she got instead, however, was a whip-thin young man, probably her own age. With white tennis shoes, a sea blue blazer, tight black pants, and a lighter blue sweater with a V-neckline and a silk cravat—*a cravat? Really? Who wore those?*—the young man brushed invisible specks of dust off his clothes. His thick, bleached silvery-blond hair pointed upward in airy waves at least three inches high in a mainstream hipster hairstyle, and his gray eyes sparkled behind clear plastic-rimmed, round glasses that stood in stark contrast to his sleek, angular features. He smiled a half-amused, half-downright-lecherous grin.

"Oh. Oh." He sounded surprised as his gaze raked over Lacey.

For her first day she had planned on wearing something unassuming and conservative, but Bro had effectively torpedoed that design right out of the water. He'd told her anything other than a dress was uncharacteristic and false of her, and it was an artsy college, so people must wear weird bohemian things daily. They were good arguments, and Lacey had felt confident enough to put on long stockings, a tight long-sleeved shirt, and an equally body-hugging tunic on top, all muted earth tones of brown and green. They were among her favorite autumn wear.

Now she wondered what this new arrival saw in her.

"Oh," he said again, his smile so wide his white teeth gleamed. His look was friendly and appreciative. "I was about to curse the gods for making me such a hopeless klutz, but now I see they had a plan. Oh yes, a design of epic proportions to introduce me to the loveliest girl in the world." He took her hand and bussed the skin like a gentleman, barely gracing it with his lips. "Oh, my sweet, aren't you the very picture of Aphrodite. I am enamored." He placed his palm over his heart in a theatrical manner, and his expressive face depicted the deep (feigned) longing of a lover missing his one and only.

Lacey was still staring. Then she burst into hopeless snickers. "Thank you. I think."

"I, my naughty nymphet, am Parker Endicott, a gentleman of leisure, at your service." He bowed in a gauche, exaggerated manner and added a large wave of hand through the air.

Lacey covered her mouth to prevent any more giggles. "Hello. I'm Lacey Adair."

Parker quirked an eyebrow. "New?"

Lacey pursed her lips and said challengingly, "I wasn't born yesterday, no."

Parker chuckled. "Touché." He glanced at her hands, apparently searching for a sign of her instrument and finding none. "Vocal?"

"Violin. Left it at home. You?"

"Piano. Came here for the jazz focus. How about you?"

"Violin performance. And… this school is close to home." It was an admission, but she didn't felt like it was anything to hide.

"Ah. And where might thou wondrous realm be, dear lady?"

Lacey rolled her eyes, sensing these antics were just that, theater for an audience. "DC. You?"

"Baltimore boy, born and raised, from the original, not the new, Northwood."

Lacey tilted her head in contemplation. "I'm sorry. I don't know the area well. Or at all, to be precise."

Parker grinned. "Northwood is one of the wealthier neighborhoods in town."

"Oh? So, you're a rich hometown boy. Is that what you're so delicately trying to hint at?" Lacey teased, not really caring either way.

Parker's tone lowered to husky, seductive. "You like rich boys?"

Lacey snorted. "Makes little difference to me. But I already have a boyfriend."

"Oh, what a shame!" Parker exclaimed miserably, looking utterly crushed, but Lacey had a feeling it was mostly pomp and circumstance. "Just when I find the cutest boy on campus, and one that looks so pretty in a dress, I have to contend with the worst rival of them all: a high school sweetheart! I sure hope he appreciates the gift that is you, milady."

Well, no secret decoder rings needed for that remark, Lacey thought. Parker was gay and had seen through Lacey's feminine appearance right from the start. "Oh, Bro and I, we keep giving each other *the gift* every day and night."

Now Parker looked decidedly wicked, like an age-old satyr, promising dirty fun with every fiber of his being. "Oh, do tell, girlfriend!"

Lacey laughed. "Do you always talk like that? Really?"

Parker waved a dismissive hand about, taking on a faux snobbish expression. "I have a style, dear lady. I shall not compromise my sense of self for anyone." Then he looked down at her and couldn't keep the smile off his face. "Well, I'd do it for you, beautiful."

"That's sweet… sort of. But I'm not looking to shift boyfriends. I could use a friend, though, if that idea is not too pedestrian for someone of your social status." Lacey was surprised how easy it was to flirt with and needle a guy she had just met, but Parker made it effortless and natural. She had an inkling he wasn't truly trying to get between her and Bro, which would help to facilitate a friendship. And he was kind of growing on her.

Parker cocked his head, pensive. "A friend, eh? I'm assuming you don't mean a friends-with-benefits type of arrangement?" Lacey pursed her lips in silent chiding, and Parker just grinned. "Sounds… intriguing. I must warn you, though. You might experience serious difficulties resisting my raw animal magnetism."

Lacey laughed again. If nothing else, the guy was funny and certainly not boring, if way over the top. "I'll be sure to keep a taser in my pocket just for you."

Parker growled like a big cat on purpose, showing off his white teeth.

"Um, am I interrupting…?" Mr. Teasdale asked, having returned from the men's room, and his look was completely flummoxed as it shifted between Lacey and Parker.

Lacey hurried to explain, "No, not at all. This is Parker Endicott, a new friend. Parker, this is Mr. Teasdale, my violin teacher."

Parker's plucked and bleached eyebrows rose as he measured the man whose hand he was shaking. "From this conservatory? I don't think I've seen you around before."

"No. I'm Lacey's high school teacher—"

"You do look kind of familiar though…," Parker continued, as if he hadn't been cut off at all, and his eyes narrowed in sharp inspection.

Mr. Teasdale looked sick and pale, so Lacey asked, "You're second year, then?"

Parker's attention returned to Lacey, and he smiled. "Yes. I can be your mentor into the many facets of college life, party central away from home, as it were."

Lacey resisted the temptation to once again roll her eyes. "I'm not really into parties. I always end up being the piñata."

Though she had tried to be flippant and humorous, Parker grew serious, and even his eyes darkened. "That's not how I roll, milady."

Now Lacey was confused. "Are you a gentleman gangster now?"

Parker took a step closer, almost invading Lacey's personal space. "I have many facets, my dear, most of them conflicting. Does that make me a fashionable schizophrenic? Maybe. I must state, however, that I will never do wrong by you, nor will I allow anyone to harm you in any way, shape, or form. Consider that my credo." He thumped his fist to his chest in a vow.

Lacey was quite moved by the gesture. "Thank you, Parker."

"Are you headed for orientation?"

"Yes, I am. You too?"

"Oh, been there, done that." Parker sighed dramatically, with a bored expression. Then he smirked. "But I can keep you two company on the tour, and give you all the dirt and innuendo while our guide gives us only the tedious bits."

Lacey chuckled. "I'm looking forward to that show, good sir."

"I'm not that good." Parker winked. He was sort of an oddball, but Lacey found she liked it a lot.

"Neither am I," she teased right back, and Parker feigned puritan shock. "Well, since you know where orientation is, lead on."

"As thy heart desires, dear lady." Parker bowed theatrically again.

As Lacey hid her giggle behind her hand, planning on enjoying the day for all it was worth. A new friend definitely improved the day, and she was eager to learn more about Parker, the apparent life's drama major.

At the same moment, the door to the admissions office opened, and a young man came out, studying a stack of papers he was holding. He was handsome in a natural, no-nonsense kind of way, with translucent green eyes, dark golden hair gelled into trendy spikes above his head, and a man's square jaw with a tiny indentation on it. He had huge shoulders, a barrel chest, and arms and thighs like tree trunks, and the rest of his muscular body was equally riveting.

Too bad Lacey knew the real guy beneath the hot veneer. "Deacon...?"

Chapter 18

ABOUT the same time, Bro was hanging out with his best friend, Bradley Carlisle, and Bradley's girlfriend, Audrey Thorne. They were all going to attend Howard University in DC, and they'd had their orientation two weeks ago. Now they were all simply strolling around the college grounds, searching for the best places to have a bite to eat, hang around and chat, and study in relative peace and quiet.

"I'm hungry," Bradley complained for like the thousandth time in thirty minutes.

Bro rolled his eyes. "We just had lunch at the cafeteria."

"That was hours ago!"

"A little over one hour, actually," Audrey teased, making an exaggerated gesture of checking the time from her iPhone.

Bradley glowered down at his girlfriend, who smirked shamelessly. Where Bradley was the embodiment of an all-American jock, tall, broad-shouldered, and imposing with his short dark hair, light-brown eyes, and rugged features, Audrey was a total babe, though a head shorter than her boyfriend. Her long black hair was free today, cascading down her back, and this illusion of height was only accentuated by her long jeans-covered legs and the skimpiest shirt that could still be called a shirt, definitely exposing the shape of her perky breasts.

The two of them were young and beautiful, and as high school sweethearts, they seemed to live and breathe for each other. They were a picture-perfect couple.

Even their constant bickering was sort of endearing, Bro mused.

"Just because you eat like a mouse doesn't mean the rest of us should go without," Bradley countered from on high. He was only an inch taller than Bro, though.

"I thought she ate like a rabbit, only salads and stuff. You know, rabbit food?" Bro cut in, knowingly aggravating Audrey.

"Men!" Audrey huffed. "Silly carnivores. When you all die out when there's no more meat left, we vegetarians will rule the world."

"No meat left?" both Bradley and Bro exclaimed loudly, shocked.

Audrey laughed her wicked, taunting laugh. "Guess you two will have to resort to cannibalism to survive."

Bro and Bradley stopped midstep, stared at each other warily, and in unison shouted, "I call dibs on white meat!" Then they started chortling, and Audrey shook her head with a playful scolding.

"I'm gonna head out to the undergraduate library, guys," Audrey hollered at them, and was off before either man even got his shit together.

Bro stared at her receding back. HU Law School was, unfortunately, not close to the rest of the campus, about half an hour away on bike. As a pre-law undergrad, Audrey had some classes there, so she got herself a bike to facilitate moving between the two areas, and she lived with Bradley about halfway between, at a small but convenient double overlooking Piney Branch Park. "Dude, I can't believe you're dating a law student."

Bradley growled. "Why's that funny?"

Bro snorted. "'Cause you're not exactly the most law-abiding—"

"She'll protect me when she becomes a defense attorney."

"What if she decides on being a prosecutor instead?"

"No money in that."

"Since when has Audrey been interested in making a profit? She's got ideals and values and stuff."

Bradley sighed, but with a happy, lopsided grin. "Yeah…. She's great."

"Not my cup of tea." Bro shuddered at the mere thought, but unsure if the reaction was because Audrey was a girl or because she was like his sister, being his best friend's girl and all.

"You don't know what you're missing, brother." Bradley smiled at Bro with a dare.

Bro sneered with amusement. "Right back at you, man."

Bradley frowned with a contemplative look. "Lacey, huh? Hmm. I wonder if—"

"Don't even think it, dude!"

Bro's fierce countenance seemed to only egg Bradley on. "But you just said—"

"Fuck that! You touch Lacey, and I'll rip your arm out of its socket and beat you to death with it."

"Wow. That's… graphic." Then Bradley chuckled and slapped Bro mildly on the back in comradely fashion. "Come on, pal. You know I've got no interest in sucking dick, only eating pussy."

"Eww!" Bro's stomach flipped unpleasantly, but at least he tried not to grimace as hard as he wanted to.

Bradley laughed with a deep rumbling sound. "My thoughts exactly. Okay, now that we've established our respective girlfriends are safe from any flirtations by us, what do you wanna do?" He nodded toward the blue waters of the reservoir. "Wanna sit down?"

"I thought you were starving."

"Well, we can get something from the closest cafeteria, and then sit down."

Bro chuckled, and that was exactly what they did.

Ten minutes later they sat on one of the benches overlooking the McMillan Reservoir on the east side of the campus. Bradley was munching on a roast beef sandwich while Bro stuck to cheese and turkey. They watched the still-leafy trees, decked out in fall colors, swaying in the wind, and the few ducks that still swam and paddled away in the pool.

"Now that we're on the team, we're gonna be okay, right? I mean, we're not gonna fuck up or anything?" Bro asked after the silence had gone on too long for him.

Bradley snorted after he gulped down a bite with a swig of his Coke. "Of course. You worry too much, dude. We probably won't even get off the bench for the first year, so don't go getting your boxers in a twist. Time will tell."

At times Bro envied Bradley's confidence. Bradley had been the quarterback and team captain in high school, and he was damn good at it. Sure, the college would be full of guys equally good, or even better, but Bro doubted they had Bradley's drive or charm. He could've sold igloos to Eskimos with a single smile and a wink. Bro assumed that was why Bradley planned on a marketing major in the long run, once all the core curriculum studies were behind them.

Bro himself was still at a loss as to what he wanted. Of all the available options, he was leaning toward media studies, his focus on TV and film. He didn't know what the hell he would do with a BA in communications, but it was the only field of study that had even remotely felt like something he could get excited about amidst all the core classes he still had to muddle through.

Of course, football would take up a lot of their time. In high school, Bradley had been the quarterback, while Bro had been a tailback due to his running skills, sprinting speed, and agility to dodge opposite team members gunning for him. But they had been recruited for running back positions on the grounds of the Howard scout's judgment that they would work well together and would be most useful to the team in those roles. Howard had hotter prospects for the coveted quarterback position. Bro and Bradley would likely end up in the reserves as freshmen, but Bro figured they had a good chance to show what they could do over the next couple of years. That would be critical if Bro even wanted to get a shot at a pro football career.

Although they had a few classes in common in their schedules, Bro and Bradley, and Audrey for that matter, had not managed to coordinate them so they would all be in the same sections. It was going to be difficult to get together on campus even half as much as they all would have liked. Or at least as much as Bro would have liked, and hoped Bradley and Audrey would too.

"What's got you all down?" Bradley asked, always attuned to Bro's mood swings, since he controlled himself so damned annoyingly well.

Bro shrugged, faking nonchalance. "Nothing."

Bradley nudged him with his shoulder. "Don't make me woo it out of you. That'll just embarrass us both. And you'll end up all teary-eyed, I guarantee it."

"You jerk." Bro chuckled, returning the gesture with his own shove. "It's stupid. I kind of imagined we'd all be together in college, you know, sharing the same classes, talking about the same professors and assignments, and stuff. But now…. The three of us are going to the same school, but we'll barely be able see each other once classes start. I mean Audrey alone is gonna be half an hour away from us! Well, part of the time anyway."

At this point Bradley could have made fun of Bro's sentimentality, but all he said was, "Yeah, I know what you mean. I always thought I'd be more enthusiastic about going to college. In a way I am, but…. Of the four of us, I think Lacey and Audrey are the ones who've got it all figured out with their music and law. You and me? We're still sort of in the wind."

"Yeah." It was exactly what Bro had been reflecting on. "I know I wanna play ball, but I just wish I could be with my friends more."

"We'll see each other every day, I promise."

Bro nodded but felt less confident about their prospects. In his head, he'd imagined things would continue along the same vein as they did in high school. Now his girlfriend went to school in another town, and his two best friends would not be attending the same classes as he did at the same time. That sucked. Bro felt like things were changing too fast around him, and he wasn't being given adequate time to adjust.

Feeling blue, Bro decided to change the subject. "Where's Ricky?"

Bradley huffed out a breath, shaking his head. "He's gone completely loco. He's taking extra classes for that home ec degree he wants already, on top of his core curriculum stuff. Nutritional sciences, economics, social anthropology, cooking. He's gonna buckle under all that workload, but he's so excited I don't have the heart to tell him to take a deep breath and really think about how hard it's gonna be to juggle all those courses."

Ricky, Frederick by birth, was Bradley's twin brother. He didn't share his brother's enthusiasm for sports, as he was more home and kitchen oriented. Cooking was his favorite pastime, and it seemed he wanted to become a chef. Ricky was one of those people born cheerful, and Bro required at least three cups of coffee to catch up with Ricky's natural vivaciousness.

"He'll be fine. He's the most energetic person I know. Besides, we'll keep an eye on him. And if it looks like he can't handle it, we'll help him get through, yeah?"

Bradley smiled and nodded, his gaze aimed across the waters but not really seeing the view. "Thanks, man."

"Anytime, buddy. Anytime."

Silently, both lost in thought, they waited. A few minutes, or as much as half an hour, could have passed before Audrey found them again.

"Wow. You should see the library building. Fucking amazing." She plopped down on the bench next to Bradley and leaned into him. She was never one to mince words, and she could curse like a sailor.

"My sweet, innocent little flower." Bradley's tease was met with Audrey's swift punch on his arm.

"Hey, guys. Glad I found you. You wouldn't believe everything I found." Ricky had been exploring like the others, and now, with a gratified sigh, he dropped heavily down on the bench next to Bro. "God, my feet are killing me." Bro could picture Ricky curling his toes in his tennis shoes in his mind's eye.

Ricky was as ripped as his twin brother, but not nearly as buff, more lean and lithe. They shared the same tones as far as hair and eyes were concerned, though only Ricky's curly hair flopped down to frame his face. With his tanned skin he had an almost Latino appearance even though that wasn't his heritage.

"Wanna get out of here?" Bro suggested. He was going to be spending a lot of time on campus for the next couple of years, so he was eager to head home.

"Ready to pack it in?" Bradley asked for confirmation, and three rapid nods followed his question.

"PLEASE, man," Bro begged once all four of them returned to the loft. "Come on, Ricky. Look at us. We're dying here." He gave Ricky his best puppy-dog eyes and even managed to quiver his jaw a bit.

Ricky snickered. "Jeez, man, cut that shit out. Okay, okay, I'll make us something to eat. God, you're such kids sometimes." Huffing, he dashed to the kitchen to ransack the fridge and rummage through the cupboards in search of food items for preparation.

Bro gesticulated with silent whoops at his success while Bradley rolled his eyes at his antics. Bro jumped over the back of the couch and landed with a thump next to his best friend. The TV was on, but none of them were really watching. Bradley rested his head on the couch, yawning, while Audrey was reading a car magazine in one of the armchairs.

"Well, aren't we a lively bunch?" Bro remarked and then stifled his own jaw-breaking yawn. "Anything on TV?"

"Nah." Bradley didn't lift his head, let alone open his eyes. The TV was on mute, and it looked like another reality singing contest. Too boring to even look at.

Though tired after a busy day and yearning for a nap, Bro still needed to talk about the events of the day. "What did you guys think about Howard? You meet any new students?"

Audrey shrugged. "I met a couple of cheerleader types, but they scrammed the second they saw my tattoos. I think they were trying to break the track team's speed record." She gave an unrepentant grin. "No one to write home about, that's for sure."

"How are the old parental units taking things?" Bro was curious. He knew Audrey's parents were the squarest in the world, an accountant and a legal clerk who had never done anything to rock the boat. Audrey, the only child, was doing that for all of them. She was a rebel in her own right, who got herself into mischief more often than not.

Audrey chuckled wickedly. "You should've seen their faces when I told them I was gonna study law. I really thought they'd fall down on their hands and knees to thank the gods, atheists or not."

"You're bad, sweetie," Bradley commented with a smirk, his eyes still closed.

"A bad babe, just the way you like it."

"I'm gonna pretend I didn't hear you say that."

Bro let out an exasperated sigh at his friends. "Come on, guys. Take this seriously."

Bradley opened his eyes to look at Bro with sympathy in his eyes. "Buddy, she's gonna be home soon. Don't worry. You're not losing her, okay?"

Knowing full well they were talking about Lacey, Bro nodded, feeling miserable with longing. "Yeah."

Audrey came over to practically sit down on Bro's lap, bussing his cheek. Bro tried not to cringe or wipe the wet mark off. "We all miss her. She'll be home soon. Orientation's probably over by now, and they're on their way back."

That wasn't Bro's concern. What if she found a kind of acceptance and a new home there so she wouldn't want to come back? What if she decided to move to Baltimore to be closer to the conservatory? How would Bro survive?

Just then Bro's phone chimed, indicating a text. He shoved giggling Audrey off his lap and grabbed the cell. On it in clear black letters read "On our way home. Have I got a story to tell you. Love you." And it was followed by a heart emoticon.

Bro let out a breath, and his body released a tension he hadn't been consciously aware of. Lacey was coming home. Everything was going to be all right. A happy grin spread his lips.

"See? Nothing to worry about. Told ya," Audrey ribbed him and gave him another smooch on his temple.

"Hey!" Bradley was jealous, and that made Bro laugh. "Fuck you." Bradley gave Bro a hard push, but it was playful, and soon they were both laughing and then wrestling on the couch. Wisely, Audrey jumped out of the way, but she began calling out illegal moves like a professional referee and egging them on.

"Guys, food's ready," Ricky hollered from the kitchen.

Parting, Bro and Bradley simultaneously sniffed the air, where rich aromas wafted over them through the air conditioning. Macaroni and cheese, which was Bro's favorite. They always had those supplies handy. He dashed to the kitchen, with his best friends hot on his trail. To make themselves useful, Bro and Bradley set the table while Audrey fetched them all some sodas from the fridge.

For a good long while it was quiet as they satisfied their immediate appetites by devouring their food. For the second serving, they actually managed to converse a bit as they ate and thanked Ricky so profusely, both during and after the meal, that he blushed.

As they started clearing the table, Audrey asked, "Where are Sebastian and the guys?"

"Working still. It's early."

"Guess that means we have the place to ourselves," she said, and from her tone she obviously had naughty ideas.

Uh-oh. "Hell no, Dree! We're *not* having a party!"

"Oh yes we are," she countered in a teasing, singsong voice. She snatched her iPhone and started punching in texts.

Bro glared at Bradley, who was washing the dishes. "Would you please control your woman? I can't have people over. Bas and Jordan would kill me!"

Bradley glanced at eager Audrey over his shoulder, and then shrugged. "I know better than to get between that woman and her plans, let alone between her and her phone. Rather you die than me."

"You selfish prick."

Bradley chuckled. "Come on, Bro. Just a couple of guys and gals. It'll be fine. Where's that reckless spirit of yours?"

"Locked in a closet till I can get a place of my own."

"Well, well. And here I thought you'd been out of the closet for years."

"Fuck. You."

"Sorry, buddy. I'm straight."

"A plague is what you are. You and that missus of yours." Bro cursed under his breath as he pictured the havoc a party would wreak on his household. But then he remembered he had been on his best behavior for a damn long time, never doing anything bad or breaking the rules for fear of Sebastian sending him back to live with their mom. Of course that was a stupid fear, because Sebastian would sooner die than allow Bro to be sent back there.

Perhaps it was time to live it up a little.

With moderation.

Hopefully.

Chapter 19

AN HOUR later the loft was packed.

Half were people Bro knew from high school, half were barely
familiar faces, friends of friends. Loud bass thumped and echoed
throughout the place, rattling windows, mirrors, and paintings alike.
Someone had put a game on TV, but there was no sound, at least not
that anyone could hear. People were jumping up and down to the
music, and there were drinks passed around. From what Bro could tell,
the liquor cabinet had not been raided, though he suspected it was only
a matter of time. People must have brought their own drinks.

"Who the hell are all these people?" Bro demanded of Audrey,
who was dancing seductively with a group of her friends. A lot of guys
were openly ogling them, but not one walked up to them, content with
watching the live show.

Audrey gave the room a cursory glance and shrugged. "Want me
to throw them out?"

Bro closed his eyes. "No. Just wondering." Then he closed the
gap between them until he was right up to her face. "Something breaks?
I'm totally gonna blame this shit on you."

Audrey winked, nodded her understanding, and returned to her
dancing.

Not wanting to be a stick-in-the-mud, Bro moved off to a group
of guys hanging out, and Bradley was with them. Falling into step with

his best friend was easy, and soon they were shooting the breeze with a bunch of guys from their high school who had started a mechanic shop nearby.

It wasn't until Bro felt slender arms wrap around his midsection from behind and a half-feminine, half-masculine perfume wafted over him that he realized how much time had passed. He whipped around and came face to face with Lacey's lovely visage.

A grin he couldn't suppress emerged, and his mood lightened instantly. "Babe, you're home."

Lacey quirked an eyebrow, grinning. "Oh, is that what this is? I thought I'd taken a wrong turn somewhere, and ended up in a nightclub."

"Funny, ha-ha." Bro took Lacey into his embrace, and kissed her sweet mouth. All sound faded away.

Until... the music stopped abruptly, and then, "What the hell is going on?"

Even into the kiss, Bro grimaced at the sound of Jordan's angry voice. He broke away from Lacey and turned to find Jordan, Sebastian, Jack, and Kevin at the door. The time-honored excuse "I didn't invite them" sprang to his mind, but at least he had the good sense not to say it out loud. Though he sure was tempted.

Jordan lifted his hands, and with his tattoos, piercings, and general bad-boy attitude, he exuded intimidation. "Everybody, get the fuck out!"

With barely audible grumbling, people started filing out of the loft in surprisingly orderly fashion. It still took a couple of minutes for the place to clear of partyers until the only ones left were Bro, Lacey, Bradley, Audrey, and Ricky.

Bro walked up to Sebastian and Jordan, half-ashamed of having the party in the first place, and half-embarrassed at getting scolded by his roommates without words. "Sorry. It was just gonna be a few friends over, but...." It was a lie, and he knew it. "I've not had any parties here, ever. I just wanted one day to celebrate going to college and—"

"Bro, enough." Jordan brought up his hand to stop the flow of words. "I'm not angry you had a party. You've been the best-behaved teenager I know." Bro was dumbfounded. "But what I am angry about is you not telling us you were having a party, and I bet you didn't know half the people in here. Anything could've happened, and we were clear across town."

Bro hedged. "It was kind of an impromptu thing, you know...." He glanced behind at his girlfriend. "I missed Lacey so much, and my friends just wanted to cheer me up, and—"

"Whatever." Jordan waved a hand about. "Next time you tell us. Then, and only then, can you have your party." As he walked past Bro, he tousled his hair, making Bro mutter about being treated like a child, but not really being all that emphatic about it. "I heard that," Jordan called out from the stairs. "Next time you let us know, or we'll tell everyone we know the A-word."

It was a threat, probably an idle one, but Bro still fumed. "Fine. Bossy bastard."

"*Watch that potty mouth of yours*," Sebastian signed as he, too, passed on his way upstairs, but his happy grin was proof positive that though some rules had been broken, nothing was broken beyond repair. Before he vanished around the corner, though, he signed, "*Don't forget to clean up. Teenager's standard punishment for throwing a party.*"

Jack snickered as he walked off, but he remembered to make the rock-on gesture and whisper loudly, "Oops, busted."

Bro flipped him off, and Jack just cackled more. Kevin was the only one who offered no opinion. Stoic as ever, he merely nodded goodnight to them all and followed Jack.

Only then did Bro exhale deeply and drop down on the couch. "Fuck me."

"Is that an invitation?" Bro looked up, startled, and found Lacey smirking at him, all bubbly and happy as a clam. When Bro started to get up, Lacey stopped him by saying, "Well, it seems you've all had quite a day. Now let me tell you about mine. You will never believe who is going to Peabody with me."

Bro frowned and glanced at Bradley, who shrugged and looked at Audrey, who smiled with anticipation and stared expectantly at Lacey. "Okay, we bite. Who?" Bro finally asked.

After a dramatic pause for effect, Lacey blurted out, "Deacon Rake."

Three pairs of eyes nearly bugged out and three jaws were left hanging.

"What?" Bro was stunned, and this time he did get up. "You're bullshitting me."

Lacey shook her head, grinning. "Nope. It's the God's honest truth." She made a cross over her heart.

Bro closed in on Lacey, a storm of concern brewing in him. "What the fuck is he doing there? Is that gay-bashing dickwad stalking you or something? Did he hurt you?"

"Easy, love. Calm down." Lacey planted a kiss on Bro's lips, and the gesture did go a long way to reassuring him. "Deacon may have been a bully back in high school, but he was okay today. Well…."

"Well—what?" Bro insisted.

"He sure was surprised to see me. He was carrying this stack of papers, but when he saw me, he dropped them all on the floor. He was all red in the face while he helped me and Parker gather everything back—"

"Who the heck's Parker?" Bro interjected, confused.

"Hmm? Oh, right, Parker." Lacey blushed, and Bro had a bad feeling. "He's this guy I met at the admissions office. He's second year. He's fun and smart and—"

"And hot?" Bro bit his lower lip hard, trying to prevent himself from succumbing to a jealous temper tantrum, though he really wanted to let go.

Lacey blinked and looked a little hurt, but also a little guilty. "I guess, yes. But I'm not into him, or anything. I'm with you." There was a question in her eyes, doubt, and even fear.

Bro couldn't have that, and then he felt guilty. "Yeah, I know you are. I'm sorry. I got a little jealous." He smiled encouragingly. "Tell me about him. And Rake."

Relief and joy lit up Lacey's face, and Bro knew he'd made the right call in not letting his negativity run amok. "Parker plays the piano, and he's totally into jazz. Peabody has a big jazz program. Deacon plays the drums."

Bro snorted sarcastically and rolled his eyes. "Well, that's original." He was unable and unwilling to forget how badly the guy had treated him in high school. In his eyes, Deacon was a bully and always would be.

Lacey looked pensive, frowning. "Maybe it's therapeutic for him. Kind of like boxing. Percussion instruments can help relieve stress, or so I hear. It's nothing to sneer at."

"I wasn't!" Bro countered, his voice rising.

"Of course you were," Audrey cut in adamantly, accepting no quarter, and then took Lacey's arm and guided her to the couch, where she questioned Lacey in a soft, conspiratorial tone, "So, this Parker guy? What's he like?"

Lacey smiled, and Bro gritted his teeth, surprising even himself with the intense jealousy he felt. "Parker's a posh GQ-model type with bleached blond hair, angular features, and a silly British accent. He's sexy as sin and flirty as hell. And he's gay too."

By that point, Bro couldn't listen to any more. He whipped around and stomped off to his own room. At least he succeeded in not slamming the door shut as hard and loud as he wanted. His brain itched, his palms were sweating, and his belly was wound tight in knots of uncertainty.

Was Lacey gonna choose that sex-on-a-stick new guy over him?

With the way Bro had been acting, it was a definite possibility. He exhaled heavily, trudged to his bed, and fell down on the mattress on his stomach, burying his face in the pillows and groaning out his frustration.

All these doubts about the solidity of their long-distance relationship were nagging at him. And yet he felt silly about it since

Lacey was in actuality only an hour or so away, and she came back here every night. So it wasn't really a long-distance relationship, was it? So… why did it feel like he was losing her?

A soft knock came from the door, and Bro knew who it was. "Come in."

Lacey snuck in timidly, and Bro hated to see her act so skittish. "Bro, I—"

"No, wait." Bro got up and went to her but kept a discreet distance so as not to touch her accidentally. "I'm sorry. You had a great day, and I'm being a total asshole. I'm sorry."

Lacey threw her arms around his neck, and with a contented sigh, Bro hugged her back.

"Parker flirted with me a lot," Lacey admitted, "and I was flattered, but the only thought in my mind was that he wasn't you. I missed you."

They may have seen each other that morning, and it wasn't even very late yet, but for Bro it was as if they'd been apart for weeks. "I missed you too." Then he took a deep breath, knowing this was something they needed to talk about. "Listen, babe. We need to talk."

Lacey pulled back abruptly, her eyes wide in shock. "You're breaking up with me?"

"Jesus, no!" Bro embraced Lacey again and tenderly nuzzled her cheek. "Absolutely not. I'm not giving you up without a fight. If Parker or anyone wants you, they'll have to take you over my dead body. And even then, I'll come back as a zombie and chew their wieners off."

Lacey was shaking in his arms, and he stroked her back soothingly, scared. But then he heard her helpless giggles and relaxed. "God, their wieners? And you wonder why I love you so much?"

Bro smiled against Lacey's strawberry-scented hair and inhaled. As he grew more at ease, the topic didn't seem so tough to face after all. "This is just the first day you've been there. I've gotta grow a set and take your daily absence like a man. I can't keep getting this whiny and bitchy just because you met a guy." He paused, but then added with a growl, "A guy I don't like at all."

Lacey kissed his cheek and jaw. "You haven't even met him. Parker's a pretty great guy. And he made sure I was never alone with Deacon."

That made Bro step back swiftly. "Rake followed you around all day?"

Lacey gave him a mock reproachful glare. "Come on, Bro. As a first-year student, he had the same orientation I did. You can hardly fault him for that."

Bro shook his head, equal parts miffed and baffled. "I just don't get it. What is it you see in that guy worth forgiveness, let alone redemption? Don't you remember how he used to treat us? The name-calling, the shoving. He dislocated my fucking shoulder at football practice, and—"

"My dad's in AA."

Bro was taken aback by the strange non sequitur. "What's that got to do with anything? You father's a—"

"Bro!" Lacey chastised softly. "What my Dad was—a mean-spirited, violent drunk—is hardly the point here. He's changed. He's trying to better himself, to wean himself off the sauce. If he can change, anyone can. As far as Deacon's concerned, I'm willing to give him the benefit of the doubt."

"And if he starts his bullshit again? What if he gets physical and hurts you?"

"Then I'll talk to the dean and the police and get him arrested." Lacey reached for Bro again, and he went obediently, like a slave with no will of his own. His girlfriend's magnetism was too strong to resist. "You do remember in the spring at the mall when he apologized for his actions?"

"Too little, too late." Bro lifted his chin in defiance; he didn't want to back down on this issue. He didn't want that jerk anywhere near Lacey, but apparently he had no choice in the matter. Didn't mean he was gonna bend over and take it, though.

Lacey smiled sweetly and gave Bro an Eskimo kiss, rubbing her nose gently against his. "We could all use second chances sometimes, love. The whole time he remained close, but he didn't once invade my privacy or violate my personal space, or anything. In fact, it looked like he was more afraid of me than I was of him. I don't think he wants anyone to know the kind of person he used to be in high school. Maybe he's trying to make a clean break from his past. You know, kids fall into these predestined roles and groups in high school. The nerds, the stoners, the cheerleaders, the bullies, the jocks."

Why did she have to make so much sense? Bro wanted to grumble but couldn't. Not in the face of Lacey's reasoning and understanding. And she'd deliberately added the last group there, just to get at him. And it fucking worked too.

"You think I'm being too judgmental. That I don't think Rake could actually change."

Lacey chuckled a little, watching him with her serene, twinkling eyes. "There are only two constants in the universe. Balance and change. Everything tries to find the right balance to keep going, and everything changes."

"Everything changes but you...." Bro sang a line from a recognizable pop tune.

Lacey stared at him flabbergasted, with her jaw hanging open. "You didn't just quote 'Take That' lyrics at me, did you?"

Bro laughed, and shrugged, all mellow. "Maybe. You'll never pry the truth from these lips."

Lacey grinned, blushing. "I bet I could do a lot with those lips."

The immediate response was Bro's jeans growing snug and uncomfortable, and he was all set to go when.... "Oh, shit. Brad and Dree—"

"Left for home with Ricky when I came to find you. They knew we'd fight and then have make-up sex. It's just us here."

Mmm, those were the words Bro had been praying to hear.

But first things first. "It's been a hell of a day. How about a bubble bath?"

Lacey smirked. "A little hydrotherapy, eh?"

"Nah. Bubbles-and-Bro therapy."

"I like the way your mind works."

"Yeah, when it works and isn't blinded by jealousy, and—"

"Shut up. You know I hate it when you denigrate yourself—"

"Sorry, babe." Bro kissed Lacey before she could say anything more.

Chapter 20

IT TOOK them twenty minutes to clean up after the party, and ten minutes after that, Bro was resting his back against the smooth surface of the bathtub while Lacey leaned against his chest with *his* willowy yet masculine back. Bro swirled his left hand over Lacey's torso, caressing and relearning every line and curve, while he fondled Lacey's sac with his right.

Lacey moaned low, his head lolled back on Bro's shoulder. "God, I love it when you do that."

Bro kissed Lacey's wet cheek. "You love it when I play with your balls, baby?"

Under the hot water and piles of bubbles, Lacey spread his legs more to give Bro greater access. "Yes. Love your hands. Love you."

"Well, as long as the intimate stuff we do never gets old, neither will our relationship. We'll get through anything, even distance."

Lacey turned his head and peered up at Bro. His eyes were a bit glazed over. "I always come back to sleep right next to you. I wouldn't want it any other way."

"I know. I just...." Bro sighed, but the warm water prevented him from getting chills down his spine. "I just worry."

"My warrior." Lacey snickered behind his hand but soon grew serious. "You think I don't worry about you? Don't think I've forgotten that hunk Eddy goes to the same school as you do, and he really liked you back at Shenandoah. *Liked* liked you."

Bro chuckled and held on to Lacey tighter. "I don't want a jock. I want a pretty, dolled-up violinist who wears silk stockings and cute dresses, and who has brown eyes and blond hair, and the sweetest tasting cock on the planet."

"Uh-oh." Lacey giggled. "That sure narrows down the field. Anyone I know?"

Bro wrestled Lacey into a tickling frenzy, and water sloshed over the edges of the tub.

"Okay, I give, I give," Lacey howled amid bursts of chortles. As they resettled, water dripping from their faces and hair, he made a deep satisfied sound in his throat. "This is what adults do, isn't it? They can't spend every waking minute with each other, but they get used to it."

"I don't think I want to get used to being apart from you," Bro admitted, glum. "Yeah, rationally I know we can't be together 24/7. Doesn't mean I have to like it."

Lacey nodded, snuggling closer in Bro's embrace. "I know. Me too." Then he chuckled a bit. "But this is good, isn't it? I mean, that we had this separation anxiety crisis now, on our first day apart, instead of after a month. Then we would've really freaked out. You about me and Parker and Deacon, and me about you and Eddy."

Bro snorted. "I didn't even see the guy today. In fact, I can't even remember seeing him in orientation two weeks ago. Hmm. Of course, I didn't know him then."

"You think he's all right?" Lacey asked, concerned.

Bro bussed Lacey's cheek. "See? This is why I love you. You could've had a jealous fit about me wondering where he is, as if missing him. But instead you're worried about him. 'Cause that's the kind of person you are. Sweet, kind, loving. And you're all mine." Bro tightened his arms around his boy, and squeezed. "Mine."

Lacey giggled and squirmed, not actually intent on release. "That didn't really answer me, now did it?"

Bro maneuvered Lacey around until he was pressed against Bro, front to front. Their chests, bellies, and cocks rubbing against each other only added to the delight of a long, lingering kiss. Bro held

Lacey's waist with one hand and kneaded his firm, round backside with another. Lacey whimpered and ground against him, hard already.

Before moving off to lick Lacey's ear, Bro kissed his boyfriend with soft suction. Lacey let out a keen, high-pitched sound. "Love it when you whimper," Bro commented, buzzing with joy.

"I do *not* whimper," Lacey countered, puckering his lips in mock annoyance.

Bro kept Lacey close. "Sure you do, and you love it too." He smiled down at him. "I'm so lucky to have you." Then he paused. "Listen, baby. I know we're both gonna meet new people in college and make new friends. And… we're guys—healthy, young, horny. We're gonna find some of them totally fuck-worthy. Doesn't mean we're gonna do anything about it, right? I want *you* next to me when I go to sleep at night. I want to wake up to your face, your breath, your heartbeat."

Lacey stared at him for the longest time, and Bro started to get nervous. Then Lacey's lower lip trembled, and he bit down to stop it. "Just when I think I know all there is to know about you, you surprise me." Lacey straddled Bro's hips and cupped his face. He leaned closer until their lips were an inch apart. "I love you. Wanna get fucked by you."

When Lacey kissed him, Bro felt like coming apart at the seams. It wasn't the warm water that made him so hot he felt like exploding was a real option. It was all Lacey.

And the thought of actually pushing his cock deep inside Lacey's sweet behind made him shiver even more. But… he knew he wasn't the only one having doubts.

Ghosting his lips over Lacey's jaw and cheek, Bro muttered, "It's fucking weird, isn't it? After all that gay porn we've been watching, it's like we're expected to go for anal right away. Like we can't be a real gay couple if there's been no, you know, no penetration."

Lacey pulled back to study him, but his hands kept up their wandering ways over Bro's chest, neck, and shoulders. "Yes, I suppose. I'd be lying if I said I haven't thought about what anal sex would be like between us."

"Yeah, me too." Then he smiled, hoping to convey his calm to Lacey. "But that doesn't mean I want to rush it. We'll know when the right time—"

"How?"

"Huh?"

"How will we know when it's the right time to do that? We've been together for almost two years now. Well, we will have been by around Christmas anyway." Lacey shrugged. "We've had opportunities…." His voice faded. "So how come we haven't?"

Bro frowned. He was usually the impatient and rash one, but he'd never figured Lacey might feel the strain of steering clear of anal sex too. "I don't know," he hedged, uncertain how their talk had turned to this. Then a horrible thought occurred to him. "Would you… did you want to with Parker, or Deacon?" He swallowed hard at the last name, feeling dread pooling in the pit of his stomach.

Lacey's anger showed in the way he sucked in his lips until they all but disappeared. Then he punched Bro's arm. Hard. "You can be such a dick sometimes," he growled vehemently and started to get out of the bathtub.

Bro yanked him right back. "I'm sorry. You know me, Lace. I can be strong and brave about anything else but you. With you I'm always scared I'm gonna lose you to some gorgeous hunk who's gonna give you everything I can't."

Lacey's eyes spewed fire at him. "And what's that? What can't you give me?"

Heat rose palpably in Bro's cheeks. "Well, you know… sex."

Harrumphing loudly, Lacey sat up, still straddling Bro, and crossed his arms over his chest. "And all that stuff we've been doing for over a year and a half was—what? Coloring with crayons? If you must know, I've been perfectly happy with our sex life."

Bro stared down stubbornly, his gaze focused on the point where Lacey's caramel-colored skin vanished under the bubbles and swirling water. They had both gotten tan over their summer vacation, but Lacey's typically pale skin now glowed with the sun's kisses.

"Bro?"

Letting out a deep breath, Bro replied, "If *you* must know, since I knew we were going to different colleges I've been thinking you might want to… play the field more. Date other guys."

Lacey gasped, and his hands pressed against Bro's chest, his trimmed nails scraping on slippery skin. "You're asking me if we're having an open relationship, now that we're away in college and can do what we want? You don't want to be exclusive with me?"

Bro's eyes shot up, and his hold of Lacey's narrow waist tightened to a near painful grip. "Fuck, of course I want that! Jesus, Lace! Of course I damn well want to be the only guy for you, the only one who gets to touch you, kiss you, sleep with you, live with you, love you. Fuck, that's all I want."

Lacey looked confused. "Then why—?"

"When you mentioned about us not, um, going all the way during sex, I thought that meant you wanted a new, different, better lover. A lot of people who used to date during high school want to try something else once they leave home."

"And you just assumed I'm one of those people? That if everyone else jumped off the deep end, I'd just be a good little lemming and follow?" Lacey shook his head and then exhaled. "Okay, Bro. Let's be crystal clear about this. You are the one I love. At this point in time, I want us to be exclusive and not sleep around, no matter what kind of hot stuff we meet in college. I can't speak about the future, not with any real certainty. But I can tell you Parker may be sexy and flirty, fun and smart, but it's *you* who I'm in love with. As for the anal part…. It's true. Maybe I've allowed myself to be influenced by all that porn, as if we have to do that. Maybe I'm rushing it. I know I may have tried to pressure you into it when we were camping at—"

"What? No, Lace," Bro cut in, adamant. "No way did you try to force me! I just didn't want our first time to happen in a tent on bumpy ground with park rangers and kids in every bush." Then he pulled Lacey down and kissed his lips tenderly. "I want us to be exclusive too. No one else but us. Damn, maybe we should've had this talk before orientation day, huh?"

Bro chuckled a little at the end, and Lacey smiled back. Crisis averted.

"I'm sorry if I made you jealous—" Lacey started.

Bro shook his head. "No. I should've trusted you. If you'd really liked a guy, I know you would've told me about it. You wouldn't cheat on me behind my back. It's not in you to betray anyone like that. You're a good person."

"So are you, love." Lacey kissed him softly, threading his long fingers through Bro's thick, wet dark hair. "I think Parker's gonna make a good friend. But a secret paramour, let alone a boyfriend? No." He scrunched his nose cutely, and a weight lifted off Bro's shoulders. "He's not my type. Too pretty. I like my men more muscular, dark-haired, and blue-eyed. You know, a jock type with a deaf brother and smart-mouthed soon-to-be brother-in-law, and a goofy blended family I adore with every ounce of my being."

"Hmm, well, thankfully that narrows it down," Bro joked, winking.

Lacey laughed, a happy effervescent sound Bro captured and locked away in his heart for future emergencies of loneliness and longing. "Damn straight." *Oh, Lacey cussed.* Enamored, Bro watched as pink colored his boy's cheeks, and smiled.

"Okay then. Is there anything else that needs hammering out now? Or can we please get out of here before my sausage shrivels into a cocktail wiener?"

That question made Lacey laugh harder, and he shifted on top of Bro so his half-hard cock pressed against Bro's stomach. Under the camouflage of water it was easy for Bro to fist the delicious piece of meat stiffly and tug a few times with squeezing pressure. Lacey's giggles morphed into moans, and his hips jerked.

The question was hanging in the air, and Bro felt the tension sizzling between them.

He took a chance. "We've got the weekend before school officially starts. You wanna, maybe, try that... you know?"

Though Lacey let out a snicker, it was obvious he was serious too. "If you can't say it, you're not ready to do it. Isn't that how the saying goes?"

"Come on, Lace. I'm being serious here."

"Me too." Lacey dipped down to rest his slender form against Bro's sturdier frame and wrapped his arms around Bro. "Every time I think about it, when we're not in bed together, it seems so easy, like I can't figure out why we haven't done it already. But when we're naked? I get all worried and doubtful and wigged out about it. I mean, from my point of view, there's nothing wrong with our sex life as it is. I don't feel like I'm left wanting more when I come."

"Me neither, babe." Bro placed a kiss on Lacey's forehead and kept him close with a hug as he let go of Lacey's penis. "Usually just having you naked against me makes me so fucking hot I about come right then and there."

Lacey giggled a little. "Me too. I love your hands on me. When you're on top of me, just grinding and taking my cock in hand, that about does it for me every time. In those moments I never think about what more we could do."

"In those moments I can't think at all!" Bro exclaimed, huffing out a chuckle that was almost a snort.

Lacey bussed his jaw and tittered. "You're the best. And I'm not just saying that 'cause you're the only guy I've ever been with."

"Right back at you, babe." Bro breathed a few times before asking, "So… not tonight, then?"

Lacey looked up, smiled, and caressed Bro's cheekbone and jawline. "It's Friday, and it's been one long-ass day. Let's go to bed, make love, and sleep till noon. We'll think about the rest tomorrow, all right?"

Bro smiled and nodded back. "Sounds good to me."

Chapter 21

"READY to start your lessons?"

Parker's singsong voice made Lacey roll her eyes, but she still smiled, for Parker had a knack for making Lacey do that. "Hold your horses, cowboy."

"Wow. No one's ever called me that before. Hmm, how would I look in chaps?" Parker's voice took on a dreamy tone, and he held his hands together, as if deep in prayer, and stared up at the ceiling as if seeing past it into heaven. "I'm so moved right now, so damn touched. No, don't look at me." With an exaggerated sniffle, he buried his face in his arms, shuddering violently.

"Parker, knock it off," Lacey ordered, barely holding on to her laughing.

"Fine. Be a bitch about it." The way Parker whispered the ugly word loudly, with his melodious voice, Lacey knew full well it was all for show.

"You're being such a drama queen. Why you didn't just head to the first bus toward Broadway I'll never know."

"New York, New York. What a wonderful town," Parker sang, and he sounded more than halfway decent. "You think I could've made it big as a drama major?"

"Absolutely." Of that Lacey had zero doubts.

She dipped the paintbrush into the can of gray paint, pulled it out carefully, dripping wet, and continued to coat the flat. They were on stage at the conservatory, part of a team of volunteers working on the set. Apparently, a group of musicians at the school wanted to try something avant-garde, a musical composed by a third-year student, with full backdrops and everything, so here they were, painting away.

"Are you going to help me or not?" Lacey asked Parker, who stood in place, swaying to music only he heard. Lacey had learned a lot of people at the school seemed to be lost in their own musical works, and it was best not to interrupt them. Parker, however, was a special project, and Lacey got a certain sense of satisfaction every time she roused her friend from whatever ethereal plane he was lost in.

"What?" Parker blinked and then refocused on her. "Oh, right. Yes, of course." He played the innocent, wetted his brush, and resumed his painting, though his former work was already dry. "I notice you didn't answer me."

Lacey took a deep breath but didn't reply. Parker had been teasing her for a month now about this. Bennett Marchand was a world-famous violinist whose many successes included a nigh-on impossible medley of concertos by Shostakovich, Beethoven, and Tchaikovsky, performed for the Queen of England and the royal family, not to mention celebrities from all possible fields of entertainment. He was also one of Lacey's professors—and a personal idol of hers.

"I know you can hear me, Lacey. Pretend all you want, but I've got a big mouth, and an incessantly nagging voice, so I can go on for—"

"Butt out, Parker. I mean it." Lacey gritted her teeth, trying not to snap harder.

"Whatever do you mean? My butt is always out." Parker waggled his bubble butt, and even stroked it lovingly. "See? Perfectly perky. You could bounce a quarter off these buns."

At that Lacey giggled, unable to help herself. "Jeez, Parker. Lay off, will you?"

Parker leaned closer, and his expensive woodsy cologne wafted over Lacey. "It's not uncommon for students to have crushes on their teachers, especially ones they've idolized for—"

"I do *not* have a crush on Professor Marchand!" Lacey turned to wave her paintbrush in his face, barely controlling her voice. "He's a fabulous violinist, but I am not attracted to him. I'm not! And all this talk isn't going to change that." She glared at Parker with every bit of her strength of will, which she had in abundance, thankfully.

"Lace, is this guy bothering you?"

Startled by the new, rough voice, Lacey swiveled around and found Deacon standing a few feet away, his eyes alternating between her and Parker.

"Oh, no," Lacey hurried to say. "Parker's just… being a total butthead." She glared at Parker as she uttered the childish taunt.

Parker burst into hearty laughter while Deacon grimaced and frowned. "You sure?"

"She said so, didn't she?" Parker needled, his gray eyes flashing like swords.

In horror Lacey watched Deacon's eyes, green like tropical pools, narrow, and the line of his square jaw strain. She was certain he was going to start throwing punches any second. His hands fisted at his sides, and Lacey opened her mouth to speak.

The moment she did, though, Deacon's attention turned to her, and his tension eased. "If you're sure." That was all he said before he offered a curt nod and stomped off to the edge of the stage. Yet, he stuck around, talking to some guy by the stands but giving Lacey and Parker furtive glances.

Lacey sighed. "God, Parker. Why do you have to rile him up every time you see him? Can't you see he's—?"

"Oh, Lace," Parker interjected, his gaze meandering toward Deacon. "Just look at him. That Neanderthal's brooding brow, those bulging warrior muscles, those monosyllabic grunts. Oh, he's too easy to tease. And that's not my fault. It would be like ordering you not to jump into a clear cool pond in the middle of a hot summer's day. The temptation is too hard to resist."

"Oh my God, Parker! Cut it out!" Lacey snapped.

"Why?" Parker faced her, eyes wide and totally without fault or blame. "You can see he's got the hots for you, dear, can't you? Why do you think he's always around, skulking in every dark corner, ready to jump to your aid at the drop of a hat? Any hat? He's such a would-be knight in furry-chested armor."

Lacey blushed. "He does not. You're being so obnoxious. He's just looking for a friend, that's all."

"He's looking for something, all right." Parker winked salaciously at her.

"Arrgh!" Lacey damn near screamed. "I can't even stand next to you right now." She moved off to paint another segment of the background, carefully avoiding looking at either man.

Yet her eyes strayed.

And Deacon was staring at her, and his gaze darted away when he was caught.

At the same time, Parker was watching Deacon, and he had that annoying, lecherous, lopsided grin on his face again.

That one gesture boded trouble, every single time.

Like the time Parker built a huge cock and balls out of papier-mâché, painted it in rainbow colors, and superglued it on the top of the dean's car. Or when he switched the handles on the classroom doors from one side to the other, thus enticing everyone to pull on the hinge side so none of the doors would open. Or when he attached silly string throughout the main entrance hallway, from every lock, hinge, handle, and possible point of attachment, creating an intricate web no one could see through, let alone get through, until the janitors cleared it up.

Lacey had a bad, bad feeling.

She wasn't sure which was the worst option, though. That Deacon had a thing for her. Or that Parker had a thing for her. Or that Parker had a thing for Deacon. Or that Parker wanted to bring Deacon down a notch with one of his pranks.

Was there an upside to this situation? Lacey sure wasn't seeing it.

"Still mad at me, my dear?"

Parker spoke, sotto voce, from right behind Lacey. He didn't sound timid, but he wasn't exactly being theatrical either. Lacey glanced at him over her should, and he did look repentant. Yes, maybe a little too repentant, with his bowed head and quivering jaw, but still....

"How could I possibly stay mad at a face like that?"

The instagrin that followed told Lacey everything. "Cool." Parker set up shop next to her and began painting again, but was quiet only for a blink of an eye. "So, are you gonna talk to Professor Marchand, or what?"

Lacey frowned, puzzled. "Why would I?"

"'Cause he's hot?"

"Oh, Parker!" Lacey pursed her lips, frustrated. "Do you want me to get mad at you? Because you're close to really irking me."

"Jerking you?" Parker looked pensive. "Hmm, sure, we could do that."

"Fine. I'm officially not talking to you." Lacey took a step to the side to put distance between them.

Parker followed. "What about unofficially?"

Lacey gave him a hard stare. "You're pushing it." When Parker drew breath for yet another comeback, Lacey cut in. "Don't even think of saying it, or I'm going to march straight over to the director's office, and rat you out." Parker chuckled, all cool like, waving his hand about in impervious dismissal. "Or… alternatively, I'll go talk to Spenser Wilcox, that straight third-year sax player, and tell him you have a major crush on him, and every time you happen to see him, you ogle his rear end."

Parker gasped in shock, his mouth hanging open and his eyes wide. "You wouldn't."

Lacey shrugged, feigning indifference. "I might. So give it a rest, will you?"

"Fine." Parker continued painting. "I'm just your best friend here, is all. I thought you might want to talk about it, how you're studying under your musical idol. But perhaps I'm just not trustworthy." He let out the tiniest sniffle, steadfastly looking away from her.

Lacey rolled her eyes. "Oh my God, Parker. Don't you think for a second I don't know what you're doing. And it's not gonna work."

Parker said nothing, just painted, his chin jutted out.

Lacey gave in, like always with Parker. "Oh, why do I do this? Look, when I said he's my idol, I swear to God I only meant in the musical sense, not in any kind of sexual sense. I do *not* have a crush on Bennett Marchand."

"Well, that's good to know."

Without needing to turn, Lacey recognized the professor's voice as it came from stage left, closing in on them. *Oh, please, God, just kill me now.* She was going to die of embarrassment—right here, right now. She was never going to live this down. Her body was all fired up, and not in a good way. Her face felt like it was burning.

"Good afternoon, Parker, Lacey," Professor Marchand said calmly, though there was a hint of amusement there.

Lacey couldn't will herself to turn around, and she stayed frozen in place, cheeks flaming.

"Professor," Parker said congenially, creating enough distraction to help Lacey get back in control. "Something we can do for you?"

"Actually, yes, you can." Professor Marchand sounded cool as ever, totally professional. At last Lacey was able to face him, and with a courteous smile, too.

The renowned violinist epitomized cool sophistication, wealth, and breeding. His gray pinstriped suit, gray silk tie, gray vest, and black shoes probably cost more money than Lacey's yearly tuition. Marchand's dark hair was gray at the temples, but apart from a few laugh lines around his eyes, he could've been in his thirties instead of late forties. Distinguished was the word that came to mind, or sexy if you preferred.

"What is it, sir?" Lacey asked and remembered to thank her lucky stars for keeping her tone neutral.

"I'm hosting a party two weeks from now. It's an annual event. I typically invite a few of the top musicians in my class to play there— for pay, of course—and this year I've got my eye on you, Lacey."

Lacey all but swallowed her tongue, unable to find her voice for anything but a totally undignified squeak.

"Lacey, you are a fine violinist. I'd be honored to host your first formal performance, though at a less than formal setting." Before Lacey could stutter a yes or a no, Professor Marchand faced Parker. "Your teachers speak very highly of you as well, Parker. I could use a pianist."

Parker glanced at Lacey warily. "With all due respect, Professor, as much as we would love to help you out, Lacey's musical style and genre are very different from mine. She's a classical violinist. I'm a jazz pianist."

Professor Marchand smiled. "I was hoping for some fusion that night anyway. Consider it thematic for the evening. If you two agree, I only need to find a drummer and a sax player."

"I know where to find a saxophone player." Lacey smiled sweetly, glancing at Parker, who looked positively ill then. The idea of spending a night playing next to his straight-guy crush was probably not what Parker had had in mind when suggesting they accept this offer.

"And I'm a drummer, Professor Marchand," Deacon said, coming into view behind them. "Sorry. I didn't mean to eavesdrop, but I couldn't help but overhear. I play jazz and alternative rock."

"Great, a quartet in one fell swoop," Professor Marchand said, exalted. "I'll inform you of the details in a day or so. Thank you all." Without waiting to hear if any one of them actually agreed, he walked off, humming happily.

"Well, I guess we all have to learn how to get along after all." Parker said this with his usual flare and sarcastic humor and gave Deacon a slow once-over. That look had Lacey crawling up the walls. Deacon snarled silently, revealing his teeth. Parker smiled back, also showing teeth.

Lacey sighed. True enough, they were committed now. In for a penny, in for a pound.

Chapter 22

"HEY, Bro."

Practically jumping out of his skin, as he was reading, deep in thought, Bro looked up to see Eddy walking toward him and then sitting down across from him at the narrow table of the library. "Hi, Eddy."

What had at first seemed like a pretty decent friendship had become something a bit more uncomfortable for Bro as he observed Eddy flirting with him at every opportunity. The guy was damn fine, but the truth was he wasn't Bro's type. Bro wanted a pretty little thing like Lacey. A petite, feminine boy whose cock made him turn inside out with a mere thought.

Eddy leaned forward over the table to see what Bro was reading. "What you doing?"

Bro harrumphed. "This is in the syllabus. Mandatory reading." He offered the cover of the book about media management and marketing. "It's not even half as exciting as I thought film studies would be." He sighed. A lot of things were different from the way he'd imagined them. It had been naïve of him to assume all he would be doing was watching films and TV all day. Now he knew better.

Eddy's green eyes sparkled with interest. "Yeah, I hear ya, brother. It wasn't what I was expecting either."

Another surprise Eddy had sprung on Bro had been him enrolling
into the same class in communications studies as Bro. Eddy had said he
was planning to major in computer science, but now he was talking
about a double major. In an effort to avoid giving Eddy the idea he was
interested when he wasn't, Bro had volunteered at the HU Speech and
Hearing Clinic. Considering he knew ASL like the back of his hand, so
to speak, he'd been warmly welcomed, and he felt useful and on track
again after getting lost in a sea of scholastic oddities.

"Mmm," Bro muttered noncommittally and resumed reading.

"Wanna go for a run, maybe? Just to get your mind off this for a
while."

A month into their college lives, Bro had realized Bradley was
awfully busy with his own studies and watching over his twin, Ricky. It
had been more difficult than he'd anticipated to arrange time for even
minimal hanging out together, even though they were both on the
football team. Practice was regimented and gave them little time to talk.
Eddy had been eager to fill the void left by Bradley, and they had
started running together in the mornings or when they had time to kill.
Eddy ran track, so he needed to run, while Bro also needed to keep up
his running skills for football. Therefore, it was natural for them to
practice together.

Bro frowned. "I can't right now. I really have to read this chapter.
It's gonna come up next class."

"Fuck. You're no fun." But Eddy grinned as he said it and evoked
a similar response from Bro. Eddy's tone dropped and turned husky.
"Come on," he enticed seductively. "You know you wanna go out for a
spin. Just a few miles. Then we'll come back and hang. Or you can read
your boring book again."

The idea of letting his mind wander as he put his body to the test
did sound appealing to Bro, and not just a little. In a month of college,
he'd spent more time reading than in any six months of high school,
and he was exhausted. His brain felt like it was oozing out through his
ears to avoid serious cramming situations like these. Maybe he simply
didn't have a school brain, but a sports brain. That wouldn't surprise
him at all.

Bro closed his eyes and willed himself to relax. *I love to read. I want to read this book. Yeah, I fucking want to read this stupid, stupid book, and learn all this stuff, and become a responsible adult, and....* He couldn't even finish the thought before he was groaning with boredom.

"Okay, let's go."

TEN minutes later, Bro may have been running on adrenaline, but he was floating high on endorphins, just glad to have his body in motion. Running was great. Bro was a fast runner, and he let himself go. His muscles strained at first, but he soon grew to love the bitter juices and the coppery taste of blood in his mouth. It was always like this. Then he fell into the zone, and it was all good.

On account of his brain having checked out to lie on the beach of the sea of tranquility, it took Bro a moment to realize Eddy was speaking to him.

"What do you wanna do after?"

Huh? After what? Oh, right, the run. Suddenly Bro wasn't floating anymore. No, he was plummeting down toward inevitable reality. They needed to have this talk right the fuck now, even at the risk of spoiling his high.

He slowed down to a gentle jog, and immediately Eddy matched his speed. "Listen, dude. I'm glad we're friends, you know. But I'm with Lacey. And that's not gonna change anytime soon."

At that Eddy stopped, leaning on his thighs and panting roughly for a few breaths, but then he straightened up, with the help of his hands on the small of his back. "What are you talking about?"

Bro stopped as well and considered his friend. Did the guy not know he was constantly flirting? How could he not know? "If I got this wrong, these vibes I'm getting from you, then hey, I'm sorry."

Eddy didn't look at Bro, who got a funny feeling. Eddy was staring out across the waters of the McMillan Reservoir. "Look, Bro...." Eddy sure sounded unsure, and his tone had dropped to a near whisper. Then he looked down at the ground and kicked a few pebbles with the tip of his shoe. "Yeah, okay. I'm into you." He shrugged, but his body language screamed discomfort. "I know you're dating Lacey. I just... I can't help the way I feel, you know." He swallowed hard and looked really pale and nauseous. "I'm sorry, Bro, if I made you feel bad."

Bro closed his eyes and prayed for patience and the right words. He didn't want to fuck up a friendship, but there was no chance this was happening between them. Not now anyway. "Eddy, I'm not offended or angry, or anything. I just wanted to clear the air. Right now I'm with Lace, and I love her, man."

Eddy managed to look more miserable, crestfallen even. "Yeah, I know."

"I don't know what's gonna happen down the line, a week or month from now, or a year. Maybe me and Lacey won't last." *God, please don't let me lose her.* "But at this point in my life, I can't be with you. It wouldn't be fair to anyone." Bro really hoped Eddy understood. He liked Eddy a lot as a friend. They had similar interests, and they had fun together.

Suddenly Eddy barked out a self-deprecating laugh. "I guess friends with benefits is also out then, huh?"

Bro moved closer and placed a hand on his friend's shoulder. "I've never been with anyone but Lacey. But if I were to consider it, I'd go for you." That may very well have been the dumbest thing he'd ever said, but he wanted Eddy to feel good about himself, not rejected and hopeless. Although Bro didn't want to give him any false hope, either.

But thankfully Eddy did seem a little perkier. He looked up at Bro through his dark bangs, and a flicker of a smile turned up his lips. "Yeah? Well, I guess I'll have to settle for that."

Bro clapped Eddy's shoulder in a show of camaraderie. "Jesus, man. This place is crawling with hotties who'd bend over the second you winked at them. Plenty more fish in the sea."

Now Eddy's smile was a full-on lewd grin. "Yeah, that's right." Then he gave Bro the once-over. "Yeah, I think I can do better than your scrawny little ass."

Then he took off running, cackling maniacally, and Bro dashed after him, cursing like a sailor.

READING the interrupted book back home was a grueling experience, and he despised it with every fiber of his being. When he heard the door close, he knew he'd gotten his reprieve for the time being. And sure enough, a minute later his door opened and Lacey stepped in.

"Hey, welcome home, stranger," Bro said with a smile. The night was getting darker, and the streets lights outside cast a yellowish glow on the ceiling. Up at the loft this was as close as they could get. But the white ceiling reflected some light down, and the beams illuminated Lacey so beautifully Bro's heart leaped up to his throat, and he had to swallow convulsively.

"Oh God, Bro, I've missed you so much." Lacey kicked off her shoes, ran toward the bed, and jumped on it, almost squishing Bro. But he sure didn't mind as he wrapped his arms around his girlfriend.

Then they were kissing, and the outside world faded away.

When Bro flipped Lacey onto her back and lay on top of her, Lacey let out a sweet sigh, as if satisfaction were finally at hand. "You okay, babe?"

Lacey smiled up at him. "It's just been one of those days."

Bro rolled his eyes, knowing exactly what to expect. "Parker?"

"He thinks I have a crush on Bennett Marchand, the professor I was telling you about, the world-famous violinist." Lacey paused, waiting for a reaction, and Bro nodded. "Well, anyway, Parker got me so wound up I pretty much shouted out loud I wasn't into Marchand. Guess who was standing right behind me?"

Bro bit back a laugh. "No! Really?"

"Yes." Lacey's cheeks colored pink with shame, and the furrow between her brows grew more pronounced. "I was so embarrassed. I could just strangle Parker sometimes!"

"What did the dear old professor do?"

"He pretended nothing happened. And then he invited me, Parker, and a few others to play at this shindig he's throwing for some social bigwigs in a few weeks." Lacey's eyes widened at this point, the wooden hues all but melting into various shades of green. "Oh, Bro. I'll get to perform in front of people. Real people. Important people. I'm so scared."

Bro kissed Lacey softly, loving the feel of her pliable lips beneath his own. "You've got nothing to worry about, baby. You're really good. You'll do great. I know it."

"But—" Lacey started, all worried and keyed up.

"No buts," Bro cut in, adamant. "You don't want to call me a liar." Then he softened his tone and gave Lacey an Eskimo kiss. "You and Parker will practice, and it'll be fine."

Lacey gave a shy smile. "We're gonna get paid for it, too."

Bro's grin grew. "Hey, even better!"

Giggling, Lacey covered her mouth with her hand. But then her fingers stole out to ghost over Bro's lips, as if retracing the shape, texture, and warmth. "I love you, Bro. If anyone else told me this, I don't think I'd believe them. So… how was your day?"

Growing serious and moving off to lie at Lacey's side, Bro wasn't sure how to have this conversation. He only knew he didn't want to keep secrets from the boy he loved. "Eddy told me today he had feelings for me."

Lacey's whole body tensed next to him, but she kept her face neutral. Bro could see how this feigned coolness cost her. "Oh?"

"Yeah." Bro laid his head on the pillow next to her, and Lacey turned to face him. "I told him I was with you, that I loved you, and how that wasn't going to change. I told him I could be his friend, but that's all."

Lacey swallowed, and she worried her lower lip. "And? How did he take it?"

Bro frowned. "He said he was okay with it. I told him there were plenty of other guys out there, and he seemed fine then. So, I guess we're still friends."

Lacey managed a small smile. "You're glad about that, aren't you?"

Bro lay on his back and stared at the ceiling, where light and shadow danced. "Yeah, I am. Brad, Dree, and Ricky all have their own things most of the time. Some days I barely see them for more than a minute or two. It sucks. Eddy's there." He turned to look at his girlfriend. "You think that's not reason enough to hang with him? Availability?"

Lacey snuggled up next to him, and her arm came around his waist. "I don't know. So far he's seemed like a good friend to you. I suppose if he has ulterior motives or any other plans in store for you, they'll come out eventually. But I know I'd hate it at Peabody if I didn't have Parker's friendship. And he's sort of available, too, so...."

"You miss Audrey?"

"Yes. Could we do something this next weekend, just the four of us? Like a movie or something? The weekend after that is the party when I'm supposed to perform."

"It's during the weekend?"

"Saturday."

"Good thing you're getting paid. I hate to lose even one day with you."

Lacey bussed his cheek and cuddled closer. "I know. Me too."

Bro stared at the ceiling. "You think we're being too codependent or something?"

Lacey snickered. "You mean 'cause we miss each other like crazy when it's just half a day when we don't see each other? Maybe. But I don't want to stop." Then she wiggled. "Unless you think I'm being too clingy."

Bro huffed out a breath, amused at their similarities. "And here I was thinking *you* thought *I* was too clingy and needy." They were on the same wavelength, had been since day one. It was wonderful to have it confirmed yet again.

That got Lacey laughing. "Oh, Bro. We're just two peas in a pod, aren't we?"

Bro hugged Lacey tight and inhaled the scent of her hair. "We sure are, baby." Then, on a whim, he added mysteriously, "Next weekend, I wanna try something different with you, Lace. You know, sexually. You up for that?"

Shuddering, Lacey nuzzled Bro's neck, and he had his answer.

Oh, Bro couldn't wait.

Chapter 23

WHILE Saturday was going to be reserved for movie night with friends, Friday was for Bro and Lacey alone.

It seemed like they had the loft to themselves as well. Jordan and Sebastian had gone to a spa for the weekend, at Sebastian's insistence—the scene with a grumbling, seething Jordan had been worth the show 'cause according to Jordan, real men didn't do bubble baths, or something to that effect—while Jack and Kevin had gone to a nearby dude ranch for horseback riding, and another kind of riding too.

As a result, come nightfall the house was silent to the point of eeriness.

Once they had checked that all the doors and windows were locked and the security system turned on, Bro led Lacey to the bathroom so they could clean up. It wasn't even seven yet, but the nights were getting darker and chillier. The concrete floor was cold to tread on even with the carpets, so they hurried to the warmth of the bathroom's heated floor.

His blue eyes darkening, Bro watched Lacey with intense hunger as he undressed her, and she shivered right down to her tippy-toes. Biting her lower lip, she lifted her hands above her head and allowed Bro to remove her dress.

She looked down at herself and saw the boy *he* was naked, all long legs and slender arms, caramel-colored skin and barely visible muscles. Lacey had always felt a little bit awkward, skinny, and somewhat androgynous. But his erection was proof positive he was indeed male, and he wasn't petite all over.

"Mmm, you look delicious." Bro's appreciative gaze had dropped to Lacey's cock, and he stared at it voraciously, licking his lips.

Lacey frowned, worried his lip some more, and glanced down. Yes, erect he was quite impressive. Yet he sometimes thought that pink piece of cut flesh could have looked more, well, manly. Why did it have to be pink? He groused at the view.

But then…. "Stop it, Lace. I know exactly what you're thinking. That pout's such a telltale sign. You have a perfect dick, and it's all mine."

With that, Bro sank to his knees on the bathroom floor, took hold of Lacey's hips, and swallowed the cockhead in one move. Lacey moaned and grabbed hold of Bro's shoulder to keep himself upright. His knees wobbled, as if made of jelly, but he managed not to fall on his face.

Bro took his time. He kissed all over the hard length, wetting the member to the point of dripping with saliva, and then used his hand around the base to squeeze Lacey's pleasure slightly toward pain. God, it was good, Lacey mused, happy with the sweet torment. Then Bro began to tug Lacey's cock in sync with his mouth bobbing up and down, and Lacey flew up high.

"See? Look at you. All pretty purple for me, all that blood gushing to your dick. Yeah, you're delectable, Lace."

Bro wasn't watching Lacey's face as he looked down, hot all over. Instead, Bro was ogling Lacey's dick with unabashed desire as he continued to jerk off his boyfriend. Then Bro's tongue came out and stole a few drops of precome gathering at the top, which was now dark red and engorged with blood. Bro's thumb brushed over the sensitive slit and even pressed down a bit to deliver delightful pressure.

Lacey all but tumbled over as he groaned. Pleasure ripped through his body from the tip of his dick and expanded throughout until he was sweating with the heat of it. "Oh, yes. That's so good. Please."

But that was when Bro stopped and stood up. Lacey may have mewled disapproval.

Chuckling, Bro steered Lacey into the shower stall and turned on the water, the cool spray taking a moment to warm up. "First things first, yeah?"

Lacey was covered in goose bumps, some from the slowly heating water, some from the teasing blowjob. "I hate you," he spat out, sulking again.

Bro laughed as he covered Lacey's back with his front, keeping him tucked close. "No moping tonight, baby." Then, without waiting for a snarky comeback, Bro moistened and soaped up a loofah, and began to wash Lacey from head to toes.

It was pure heaven.

Lacey let himself be indulged by the gentle touches of his lover. And there was still the surprise Bro had promised, or hinted at, to be precise. Something new sexually. What could it be, he puzzled. But tension fell from his shoulders along with the suds as Bro relaxed him with his tender ministrations.

"My turn," Lacey demanded when Bro was done.

He brushed his hair out of his eyes and made sure Bro was standing right in front of him, all wet and glistening. And the smug grin on his face was just icing on the cake. Lacey liked it when Bro got all confident with his boyfriend. Not quite arrogant, but self-assured.

With slow circles and leisurely strokes, Lacey washed Bro's body, covering it with gel and suds. He trailed the sponge over hard flanks and defined lines, over bulging muscles, smooth grooves, and silky indents. The best part was when he dropped to his knees and traced the V-shape dipping down to his groin, and with soapy hands palmed the stiff erection almost poking his eye out as it stood straight up, nearly kissing Bro's belly button.

When Lacey's fingers rubbed over the head of Bro's penis, Bro let out a guttural groan. Then he whipped his hand out fast and stopped Lacey cold. "No more, baby. I don't want come in the shower. I have plans."

With reluctance, Lacey nodded, stood up, and finished washing Bro.

Together they rinsed, dried off, and went to bed.

Once there, Lacey lay on his back, simmering with anticipation. What was Bro up to? The fact that he couldn't guess only heightened the wonderful hot pressure building in his groin. For a moment, he thought perhaps tonight was the night they'd go all the way. Yet Lacey couldn't be sure, so he simply forced himself to lie still and wait patiently.

While Lacey was busy conjuring calming images, Bro moved about in the room as if in search of something. When he finally stopped at the foot of the bed, Lacey gasped.

Bro was holding a tube of lube and a big white terry towel. As he stood there, looking all masculine and perfect, Lacey could barely hold still. He wanted to lunge at Bro, and yet he was too anxious to do so.

"You okay, Lace?" Bro asked, his tone low and hesitant.

"I'm fine," Lacey vowed, and was able to produce a halfway decent encouraging smile. "So… tonight, then?"

Bro smiled, but then surprisingly shook his head slowly. "Not quite." Then he knelt on the bedspread, close to Lacey's feet. "Lift up." After Lacey obeyed, Bro rested the towel on the bed, smoothing out wrinkles carefully. "Lie down." Once again Lacey did as he was told. There was no reason not to. He trusted Bro. On his back again, with the slightly ticklish and rough towel beneath him, Lacey watched Bro, who placed the lube on the comforter. Then he stopped, kneeling still between Lacey's legs. "Okay. Here's what we're gonna do. I know this is different from other times when we've had sex. You can say no or stop at any time. I will stop, okay?"

Lacey nodded, feeling the damp of his hair against the towel, or it could have been sweat, since he was hot all over, tingling. "What *are* we gonna do?"

Bro took a deep breath and nodded, as if confirming his own intentions. "I'm going to eat your ass. And then I'm going to put a finger inside you. Lubed up, of course. Nothing more. Just that. Like a test, you know. I mean… it's not like we've never touched each other down there. We've just never gone… in. Now I will. With you." Then he was deadly serious. "Unless you don't want me to. Just say the word. It's okay. I won't be mad or anything. I want this to be a good experience for both of us." Then he visibly swallowed, and Lacey saw how nervous his guy really was. That was kind of a relief. "So... what do you think?"

Lacey took a deep breath, too, and shivered all over. His pucker was already twitching at the idea. "I think I want to do that. I want *you* to do that to me." Then she had a doubt. "But what about you? Will I...?"

"No." Bro shook his head. "I was gonna make this night all about you." Suddenly he shook his head furiously and rubbed a hand over his face. "God, that sounded so stupid. I didn't mean to say I would never bend over for you. 'Cause I totally would. It's just... I just wanted to do this for you tonight. Well... I'm not being completely selfless here. A lot of it will be for me too, obviously. After all, I'll get to... to be inside you. For the first time. Your first."

All of a sudden Lacey felt a tightening in his chest, right where his heart was. Sure, there was an emotional lump lodged in his throat as well, but this was different. The kind approach his boyfriend had to this, their first attempt at anal sex, was somehow exactly what Lacey needed to calm his nerves.

They were going to do this. "All right." Lacey spread his legs more, revealing all of his nether regions to Bro's view. "Bro? I love you."

Smiling and letting out a breath, Bro nodded. "I love you too." He scooted up closer to Lacey's groin, and his knees bumped Lacey's thighs, pushing them even farther apart. Then Bro frowned, his hands wavering. "Should we, um, just try it, or do you want to make out first?" Lacey bit down a giggle of happiness threatening to burst out, but Bro quickly added, "'Cause I'm fine either way. I mean it's not like making out with you is ever a chore, you know." He chuckled at the end, and Lacey felt even more at ease.

"Come up here and kiss me," Lacey beckoned, and Bro did as requested. Their body parts lined up, pressed against each other, and then they were kissing, slow and easy, like they had all the time in the world. Both their skins were hot and coated with a sheen of sweat, and their mutual rubbing was slick and effortless.

All too soon, Bro pulled back, but Lacey let him go. "Had you kissed me one more second, this would've been over with a bang," he commented, breathless.

Bro chuckled at that, but he was partly gasping too. "Why do you think *I* stopped?"

Lacey sighed, lifting his hands above his head, and gazed up at Bro dreamily. "We fit so well together, don't we?"

"Like the birds and the bees," Bro joked, winking.

Lacey rolled his eyes. "Gosh, that had to be silliest—"

Bro kissed him just long enough to silence him, and then he withdrew.

His hands landed on Lacey's thighs, and his corded muscles jumped at the contact. But Bro seemed pensive. "Hmm, should you, maybe, turn around?" Lacey didn't get a chance to comply or refuse when Bro nodded decisively. "Yeah, on your stomach." Without argument, Lacey rolled over on his belly, wiggling to get comfortable on the slightly scratchy towel. Then he heard it. Bro inhaled sharply. "God, that's fucking beautiful."

The moment the utterance echoed around the room, Bro's mouth had already latched onto Lacey's backside. Lacey shuddered violently and gasped, blinking hard as he stared into the pillow. It wasn't exactly an out-of-body experience; he was firmly rooted in place under his lover's ministrations.

At first, Bro licked long lines up and down the globes of Lacey's ass, shoving at his thighs to push his legs out of his way. Lacey tucked his knees under his belly a bit and spread himself wide open. Bro murmured appreciatively as he sank his teeth into Lacey's ass cheek. Lacey jerked, and then he moaned, a full, wanton sound that escaped from deep in his very being. The nibbles continued, and so did the licks. Lacey's body trembled, and he wondered if anything had ever felt so good.

Then Bro's tongue swirled around Lacey's hole, flicking right across the puckered skin to send Lacey's channel into a clenching frenzy.

In passing he wondered what Bro must have tasted right then. Did Lacey taste good or bad? He had showered, so it should be just skin, right? He honestly had no idea. While he had sampled Bro's ass cheeks several times in the nearly two years they'd been together, that had been different. This was his hole, his body's exit point—and apparently entry too. After all, if God hadn't designed the ass for this kind of play too, then why did Bro eating his ass feel so damn good?

Lacey was about to come apart at the seams. He clutched at the sheets, heat coming out of his every pore, and blood thundered in his ears, deafening him to every other sound.

Suddenly Bro stopped and leaned back on his haunches.

Surprised, confused, and disappointed, Lacey pushed up on his arms and glanced over his shoulder. "Did I do something wrong?"

Bro scrambled out of bed, but halted in midmotion. "What? Fuck, no! I'm just getting a pillow." Lacey barely got a breath of relief out before Bro stuffed a pillow under his hips to lift him up, most likely at a better angle for Bro. Lacey's assumption was confirmed when Bro made a hard hungry noise, knelt back on the bed, used his hands to part Lacey's buttocks, and dove right back in with gusto.

That was when the slurping sounds began, and Lacey's eyes flew open in something akin to shock. He had never heard such sounds, not even when either of them were sucking cock. Bro was doing things with his lips, delivering heavy suction, and his teeth nipped, and his tongue laved and licked and probed. And all the time there was that *sound*. It was so incredibly dirty, and sort of erotic, and more than a little obscene, but Lacey was getting harder by the second listening to it. In fact, his cock was so hot and straining he ached.

"Bro, please," he mumbled, his words slurred with pleasure. He felt if he were any more relaxed and open for his boyfriend, his DNA would unwind.

But Bro wasn't done, not by a long shot. "Not yet, baby." Then he went right back to his meal, and his hands kneaded Lacey's ass cheeks so roughly, they would be bruised for weeks. Yet every sensation given, even the squeezing pain, only heightened his pleasure.

Lacey shook all over, unable to catch his breath, and his heart thudded. He let out a whimper that tried to be a coherent plea but ended up a moaning gurgle.

When Bro pulled back, just an inch or so, Lacey suddenly felt cold liquid touching his hole, circling it. *Lube.* Lacey closed his eyes tighter and pushed back against the gentle brush.

But Bro wasn't having any of Lacey's urgency. Every time Lacey tried to shove back to get that teasing finger in, Bro withdrew.

Then he just couldn't take it anymore. "Damn it, Bro! If you don't give it to me now, I'm never speaking to you again!"

Bro stilled for a second. Then that smug chuckle sounded. "Guess you're ready, then."

Lacey was about to give the flippant boy his comeuppance when that wet digit, warmer now, pressed on his sphincter, insistently this time. Unfortunately, against the weight of it, Lacey's hole clamped shut tight.

"No…," he complained, his voice muffled into the pillow.

"It's okay, Lace. Just relax. I won't hurt you." Bro's soft, crooning voice was unlike anything Lacey had heard before. Bro's other hand came to rest on the small of Lacey's back, and it was as if a connection was drawn. A line of fire between his two hands, and that warmth spread all over Lacey, easing the sudden tension.

Then he heard yet another new sound. A wet suction, as if his ass was trying to get the invader in. A pop rang in his ears when he felt Bro's finger slip inside.

Lacey shivered. He'd expected pain, but there was none. Yes, a mild discomfort and a strong urge to push out, but no pain. "H-how far in…?"

"Just the tip." Lacey heard the strain in Bro's hoarse voice, and he peered at Bro over his shoulder. Bro was staring down, rapt, undoubtedly at the point where they merged. There was perspiration all over his tanned skin, and his muscles were taut. He was concentrating deeply, and yet the lust was fully visible in his eyes, now dark as midnight skies.

He wants this as much as I do, maybe more. That thought gave Lacey enough courage and comfort to loosen up entirely.

Then Bro's finger entered him all the way. Lacey felt him greasing the walls of his ass, lubing him up for more. God, there was gonna be more. He pressed his face against the comforter and closed his eyes, sighing with contentment.

"You okay, Lace?" Bro asked, his voice raspy and breathy. His hand on Lacey's back trembled. Perhaps his control was waning too.

"Yes. It feels good."

"Yeah?" Bro sounded happy and relieved. It occurred to Lacey maybe they had both worried about doing this, just differently. Lacey had felt anxious about penetration, about pain, about lasting effects. Now he realized Bro must have dreaded the idea too, only that he wouldn't be able to give Lacey pleasure, to make their first time good, to have them enjoy this first time.

"Oh, yes. Please, Bro. Give me more."

Bro hesitated, his finger stilling inside Lacey. "You sure?"

Lacey nodded. "I'm sure. Want more."

He heard Bro taking a deep breath and then felt him easing another finger against the lubed-up entrance. Then he pushed in.

Oh, pain. Lacey closed his eyes tight, gritted his teeth, and willed his body not to try to run. It would feel good again soon, right? He'd always wondered what the burning sensation meant. Now he knew. It was as if someone was holding a flame to all the nerve endings of his entire body at the same time, and then adding pressure to them, more and more weight until he thought he was going to climb the walls just to get away.

But then he heard Bro's timid voice. "You okay? Does this hurt?"

Trust and love overwhelmed Lacey, like soothing waters cascading over the wildfire. The pain eased as he relaxed. "Yes. Yes. I'm all right. Just took a moment, is all. I'm fine."

Lacey more felt than saw Bro release the breath he was holding. "Thank God."

Then his fingers began to move again. First in and out, but then swiveling around a bit. It was the most curious sensation. Lacey couldn't think, only feel. His imagination about this part of his anatomy getting probed and felt up by another person had been lacking. This was *so* much better in real life. It took an act of faith, of both trust in Bro and confidence in himself, to give them this experience.

Bro twisted his fingers inside Lacey, and it felt damn good. A strange kind of heat and pressure, but good nonetheless. Then again, this was only two fingers. How on earth was a thick hard cock like Bro's ever going to fit in?

"Where is it…?" Bro muttered, his tone impatient and frustrated.

Where's what? Lacey frowned in puzzlement. Then his fried brain provided the needed information. Right, the prostate.

And at that exact moment, Bro found what he was looking for. His fingers bumped on Lacey's sweet spot.

"Oh my effing God!" he cried out. His body jolted when electricity shot through him and consumed him in flames. His groin was lit up like a Christmas tree when the lights were flipped on, and his dick shot out precome in a spurt. *God, I almost came.*

Bro chuckled a bit, panting. "Oh yeah. Right there, huh?"

"Please, do it again." Lacey wasn't above begging, not when that much pleasure was in his grasp.

So Bro did. With relentless fingers, he doled out so much attention on Lacey's prostate there was no doubt about coming. In fact, Lacey was right there, hurtling into the unknown of the kind of sex he'd only ever dreamt about. *Why haven't we done this sooner?* But he knew they hadn't been ready before. Every time they touched, the fiery urgency was there, controlling their instincts, pushing them to come. Patience was something they'd had to learn.

"Oh, God, yes," Lacey groaned and started to shove his ass back toward the hand that was giving him such delight.

"You like?" Bro sounded pleased with himself again, and that self-assurance definitely calmed all of Lacey's fears. His lover was giving him time, attention, tenderness, and enjoyment beyond belief.

"Yes. Yes. *Yes!*"

Then Bro shifted his fingers so he was able to stroke in and out while simultaneously pressing his thumb against Lacey's perineum. He was pushing on that secret sex button inside and out. Lacey was pretty much mewling then, letting out half gasps, half keening noises.

Lacey moved up his knees so he was essentially shoving his ass up and back for Bro's taking. That move also allowed him to fist his own cock and beat it in time with those agile fingers inside him, owning him. His hips worked involuntarily, thrusting back and forth on pure instinct.

"Mmm, nice." Bro's compliment only added to Lacey's desire. Then Bro used his other hand to grab Lacey's balls, the sac wound up tight and high, ready to blow. "Love your balls. So cute."

"Huh?" Lacey thought he might have misheard, but his squeak was loud and angry.

Bro chuckled and planted a sloppy, wet, hot open-mouthed kiss on Lacey's left cheek. "You heard me. Your balls are so pretty. All pink and tight and small."

Now Lacey was getting pissed. What guy wanted to be told his balls were tinier than a bug's penis? He wasn't that much of a girl, petite or no. "Get off me, you oaf."

Bro wouldn't let up. "I love you, Lace. I love how your balls are the perfect size for me. I can always get them in my mouth at the same time. Love that about you."

And just like that, Lacey's righteous fury evaporated, and he was left with a mushy, happy feeling centered on his chest. "Bastard."

But grumbling never worked with Bro, who laughed. "Love you, baby."

And then he dipped his head and licked Lacey's balls from behind.

That, Bro's words, and his fingers on Lacey's sweet spot was all it took.

Lacey shouted, eyes screwed shut, and started coming. His cock twitched and jerked as his balls drew up and released all that pent-up sexual tension and white seed out through the slit onto his hand. He kept coming for ages, spilling out jets of semen with every spasm, again and again, until his balls and dick were wrung dry and his groin hurt from the exertion. He had nothing more to give, so he slumped on the bed, whimpering.

"Fuck, that's the hottest thing I've ever seen."

Lacey barely heard Bro's words through the drumming in his ears, but he was pretty sure Bro's fingers had dislodged from inside him. He felt empty, almost bereft at the loss.

What he also felt, curiously, was his wet cheeks. *I just cried through an orgasm.* It was a heady realization. He had never blubbered during sex. Lacey had to admit this time Bro had really hit a home run. As surreptitiously as possible, he wiped the remaining moisture away.

Not only did he need to reciprocate, he wanted to.

With a groan and protesting muscles, Lacey rolled over slowly onto his back. Bro was sitting on his haunches at the foot of the bed, a goofy grin gracing his lips, and his glazed-over eyes sparkled.

"You okay, Lace?" His concerned words belied his complacent stance.

Lacey opened his mouth, but only harsh breaths came out. He felt flushed all over, his skin sparking and tingling. "Mmm-hmm." Then he weakly started to force himself to sit up.

"What are you doing?" Bro stopped Lacey with a hand on his thigh.

Lacey looked up at his eyes. "Don't you want to…?"

Bro looked amused and bemused, tilting his head. "Want to get fingered, or to come? 'Cause I already did the latter."

Confused, his eyebrows rising to his hairline, Lacey looked down. Bro's penis lay on the groove of his hip, limp and sated, with white blotches of come on it, on his thigh and belly, and on the sheets. "You came…."

Bro chuckled and nodded, surprised. "Yeah, I did. While I had my finger in your ass. That was the most amazing thing I've ever had the privilege of witnessing. If I thought you could muster up the strength, I'd do it to all over again."

Lacey gulped, wide-eyed. The buzz in his body was getting louder as Bro added fuel to the fire with his enticing words. "I…."

Bro laughed, shaking his head. "I'm gonna get us both cleaned up, and then we can get some sleep, yeah?" He bounced up on his feet, happy as a clam. Just as he opened the bedroom door to go across the hall to the bathroom, he turned around and stared at Lacey with pride. "I'd say that was a successful test, wouldn't you?"

Lacey laughed too, though still trying to catch his breath. "I'll be up for more research whenever." Then he stretched like a feline. "Well, after a nap, that is."

Even after closing his eyes and beginning to drift off, Lacey heard Bro's chuckle from down the hall. And as annoyingly self-satisfied as his boy was, that sound still made Lacey's heart fly.

Chapter 24

"WE SHOULD form a band," Parker announced out of the blue.

In shock, Lacey glanced over her shoulder to the backseat, where Parker sat next to a displeased, grumpy-looking Deacon. "What?"

Parker smiled charmingly. "The past two weeks of practicing for this shindig has gone extremely well, hasn't it? You must all admit the four of us work well together."

Lacey sat back in her seat, wondering if that was indeed true. From a certain point of view, it was. They had created a set where each instrument—violin, piano, drums, and sax—got its chance to shine. And from the planning stage to the practical, it had all gone off without a hitch. So maybe there was a grain of truth in Parker's statement.

Still, where Parker and Spenser Wilcox raved about jazz, Deacon leaned toward rock, and Lacey was never going to abandon classical. As a band, their music wouldn't be a fashionable eclectic fusion, but a mishmash of clashing styles, all desiring to be dominant.

"Parker, we might have been in sync during practice, but putting together a group out of people with such varying interests wouldn't get very far," she said, appealing to his reason.

Parker snorted. "Aw, you're no fun. Always focusing on the negative."

"I do not," Lacey denied, pouting at the accusation.

She turned to see what their driver, Spenser, the third-year sax player, thought about the discussion. But the massive black guy with dyed red hair had his white earbuds in, hooked up to his iPod, and his head was nodding slightly, moving to the music. Clearly, he was above such petty conversation. In fact, when he'd first met Lacey, he had given her a contemptuous look—not of disgust at the petite queer boy in a dress, but of his disdain at having to play with first-year students. What a snob, Lacey had thought. Yet she had to admit he played the sax rather well.

"Seriously though," Parker continued after a brief silence. "Wouldn't it be fun to travel the country and play, just for the fun of it?" A hint of longing tinted his tone.

Lacey felt for him. "Could you, or any of us, just pack up and leave to play gigs at bars and small stages all over the country? Come on, Parker. Be reasonable. What about your studies and degree? What about your family and friends?"

Parker stared out the window, his face blank. Lacey was worried she'd gone too far. It wasn't her business to shoot down his dreams. She was ashamed of herself.

But Parker spoke first. "My parents love me, but they ignore me."

"Oh, Parker. I'm so sorry." Now Lacey felt even worse, and she shrunk into the seat.

Parker shrugged, making a noncommittal noise in his throat. "Doesn't matter, and sure doesn't bear mentioning. Poor little rich boy is such a cliché." His voice took on a mocking tone.

But Lacey had her own reasons for feeling empathy with her friend. "It's nothing to sneer at, Parker. At least they love you. That's something."

"Is it?" Parker said sharply. "I sense a story there." Lacey didn't need to turn around to feel Deacon fidgeting in his seat. Naturally, Parker noticed. "What's the matter with you? Ants in your pants?" Deacon's harsh, quickening breathing was full of emotions held back, and Parker just had to go poking the sleeping bear. "Does all this family talk make you uncomfortable? Or maybe it's Lacey who gets under your skin so?" His voice lilted at the end, a decidedly feminine quirk.

"Must you be so…?" Deacon spat out, angry. But at least he didn't finish.

"So—what, Mr. Rake? Garish, gaudy, flaming, flamboyant, outspoken, opinionated, smart, funny, stunning? Do tell." Parker was just getting started, and Lacey cringed. They were both big boys and could handle themselves. Should she still cut in and play peacemaker?

Deacon said nothing, just sat there ramrod straight, seething quietly.

Parker didn't leave it at that. "This Neanderthal act is so tedious. These grunts and all that rage? You're going to blow a blood vessel or a brain cell. Tell me, Mr. Rake. So—what?"

"So obvious!" Deacon shouted. He was so angry, he was shaking. Lacey could see it in the mirror.

But Parker was not deterred. "Oh? As opposed to your is-he-or-isn't-he act?"

Deacon was stunned. "My what?"

Then they were both snapping loudly and vehemently at each other, their rising voices evenly matched, and Lacey couldn't distinguish a single word from the argument.

Spenser shook his head and pursed his lips in obvious vexation. "Kids."

Depressed, Lacey sunk deeper into her seat, sighed, and prayed they would reach their destination within the next five minutes, before the two guys in the backseat killed each another.

TWO hours later, the party at Professor Marchand's swanky mansion was in full swing.

Even while busy playing her violin, Lacey recognized several faces from the society pages and gossip columns. She'd had no idea the professor was so well connected, but with the level of charm and sophistication he sported, it made sense. Academics and artists today needed to network and expand their circles of colleagues and allies. That was in Lacey's future too.

They played all kinds of musical pieces, from classical concertos to popular songs. When it was time for one of them to perform solo and shine in their particular musical genre, the partygoers always seemed to halt and listen. And then they would clap for a while to show their appreciation, and immediately after start mingling and chatting again until the next solo.

Lacey had agreed to do a violin sonata with Parker accompanying her on the piano. She had already performed her piece, Matthew Davidson's *Bergamasques* for solo violin. It was a modern piece with some interesting passages. They had decided beforehand they would focus on newer compositions, rather than the older classics.

But now, with Parker, they were going to play *Meditations* by Thais to bring the rowdy mood back down a bit, since the Saturday night was still relatively young at 9:00 p.m.

As they began and the sublime notes echoed through the halls, people stopped what they were doing and stood there, listening. Though some appeared bored, most frowned in concentration, and a few were obviously moved—their jaws quivered and they blinked hard. The mournful piece was one of Lacey's favorites, but she rarely had anyone to play it with since she couldn't play the piano, and even if she could, she only had two hands. The soulful tune sounded simple, but it was technically difficult to coax the right mood out of the instrument. Every single nuance of the phrasing demanded emotional presence from the musician, and thankfully, this was a lesson Lacey had already learned. In the end, it sounded as if the violin was weeping in her hands, and the audience felt it.

As they finished, silence filled the house for a blink of an eye. Then a shudder seemed to run through the crowd, like a wave, and an awakening occurred. The applause that followed was thunderous and eager. Lacey couldn't keep the smile off her face as she bowed.

It was time for their break between the hour-and-a-half sets.

Recorded jazz music started to play from speakers throughout the mansion as soon as the musicians stepped off stage.

They stepped into the shadows of the hallway reserved for performers and servers, and Parker laughed and hugged Lacey so enthusiastically he lifted her off her feet. "Wow. We totally owned the room. We rocked."

Lacey beamed. She agreed. They had played remarkably well. It was official: her first formal performance was a raving success. "We definitely did." She took deep breaths to calm her frayed nerves. She'd been so nervous in the beginning, but as time had gone by she had grown more relaxed. "Oh, Parker, you were brilliant. Your interpretation of Liebermann's sonata for piano and flute, only with Spenser's sax instead, was incredibly masterful. Amazing."

Parker actually blushed. "Thank you kindly, dear lady." He glanced over his shoulder at the stage. "Pianoforte is not my specialty, but yes, I think I did rather well." He used his most posh voice and raised his chin in an imitation of snobbery, but his lips, twitching with pent-up laughter, gave him away.

Lacey chuckled and nodded her agreement. "You did indeed, kind sir."

Parker seemed ridiculously pleased, and he bowed his whole upper body. "Oh, milady, I knew I'd win you over eventually." Then he winked. "I'd love to play some Dvorak with you."

Lacey smiled. "Me too. Sounds heavenly."

"Oh, how come I only ever hear those words from your sweet lips when we're talking about wretched music, my dear, and never about sex?" Parker pouted dramatically, his exaggerated expression downright despondent.

Lacey chuckled and bussed his cheek. "Because we're friends, not lovers."

"Ah, I suppose that's true," Parker said wistfully.

"All right, I'm going to the bathroom. We're on in fifteen again, right?"

"Twenty."

Out of the corner of her eye, Lacey saw Deacon hovering close by, obviously having eavesdropped on them because the moment their gazes connected, Deacon flushed red and hung his head to hide it. Lacey didn't know what the guy's problem was now, so she headed for the bathroom to get some relief.

Once she was done with her business, she unlocked and opened the door, only to find Professor Marchand standing on the other side, perhaps waiting to get in. Strange. Surely the man had other bathrooms in his own place.

"Professor," she said congenially and offered a polite smile. "Thanks again for having us here tonight. It's been wonderful to play in front of people."

Professor Marchand chuckled lowly and then leaned forward a bit, as if taking Lacey into his confidence. "Even if all these people are here to be seen, to mingle, and to drink, not to listen to the finest musicians of the decade?"

Stunned, Lacey didn't know which part to respond to first, the curious compliment or the disparagement of his own friends and colleagues. "Um...."

But the dashing man merely smiled, waving a hand about. "No need to answer. I'm just on my—" He frowned, contemplating the drink in his hand. "— fifth drink of the evening, and I do believe the good stuff is really good tonight." He winked.

Lacey smiled again, though the gesture was forced. She smelled alcohol on his breath, and since her father was a recovering alcoholic with homophobia and violence issues, the odor was enough to bring forth bad memories. "Yes, of course." She peeked past him to the empty, dimly lit hallway and tried to plan her escape from the company of her drunken idol.

But then Professor Marchand said admiringly, "Your performance tonight, Lacey, was spectacular. More than I could've hoped for."

Lacey's gaze flew to him, eyes widening. That was so great to hear. "Really?"

"Oh yes." The man nodded, smiling. "You moved so beautifully, so fluidly. Your bow hand, your body. It was like you embodied music. Like you became one with your instrument. And you were emotionally present, all the time. Your stage presence was so natural. You have a real gift for performance."

Lacey beamed. "Thank you."

"I mean, I could feel your passion for the notes, the harmonies, the phrasing, all of it." He sounded so impressed with her Lacey was all but bouncing with glee. "The way you cajoled and seduced the music from the violin, oh, it was as if you were making love to your violin."

That remark made Lacey blush. No one had ever characterized her playing in such a way. "Um, thank you...." *I think.*

"No, thank you." Professor Marchand leaned closer again, and his tone dropped lower as he went on. "Watching you play was so damn close to a sex act with music I almost felt like I was watching a live porn show at a strip joint."

"What...?" Lacey wasn't smiling anymore. The high she'd been on was gone. This wasn't good at all. This was something darker, dirtier, cheapening his previous compliments.

Professor Marchand sounded excited about his interpretation—and then his hand came up to wrap around Lacey's wrist, and his fingers slowly inched up her arm, bare up to the elbow. "I'd love to have a private performance. And perhaps, who knows, we could make some music of our own. Together. Tonight. After the guests leave. What do you say?"

Bile rose up in Lacey's throat at the thought of being crushed under the heavy weight of a drunken man wanting to fuck her. Her first reaction was to run, hide, and cry.

But then nausea gave way to anger, and her second reaction was part girl power, part entirely male. Dressed as a girl she sometimes forgot how much strength she had within *his* manly physique and mentality. Now she used it and shoved him off hard to put distance between them. "Get off me."

As he stumbled backward a few steps, Professor Marchand spilled some of his drink on his expensive black tie. "What the fuck?" The shock of rejection indicated this was obviously not what he'd expected from this encounter.

As he was wiping the front of his jacket with his napkin, Lacey growled out, "Don't you ever touch me again, or I'll rip your balls off. I can't believe I used to believe that because you were the most amazing musician in the world, you'd be an honorable person too. I can't believe I looked up to you. I'll go to the dean about this."

Still busy cleaning himself from his spillage, Professor Marchand nonetheless let out a breathless laugh. "Oh, sweetheart. I'm a famous composer, and you're a little first-year student with no name. You can say what you want, but I'll spin the story until it appears I gave you a bad grade, or something, and you're lashing out in jealousy, envy, and revenge. No one's going to believe you."

Lacey swallowed hard, so angry she was shaking. What he said was probably true. Those in power who had the right connections banded together and got away with everything. Still, she wasn't going to be a victim ever again.

"My name is Lacey Adair. And if you so much as brush up against me, by the time we're done you will remember my name."

Undeterred, Professor Marchand grunted, chuckling even. "Whatever. Your second set's about to start. Better hurry." Dismissing Lacey with an impatient wave, Professor Marchand continued his cleaning in between sips of what was left of his drink.

Lacey felt physically sick, and her arm was itching where he had touched it. Without another word, she rushed off, wanting to get away, not just to get a breath of fresh air, but so she wouldn't kick the man in the groin so hard his nuts would become internal organs.

She was still shaking when she reached the low podium serving as a stage.

Deacon saw her first, and immediately he came up to her, frowning with worry. "Hey, you okay?"

Mulling over how much to share, since Deacon would probably storm off and beat the guy to a bloody pulp, Lacey made a decision and put on her best casual expression, even smiling a bit. "I'm fine. Just indigestion, or something. I'm good. Are we on?"

"Yeah." Deacon didn't look convinced, but he nodded and walked back to the drums.

Parker, however, was standing close by, and his worried look differed from Deacon's protective one. Parker's look was darker, more suspicious, and definitely not gullible. "What's wrong, Lacey?"

"Nothing. Let's just do the set. I'm getting tired, is all. Been a long week." Excuses flowed out of her mouth. No, not excuses. Lies. It was surprisingly easy. But she was determined not to be pitied simply because a mentor and an idol had busy hands and got fresh with her when no one was looking. She wasn't a victim anymore. Her father may have hated and even hit his gay son, but no one else was ever going to see her that weak and vulnerable.

Except maybe Bro. He understood. He was safe for her to share secrets with. *God, Bro, I miss you so much right now.*

Then Parker's sharp, knowledgeable gaze veered past Lacey's shoulder, and out of the corner of her eye she saw Professor Marchand appear from the dark corridor, slightly disheveled, still smoothing out the wrinkles in his clothes.

Lacey felt the tremors of pent-up rage again, and her face went stony as her hands fisted hard. How could he just stroll along as if nothing had happened?

But the arrogant professor's award-winning smile was firmly in place and actually amped up in wattage as he passed them. This was the face of a man who believed he had asked for no more than his due. *Devil's due, more like.* Lacey wanted to scream.

"Nothing wrong, eh?" Parker watched the man as he walked by and then looked at Lacey with perceptive eyes. "I see."

Swallowing down her disappointment, Lacey ignored Parker's insinuations. Instead, she picked herself up, took her violin from the dresser, stepped onto the stage, and gave the second set her full and undivided attention. She was going to shine even if her heart was swamped by the filthy darkness of an unwanted touch.

Still, she couldn't wait to get out of there.

Chapter 25

"COME on, brother. Just one more." Eddy's teasing was starting to irk Bro.

Nonetheless, he allowed his plain plastic cup to be refilled from the keg until it overflowed and foam ran down over his fingers. "Fuck!" he cursed. He grabbed a napkin and dried his hand. Then his accusatory gaze landed on his friend. "If you or anyone starts chanting 'chug, chug, chug,' I'm gonna chuck something hard and heavy at you."

Eddy chuckled and lifted his hands, palms up in a surrendering gesture. "Sorry." But he didn't look apologetic at all, just mischievous.

Bro took another sip of his beer—*yuck, warm!*—and looked around the crowd. They were at a noisy kegger at Carver Hall, Eddy's all-male dorm, where Eddy had lured Bro when he was feeling melancholy at losing a perfectly good Saturday with his girl while Lacey was performing at her classy soirée. After Eddy discovered the cause of Bro's bad mood, he had been insistent that Bro come with him to the party. Though open to all races, Howard University was a historically black college, so the crowd was predominantly African-American.

Unfortunately, Bro knew next to no one there.

At least, not until he spotted Bradley and Audrey, as well as a couple of his teammates, in the crowd. He hailed them with his drink.

Bradley noticed him and gave him a comradely chin lift as he approached. "Hey, you. I thought you were staying in tonight."

They bumped knuckles. "Yeah, I was supposed to, but this dickwad wouldn't leave me alone." He aimed a thumb at Eddy, who had followed him over and smirked at the insult.

"How's Lace?" Audrey asked sweetly, her gaze flickering to Eddy briefly. From the flash in her eyes, Bro could have sworn Audrey didn't think much of the guy.

"We spoke just before she left. She wasn't overly fond of having to spend her free day at some god-awful party, either. I texted her when I came here, but she hasn't texted me back." He rechecked his cell as he spoke. Nothing. No texts or missed calls. He shrugged but felt unhappy. "Guess she's still busy."

Audrey patted his shoulder. "It's only eleven. She'll be fine. She's a great violinist."

"Yeah, she is," Eddy cut in, chuckling, and Audrey's smile vanished as she frowned. "I heard her play at Shenandoah. Fucking amazing." He sounded sincere enough to Bro, but Audrey did have a knack for detecting bullshit artists. "Want another beer?" he asked Bro, his eager smile as wide as ever.

Bro shook his head. "Nah. I'm good."

Eddy nodded, watching Bro and chewing on the inside of his cheek.

"I could use one," Audrey said cutely, smiling.

"I'll get—oomph!" Bradley started to say when Audrey punched him in the ribs with her elbow, and he grabbed his side, grumbling.

"No, no. Eddy can get it for me, right?" She batted her eyelashes.

Befuddled but amused, Eddy nodded. "Sure. Be right back." He waded through the crowd, disappearing into the sea of bodies.

"What the hell was that about?" Bradley insisted, growling.

Audrey didn't pay any attention to her boyfriend. Her eyes sharpened like knives as she directed them at Bro, who took an instinctive step back. "What the hell do you think you're doing?"

"What do you mean?" He lifted his half-filled cup of beer. "Having a drink?"

Audrey slapped him on arm, hard enough to sting. "You stupid idiot. That guy's got the hots for you. He wants in your pants. Are you that blind?"

Rubbing his arm, Bro leaned closer and lowered his voice. "I know that, okay? I know. He told me. But I told him I'm with Lacey. He's fine with it. We agreed to us being just friends. That's all."

Audrey looked pained. "Oh my God. Guys are so stupid sometimes," she huffed out, brushing her forehead, obviously taking great pains to stay in control. "As he keeps shoving beer down your throat, how long do you think it's gonna take before he quietly escorts you upstairs to sleep it off and then…?"

"Jesus, Dree. You're being freakishly paranoid." Bro was doing his best to keep his own voice low and not shout at his friend. "Eddy's a nice guy. He wouldn't do anything like that."

Audrey grabbed his arm, but Bro shook it off, snarling. "Mark my words," she said. "He's gonna make a play for you tonight. You'll see." She had that mixed look of hurt and disappointment women sometimes got when they looked at a man.

That made Bro grit his teeth. He refused to believe his instincts about Eddy could be so wrong. "You're being ridiculous."

Audrey drew a sharp breath as if she had more to say, but then she huffed and shook her head. "Fine," she said and stomped off, cursing and steaming as she went.

Bro watched her go and couldn't avoid the nausea rising. He felt uncomfortable, and he didn't want to lose a friend over a quarrel. "No offense, man, but your girl's insane."

Bradley didn't say anything at first, not until Bro looked at him. Bradley was always the composed one, his deep voice serene. "I don't know. Eddy does give you the weirdest looks sometimes."

Bro blushed. "Look, Eddy may have the teeniest crush on me. But that's it. And you know I would never cheat on Lacey. I love her, man."

Bradley glanced at the half-empty cup in Bro's hand. "With enough booze—"

"I'm not gonna get wasted," Bro interjected defensively, a bit hurt. He couldn't fathom why his friends were ganging up on him. Didn't they trust his judgment or self-restraint?

Bradley shrugged and then downed his own single cup of beer in one, grimacing as he swallowed. "Eww, this shit's warm." He studied

Bro quietly for a moment. "Look, man. I don't doubt your love for Lacey. You've got it bad for her. But I see Eddy looking at you, and I can't help but see exactly what Dree sees. I don't think it's impossible to reason the guy tempted you here to make a move on you. Now, I'm not gonna claim you'll succumb. Just saying… watch your back."

Bro stared at his best friend. Only once had he ever seen Bradley lose his self-control, and that had been when Lacey's father had attacked Lacey and Audrey at their high school football field. Even now he was cool as cucumber. And Bro did trust him. Because of his placidity Bradley had an eye for people's true natures. Kind of like Audrey's living lie detector mode.

Hadn't Bro already had this talk with Eddy? What more was there to say? Did they have to sever their friendship entirely to ensure nothing happened between them? Because Bro did not want to start any shit with Eddy. Sure, the guy was hot and into him.

But Bro wanted Lacey, and only Lacey.

"Hey, where's Audrey? I brought her drink." Eddy stepped to Bro's side, his confused gaze searching the masses for Audrey.

Bro started to say, "She went to get some fresh air—"

At the exact same time as Bradley said, "She saw a friend and went to talk—"

They stopped at once, and looked at each other. *God, we need to get back in sync*, Bro thought glumly. From Bradley's morose expression he must have thought the same.

Eddy stared at them, frowning, perplexed, and a bit suspicious. "Um… okay…."

Bro sighed sadly. There really was no way out of this conversation—again. "Come on. Let's go outside. I need to talk to you."

Without waiting for Eddy to accept, Bro walked toward the back door. It wasn't until he walked outside to the large backyard with its trimmed lawn, tall trees, and winding footpath that he realized how late it really was. Stars shone in the black sky, but Bro saw no sign of the moon, and the back terrace lights didn't offer much illumination. A few small groups of people stood or sat nearby, but none farther out toward LeDroit Park.

Bro headed for the privacy offered by the park. He stopped under a tree, staring at the dark emptiness across from their little shelter of nature. No one was about, not even on the footpaths. A clamorous city was not far from their seclusion, but here all was still.

"You okay, brother?" Eddy asked, concerned. Only then did Bro notice the guy had indeed followed him out, as requested, or ordered, more like. "Have I done something wrong?"

Bro needed a moment to collect his thoughts. He didn't want to end their friendship, but if Eddy insisted on pursuing this line of so-called association....

The silence dragged on, and Eddy fidgeted. "What is it?" When Bro still didn't reply, he moved into Bro's line of sight, facing him. "Talk to me."

Looking straight into Eddy's eyes, Bro asked slowly and steadily, "Did you ask me here tonight to... to make a pass at me?"

Eddy blinked hard and bit his lower lip. That told Bro tons. "I...." He looked down, and then everywhere else but at Bro, until finally the dam broke. "I'm sorry, Bro. It's true. I did ask you here so I could see if we—"

"There is no we, Eddy," Bro cut in, reining in his temper. How could he get mad at his friend, who was caught in the throes of unrequited love? "I'm with Lacey. She and I are meant to be. I love her."

Eddy cleared his throat, still staring down at his feet, looking distinctly uncomfortable. "But isn't she a little... you know, not manly? I mean, you're gay, and she's—"

"I may refer to her as she, but Lacey's *not* a girl. She's a man. My man. I honestly don't know how to make this any clearer."

Eddy looked even more forlorn, and Bro was having a hard time staying angry at him for meddling and for this attempted frat-boy seduction routine. "But you two have nothing in common," Eddy argued. "You're going in different directions. You think she's gonna stay in DC just for you if she gets all famous and shit? She's gonna travel, and you're having trouble not seeing her during the day as it is. What if she moves to another town, or another country, or abroad to Europe? That's where musicians like her get noticed. What are you going to do then? Follow her around while she gets to live her dream as a violinist, and you drop your dreams of a career in football in favor of all that? Come on, Bro. Be serious. That can't be good for either of you."

Bro had to hold his head. His forehead was hot and he felt feverish. Why the fuck was this so damn hard?

And why did his prick of a friend have to start making sense? It wasn't like Bro had never asked those kinds of questions himself in the dark, lonely hours of the night when Lacey was at his side. Yeah, he did fear losing her, and there was no chance he would stand in the way of her dreams.

But what about my dreams? Bro sighed inwardly. Apart from Lacey, he didn't even know if he had any dreams. Football was fun— but as a career?

Bro could be driven, he could be passionate. He loved football, but to be a professional football player required extraordinary skill, and the career expectancy wasn't very long. There would be injuries. One busted knee or shoulder or whatever, and he would have to kiss that career good-bye. And in all likelihood, that could happen at a very young age, and then where would he be? What backup plan did he have to fall back on?

Not to mention the fact that he was gay. Openly gay football players had a hard time fitting in no matter how great their skills, stamina, and strength of will. Bro had already seen his share of hate for being gay. How much more would there be ahead of him if he wanted to be allowed to be who he was and live and work the way he desired? Hatred, bigotry, and discrimination ran so deep in society, it was daunting, and in sports it was doubly, even triply, so.

Bro sighed again. He felt tired. It was almost midnight, and he longed to hold Lacey in his arms. He didn't need any answers, then. She was answer enough for him.

"Bro, did you hear me?" Eddy asked, his voice at once shaken and insistent.

"Yeah, I heard you, man." He locked gazes with Eddy, stern and decisive. "But that's not gonna change my mind. I'm with Lacey. And as far as my career plans go, well, they're my business, and no concern of yours."

Eddy looked hurt. "I was just trying to point out how different you guys are. In the long run, commonalities are better for a relationship—"

"Yeah, I know that, okay? I know." Bro stifled a growl. "But the knowledge doesn't affect my feelings for Lacey." He exhaled. "Yeah, maybe she and I will go our separate ways one of these days. But that day isn't here yet. And I love her. I'm not gonna push her away just because we *might* break up one day down the line. That's just stupid."

Eddy nodded slowly, worrying his lower lip. "I guess you don't wanna be my friend anymore."

"That's up to you, man. If you keep doing this…." Bro shook his head, hands raking through his hair angrily. "I get it that you're into me. But it's a crush, right? There are plenty of other guys out—"

"You want Lacey. I want you." Eddy sounded more adamant now, even stubborn.

Bro didn't know if he was angry or sad. "You don't even know me—"

Eddy chuckled at that. "I do know you, Bro. We've got a hell of a lot in common. We hang out together all the time. We run, exercise, talk, even eat alike. We could be good together. I think you know that too, and that's why you're declaring your love for Lacey so loudly. A part of you wants—"

"Don't even think of finishing that sentence!" Bro ground out, resisting the urge to grab the guy by the collar, lift him up, and shake him till his teeth rattled. "I've tried being nice and understanding, but you—"

Eddy kissed him. A firm press of lips hit Bro right smack in the mouth, and then a tiny flick of tongue followed, coaxing Bro to open up.

Bro yanked back and shoved Eddy off hard with both hands on the guy's chest, making him stumble back a step or two. "What the fuck, man?"

But Eddy was looking over Bro's shoulder, a wealth of emotions on his face.

Bro felt the hairs on his nape stand as he turned around and saw three people he loved standing on the terrace steps. With his arms crossed over his chest, Bradley looked calm even though he was frowning, but Audrey had her hands on her hips, and she was seething mad.

Only Lacey looked blank, just staring, blinking.

But the moment their eyes met, it was as if a switch was flipped on in Lacey, and she came to life. She walked over to them, glancing between Bro and Eddy.

When she stopped, just short of touching distance, Bro opened his mouth to speak.

But Lacey got there first, addressing Eddy. "Hi."

Swallowing hard, Eddy fidgeted in place. "H-hi…."

"You do know that was my boyfriend you just kissed, right?" Her voice was neutral.

Eddy's lips thinned as he tried to control his emotions. "Yeah. I know."

Bro observed Lacey, who for some reason looked older tonight, more tired and weary, and definitely sadder than before. She couldn't think he would ever…? Could she?

Lacey smiled ruefully. "Look, Eddy. Unrequited love's a bitch, and—"

Eddy snorted out a disdainful, broken laugh. "How would you know?"

Lacey let out a breath, looking down. "Because for years I've loved my father, and he does not love me back. In truth, he hates me—"

"He hates you 'cause he's nothing more than a drunken, violent, homophobic asshole who hits his defenseless queer son," Bro cut in, furious.

The shock was evident in Eddy's face for a moment. "He… hits you…?" Then shame and guilt replaced the surprise, and he lowered his head. "I'm sorry, Lacey." His shoulders slumped, and he looked about as defeated and dejected as a whipped dog in the rain.

But Lacey touched his arm gently. "It's all right." Then she harrumphed. "Well, it's not all right, obviously. Me being hit by my dad is hardly the same thing as you loving Bro."

"I'm not...." Eddy looked about ready to deny it, but it was as if the words refused to come out. He let out a breath, and the broken, pained look returned. "I'm sorry. I didn't mean to."

"At the risk of sounding like a cliché, the heart wants what the heart wants."

Lacey's sympathy was obviously too much for Eddy, who turned away, wiping his eyes with the backs of his hands. Yet not a single sound emerged.

"Eddy, you and Bro are friends. I don't want to come between that. If you respect and care for me as well, you won't try to come between me and Bro either."

She sounded so different to Bro. To be honest, she reminded him of the time when she spoke to her father at their high school football field, after he had attacked her. The same strength, almost casual in its indifference, was present now. And Bro wasn't a fan of this side of her. It wasn't that he needed her to be weaker so he could protect her. No, it was her odd emotional detachment that clinched it for Bro. She spoke with sympathetic words, and yet her face betrayed no feelings underneath. Not really.

Eddy looked up at Lacey, confused. "You mean.... If Bro forgave me, you wouldn't mind if he and I were still friends?"

"I don't make decisions for him," Lacey replied, and again the empathy was there, only aloof somehow, like the light of a distant star. You could see the light, but it was cold, no warmth to be had. "Bro's a big boy. He can take care of himself. We all can. Yes, I admit it did hurt seeing you kiss him—especially when I know you saw me *before* you did it."

"What?" Bro gasped in shock.

Eddy cringed, shame coloring his cheeks until they bloomed red, and his gaze darted away. "I'm sorry. I just wanted.... Just once, you know."

Lacey sighed, sadly. "Yes, I know. I've felt that way about Bro since the day we met. I wish my father loved me, too, and it hurts to be the only one doing the loving." Then she straightened up and visibly collected herself. "But now I know better than to hold my breath waiting for miracles to happen. I'm moving on with my life. This may sound harsh, Eddy, but you might want to try doing the same."

Frowning, Eddy closed his eyes for a moment. "You and Bro, you're so different. You want different things. Me and Bro? We're a lot alike. We could make it last."

Lacey smiled and nodded. "Yes, I'm aware of that." Bro started to speak, his emotions in turmoil, demanding attention. But Lacey once again beat him to it. "I think we've all heard it. The proverbs. Opposites attract, but similarities bind. The thing is, Eddy, what differences exist between me and Bro, they're superficial only. Inside? We're of one heart, one spirit. We love each other. And love, well, it smoothes out a lot of rough edges."

With a soft smile on her lips, Lacey took Bro's hand, and he squeezed back, interlacing their fingers. The constricting feeling in his chest eased, and he could breathe again.

"Yeah. What she said." And he smiled back, centered once more.

"Bro?" Eddy asked, hesitantly. "I did say before it was okay that we'd never be more than friends. Clearly I still have my work cut out for me. Can we… still be friends? Or did I totally ruin it?"

"Yeah, we can still be friends." The truth was, Bro liked Eddy, but things were going to have to change. "But let's be clear. One more pass at me, and we're done."

Blinking hard, his green eyes glistening, Eddy nodded. "Okay."

He looked uncertain, so Bro brought up his hand and allowed Eddy to bump their fists together. It was a show of trust and friendship, and he supposed it symbolized all the things between them left unsaid, but now taken for granted. No more fuck-ups.

With a cracked smile, Eddy moved past them to go inside.

Before he got three steps in, Lacey brushed his arm. "Eddy? You'll find someone. You will. Someone who means as much to you as Bro means to me. And then you'll know it's right 'cause it'll feel right, and not like you're doing something underhanded behind someone else's back. You'll find your Mr. Right. Trust me."

What at first looked like skepticism on Eddy's face soon turned into a kind of tough resolution, and he nodded. "Thanks, Lacey. And, uh, thanks for being so, you know, understanding. I don't think I could've been so forgiving if our roles were reversed."

Lacey smiled encouragingly. "It's during the bad times when you find out what kind of man you really are." Then she leaned forward a bit, as if taking him into his confidence. "I honestly don't believe you would've had it in you, Eddy, to go through with it. Betrayal, I mean. Bro's a good guy, and his judgment is rarely that off." She patted his arm. "It'll be all right."

Eddy nodded curtly, ducked his head, muttered "Good night," and was off, vanishing into the dorm.

Bro brought Lacey's hand to his lips and kissed it. "How'd you find me?"

Lacey snickered a little, but the sound was halfhearted. "You texted me? Duh."

Audrey and Bradley walked up to them as soon as Eddy was gone.

"You okay, Lace?" Audrey asked, aiming a glare at Bro.

"Fine. We're all fine." Lacey locked gazes with Audrey. "Dree, try to understand him, please? It's no fun feeling less than the object of your affection, especially when being so powerless to prevent your own emotions."

Audrey looked doubtful. "You really believe he wouldn't have tried to seduce Bro all the way?"

Lacey nodded firmly. "I do, yes. In his heart I think Eddy's a good person. But love can make you do strange things." Then she glared at her best friend. "And that kiss wasn't Bro's fault, so give him a break. Bro was trying to let the guy down easy. Surely you can understand that."

Audrey looked away, pouting, but her mannerisms were so exaggerated it didn't take a genius to realize she was already fully placated. "I guess. If you say so."

"I do." Lacey let out a tiny giggle, but again it sounded off to Bro. "So, are we gonna get a drink, or what? 'Cause I'm in the mood for—"

"Sorry, guys," Bro cut in sharply. "But me and Lace are gonna head home. It's late."

Lacey gave him an odd look but nodded in compliance.

Audrey gave Bradley a teasing once-over. "How 'bout it, big guy? One dance before we head home too?"

A widening grin from Bradley would have been answer enough, and when he pulled the naughty minx into his arms tight, that was just icing on the cake. "Come on, baby. Shake that booty for me."

Audrey rolled her eyes. "You did not just say 'booty' to me?"

Laughing deeply, Bradley pulled the affronted lady into the dorm.

But Bro and Lacey? They headed for the car to drive home. And they still had tons to talk about.

Chapter 26

BUT they had barely made it into the car and eased into traffic when Lacey said, "Bro, I love you, and I trust you. There's no need to talk about what just happened. Eddy made a mistake is all. Could've happened to anyone."

But clearly Bro wasn't having any of Lacey's distraction tactics. "Wanna talk about what's wrong with *you*, then?"

Lacey stiffened. "Me? What do you mean?"

Bro rolled his eyes and let out a dry, humorless chuckle. "I mean why you're so rigid it's as if someone stuck an iron rod up your backside."

"Nice visual, thank you."

"Lace? If you trust me...."

Her boyfriend was right, unfortunately. Lacey didn't want to go into this, and yet she knew she needed to. So she told Bro what had happened between her and Professor Marchand at the party. Once she was finished, she waited for Bro to speak.

The silence lasted a while. Lacey drove on, waiting as patiently as she could. It wasn't easy to sit still.

Finally Bro spoke. "Could he make trouble for you? At school, I mean?"

That was the part that worried Lacey the most, and she was glad Bro had picked up on it. "I don't know. I guess it depends on his reputation, and mine. I mean, if the dean or the faculty know about his, um, proclivities, it might make my side of the story more credible."

"So, you've decided to go to the dean?"

Lacey hesitated, biting her lower lip. "The dean of the conservatory is also the deputy director of the institute, and she has a lot of clout. Marchand is a violinist-in-residence, and—"

"What does that mean?" Bro asked, confused.

"When there's an artist-in-residence, it means they aren't part of the place for good, but they've been invited there to do research, or to perform, or to teach, and so on. It's about artistic exchange of ideas, and making collaborations and contacts, and that sort of thing. Broadening one's horizons. It could be a seasonal arrangement, or ongoing, or temporary. Marchand is a big name in the music world. He won't be there forever."

"So, what you're saying is that if he did something improper, he could be booted out?" Bro sounded happier just stating the conclusion.

"Possibly." She took a breath to calm herself. "That's why I want to talk to the dean. I don't know if they'll believe me, but I won't let him push me around."

Suddenly Bro's hand landed on hers over the stick shift, and the warmth of his tender touch radiated through her body. It never ceased to amaze Lacey how quickly Bro could make her feel better.

"I guess my work is done then."

Lacey glanced at him, bewildered. "Huh?"

Bro smiled that cheeky lopsided grin he sported sometimes when he knew a secret and was taunting with it. "You don't need me to protect you. You're not a girl, you're a woman. Okay, okay, a man, to be precise." He winked at the joke, and Lacey smiled back. "You can stand on your own two feet, and you can fight your own battles." He smiled a little sorrowfully then. "I am gonna miss protecting you, though. Like I had your back."

Lacey chuckled then, at ease. "Bro, if you think I don't need you in my life anymore, you're wrong. Dead wrong. The only thing on my mind after Marchand put his hand on me was you, getting back to you, because I knew you'd make me feel all right again. That the world made sense, and that there was still true love in the world. That it wasn't all just dirty lust and filthy trysts in a drunken haze. You put my world back into balance, and I'll always need and want you for that. And I love you."

"You centered me too," Bro said with a contented sigh. "The moment you held my hand outside I knew everything was gonna be okay."

Though her gaze was half-focused on driving, Lacey managed to steal a glance at Bro. "I guess we're stuck with each other."

Bro smiled back. "Wouldn't want it any other way."

EARLY Monday morning, Lacey went in search of Parker at the conservatory.

And she had a pretty good idea where he would be. Though most of the performances on any of the many stages around the conservatory were done against a simple white, gray, or black backdrop, or the red velvet curtains, some performers preferred a more theatrical setting. Lacey liked to help in that regard. Painting was surprisingly soothing. Though it was merely cheap planks and boards, with a touch of paint they became magic, a visual delight to spark the imagination while a vocalist sang his or her heart out or a musician released soulful sounds from an instrument.

As she had guessed, Parker was on stage, a paintbrush in hand.

Unfortunately, he wasn't alone. Professor Marchand was with him.

The stage was lit, while the audience space was in shadow. That was where Lacey had entered, so she remained unseen, and she stopped to listen. Yes, eavesdropping may have been wrong, but it seemed the two men were arguing, and Lacey wanted to be informed enough to jump to Parker's aid if it came to that.

What she heard chilled her to the bone.

"You meddling little shit. You won't get away with this," Professor Marchand was hissing furiously.

Parker swished a hand at him, sneering. "Who do *you* think you are, you little upstart? My family rules this town, and much of the eastern seaboard. I can make your life a living hell." Then he leaned closer to Marchand, and his finger pointed straight at the man's chest. "And if you so much as sneeze in Lacey's direction again, with a snap of my fingers I will end your petty little career."

Whatever Parker was holding in his hand, Marchand snatched it up, growling. "Don't threaten me—"

"I never threaten." Parker's voice had gone so low it reverberated around the room. "You thought you could fuck with my friend without any consequences. Now you know better. Consider this a learning experience. This is a school after all."

Marchand looked like he had way more to say, his features twisted with rage, but he seemed to think better of it. "I won't forget this, Endicott."

Parker looked relaxed, but his face was an ice-cold mask. "I've already forgotten you, Marchand. Oh, and you may keep that. I have copies." With a smirk he pointed at whatever the man was holding.

Marchand snarled, threw the object in his hand to Parker's feet, and stormed off. The door slammed shut behind him as Parker picked up the little black object from the floor.

Lacey was about to approach when movement to the left of the stage caught her eye.

"That was quite a show." It was Deacon, standing in the shadows stage left, his arms crossed over his chest, leaning against the wall, long legs crossed at the ankles.

Parker turned to face him and barked out a laugh, bowing his head like a gentleman of old. "Why, thank you, noble sir. Though usually the audience takes front-row seats so the poor performer knows where to direct his bows."

"A cunning stunt you pulled on Marchand." Deacon walked closer to Parker, or from Lacey's point of view, more like stalked. "How'd you know about the recordings?"

Parker grinned. "As it happens, Marchand fibbed about a lot of things. For one, that wasn't his mansion. I happen to know the *real* owner. Marchand is only housesitting. And second, the real owner has placed security cameras throughout the estate."

"Including the bathroom hallway," Deacon concluded.

Lacey swallowed hard. Her encounter with Marchand had been recorded by security cameras? So that was what Parker held over the unscrupulous professor's head.

Her friend had taken a huge risk for her. She nearly sobbed as the realization hit her.

"Yes indeed," Parker confirmed, watching intently as Deacon approached. "Which the good professor would have known had it been his home as he claimed. And it really was stupid of Marchand to assume his transgressions could always remain unseen by prying eyes." Deacon said nothing, and the stare-off continued. "You disapprove of my methods?"

Deacon snorted, shaking his head. "The fucker was gonna hurt Lacey's future career and her time here. Hurt *her*. Had it been me instead of you confronting him, I would've just killed the guy." He shrugged as if indifferent. "Your way's better. Wiser."

Parker was silent for a moment, but his gaze never left Deacon, who had almost closed the gap between them. "You are aware Lacey belongs to another?"

Deacon stopped midstep, his eyes narrowing. "Yeah, I know that."

Parker cocked his head. "Are you going to make trouble for her?"

Deacon started his stalking again. "No. She's nice. I don't know a lot of nice people."

Parker chuckled contemptuously, his eyes gleaming. "Funny. I didn't think nice was what you were looking for. I would've thought you'd prefer a little spice with your vanilla. A wee bit of a challenge." Then he stepped right up to Deacon and looked up at him. They were only an inch apart in height. "Or are you going to stand there and still claim you're not gay?"

Deacon's snarl exposed his teeth. "You know something, Endicott? You're just asking for it now." His hands fisted at his sides.

"Funny. Here I thought I was already begging for it." Parker's relentless gaze remained locked on Deacon.

The air around the two men sizzled, so thick with tension you could have cut it with a knife. The hairs on Lacey's skin stood on end, and her feet twitched with the need to run up and stop them before they ripped each other to shreds.

Then Deacon lunged at Parker, wrapped his arms around him, and kissed him. Well, more like devoured him. With a loud moan, Parker melted against him and entwined his own arms around Deacon. Then their kiss deepened, their bodies pressed tight against each other—and blushing, grinning, Lacey slunk out of the room under the cover of darkness.

AFTER the school day at the conservatory was done, Lacey drove up to Parker's house. She didn't think she would be intruding even if Parker and Deacon had decided to get up close and personal with each other.

The historic original Northwood district was affluent, dominated by a couple hundred townhouses and magnificent oak and elm trees. All the houses in the neighborhood had large front lawns and backyards, and the buildings themselves had multiple stories and light-colored facades.

Parker's home, similar to the others, stood on a gentle slope, and there was plenty of room to park at the curb. Lacey made her way to the front door and rang the bell.

A middle-aged woman with glasses, a white apron, and graying blonde hair in a bun on her head opened the door, a question on her face.

"Hello. My name is Lacey Adair. I'm a friend of Parker's from Peabody."

The woman stood aside to let Lacey in, no judgment or even an opinion on her face. "Wait here, please" was all she said, and she walked off, disappearing into one of the hallways.

For a few minutes Lacey waited, anxious. Still, she barely moved from her spot, doing all her pacing in a tiny circle.

"Lace?" Parker emerged from the shadows of one of the hallways. Dressed in jeans, gray loafers, and a pink cashmere sweater, he exuded casual cool even in his off-hours. His attire hinted at wealth but didn't shove it down your throat.

"Hi, Parker."

If he was surprised to see her, Parker soon recovered and gestured for her to follow. They entered a spacious lounge with three couches, a large fireplace, antique furniture, art on the walls, and a grand piano by a set of French doors. It didn't scream opulence, but rich taste and refinement came through loud and clear.

As they sat down on opposite couches, the housekeeper reappeared. "We have some excellent teas, Lace. Care to sample?" Parker asked politely.

"Um, sure, I'd love some." Lacey hadn't come to drink tea and was eager to bring up the subject she was holding back. "Parker—"

Parker raised a hand, palm up, effectively stopping Lacey cold. "Music? Scones? A massage? An erotic massage?" Parker grinned wickedly, and Lacey quirked a smile.

"No, thank you. Now would you please stop distracting me, and let me speak?"

Parker leaned back, resting one arm on the back of the couch, and crossed his legs. "I assume you've come to confess, my dear."

Puzzled, Lacey asked, "I'm sorry?"

"For eavesdropping on me and Marchand, and then on me and dear Deacon."

Lacey blushed. "I didn't intend to listen. I came to find you so you'd come with me to speak to the dean."

"About Marchand?"

"Yes. I guess that matter is now moot." Lacey kept their gazes connected, wanting to convey to her friend how grateful she was. "I don't know how to thank you, Parker. I thought I was going to get kicked out or—"

"When we panic, we often see things in black and white, do or die, life or death. Much like being a teenager, wouldn't you say?" Parker's annoyingly knowing tone made him sound older and wiser, and Lacey had an inkling that was the effect he was going for.

Rolling her eyes, Lacey chuckled. "You're a teenager too."

Parker winked. "I'm an old soul."

"You're something all right." Lacey grinned right back.

Parker laughed merrily. "Well, now that that sordid business is concluded—"

"You didn't have to do that for me. Why did you?"

Parker tilted his head, looking positively bemused. "You are my friend, my dear. What a silly question."

"You took a huge gamble. Marchand could've—"

"No, he couldn't have. My connections and wealth trump his. Simple as that."

"Simple as that?" Lacey echoed, dazed. "That's it? Just... no problem?"

"None whatsoever."

Suddenly they were interrupted by two middle-aged women, both wearing white skimpy tennis outfits, entering the foyer. The taller one with long silvery-blonde hair was skinny to the point of imminent anorexia, while the shorter one had voluptuous curves and short burgundy-colored hair cut in a bob. They stopped talking when they saw Parker and Lacey.

Parker got up, so Lacey did as well. "Mother. Ms. Denning." He bowed to the ladies.

The curvy one rolled her brown eyes. "Parker, how many times have I told you to call me Jennifer?"

"Several dozen, I believe, Ms. Denning."

"How many more are required?"

"A few dozen, Ms. Denning." Parker grinned and then gestured at Lacey. "Mother, Ms. Denning, this lovely young boy is Lacey Adair. You had the pleasure of hearing her play the violin on Saturday."

"Ah, yes, now I remember." Ms. Denning came closer, extended her hand for Lacey to shake, and nodded in recognition. "You played exceedingly well, Ms. Adair. Though I liked the Thais with Parker here, I must admit your *Bergamasques* was dazzling."

Lacey felt charmed herself. In addition to being the CEO of *Boudoir*, a worldwide fashion magazine she had created and spearheaded for twelve years, Jennifer Denning was also rich, famous, and a well-known patroness of the arts. Just meeting her was a privilege. She had her hands in a lot of trendy areas of life, from fashion to film, from music to art, from men to women. Her reputation held a hint of notoriety.

Lacey swallowed down the lump in her throat and prayed her hand wasn't too sweaty. "Ms. Denning, it's an honor to meet you."

The woman smiled, pleased. "I see I don't need to tell you who I am."

Lacey shook her head. "No, ma'am."

"I'm so glad I got the chance to meet you in person. Parker here has been glorifying you from here to there." Lacey stared at Parker, stunned into silence, opening and closing her mouth like a fish on dry land. Ms. Denning continued, "As it happens, I had no other reason to stay at that dreadful, tedious party than to listen to the new talent of the eastern seaboard. I don't know if you are aware, but I have often recommended live fusion music at fashion shows."

"Yes, I know." Lacey smiled eagerly. "I've seen a few of those shows on TV."

"Are you interested in fashion?"

Lacey had to bite her lower lip. "Um, no, not really."

Ms. Denning only looked more pleased. "I'm happy to hear that. Most all of the young talents I nurture tend to think I'm a first-class ticket to high society and haute couture. They aren't wrong, of course, but the assumption is so dull and cliché."

"Yes, of course." Lacey had no idea where this conversation was heading.

"But I see Parker did not exaggerate about your skills, Ms. Adair. I would be more than happy to sponsor you and introduce you to the right people, those who can send your career into a steady climb towards stardom. Tell me, Ms. Adair, is fame what you seek?"

Lacey felt like she was caught on a merry-go-round, and everything was spinning. "No, I don't really care about fame or money. I just want to play the violin. In front of people, naturally." She blushed because the last part sounded so silly to her ears, but it was too late to take it back.

Ms. Denning smiled, her smile as sly as a cat's. "Hmm. I didn't think such innocence still existed. I was sure it had gone the way of the dodo."

"Don't be snarky," Parker interjected, waving a scolding finger before her face, and Ms. Denning laughed in response, a curious jingling sound, like little silver bells.

The other woman placed a thin hand over Ms. Denning's arm. "Come, Jen. The court is free, and I have an appointment later."

"Oh, yes." Ms. Denning straightened up, although it wasn't like she'd been slouching all this time. She studied Lacey with those sharp eyes as she gave Lacey her business card. "Call me in a few days, and we'll set up a meeting. There are some people I'd love to introduce you to. One or two performances, and we can assess how to best aid you in your path to prestige." She held up her hand for another handshake, and Lacey responded. "It was lovely to meet you."

"You too, Ms. Denning," Lacey said with a shaky voice, but the two women were already walking away. As they disappeared, clearly to play tennis, she turned to Parker. "Oh. My. God."

Parker chuckled but helped Lacey take a seat again, sat down next to her, and offered her a cup of white tea. "Here, drink this. You'll feel better. Tea cures all ills."

With trembling hands, she cradled the cup and sipped her tea, the sweetness surprising her. "This is good." Parker nodded but said nothing, just watched her amusedly. "You…."

"Me…?"

Lacey was breathless with excitement and could barely speak. "You…. What you did with Marchand. And now with Jennifer Denning? Do you have any idea—"

"Oh, yes, a very, very good idea." Parker shrugged, nonchalant. "Jen is looking for a new protégé, and you fit the bill. Besides, under her wing, not only will you be guaranteed fame and fortune, you will be immune to whatever Marchand might come up with. He is flighty, but he may decide to seek revenge. I vowed to make sure he wouldn't get that chance."

Lacey frowned. "And now those vengeful plans will be directed at you. Parker, no. I don't want you to get hurt because of—"

"Aww, aren't you the sweetest little thing—"

"Parker, I'm not joking!"

"I know, Lace. I know. But… from my standpoint, I am far better equipped to handle him than you. Not only do I love a challenge, but his attempts at me will only amuse me."

"Is everything a game to you?"

"All of life is game, my dear. And I know how to play. Marchand doesn't." Parker took a sip of his own tea. "You need a patron, and Jen will be that for you. She's legit, believe me. No, that doesn't mean she won't have her own financial and artistic interests mixed with yours, but she'll do the minimum amount of screwing you over, that I promise."

Lacey's mind was whirling. In that raging sea she turned to a calmer topic. "Was that your mother with her?"

"Yes. Vivien Endicott, socialite." Parker sounded snobbish, but Lacey sensed a kind of sadness under the surface.

"She didn't speak to you."

"My mother loves me. But we aren't a hugging type of family. And Vivien likes new shiny things. She's already seen me. The novelty has worn off." Though Parker jested, Lacey was sure this was a subject that caused heartache for him. She took his hand and gave it a tentative squeeze. Parker looked at the hand, frowning as if faced with a puzzle he couldn't understand, but then he looked up and smiled, a genuine smile with no guile behind it. "Thanks, Lace."

Lacey smiled back. "I owe you many, many thanks."

"Nah." Parker looked away, shrugging, but his cheeks pinked. "It was no problem."

"Even if it was, you'd just run into the fray, no doubt. Because you love a challenge." Parker bowed his head to acknowledge Lacey's characterization. "And what better challenge than a certain boy I saw you kissing on stage today…." She let her suggestive voice trail off.

Parker laughed, and his cheeks grew redder. "I don't know what you're talking about." Then he looked at Lacey shyly. "Would you like to stay for dinner?"

It was late in the day, and she had a long drive ahead, but Lacey had only one answer to the invitation. "I'd love to."

Chapter 27

"I'LL be home late."

Bro read the text as he was sitting down to have dinner with his family. He smiled. He had received the earlier gushing call about what Lacey had seen with Parker and Marchand. Bro knew Lacey was going to Parker's house to thank him, and he was fine with that.

One night here or there would hardly make a dent in their rock-solid relationship.

Besides, he had other things to deal with tonight.

As they ate, Jack and Jordan argued about the reckless behavior of paramedics, but Bro didn't really listen. He was happy for Lacey, glad things had worked out for the best. Well, not for the best, but still pretty good.

With her problems sorted, Bro realized he still had his own to deal with.

No, it wasn't Eddy who dominated his thoughts. He was relatively certain Eddy would not try anything else. Bro was confident all Edwin had to do was think about his father, Irwin, and wonder what the man would think about his underhanded attempt at coming between an established couple, and Eddy would reform his ways. Yes, Eddy may have chosen communications to be closer to Bro, but he doubted Eddy would sacrifice everything that was good in him for a quick, illicit assignation with Bro.

No, as far as Bro was concerned, Eddy was a nonissue.

"Penny for your thoughts." Sebastian smiled at him from across the table.

Bro smiled back and then couldn't hold it in anymore. *"What if I never figure out what I want to do with my life?"* Bro signed. *"I'm taking media studies 'cause I like films, and I practice football 'cause I like to run like the wind, but I don't think I want a career in either. I'm wasting money we don't have by going to college and doing things I don't know if I want, and—"*

Swiftly Sebastian had moved to his side of the table. Bro didn't notice until Sebastian sat down and placed his hands over Bro's, which were signing frantically. "Easy now. Deep breaths," Sebastian spoke out loud, soothingly.

Bro did as he was told, and for a good minute he did nothing but focus on breathing in and out, steady and slow.

"Better?" Sebastian signed.

Bro nodded. *"Yeah. Sorry about that. I guess it's all been on my mind for a while."*

"It's natural to have doubts. No one expects you to have everything sorted out in your life when you're only eighteen. We'll talk again when you're twenty-eight."

Sebastian always was the reasonable one. Bro sighed and nodded. "I guess."

"Come on. Let's go play Twister."

"Huh?"

Sebastian's evil grin was daring, and Bro felt like accepting. Sebastian dashed off to find the plastic mat, and Bro followed, chuckling. His mood had lightened already. If he could get himself out of a twist, maybe he could find his way out his problems too.

His brother sure was crafty.

For the next half an hour they played Twister. It was way harder now that their bellies were still full from dinner. Not to mention having Jordan, Jack, and Kevin egging them on with their shouts and wolf whistles, and chortling with every new odd position. Bro almost cursed them all to hell. Then he didn't because they were his family, and he loved them to bits.

"Left hand red," Jordan called out, smirking. *Smug bastard.*

Bro was nowhere near red. He tried to crane his neck to see where to go but Sebastian was blocking his view. *Dammit, I'm gonna lose.*

"Giving up, squirt?" Jordan teased, grinning.

Bro would have flipped him off but couldn't from his position. Instead, he growled as loud as he could. "What did my brother promise you if he won?"

Jordan chuckled. "Not telling."

"Fucking cheaters." Bro didn't think they would actually cheat, as it was just a game, but he wasn't 100 percent sure, either. Turning his head didn't yield any better results as his view was still obstructed.

But he did think he caught a glimpse of red somewhere close to Sebastian's right leg. Shifting his weight around, Bro managed to see red. He was close, but not quite that close. This was going to be hard.

"Fuck," he muttered, then lifted his left hand off the mat just long enough to get it to land on red. His weight was completely off, and his right hand was shaking and slipping.

Jordan flicked the spinner into motion. "Right leg green."

Bro flinched. To get there Sebastian would have to either throw his leg over or slide it under him. Neither option was appealing.

He more felt than saw from his position Sebastian twisting his head around, searching for the best avenue of movement.

Then Jordan mumbled, "Fuck," and Bro grinned. He had won. No way was Sebastian going to get his right leg on green.

"I win," he exclaimed loudly, and let out a whoopee.

Huffing in frustration, Sebastian tried to get his limb where it was supposed to go, but nothing came of it. After a few minutes of twisting and turning and shifting, Sebastian let out a hiss and then crumpled onto the mat.

Bro jumped up and bounced in place several times with a shit-eating grin on his face. "I win!"

Jack laughed and clapped, and Kevin clapped as well, while Jordan helped his fiancé off the floor.

As soon as he was upright, Sebastian smiled at Bro, and signed, *"See? Something went your way today. And it's gonna every day. It's all about attitude. Answers will come. Give it time. Give yourself time to sort things out. It's only been two months. Fall break's gonna be here soon.*"

Bro narrowed his gaze and felt some residual vehemence boiling inside him. "Now I know you didn't 'let' me win. I won fair and square." He used air quotes on "let" and glared at his older brother.

Sebastian chuckled and winked. "Maybe I did. Maybe I didn't."

"Aw, hell no!" Bro shouted, pouting.

Sebastian rushed up to him and grabbed him into a fierce bear hug. Bro hugged him back.

It was good to be home and with family. Though he didn't know all his directions in life yet, that didn't mean he was never going to. If he believed in himself and stayed positive, it was all going to work out.

Funny how he went to college, but still learned his most important life lessons at home.

LATER that night, at around ten, when Lacey still hadn't come back, Bro came to the conclusion Lacey was spending the night at Parker's place. He wondered why he wasn't worried about it. Perhaps they really had come further in their relationship than they thought. Perhaps they had grown up a lot in the past six months.

Sebastian peeked his head through the open doorway. "Hey, still awake?"

"Yeah. Hard to sleep without Lace." He sighed. His body wasn't the only one missing her. Bro's heart was too, and the ache was unpleasant. Not overwhelming, just uncomfortable.

Sebastian nodded. Then he came into the room and sat down on the bed next to Bro. "You still worried about school?" He didn't sign it this time. His hollow voice was always hypnotic in a way. Lacey found it fascinating, and Bro thought it might be the musician in her. Bro himself rarely focused on it, but sometimes, when it was really quiet, he did hear the lack of most of the nuances that made up a so-called regular voice.

"Yeah, a little. I suppose I'll continue to be until I figure out what it is I really want."

"But not football?" Sebastian only sounded curious, and his expression verified it.

Bro smiled and huffed out a laugh. "Crazy, right? I've been into football as long as I can remember. And here I am, on a college football team, and... the spark's just not there. Not the way it used to be. I mean, I still like it, and I want to play. But to make a career out of it?" He gave his brother a look. "Is that stupid? I mean, I'm there on a football scholarship, and I'm good at it. I should want to make that into my future, right?"

Surprisingly, Sebastian shook his head, always with that kind smile. "I don't know, Bro. A person can be good at a lot of things, but still not make them into his whole life. Sometimes I think we choose a career and a future in things that make us challenge ourselves. Things we aren't quite so good at. It would be easy to do only things you excel in. But to choose to pursue something that isn't an automatic, guaranteed win? That's much harder. But also ultimately more rewarding."

"Like when you went to work for the police?"

"Yes. That wasn't easy. I knew I'd get a lot of flak about that, being deaf and all, but I really wanted to do something that matters, you know? Something with substance. At the end of each workday I can say to myself I did something worthwhile. I help people. I help the men and women who protect and serve us and our city. That's important. No, I may not be on the streets at their sides, but every little bit helps. That's how I see it."

Bro listened carefully. That was what he wanted too. To do something meaningful and with a purpose. To go to bed at the end of the day and know he had made a difference.

Sure, he could do that by playing professional football as an out and proud gay man. That would definitely be a challenge. But he also realized then and there that he had other options too. In fact, he had a lot of them. Howard University offered plenty of options to choose from. All he had to do was study them and make an informed decision.

And best of all, he could always change his mind later, because nothing was written in stone. And he had the backing of his friends and family.

And that sure as hell mattered a lot.

He recalled what he had learned volunteering at HU. "I was looking at media studies to begin with, but I've been thinking about the Speech and Hearing Clinic too. I know ASL, and I've enjoyed working there a few hours a week. Maybe I should look into their degree program. I could do some good with that."

The proud and happy look Sebastian got then made Bro's chest tighten, and he had to blink away unshed tears. "Bro, you do whatever makes you happy, and we'll all be happy for you. That's all I want."

The decision came easily after that. "Cool. I'll check out HUSHC tomorrow."

Sebastian nodded. Bro knew his brother would have exhibited the same pride in him had he chosen to become a garbage man or the next president of the United States. As long as he was happy.

Then Sebastian checked the time on his wristwatch. "Is Lacey still coming tonight? It's awfully late to be driving. Especially since she has to be right back to classes in the morning."

Bro shook his head. "She texted she might be late. I think she's gonna spend the night at Parker's. I'll call her in a minute to confirm."

Sebastian studied him coolly. "Are you okay with that?"

Bro didn't get a chance to answer when his cell phone vibrated. "Gimme a sec." It was Lacey. Bro answered with a quick hello. "What's up, baby? You staying over?"

There was jazz playing in the background, and Lacey sounded like she was smiling. "Yes. It's really late, and Parker didn't think it was a good idea for me to drive home so late, you know, in the dark."

"That's good. I would have told you the same."

There was a pregnant pause. Then Lacey asked, hesitant, "Are you all right with that?"

Bro chuckled. "Funny. Bas said the exact same thing a second ago. Yeah, it's fine. I'm just glad you're safe and sound." Then he added on a whim, "But you better tell Parker no hanky-panky, or I'll make sure he doesn't play the piano ever again."

There was hearty laughter in the background, and then a lilting voice said loudly, "Oh, are you sure you two are exclusive? You know, we could totally have a threesome—oomph!"

There was rustling on the line, and Lacey called out breathlessly, apparently amid a tussle, "Oh, please. Don't you mean a foursome? Me, Bro, you, and Deacon?"

That remark, not aimed at him, left Bro with his jaw hanging open. Deacon was gay? Since when? "Um, Lace...? You still there?"

Some maniacal cackling followed, and then Lacey returned to the line. "Sorry about that. I had a crazy person to deal with. Yes, I'm talking about you!" she yelled at someone, and Bro knew the target was Parker.

"Um, can we get back to the part about Deacon being gay?"

Suddenly Lacey chuckled evilly. "Oh, yes. Did I forget to mention that? I totally saw Parker and Deacon making out on the stage at—ouch, gimme that!" Her voice faded suddenly, so clearly Parker had tackled the phone out of her reach again.

A breathy voice came on. "Hi. Bro?"

"Yeah. Parker?"

"Yes indeed. Hi. Listen, I'm not trying to get Lacey, all right?"

"You and Deacon, huh?" Bro didn't know whether to laugh or groan. A chuckle won.

"Ah, well, we'll see." More rustling, and then running feet on parquet floors, and more hyena-like chortling. "I'm gonna give the phone back to Lacey now, all right?"

Bro laughed. "Might be a good idea, yeah."

A second later Lacey was back on, panting. "You little tosser!"

Parker chuckled in the background. "See? I'll bring that British lady out of you yet. Call me Professor Higgins."

"I'll call for a funeral service if you don't get away from me!" Then Lacey focused on Bro. "I'll see you tomorrow, all right? I love you, Bro. So much." Before Bro could comment, someone was making lewd kissing sounds in the background. "Parker, shove off! I mean it."

Bro kept on laughing too. He hadn't met Parker yet, but he was coming to the conclusion he liked the guy. And if he and Deacon were getting it on, that was another show he didn't want to miss. "Babe? Good night. Sleep well, okay? See you tomorrow."

In the background, Parker's voice called out, "Drop that pillow, you wicked wench."

"I'll shove it down your windpipe!" Then a sound that had to be a pillow getting tossed across the room, and finally Lacey came back. "Love you, Bro. I'll tell you everything tomorrow. Good night. I love you."

"I love you too," Bro said. Then the line disconnected.

He may have been apart from Lacey for one night, but he still couldn't stop grinning.

Friends and family truly were everything that was important. With that thought he felt confident about getting a good night's sleep after all.

Chapter 28

BEFORE they knew it, October had rolled around the corner, and the long weekend of fall break had come along. No classes to attend, and a four-day vacation ahead. Both Lacey and Bro had waited for it impatiently.

Encouraged by their family members, they had opted to spend the time at a four-star hotel, Lansdowne Resort. The place was situated outside Leesburg, about an hour away from DC. They were going to stay in an alcove suite with room service and a king-size bed, and that was all they really needed. The suite had a country-manor-style decor with brown, green, and orange tones dominating the small space. There was a bedroom, bathroom, and a tiny living room. It was rich but not lavish to the point of extravagant.

After driving over late Saturday afternoon, checking in, and unpacking, they both decided to take a shower. And to avoid any temptations, they went in separately.

Bro went first, washed up quickly, and gave the place to Lacey with a wink. Once he got dressed in jeans and a T-shirt, he opened the bay window a crack, sat on the cushioned window seat, and inhaled the chilly night air. Autumn was well underway, and the foliage of the trees below in the riverfront park and valley were vast canopies of greens, yellows, and reds. The wind blowing in from the Potomac River was crisp, and Bro shuddered and closed the window, then sought refuge in the room behind him.

He was ordering dinner from room service just as Lacey came out of the bathroom with only a towel around her hips, and a cloud of steam wafted from behind her. "Hey, babe. Just getting us some chow. How does a whole fried organic chicken with black truffle sauce, macaroni & cheese, crispy roasted Brussels sprouts, and cheesecake with strawberries sound?"

Lacey licked her lips hungrily. "Heavenly."

Bro chuckled and finished the order. As he put the phone down, he sighed happily. "I love our family."

Lacey dried her hair fastidiously. "It was really sweet of them to do this for us."

Bro grinned. "I think they wanted us out of the way so they could have some adult fun forbidden for the likes of us."

Lacey giggled, her hand rising to cover her mouth. "You really think so?"

Bro grinned and plopped down on the bed. "Abso-fucking-lutely. Where do you think I learned all my underhanded stuff?"

Rolling her eyes, Lacey smirked. "If you say so."

"Now that's an alluring dare." Bro gave Lacey a seductive come-hither chin lift, and Lacey approached, snickering but wary. "Oh, come on, baby. Don't be shy."

"I'm not shy. I'm concerned. You have that 'I'm gonna eat you up' hungry look in your eyes." Lacey laughed. "You make me feel like Little Red Riding Hood."

"Guess that makes me the Big Bad Wolf." Bro winked and gave a sharp wolf whistle. Then he grabbed the hem of Lacey's towel and yanked it off fast. Lacey was left naked, standing in the middle of the floor.

"You jerk!" Lacey cried out angrily, but then she jumped on the bed, right on Bro's lap, cupped his face, and kissed him.

For a while they tumbled on the bedspread and kissed and fondled their way around each other's bodies.

Lacey tugged on the hem of Bro's T-shirt. "Take this off."

But Bro smoothed the fabric back down. "No. At least one of us shouldn't be buck naked when room service arrives with our meal."

"Fine," Lacey huffed, indignant, and tried to move off.

Bro kept her on top of him, and then rolled her underneath him. "I'm the big bad wolf, remember? Can't let you leave." His arrogant smirk was firmly in place as he held Lacey's hands above her head with his own, and his gaze raked all over her body. "Mmm, nice."

At first Lacey wiggled, trying to dislodge Bro, but then she remained still, deceptively so. "Well? Are you going to molest me or not? Tease…."

Bro chuckled. He loved playful Lacey. "All in good time. Right now I just want you near."

Lacey's features softened, and love shone from her eyes. "I love you."

"I love you." Bro slipped to Lacey's side but held her close. Their foreheads touched. "So, what's the story with Parker and Deacon?"

Lacey shrugged. "I don't know. I saw them kiss once. That's it. Parker's a bit flighty, and Deacon's… well, who knows what he is."

"If he kissed a guy, he's gay."

"That's not always how it works."

"Hmm, I guess." Bro kissed Lacey's lips and smelled the strawberry scent of her hair and the peach of her skin. "The past few months have been…." He couldn't quite find the right word. A lot had changed, and they had faced challenges, hurdles, and temptations. Yet, from his point of view, they had come out on top. And best of all, they had accomplished it together, as a stronger couple.

"Yes, I know. A lot going on." Lacey nodded and kissed him back. Her hazel eyes locked with his blue eyes. "You've seemed happier lately."

"Oh?"

"I mean, before, when we started college you seemed to be a bit down, a little more every day that passed. I hated leaving you, sensing that everything wasn't all right with you."

Bro was impressed. They were on the same wavelength all right. Lacey knew him so well. "Yeah, that's true, I suppose. I didn't want to trouble you with—"

"That had better be the start of a joke. And by the way, it's not funny." Lacey's eyes held a spark Bro adored and feared.

"Sorry. It's just…." He wracked his brain trying to word things right. "You have it all figured out, you know. Your violin, your future career as a performer and a lead violinist, and now you even have a sponsor who's got your back. Me? I thought I wanted football. I still do, in a way, but I don't think I want to make a career out of it."

Lacey frowned. "Let's skip the discussion about why you didn't tell me. We'll have *that* talk later, though, mark my words. But, Bro… if what you want isn't clear to you, why do you look and sound so happy these days?"

Bro smiled. "Because Sebastian and I talked about it. And I'm in no hurry. I have time to figure things out. It'll all work out. We're young, babe, and we've got the world in the palm of our hands."

Upon hearing that, Lacey kissed Bro. "See, this is why I love you. You always see the bright side of things."

"I don't always—"

"Most of the time, and that's important." Lacey wound her arms around Bro and held on tight. "I may become famous. I may become a nobody." Bro tried to cut in, ready to argue, but without success. "So could you. But it doesn't matter as long as we're together. Yes, we've encountered our own set of troubles these past few months, but we've come out stronger for it, I think."

Bro smiled, again happy that they indeed were like two peas in a pod. "That's exactly what I was thinking." Their food would arrive soon, but the moment was perfect. Bro jumped off the bed, dashed to the wardrobe, dug into his suitcase, and pulled out the little square box. Then he bounced right back to Lacey, who sat up, leaning on her elbows. "Here." He offered her the box.

It was easy to tell what kind of gift it was, and Lacey's eyes shot up, widening, and her jaw dropped in shock. "B-Bro…." Her voice cracked and faded away.

"Open it," he encouraged her, joyous and nervous at once.

With trembling fingers Lacey popped the lid of the blue velvet box open, revealing a gold engagement ring with six different gems in the colors of the rainbow.

Lacey was obviously stunned to silence, and for the first time Bro had known Lacey she covered her mouth for a reason other than to hide a smile.

To break the tense silence, Bro said, "The gems represent the colors of the gay pride rainbow flag. The red's for life, orange for healing, yellow for sunlight, green for nature, blue for serenity, and violet for spirit. All of which you have in abundance, Lace. You're the most beautiful, the strongest, bravest, kindest person I know. I'd be an idiot if I let you slip through my—"

Bro was interrupted by Lacey crying, throwing her arms around him, and generally smothering him with kisses all over. "I love you, Bro. Oh my God, so much. Every day. Love you. More and more." She kept mumbling endearments and vows of affection in between smooches, and Bro was high as a kite.

"So, I take it your answer's yes?"

Lacey laughed and sobbed at once. "You haven't asked anything yet."

Bro chuckled. "Oh, yeah, right. Sorry. My bad. Lacey Adair, I love you with all my heart, body, and soul. Will you marry me? Obviously not yet, but one day, relatively soon-ish, maybe during spring break, or when we finish our first year, or when we get our own place, or—"

"Yes, Bro. Yes!"

After that Bro was able to breathe easy again, and he wound himself around the naked beauty in bed with him. Then they were kissing and touching, and things were heating up fast.

There was a knock on the door. "Room service," a faint voice called out.

Bro pulled away from Lacey, who pouted. "Hold that thought, Lace. I'll be right back, and then we can have a picnic in bed, and feed each other—"

"Oh, no. No crumbs in bed," Lacey cut in, and hopped off the bed in search of clothes. "There's a perfectly good parlor with a table. We're not animals. We're eating at the table like decent folk."

At that, Bro laughed, unable to help himself.

AN HOUR later, their tummies sated, Bro and Lacey lay in bed together, naked, watching the news on the widescreen TV in the armoire. It was still early, and neither was willing to retire for the night yet.

What started as casual caresses and gentle holding soon turned to tender kissing and slow touching. Until the flame burned bright between them, and their passion roared into life. Bro kissed Lacey with all his might, practically devouring *him*, and they held on for dear life.

Suddenly, without either of them needing to speak, they stopped a hair's breadth away, looked into each other's eyes, and knew. Tonight was the night.

Since the first fingering experiment, they had done it several times, growing accustomed to the eventuality when it would present itself. That time was at hand.

Lacey bit his lower lip. "Please, Bro. Love you. Want you now."

Nodding and clamping down his fraying nerves, Bro dipped his hand into the drawer of the nightstand and pulled out the tube of lube and a packet of condoms. He wondered if they were going to use the latter since they were exclusive, neither of them had done this before, and it was unlikely they'd be searching for other lovers anytime soon.

"Um, Lace…?" He lifted the condoms up in view, with a silent question on his face.

Lacey worried his lower lip, and his gaze flicked between Bro and the rubbers. "I, uh, I don't think we need those. I mean, I haven't with anyone else. Wait. I mean, I haven't *been* with anyone else, not that I've been with others and not used condoms."

He was babbling, and Bro placed a hand on Lacey's thigh to calm him. "It's okay, Lace. I get it." He tossed the condoms over his shoulder. "Problem solved."

Lacey giggled at that, and the temporary tension was gone. "You could have a career as a professional problem solver."

Bro quirked an eyebrow. "Well, that's something to consider. Tomorrow."

"Nu-uh. On Wednesday. For these four days you're mine." The raw hunger in Lacey's voice made Bro shiver, and all he could do was swallow convulsively and nod.

Then he stared at Lacey with wide eyes, lust swelling in his body. Lacey was indeed a sight to behold. Now, without the makeup and the dresses, all traces of the dolled-up femininity gone, Lacey was all man. His slender arms and legs had strong and defined muscles, usually buried under soft fabrics. His hair was cut in a feminine style, but now all mussed up, it was manly. Having shaved this morning, Lacey sported next to no body hair anywhere but around his groin, and even that was a mere tiny patch. He never really even had stubble. But his cock, pink and cut and dripping precome, destroyed all illusions of womanhood.

Lacey was a young man. Beautiful, yes, but still a man.

Bro leaned forward and followed the lines of bones and curves of muscles until he got to the delectable V-shape of Lacey's lower abdomen and groin. There he buried his face, inhaling the sweet, musky odor and nibbling a bit.

Lacey groaned, his hips bucking up a bit, shaking. "Oh…," he sighed, and the wanton tone was music to Bro's ears. Wanting more, Bro kissed his way up to Lacey's belly button and circled it with his tongue.

Lacey giggled breathlessly. "That tickles. Stop it." Despite his words, Lacey kept his hands in Bro's hair and held him in place.

Chuckling, Bro shook his head to dislodge the hand and kept on moving up. When he reached a nipple, he lapped at the soft nub like a dog until it pointed up hard, redder than before, the skin silky and hot. Then he repeated the maneuver on the other nipple.

"Oh, oh, oh…." Lacey kept chanting, his back arching toward the hungry mouth. Bro wet his fingers and tweaked the nipple he wasn't sucking. "Oh God."

Delivering delight upon Lacey was easy because he was so responsive. The direct line from his nipples to his groin was an invisible carnal connection Bro often took advantage of.

Then he moved his hand down between their bodies and took hold of Lacey's cock. The silky, hot piece of meat twitched and pulsed against Bro's palm as he glided his hand up and down. On top he rubbed at the slit, where precome pooled, with his thumb and then spread the sticky moisture all over the shaft. When he pressed his thumb a bit harder on the sensitive spot beneath the ridge, Lacey moaned loudly, and his body jerked.

Weighing the choices in his mind, Bro decided it was better he didn't make Lacey come before they got down to business as opposed to having Lacey come twice. From his research he knew not all guys came during anal, but Lacey was close to the edge already. That increased the odds of them both finding pleasure and climax in this.

After a soft kiss on Lacey's luscious lips, Bro backed off, despite Lacey's keen protests, and found the lube. Though his hands trembled, he managed to moisten his fingers. He pushed one of Lacey's legs up to expose his taint and carefully started to circle the pucker.

"Oh, so good," Lacey whispered just before he hooked his arms under his knees and brought them up to his chest.

Bro thought he swallowed a moan, but was unsuccessful as a guttural groan, "Nghh," escaped anyway. Open and exposed, Lacey was indeed a sight. And the pink starburst pattern of his tiny hole was so vulnerable Bro almost hesitated touching it. But they had done this before, so he soldiered on and started pushing against the initial resistance.

"Mmm," Lacey mumbled, and Bro felt him pushing back, trying to take the finger in. And like the half a dozen times they had done this before, Lacey opened up to swallow Bro's finger, sucking it in with strong muscles. The tight heat around him was indescribable.

Careful to get every inch of Lacey's channel coated with lube, Bro was soon able to add a second finger, and then a third. Groaning, Lacey obviously willed himself to relax, because there was almost no pause between the first second of tension and the following loosening up. In no time at all, after some prolonged prostate teasing by Bro, Lacey was ready to go—or ready to go off, Bro thought with an inner chuckle.

Am I ready? Bro felt like hyperventilating, and his body seemed to ooze sweat out by the bucket loads. Yet his hands shook and felt cold and clammy.

As always, Lacey was in tune with Bro. "Hey, love. Look at me." Bro did as he was told, and two hazel eyes stared back at him with love, warmth, and trust. "It's just us. You and me. There's nothing to worry about. Come inside me, Bro. Make love to me."

Taking a shuddering breath, Bro licked his dry lips and nodded. He could do this. It was just sex, right? "P-promise me you'll tell me if it hurts, okay?"

Lacey's hands landed on Bro's arms and squeezed gently. "I promise."

Gathering his courage, Bro inched into place, sitting on his haunches between Lacey's legs. As he watched, Lacey spread them more to accommodate Bro's bigger size. *He thinks of everything, my sweet love.*

Holding his breath, Bro lubed up his own cock, closing his eyes tight and squeezing the base so he wouldn't blow his load prematurely. The mere thought of what they were about to do, how much Lacey loved and trusted him, was enough to push Bro over the edge.

Finally, he was able to say, "Okay, I'm coming in."

The sweet smile on Lacey's lips encouraged him, so he aimed his blunt, fat cockhead at the quivering hole and started pushing. Lacey whimpered, and then, in a heartbeat, Bro was in.

I'm inside Lacey.

His head buzzed, no coherent thoughts anywhere, as he kept an almost bruising grip on Lacey's thighs while holding still and giving Lacey a chance to adjust. With only the tip of his cock inside the maddeningly hot, tight space, he felt his boy's muscles clamp down on his, as if trying to squeeze the very life out of him.

"Nghh, go," Lacey whispered, his tone raspy and wavering.

With a nod, though Lacey couldn't see it with his closed eyes, Bro slowly insinuated himself deeper. He had to trust Lacey would speak if things were going too fast or too painfully. But Lacey said nothing and only made soft, breathy, ardent sounds that provoked Bro into entering farther, until he was buried in loving flesh to the hilt, his balls hitting Lacey's ass.

Right at that moment, when their bodies touched, they both groaned sharply. And it was a sound of pure pleasure.

"Oh my God," Bro muttered, engulfed in heaven, a viselike hold that surrounded his whole length. A mouth on his dick was great, but this was something else. Being inside the body of his lover, his girl, his boy, his partner, it was a heady epiphany, and he started chuckling with the lightness and happiness of it.

"Oh sweet Jesus," Lacey cried out, his back arching, his muscles straining, and his head thrown back on the pillow. "I swear, you've grown a couple of inches. God, so deep." Then he too chuckled lowly, breathlessly.

"It's okay, though, right?" Bro asked, panting with the exertion and feel, and praying he hadn't hurt Lacey in any way. He held Lacey's legs high, on his shoulders, and kissed the sole of the nearest foot, and then the other.

Lacey's eyes flew open, and the intensity of that gaze almost did Bro in. "Yes. Perfect. Love you in me. Move."

Nothing in his range of experience could have prepared Bro for the awesomeness of moving his cock in and out of Lacey's quivering channel. Every nerve ending of his dick was on fire, sparking along the length of the shaft, and the heat and pressure from Lacey's passage spread to all corners of his body.

At first, he moved in short, shallow thrusts, getting the feel of it. He wrapped his hands around Lacey's legs and held on for leverage. As he got into it, lost in the sensation and motion, he picked up the pace and pulled out more, only to shove his way back in harder, faster, stronger.

"Oh, God, yes!" Lacey exclaimed, his voice hoarse and edgy. His fingernails dug into Bro's arms, chest, shoulders, and back, wherever they roamed, and the sting of the touch awakened pain and brought out blood. But those new, sharper, darker feelings only enhanced his pleasure.

And then Bro hit the jackpot.

"Oh, God almighty, right there, right there!" Lacey shouted, his body galvanized and energized. Bro grinned at the knowledge he had found the right angle, and he aimed his thrusts at the sweet spot, again and again, losing himself in the rhythm of sex.

When he nearly dropped on top of Lacey, he felt the need boiling inside him, the lust spiking fast, demanding more. Bro chased his own orgasm as fiercely as he sought to feel Lacey's. They would come together, he decided firmly.

Lowering himself, Bro crushed his mouth over Lacey's delectable lips and plunged deep into the opening mouth, taking, craving, unwilling and unable to stop. The hunger was a beast, ferocious and relentless. But Lacey must have been on the same page since he delved deep into the kiss as well, with reckless abandon and wanton moaning.

Without a doubt, tonight the sex went beyond any gratification they had sought before.

The passion and yearning built and built, and they rose higher and higher toward the inevitable crescendo, their bodies moving as one.

Bro snaked his hand between their bodies, fisted Lacey's cock, and tugged with swift determination. Lacey groaned into the kiss, and then his hand covered Bro's, and they jerked Lacey off together.

The new position, the movements, the harsh fucking, it all took a toll on Bro, and he felt his body aching for release. His muscles quaked, and he was certain he couldn't take a second longer without melting into a pile of goo.

"Lacey, please," he mumbled against Lacey's kiss-swollen, puffy lips.

"Harder, Bro. More." Lacey's urgency was as evident as his own.

A single breath they shared, and then they were both coming.

Lacey cried out, shrill. His balls drew tight between them and then his cock erupted. Creamy white ejaculate landed between them, coating them both with hot, sticky droplets.

His lover coming all over them both felt as wonderful as ever, but what Bro felt with his cock was something else. Lacey's body was determined to choke the come out of him, and those inner muscles clenched tight around Bro's buried length.

That constricting hold pushed Bro over the edge of delight.

With a hoarse shout, Bro orgasmed so hard his eyes rolled to the back of his head. His balls pulled so high up he wondered if his body had swallowed them whole. He spilled his hot seed deep inside Lacey's lovely body, his cock convulsing with involuntary jerks to push out more, his hips working overtime. Lacey's ass kept on milking Bro's cock until his balls were siphoned dry.

Only then did he gasp and fall down on top of Lacey.

"S-sorry, baby...," he whispered, unable to speak, move, or think. The only thing he was able to do was breathe, his chest heaving hard, and his frame felt like it weighed a thousand pounds.

Lacey swiveled beneath him, chuckling breathlessly, and managed to tilt them both to their sides. "It's okay. I wanted you lying on top of me."

"Crushing you?" Bro worried, and felt his limp, spent dick slipping out of Lacey's ass.

"No, silly." Lacey giggled, snuggling in close, and nuzzling Bro's neck. "Loving me."

Bro held on tighter too, fearing the nimble nymphet in his arms would disappear if he so much as blinked. "You're such a kook sometimes."

"Takes one to know one."

Bro kissed Lacey's hair, temple, cheek, and finally lips. "You okay? Does it hurt?"

"No, not really." Lacey frowned, his look pensive. He wiggled about, as if trying to find a comfortable position. "Feels strange. Kind of empty. Not pain, but a sort of... softness. A bit throbbing, but not bad. Sort of abused and tender, but nothing I can't live with." He sighed. "Yes, maybe tomorrow I'll sing a different tune, but for now I'm fine."

"Don't you mean you'll *play* a different tune?" Bro joked, glad everything was all right. His fingers sought Lacey's entrance and gently massaged the tiny hole, hoping to ease some of the ache that might be there.

Lacey sighed again, this time with deep satisfaction, or so the exalted expression on his face seemed to suggest. "I feel you inside me still. Not just the pounding, but your come. I feel it filling me, seeping into me, and dripping out of me."

"Dripping?" Bro sat up in a hurry, and immediately he saw the white trails of semen flowing out of Lacey's hole as it opened and closed with tiny intermittent spasms, pushing out new small streams. Suddenly he couldn't breathe, and his voice stuttered as he said, "That is abso-fucking-lutely the most awesome thing I've ever seen."

Lacey burst into a fit of giggles, and Bro joined him. Then Bro used a warm washcloth to clean them both up a bit, gently swiping away the come from Lacey's backside. It was only the gentlemanly thing to do.

"What are we going to do tomorrow? I don't think my ass could handle another round so soon." Lacey spoke sleepily, and Bro gathered him close.

"I booked us a few spa treatments over the next couple of days. Hot stones, of course, and aromatherapy, and a mani-pedi for men."

"Mmm, sounds heavenly," Lacey whispered, sighing happily.

Bro snuggled in close, letting out a breath and relaxing.

Everything the two of them had achieved in the short time since starting college reached Bro's awareness. They had faced daily separation, new friends, possible love interests, uncertainties about their future careers, bad role models, new sexual frontiers, and the prospect of ending up apart, sad and alone, and not knowing what was in store for them.

But they had prevailed.

And Bro and Lacey had done it together. Now they were stronger for it, an engaged couple who stood together on the threshold of adulthood, with new responsibilities and obligations ahead. Yet they also got the chance to remain children at heart with the support of their family, and would get to enjoy the liberties and joys that came with growing up.

As he cuddled closer to Lacey, Bro anticipated the enjoyment of the fall break *and* the rest of their lives together. If distances, jealousies, doubts, and fears couldn't keep them apart, what could?

"Stop thinking, love. You're keeping me awake," Lacey mumbled with blurred words, halfway off to dreamland already.

Bro smiled and wrapped himself around his lover.

The answer to his question was that nothing could separate them because they had everything, their futures and the whole world, still ahead.

SUSAN LAINE, a Finn through and through, was raised by the best mother in the world. She told her daughter time and again that she could be whatever she wanted to be. It still took Susan until her thirties to find the spark for serious writing when she discovered the gay erotic romance genre.

Her formal education revolves around anthropology, but she wishes to be a full-time writer sooner rather than later. Susan enjoys hanging out with her sister and friends in movie theaters and bookstores. Her other pastimes include walking, swimming, and fantasizing about sizzling hot manlove. Some of her likes are pop music, chocolate, and doing the dishes, and a few dislikes are sweating hot summer days, tobacco smoke, and purposeful prejudice.

Visit Susan's website at http://www.susan-laine-author.fi/ or write her an e-mail at susan.laine@hotmail.com.

Senses and Sensations from SUSAN LAINE

Sounds of Love

Susan Laine

http://www.dreamspinnerpress.com

Senses and Sensations from SUSAN LAINE

A SENSES AND SENSATIONS MYSTERY: 2

Love in
Plain Sight
Susan Laine

http://www.dreamspinnerpress.com

Senses and Sensations from SUSAN LAINE

A SENSES AND SENSATIONS MYSTERY: 3

A
Luminous
Touch

Susan Laine

http://www.dreamspinnerpress.com

Lifting the Veil from SUSAN LAINE

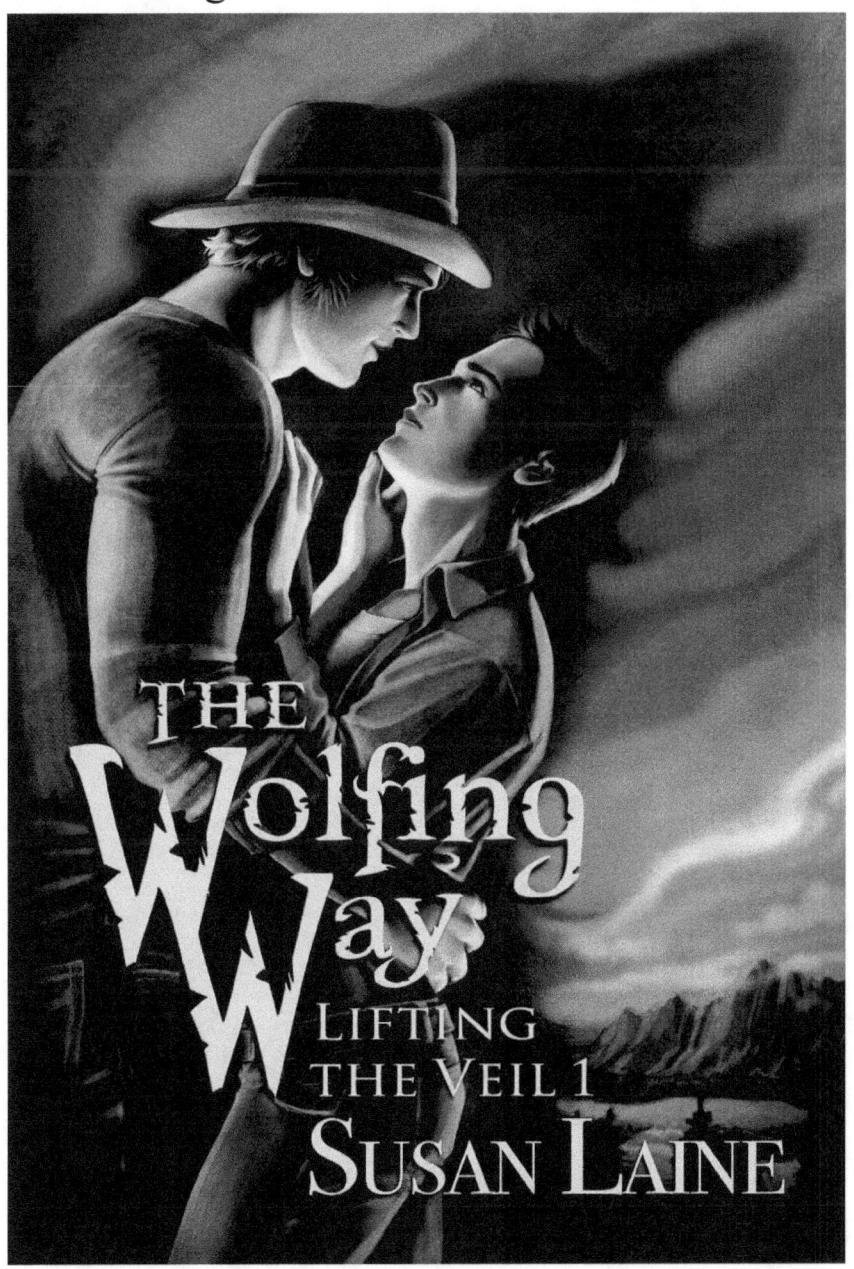

THE Wolfing Way
LIFTING THE VEIL 1
SUSAN LAINE

http://www.dreamspinnerpress.com

Lifting the Veil from SUSAN LAINE

Genie's Wish

LIFTING THE VEIL 2

SUSAN LAINE

http://www.dreamspinnerpress.com

Lifting the Veil from SUSAN LAINE

LIFTING THE VEIL 3

Hunter's Moon

SUSAN LAINE

http://www.dreamspinnerpress.com

Also from SUSAN LAINE

http://www.dreamspinnerpress.com

In Italian from SUSAN LAINE

NON C'È DUE
SENZA... TE

Susan Laine

http://www.dreamspinnerpress.com

For more of the
best M/M romance,
visit

Dreamspinner Press

www.dreamspinnerpress.com